CW00506002

Terrier

Book 2 in The Angel of Camden Series

Keith A Pearson

Inchgate Publishing

For more information about the author and to receive updates on his new releases, visit: www.keithapearson.co.uk

Copyright © 2024 by Keith A Pearson. All rights reserved. This book, or any portion thereof, may not be reproduced or used in any manner whatsoever without the express, written permission of the author, except for the use of brief quotations in a book review.

Author's Note

Sorry to stall your reading. Just a couple of quick points if I may.

This is the second book in *The Angel of Camden* series and whilst it's a standalone story, you might prefer to read the first title, *Eminence*, before getting stuck into this one.

I should also point out that the central character, Clement, is a man of his time – that time being the 1970s. He's a decent bloke at heart, but his language and views might be considered outdated by modern standards. Personally, I prefer characters to be authentic but if you're easily offended, this probably isn't a book for you.

I hope you enjoy the story.

Keith

Chapter 1

Life is full of illusions, and most should remain as such.

When I was a child, maybe five or six years of age, Mum took me to see Father Christmas at a department store in town. To this day, I can still remember the fizz of excitement as a suspiciously tall and pimply elf escorted me into the grotto, and I first clapped eyes on that jolly man in a red suit. The colouring book I received wasn't quite the present I'd wished for, but I still got to meet Father Christmas, and that in itself was amazing enough.

We left the department store a little later, and that's when I happened to glance up an alleyway at the side of the building. To my astonishment, I spotted Father Christmas and two of his supposed elves, chuffing away on cigarettes. Being a child, I could almost accept that maybe Father Christmas did enjoy the occasional smoke, but I wasn't stupid — you can't remove a beard and keep it in your pocket.

Now, I fear another illusion is under threat.

I love receiving flowers but, having just stepped through the door of Penny's Petals, any future floral gifts will be tainted by the vision before me. Early twenties, I'd guess, there's nothing remotely romantic about the florist's greasy hair, stained t-shirt, or the tattoo of a scorpion on her neck.

"Mornin'," she says flatly as I approach the counter. "Can I help?"

The lopsided badge fixed to her t-shirt is printed with a single word: Rebel. I can't say for certain if it's the woman's name or a life goal, but I presume it's the former.

"Yes, I'm here to collect a bridal bouquet. The surname is Jackson."

"When did you order it?"

"My mum popped in last week. Thursday, I think."

"Gimme a minute."

Without explaining where she is going or why it'll take a minute, Rebel disappears through a doorway to the side of the counter. I'm not naturally impatient, but I can't resist a glance at my watch. It's almost eleven o'clock, and the wedding is at three this afternoon. Fortunately, this is the last errand on my to-do list.

Rebel defies her slovenly appearance by returning promptly. She then places a cardboard tray on the counter and verbally checks the contents against a hand-written note taped to the side.

"One blush rose bouquet."

"That's it," I confirm.

"Are you paying by card or cash?"

"Card."

She steps over to the till and taps a series of keys. "That's £74 to pay."

I look down at the modest spray of flowers and then at Rebel. "Sorry?"

"It's £74."

"For a small bouquet?"

"Yeah."

"Are you sure? That seems ridiculously expensive."

"I'm sure," Rebel huffs. "And I don't set the prices. If you've got a problem, speak to Penny."

"Fine. Can I speak to Penny?"

"She's out on deliveries. She'll be back around four."

"An hour after the wedding. Great."

I quickly consider my options. Penny's Petals is the only florist in town, so those options are limited: return home without the bouquet or accept that I'm about to become the victim of daylight robbery.

"Doesn't look like I have much choice," I mutter while rooting around in my handbag.

I find my purse and, with unbound levels of reluctance, slide my debit card into the payment terminal.

"Would you like a receipt?" Rebel asks.

"Yes, and considering how much you charge, I assume it'll come in a gilded silver frame!"

She hands me a dog-eared slip of paper.

As a mark of protest, I snatch the cardboard tray from the counter and depart without a word of thanks.

After hurrying back to the car, I place the tray on the back seat and double-check my list. Four errands, all completed. Now, all that remains is to return to Mum's and get ready. Unlike everything else about this wedding, at least we won't have to rush our hair and makeup.

I start the car and set off on the short journey to Windsor Gardens.

With little on the radio to distract my thoughts, they turn to the peculiarity of my situation. At the age of thirty-three, I should be the one about to walk down the aisle, and my mum should be rushing around with a list. Life, though, doesn't always play out the way you expect it to. In Mum's case, life over the last twelve months has been nothing short of a whirlwind. Never in her wildest dreams would she have imagined that today, the eighteenth of July, she'd be about to wed a man who doesn't even live in the UK.

4

Last summer, Mum was set to visit New York with her best friend, Paula, right up until three days before their departure when Paula sprained her ankle. Not wanting to disappoint Mum, she insisted I take her place.

Mum thinks it was fate, but on our second day, I suggested we visit an art gallery. She'd never have visited that art gallery with Paula, nor would she have popped into a nearby coffee shop afterwards. It was in that coffee shop she met Bruce Franklin — the man she's set to marry in a little under four hours' time. Fate, alas, still hasn't introduced me to my happily ever after.

I pull onto the driveway of number four Windsor Gardens and get out of the car. Mum moved into the detached bungalow with my granddad, Ray, seven years ago, although he only got to enjoy it for five years. Even now, whenever I hear the word Covid, I'm cast back to the moment when I first heard Granddad had lost his battle against that fucking virus. Never a day goes by when I don't picture his face, and I miss him terribly.

"Happy thoughts, Gina," I whisper to myself.

Mum opens the front door as I'm unloading the fruits of my morning's labour. She's wearing a silk dressing gown that's maybe a little on the short side — a gift from her fiancé, I believe.

"Did you get everything?" Mum asks from the doorway.

"Yes, including one bouquet from the Dick Turpin florist shop."

"Pardon?"

"You might have warned me about the price."

I carry the tray over to the door so Mum can inspect the object of my ire.

"Seventy-four quid," I huff. "I can't believe you agreed to pay that much."

"It's only money, Gina, and it looks lovely."

"As long as you're happy, but I'm never buying anything from that florist again. It's a rip-off."

"True," Mum chuckles. "But then everything related to weddings is a rip-off."

She isn't wrong, as we've discovered over the eight weeks we've been planning this wedding. If you want a decorated cake for twenty people, the cost is £100. Tell them it's a wedding cake and suddenly it's £300. It's amazing that you can attach a simple, two-syllable word to any product or service, and it magically trebles in price. I'm amazed some bright spark hasn't yet created wedding-themed toilet paper so guests can wipe their bits and bobs at the reception. Of course, it'd likely cost ten quid a roll.

I transfer the flowers to the kitchen table and return to the car for the rest of my haul, including a simple but hideously overpriced wedding cake. Mum then hands me a glass of Prosecco.

"It's not too early, is it?" she asks. "I need something to take the edge off my nerves."

"It's never too early."

We take our glasses through to the bedroom, and Mum takes a seat at her dressing table, facing her bed. I sit on the edge and lean forward, tilting my glass towards Mum's.

"Here's to you, Mum, and a wonderful day ahead."

She clinks her glass against mine. "I'll drink to that."

"You'll drink to anything," I joke.

"Cheeky mare," she replies with a broad smile before proving my point. She gulps back half the glass.

It's a bit of a cliché, but my mum is also my best friend. My so-called Dad walked out on us when I was still in nappies, so Mum is the only parent I've ever really known.

"Is Bruce feeling the nerves too?" I ask.

"I had a brief chat with him an hour ago. I don't think he knows how to be nervous."

She glances over her left shoulder towards a framed photo on her dressing table. It features the face of the man Mum fell in love with from the first moment they met. I have to admit that, even though he's recently celebrated his forty-seventh birthday, Bruce Franklin is a good-looking man. With misty-grey eyes and a winning smile, Mum has often joked that if Bruce ever decided to stop practising law, he could earn a living as a catalogue model.

"You'd think he might be just a little bit nervy," I remark. "It's not just the wedding — he's uprooting his entire life and relocating to the UK. I know I'd feel more than a bit apprehensive if I ever had to move for love."

"You know Bruce," Mum says. "He takes everything in his stride. That's one of the reasons I fell in love with him."

"Well, I think he's a lucky man."

"I'm the lucky one," Mum replies, shooing away my compliment. "I thought my chance of happiness had passed."

"You're fifty-two, Mum — not eighty-two."

"That's not what I meant. I've never felt like anyone's idea of the perfect wife."

"Why?"

"Look at me," she snorts. "I'm overweight, and I've got more lines on my face than a map of the underground."

"Stop that," I chide. "You're beautiful, inside and out, and I stand by what I said. Bruce Franklin is the luckiest man alive."

It's an odd dynamic of our relationship that even when I was an angsty, hormone-addled teenager with a face full of spots and unmanageable hair, it was Mum who felt most insecure about her looks. I've spent most of my adult life trying to bolster her self-esteem, but my dad did such a grand job of destroying Helen Jackson's confidence that the project remains a work in progress.

We share a hug, and with that, Mum seems to remember her appointment at the registry office in a few hours.

"Right," she says breezily. "Time to slap some lipstick on this pig."

For all of Mum's issues with her body confidence, she has developed her own style of self-deprecating humour. Despite myself, I can't help but laugh.

After a quick shower to freshen up, I set about fixing Mum's hair. I'm no hair stylist, or a makeup artist for that matter, but Mum didn't want some random stranger involved in her wedding preparations. Once I've finished, she admires my handiwork in the mirror.

"See, I knew you'd do a great job," she remarks while examining her face in the mirror. "You're a naturally gifted artist."

"Maybe, but my usual medium is canvas. I'm nowhere near good enough to make a living applying makeup, that's for sure."

Truth is, I barely make a living applying paint to canvas, but I love it too much to give up my dream career.

With her hair and makeup sorted, Mum heads to the kitchen to top up our glasses. As I'm not the bride, I doubt anyone will care about how little makeup I'm wearing or if my coppery locks aren't styled to perfection. I apply a little eye shadow and a half-price lipstick I snared in a department store sale. The coral colour isn't a shade I'd usually go for, but I can't resist a bargain. That trait is probably genetic, as Granddad earned his living in London's East End through wheeling and dealing.

Mum returns with fresh glasses of Prosecco, and we natter about nothing in particular until both glasses are empty. We resist another top-up and, with time getting on, slip into our respective wedding outfits. Then, we stand shoulder to shoulder in front of a mirror.

"You look amazing, Mum," I remark.

"And you look lovely, too, but you always look lovely. How you haven't been snapped up is beyond me."

Here we go.

"When I toss the bouquet," Mum continues. "Make sure you catch it. It might be the stroke of good fortune you need."

"Mum, if you throw that bouquet in my direction, I warn you that I'm likely to take it back to the florists and demand a refund."

"I don't think they do refunds."

"Okay, I'll shove it up Penny's arse, then."

Mum playfully rolls her eyes and then plucks her phone from the dressing table.

"I don't know if I'll ever look this good again," she says. "So, I'd like a photo with my favourite daughter."

"Your only daughter. Your only child for that matter."

"Ahh, but you'd still be my favourite, even if I had a dozen children."

Mum fiddles with the phone but can't seem to get the camera working.

"Silly thing," she groans. "It's too complicated."

The sleek Samsung phone is only a few months old, and another gift from Bruce. It's a significant upgrade on Mum's old phone, and she still occasionally struggles to operate it.

"Give it here," I chuckle. "I'll show you ... again."

I open the camera app, and we both smile as I capture a selfie. I then show the photo to Mum.

"Aww, it's lovely," she coos. "And it's the very last photo before Helen Jackson becomes Helen Franklin. I'll treasure it."

On cue, the doorbell rings. I check the time.

"That'll be the car. Are you all set?"

Mum takes a final look in the mirror and draws a deep breath.

"I'm set."

Chapter 2

The car I hired for our trip to the registry office was supposed to be a nice surprise for Mum. I wasn't expecting her to choke up the moment she clapped eyes on the Mark II Jaguar. In hindsight, the choice of wedding car, whilst poignant, was perhaps a mistake.

Granddad always wanted to own a Mark II Jaguar, but it wasn't until he retired and moved to Brentwood to live with Mum that he finally realised his dream. Sadly, it was short-lived. His arthritis prevented him from driving as much as he wanted to, and within two years, he had to quit driving altogether. Selling that car broke his heart.

Standing on the driveway, with our driver holding the rear door of a racing-green Mark II Jaguar open, Mum is struggling to hold back the tears.

"I didn't mean to upset you," I say, putting an arm around Mum's shoulder. "I'm so sorry."

"I'm not upset," she replies, swallowing hard. "I was just thinking about your granddad and how chuffed he'd be that you arranged this."

"That was the idea."

"And I'm grateful. It's a lovely thought, Gina."

Relieved that my nod to Granddad paid off, we say hello to Eric, our driver, and take a seat in the back of the Jaguar.

"It's such a lovely car," Mum remarks once she's made herself comfortable. "It even smells the same as Dad's."

"All classic cars have a distinct scent," Eric replies from the front seat. "It's a combination of leather, petrol, and midlife crisis."

"And Brut aftershave," I add. "I bet whoever originally bought this car in the late sixties wore Brut, and probably most of the owners since."

"More of an Old Spice man myself," Eric chuckles.

We set off, and within a few hundred yards, Mum's phone trills to signify an incoming text message. She wrestles it out of her clutch bag and prods the screen.

"Is that from your husband-to-be?" I ask. "Checking that he won't be left standing at the altar ... although I don't think a registry office has an altar, come to think of it."

"No, it's just some stupid spam message. Bruce messaged first thing this morning to double-check I wasn't about to have a last-minute change of heart."

"He's never struck me as the insecure type."

"He was only joking. As if I'd change my mind."

"Are you sure?" I reply with a wry smile. "Might be an idea to tell him you're on your way."

"I might send him a quick message, yes."

Smiling to herself, Mum begins composing a message to Bruce. She hasn't seen him since his last visit to the UK, eight weeks ago, and it was during that visit that Bruce surprised everyone by asking Mum to marry him.

I initially had reservations about his proposal because I'd heard all manner of horror stories regarding foreign men marrying British women to either secure an immigration visa or fleece them financially. However, Bruce Franklin is a partner in a successful New York law firm, and he owns a luxury apartment in Manhattan. As Bruce himself pointed out, he has far more to lose than Mum if their marriage doesn't work out. He's also prepared to move to a new country just to be with the woman he considers his soul mate. I couldn't fault his logic, and he won my blessing.

As Mum taps away at the phone screen, I take a moment to enjoy the brief but nostalgic journey across town. The idea of hiring an old Jag was as much for my benefit as Mum's. When Granddad admitted defeat and put his beloved car up for sale, I suggested we take it out for the day — one final hurrah before the Jag moved on to a new home. So, on a glorious June morning, we packed a picnic and set off for the seaside town of Broadstairs in Kent. Granddad managed to drive the first hour before gracefully suggesting I take over. Despite my somewhat nervy driving style, we reached our destination in one piece and enjoyed a wonderful day together. We didn't know it at the time, but there wouldn't be many more.

Mum returns the phone to her bag.

"Should I feel so nervous?" she asks.

"I wouldn't know. How did you feel when you married Dad?"

"It was a long time ago. I can't even remember the name of the hall where we held the reception, let alone how I felt on the drive to the church. Besides, that man is the very last person I want to think about today."

Mum's marriage to Paul Hewitt, my dad, didn't so much as end but implode in devastating fashion. They met in the late eighties at a nightclub in Canning Town and married a year later. Dad was from Billericay in Essex, and that's where they began their married life, in a small one-bedroom flat. I then arrived and we moved to a terraced house on a council estate. Back then, having just one child was uncommon, but the reason I don't have a sibling is that for the best part of a year, my dad was shagging Mum's younger sister, Lynn, rather than his wife. Mum only found out about the deceit when she came home from work unusually early one afternoon and found them in bed together.

If that betrayal wasn't destructive enough, Dad and Aunt Lynn decided to set up home together in Manchester.

Understandably, the ensuing drama tore our family apart. It remains a blessing that I was too young to understand what was going on, but some years later, when Mum eventually told me what my dad had done, her pain was still evident, still raw, to the point we both disposed of the Hewitt surname because it served as a reminder of what that man did.

I didn't see my dad again until I was in my early teens, and even then, it was only for a few hours. Lynn, however, returned to Billericay after four years when Dad, to no one's great surprise, left her for another woman.

It took a long time, but Mum did find it in her heart to forgive Lynn. The catalyst was my nan passing, and although she's never said as much, I think Mum initially offered an olive branch purely for Granddad's sake. They seem to get on okay these days, but it's telling that Lynn is merely a guest today when, under any other circumstance, she'd be Mum's matron of honour. Some wounds are so deep they never truly heal.

"Sorry," I reply. "I don't know why I mentioned his name."

"It's okay," Mum says, squeezing my hand. "I just want today to be perfect, and so far, that's exactly what it's been."

"No reason it won't stay that way ... unless the best man forgets the rings."

"Just as well that I double-checked with Bruce last night. As I said, I don't want any hiccups today."

Bruce and his best man, Daniel, only arrived in the country yesterday afternoon, and although Mum was desperate to meet them at the airport, Bruce is a stickler for tradition. He thinks it would be bad luck for them to see one another before the big day, so the groom and his best man stayed in a hotel last night.

"I was kidding about the rings, you know."

"I know you were."

"Today *will* be perfect for no other reason than you deserve perfect."

"The perfect day followed by the perfect life with the perfect man. I can't believe my luck."

Despite Mum's optimism, there is one slight blot on the horizon, although it's more a technicality than a blot. Bruce still needs to apply for a visa so he can reside permanently in the UK. Being he's a lawyer with a healthy bank balance, and he'll be married to a British citizen within the next thirty minutes, it should be a formality by all accounts. I have no doubt it will be, but Bruce is yet to experience bureaucracy on this side of The Pond. I don't envy him,

We reach the registry office, and Eric slows the Jag to a standstill outside the main entrance. Being a public building, it's not exactly what you'd call romantic, but then again, Mum married Dad in a quaint little church and that counted for nothing in the end.

"All set?" I ask Mum as Eric hurries to open her door.

"One hundred per cent."

She picks up her bouquet and steps out of the car. I don't wait for our driver and open my own door before joining Mum on the pavement.

"I'll park up and wait," Eric confirms. "If there's a delay for any reason, just ping me a text. I've nothing on for the rest of the afternoon so there's no drama if the ceremony over-runs."

"Thanks, Eric," I reply.

Our driver's second task of the day is to transfer the newly-weds back to the bungalow where we're holding a small reception. With only twenty-odd guests in attendance, it seemed pointless hiring a venue when Mum's home has a sizeable garden available. Thank God the great British weather is behaving itself for once, and it's as pleasant a July afternoon as we could have wished for.

Our driver departs and Mum locks her arm with mine.

"Would you like me to sing *Here Comes The Bride* as we enter?" I ask.

"Darlin', I've heard you sing," Mum chuckles. "I'm okay, thanks."

We reach the steps of the registry office just as a figure bustles out of the main door.

"Wait up," Aunt Lynn says as she moves gingerly down the steps in heels that are far too high. "You can't come in yet. Bruce isn't here."

Instinctively, I glance at my watch. We're only four minutes away from our allotted appointment with the registrar.

"He's cutting it fine," I remark. "But why can't we come in?"

"Because it's bad luck if the bride arrives before the groom."

"Mum arrived after the groom at her first wedding, but that didn't stop—"

"It's fine," Mum interjects before I finish my barbed response. "I'm sure there's somewhere I can wait, and Bruce will be here any moment, anyway."

Lynn responds with a sharp nod, and the three of us make our way inside where the guests are already seated in the room where the ceremony is due to take place in a few minutes.

"Hi, everyone," Mum chirps. "I'm unfashionably early, so we're just waiting for Bruce and his best man."

Before any of them can reply, Mum's phone trills from inside her handbag.

16

"You should probably turn that off," I suggest. "You don't want it ringing halfway through the ceremony."

"Yes, you're right."

Mum retrieves the phone and then stares at the screen. She taps it once, and suddenly a deep furrow forms across her forehead.

"Something up?" I ask, stepping close to her.

Mum doesn't answer, probably because her hand is clamped across her mouth.

"Mum? What is it?"

Ashen faced, she passes me the phone. There's a message on the screen from Bruce — *In an accident, can't get...*

"Oh, my God," I gasp. "Can't get what?"

"How the hell should I know," Mum cries. "But we need to go."

"Go where?"

"I don't know ... the hospital."

"We don't even know if he's at the hospital, never mind which one."

Aunt Lynn then arrives on the scene.

"Is there something wrong?"

"We're not sure," I reply. "Bruce messaged Mum to say he's been in an accident."

"That's awful. Where is he?"

"We don't know."

"Have you tried calling him?"

I'm annoyed that I didn't think of such an obvious step. I return my attention to the phone and tap the call icon next to Bruce's name. Before a single ring, a voicemail message kicks in.

"Bruce, it's Gina. Can you call me or Mum the second you get this message, please? We're all worried about you."

I attempt to return the phone to Mum, but she's staring into space, clearly in shock. Slowly, the group of concerned guests encircle us. Mum's best friend, Paula, breaks from the pack and steps forward.

"Sweetheart, what's wrong?" she asks Mum, placing a hand on her shoulder.

Paula's presence seems to shake Mum from her trance, but the rapid breathing isn't a good sign. I need to intervene before the now-uncertain bride-to-be suffers a full-blown panic attack.

"Paula, it seems Bruce has been in an accident, but we don't know any more than that. Can you take Mum and sit her down while I work out what we do?"

"Of course."

Paula leads Mum to a chair at the back of the room while I update the guests. Aunt Lynn's husband, Stephen, is the first to pose a question.

"What can we do?" he asks.

Whilst I struggle to like Lynn, her husband is the epitome of pleasant: always helpful, always considerate.

"Could you find the registrar and tell her what's going on? I think it's fair to say there won't be a wedding this afternoon."

"I'm on it," Stephen replies before dashing off. His wife remains at my side.

"Would you like me to call around the hospitals?" she asks. "If we can find out where Bruce is, at least we can get your mother over there to be with him."

"Please. Yes."

Lynn bustles away, and I turn to the guests.

"I'm so sorry, everyone, but it looks like the wedding is off … for today at least."

A few of them ask if there's anything they can do while the rest ask to be kept informed as soon as there's news on the groom's whereabouts. Concerns lodged, they all filter out of the room.

With Paula keeping Mum calm, Lynn calling the hospitals, and Stephen dealing with the registrar, I don't know what to do with myself. All I do know is that no one deserves this less than my mother.

I look up at the ceiling. "God, why are you doing this?" I whisper.

He doesn't reply.

Chapter 3

I've never felt so helpless, so useless.

Sitting next to Mum on a sofa in the registry office reception area, all we can do is wait for news. The first bearer then returns as Stephen strides across the tiled floor towards us.

"I've spoken to the registrar," he confirms. "She was very nice about it and gave me her card so we can reschedule once we know Bruce is okay."

I admire Stephen's optimism, but it's of little consequence until his wife reports back after calling the local hospitals.

"Thanks, Stephen," I say. "Could you see how Lynn is getting on? I think she stepped outside to get a better phone signal."

"Sure. I'll be right back."

He's about to head off, but his eyes linger on Mum, sitting with her head in her hands.

"Keep positive, Helen," he says softly. "We'll find Bruce, and I'm sure he'll be just fine."

Mum looks up at him and replies with a smile so feeble it barely registers. Stephen returns the smile and hurries off to find his wife.

"He'll be alright, Helen," Paula says, although the glance she shoots in my direction suggests she's less than convinced.

"Absolutely, he will," I add. "If he was badly hurt, how could he have sent you a message?"

"But he didn't send a message," Mum replies, still tearful. "He sent half a message. Why didn't he finish it or call me if he's okay?"

"Maybe his battery died?" Paula suggests. "It would explain why Gina's call went straight to voicemail."

"Or maybe *he* died," Mum sobs.

"Don't say that, Mum. You're thinking the absolute worst with no good reason. Let's just see—"

Lynn bustles back into the reception area with her husband trailing behind. I try to gauge her expression as she closes the yards between us, but there's no obvious clue if the news she's about to deliver will be good or bad.

"I called The Community Hospital and Queens," Lynn begins. "Neither of them has admitted a Bruce Franklin today."

It's not bad news, but neither is it good.

"Where is he, then?" Mum asks to no one in particular.

"Maybe we should go back to your place, Helen," Stephen suggests.

"You think?"

"There's not much we can do here, is there?"

Mum nods and then slowly clambers to her feet.

"I'll come back with you," Paula says.

"So will we," Lynn adds. "At least until we know Bruce is okay."

With some semblance of a plan in place, my thoughts turn to a more obvious task that no one has yet mentioned.

"I think it might be worth informing the police."

"What can they do?" Lynn asks.

"If Bruce has been in an accident, someone must have reported it."

21

"We don't even know what kind of accident it was. For all we know, he might have fallen down the stairs at the hotel."

"We have to do something," Mum interjects. "We can't just sit around and hope he turns up."

"That's settled, then," I reply, fixing Lynn with a suitably defiant glare. "You four head back to the bungalow, and I'll walk up to the police station."

"Whatever," Lynn huffs. "But I think you're wasting your time."

I ignore my aunt and give Mum a hug.

"It'll be okay," I say gently. "We'll find him."

"God, I hope so," she replies, her voice once again close to breaking.

I flash Mum a reassuring smile and nod goodbye to Paula and Stephen. Even if I felt like saying goodbye to Lynn, she's rummaging around in her handbag and doesn't look up.

As I hurry back across the reception area to the exit, it occurs to me that our driver is still waiting outside, blissfully unaware that he won't be driving the happy couple anywhere today. I pull out my mobile and call Eric. When he answers with a cheery hello and his name, it's obvious he's talking on a hands-free device.

"Eric, it's Gina Jackson. I don't have time to explain, but sadly, we won't need your services again today. I'm sorry to have kept you hanging around needlessly."

"Actually, I left five minutes ago."

"Oh, right."

"Your mum's sister was standing outside the registry office while I was having a sneaky cigarette, and I overheard her mention the name Bruce Franklin. Once she finished her call, I confirmed that I was waiting to drive Mr and Mrs Franklin back home. She said there wasn't much point hanging around as Bruce had been in an accident. I'm so sorry, Gina."

"Right ... thanks, Eric."

I apologise again and end the call.

It doesn't matter how Eric found out, but I'm miffed that Lynn stuck her oar in and dismissed Eric when we might have still required his services. I brush off Lynn's interfering and set off on the short walk to the police station.

Short as the walk is, I didn't plan to walk any distance today, and my brand-new three-inch heels pinch my toes with every step.

By the time I barge through the police station's main doors, I'm close to going barefoot. I approach the counter, where I'm welcomed by a desk sergeant with thinning hair and tired eyes. He confirms his name as Sergeant Berry and asks how he can help. I explain the sequence of events that led me to the station.

"We don't know what to do for the best," I say once I've updated the police officer. "Which is why I'm here."

"I'll double check with the control room, but I'm almost certain we haven't received any calls about road traffic incidents within the last hour. Would you like to report Mr Franklin as a missing person?"

"I guess so."

"No problem. Let me take some details, and I'll file a report."

"And then what?"

"One of my colleagues will pick up the report and assess our best lines of enquiry."

"Can't you just use Bruce's phone number to trace him?"

"I'm afraid it doesn't work like that, Miss Jackson. Despite what you see on TV, we don't have the powers to simply plug a phone number into our system and track someone. Besides, you mentioned that Mr Franklin is a US citizen, so it's highly unlikely his phone is even registered to a UK network."

"I hadn't thought of that."

"On that note, you might want to consider contacting the US Embassy. I don't know what support they might offer, but it can't do any harm."

"Yes, thank you. I'll do that."

"Good. Now, let's get the ball rolling so I can file a report."

It takes a good fifteen minutes to supply all the relevant information.

"What happens next?" I ask once Sergeant Berry has finished with his questions.

"As I said, it'll be allocated to a case officer, and he or she will contact you."

"When?"

"As soon as we can," the officer replies in a less than convincing tone. "We're a bit stretched at the moment, so I wouldn't want to make a promise we can't keep."

I'm about to launch a protest, but I get the impression it'd be a waste of breath. All I can do is hope that Bruce resurfaces sooner rather than later, and that the missing persons report becomes an irrelevance. I thank Sergeant Berry and depart.

Not wanting to put my feet through any further punishment, I call a local taxi firm, and a car arrives within a minute. Noting my attire, the driver assumes the obvious and starts telling me about his son's wedding plans. I'm in no mood to listen, so I tell him I'm not feeling well and reinforce the message by closing my eyes.

After a mercifully quiet journey, I pay the driver and hurry up the driveway to the bungalow. When I reach the front door, I pause for a moment and offer a silent prayer that Bruce is inside, full of apologies but no worse for whatever ordeal he's endured.

I slip the key into the lock and enter.

My first and most pressing task is to kick my shoes off. I then walk barefoot through the hallway to the kitchen. When Mum and Granddad first moved in, they had it refitted and extended so it's now almost the same size as my first-floor flat. I make it as far as the doorway when Mum appears.

"Did you find anything out?" she blusters, putting an end to my hopes that Bruce might have returned while I was at the police station.

"I filed a missing persons report."

"And what are they going to do?"

"They said an officer will be in touch soon, but as we've already called the hospitals and Bruce's phone, there's only so much they can do."

"This is a nightmare," Mum cries, flinging her arms in the air. "Where is he, Gina? Where is my Bruce?"

"I don't know," I reply, trying to portray some semblance of calm. "But we will find him."

I pull her into a hug while Paula, Lynn, and Stephen look across from the kitchen table, their expressions grim. There's only so much faux reassurance and optimism anyone can muster in a situation like this.

However, we need to do something, even if it's just to keep Mum's mind occupied. Left to dwell on the worst possible scenario, her fragile mental state will eventually crack.

"While we're waiting for the police," I say. "Why don't we conduct our own investigation?"

"What do you mean?" Mum replies tearfully.

"Let's sit down and try to work out where Bruce was when he sent that text."

Mum appears temporarily buoyed by the idea of doing something other than fretting and nods enthusiastically. I lead her over to the table and grab a pen and notepad from a drawer.

"Right, let's jot down what we know," I say, taking a seat next to Mum. "What time did Bruce message you earlier?"

She checks her phone. "12.11 pm."

"Did he say where he was?"

"No, but I presume he'd just checked out of the hotel. They had the room until noon, and the plan was to get a cab from there to the registry office."

"Where was he staying?" Stephen asks.

"The Rembrandt in Knightsbridge," Mum confirms.

"Why there and not a hotel nearer Brentwood?"

"Because rather than take a suit on the plane, he and his best man intended to buy suits in London. Knightsbridge is as good a place as any, plus there's a tube line running directly from Heathrow."

"Oh, okay," Stephen responds.

"We should call The Rembrandt and ask if he definitely checked out," I suggest.

"Won't the police check?" Paula asks.

"Probably, but why wait?"

"Good point," she replies, getting to her feet. "I'll call from the garden so you can continue."

As Paula heads outside to make the call, I open up Google Maps on my phone and locate The Rembrandt Hotel.

"Mum, you said Bruce and Daniel intended to get ready at the hotel and then get a cab to the registry office, right?"

"I think he said cab. It might have been a car."

"Either way, the journey time by road is just over an hour. When did his second message arrive, the one relating to the accident?"

Mum checks her phone again. "1.57 pm."

"So logically, he must have been close to Brentwood when he sent that message."

26

"Unless it was delayed," Stephen suggests. "It sometimes happens, especially if you're using your phone in a foreign country."

"If that's the case," I reply. "Bruce and Daniel could have been on the road anywhere between Knightsbridge and Brentwood."

I return my attention to the map and check the distance. "It's thirty-one miles."

Lynn, unusually quiet, glances across the table in my direction. She's likely thinking what I'm thinking, that thirty-one miles of road is a lot when you're trying to pinpoint exactly where an accident might have occurred.

"There's only one thing for it," I say. "We'll have to call every hospital along the route."

"You've got to be joking?" Lynn replies. "There could be dozens."

"Do you have any better ideas?"

Whether she does or not, her reply is interrupted when Paula returns from the garden.

"I'm so sorry," she sighs. "I spoke to the hotel manager, but they're unwilling to even confirm if Bruce stayed there last night."

"Did you explain the situation?" I ask.

"Of course, but it's company policy, apparently — guest confidentiality. He said they'd release the information to the police, but they can't release it to members of the public."

"They booked the room till noon," Mum repeats. "There's no reason they'd leave before then because ... where would they go?"

"Mum's right," I add. "It makes sense to contact all the hospitals along the route from the hotel to Brentwood."

"Which still seems like a mammoth task to me," Lynn pipes up.

"No, it's a good idea," Paula replies. "And what else are we supposed to do?"

A consensus reached, I use Google Maps to identify the location of every hospital along the route. There are seventeen, but more than half are private. It leaves us with a list of just eight possibilities.

"It's only two hospitals each to check," I state, throwing a snide look Lynn's way. "Not such a mammoth task after all."

I jot down the phone number of each hospital and hand a pair each to Paula, Lynn, and finally, Stephen. I then dial the number for the first of my two.

"What am I supposed to do?" Mum asks.

I glance up from the phone screen. "You believe in God, so I'd suggest now is as good a time as any to have a word with him."

Chapter 4

"Right. Thank you, anyway."

I end the call and dial the second number. As I wait to be connected, I look around the room at the other three making similar calls. I can't tell if they're on their first call or second, but the fact we're all still on the phone suggests no one has found Bruce yet.

My call connects, and I ask to speak to someone in admissions. After a painstaking wait, I ask a different hospital administrator the same question. I then wait as keys are tapped and mouse buttons clicked.

"I'm sorry, but no one of that name or description has been admitted within the last three hours."

"Okay. Thanks."

I press my finger against the phone screen and look up. Paula and Lynn are both standing with their arms folded, faces glum. Even if I couldn't understand English, I'd be able to tell from Stephen's tone that he's also drawn a blank. He ends his call.

"No joy at either," he sighs.

"Same here," Paula adds.

"No luck with either of mine," I reply. "Lynn?"

She just shakes her head.

"What do we do now?" Mum asks, her shoulders slumped.

"We wait for the police," Lynn suggests. "Not that they'll be much use."

"We could call the US Embassy," I blurt, recalling my earlier conversation with Sergeant Berry.

"Why?" Mum asks.

I don't have an answer but, as I'm out of ideas, it's at least a way of keeping Mum's hopes up.

"The sergeant I spoke to at the police station suggested it. As Bruce is a US citizen, maybe they've heard something. It's got to be worth a shot."

Mum nods, but I can tell from her face that she's not confident. I snatch my phone up from the table just as the doorbell rings. As I'm nearest to the door, I confirm I'll answer it and hurry out of the kitchen.

I half-expected to answer the door to a detective or at least a police officer in uniform. Instead, two men in bright-yellow polo shirts are standing on the doormat. There's a van parked behind them with a company name prominently displayed on the side: Finch Caterers.

Shit!

"Afternoon," the older of the two men says. "I'm Carl from Finch Caterers, and this is my colleague, Owen. We're a bit early, but we've got a wedding buffet to deliver if you're ready?"

In all the chaos, it completely slipped my mind that Mum had ordered food for the reception party.

"I'm so sorry, Carl, but the wedding never happened, so we don't need a buffet now."

"That's unfortunate, but I'm afraid you'll still need to pay the balance of the invoice."

"Can we sort this out another time? Now is not ideal."

Rather than reply, Carl checks the clipboard in his right hand.

"Are you Helen Jackson?" he asks.

"No, that's my mother."

"Can I speak to her, please?"

"No, you can't. She's ... she's indisposed at the moment."

"Fair enough, but we're not leaving until someone has settled the invoice. Your mother signed a contract, and that contract clearly states that we require full payment on delivery."

"Can't you wait for a few days? It's really not a good time."

"I don't wish to sound cold, but it's not exactly a good time for us, either. Our profit levels are shrinking by the week, and we don't have time to chase up unpaid invoices. That's why we have a contract."

As little as I need this hassle right now, I sympathise with Carl. Times are tough, especially for small businesses.

"How much is the outstanding balance?" I ask.

Carl refers to his clipboard again. "£280, to be paid by bank transfer on delivery."

"Can you take a card?"

"I'm afraid not. The charges eat into our already thin profits."

Resigned to settling the invoice, I'm about to ask Carl to give me a second while I fetch my phone when Mum steps up beside me.

"Oh no," she exclaims. "I forgot all about the catering."

"It's okay, Mum. I've told Carl we no longer require the food, and we were just sorting out his invoice."

"Seeing as they're here, they might as well deliver the food."

"Why? What are you going to do with a buffet for twenty?"

"People still need to eat, Gina. And besides, Bruce and Daniel will be famished when they show up."

Rather than argue or undermine Mum's optimism, I turn to Carl. "I guess you'd better bring the food in, then."

"And the invoice?" Carl replies.

31

"I'll deal with that," Mum says before I can respond. "I placed the order and agreed to pay on delivery, so it's only right."

"But Mum ..."

"Please, Gina," she snaps, holding her hand up. "I'm upset and worried sick, but I'm not a child that needs mollycoddling."

"Um, we'll start bringing the food in," Carl says.

"Bring it through to the kitchen, please," Mum responds.

Maybe this is my mother's way of normalising the situation — an attempt to briefly forget that her wedding buffet is now just a regular buffet and significantly fewer guests will be picking over it. I step back into the hallway and let the two men deliver their wares.

After the final tray is transported from the van to the kitchen table, I stand in the doorway while Mum signs Carl's invoice to acknowledge every scrap of food is present and correct.

"That just leaves the balance of £280 to pay," the caterer confirms.

"Give me a moment to log in to my account, and I'll transfer the funds."

"Thank you."

Mum puts on her reading glasses and then taps away at the phone screen with her index finger. It's a slow process and painstaking to watch.

"Do you need a hand, Mum?" I ask, sensing that Carl's patience is wearing thin.

"No, it's fine," she replies. "Bruce showed me how to do it when I paid for the registry office."

She continues frowning at the screen while I mouth an apology to Carl.

"Does anyone mind if I grab a sandwich?" Paula asks, possibly just to break the awkward silence.

"I'm a bit peckish, too," Stephen adds. "I skipped lunch."

"Help yourselves," I reply. "There's plenty to go around. We'll be eating sausage rolls for a week."

I spot Carl glancing at his watch and decide to intervene for my sake as much as his.

"Nearly there, Mum?" I ask, stepping up beside her.

"No, I'm not," she groans. "There's something wrong with this stupid banking app."

"Are you having problems logging in?"

"I've logged in, but ... here, look."

I lean in and study the screen. Mum has banked with the same building society for decades, and it happens to be the same one I use for both my personal and business accounts. For that reason, the app's home page is familiar, displaying two boxes at the top: one for Mum's current account and one for her savings account. They both display the same balance: £0.00.

"See," Mum says. "It must be a fault with the app."

"Give me the phone a second."

I take the phone and tap the first box linking to her current account. As of 2.05 pm this afternoon, the account had a balance of £4,917. The app then confirms that at 2.06 pm, a single payment to another account completely wiped Mum's balance. With panic mounting, I hit the back button and check her savings account. To my utter horror, a single payment left the account precisely one minute before the payment left her current account. The key difference between the two transactions is the amount — £4,917 for the current account but £1,893,200 in the case of the savings account.

"They're empty," I splutter. "Both accounts."

"They can't be," Mum replies, perhaps not understanding the gravity of the situation.

"Look at this," I reply, showing Mum the details of the payment that left her savings accounts while we were all standing around in the registry office, panicking over Bruce's whereabouts.

"I never made that payment," Mum gasps.

"Yes, I know, but someone obviously did."

"It must be a bank error. It has to be."

As we both stare at the screen, dumbfounded, Carl clears his throat. I pull out my phone.

"Give me your bank details," I demand.

It takes two minutes to settle the invoice, and the caterers don't hang around once my payment hits their account. That done, I immediately turn my attention to a graver account issue.

Mum is now sitting at the table, staring at her phone screen with Stephen on one side and Lynn on the other.

"This can't be right," Lynn says. "It has to be a glitch with the bank's computer."

"Maybe it's a hacker," Stephen responds grimly. "You hear about people's accounts being hacked all the time."

I take a seat opposite Mum. "You need to call the bank immediately."

She looks at her phone screen again, almost in disbelief, but remains inert. When I thought this day couldn't get any worse, fate has dealt another devastating blow.

Taking the lead, I google the bank's fraud department and dial the number. I then activate the speaker and place the phone on the table in front of Mum.

"I'm ringing the bank's fraud department. You need to tell them what's happened."

The sound of a trill ringtone seems to snap Mum out of her trance. "Oh ... yes. Right."

"Good afternoon," a female voice suddenly squawks from the phone's speaker. "Thank you for calling the fraud reporting team at Midland & West. My name is Rachel — how can I help you?"

"Hello," Mum says nervously. "I, um ... I think my bank account is broken."

I intervene.

"Hi, Rachel. My name is Gina Jackson, and I'm here with my mum, Helen Jackson. Her account appears to have been hacked, and whoever did it has emptied both her current and savings accounts. As you can imagine, she's in shock."

"I'm so sorry to hear that. If we can go through some security questions, I'll do my best to help."

After five minutes of utter frustration, Rachel finally confirms we've passed security. She begins by accessing Mum's accounts on the bank's system.

"I can see the payments leaving the account earlier," she confirms. "One at 2.05 pm, from the savings account, and the second, from the current account, a minute later."

"That much we know, but Mum never made those payments. She was due to get married at two o'clock, and we were all standing in the registry office in Brentwood at the time because her fiancé was ... he was involved in an accident and therefore didn't make it."

"I'm sorry about that. Give me a moment to look into the payments."

We wait in anxious silence as Rachel investigates.

"A couple of quick questions," she then announces. "If I may?"

"Go ahead," I reply.

"Mrs Jackson, have you used the banking app to make payments in the last four weeks?"

"Um, yes," Mum replies.

"To be sure, can you confirm that on the eighth of July, you made an online payment to Tomkins Window Cleaning Service?"

"Yes, I did."

"How much was that transaction?"

"£18, I think."

"That's correct. And can I also confirm that you haven't changed your phone since you made that payment, or logged into your account on any other device?"

"No, I don't think so."

"So the device you used to access your account ten minutes ago is the same device you've used to make other payments in recent weeks, including the one to Tomkins Window Cleaning Service?"

"Yes," Mum snaps. "What does that have to do with someone emptying my accounts?"

There's a brief moment of silence on the line until Rachel speaks again.

"I'm sorry, but I'll need to refer this to our fraud investigation unit. I can't offer any further assistance."

"What?" I cough. "Why not?"

"Because, Miss Jackson, both the payments from your mother's account today were made in a single session. According to our data, that session took place on her phone from a location in central Brentwood."

"No, that's impossible."

"I'm merely relaying the information on my system. It's the exact same IP address for the device your mother used numerous times in recent weeks, and the location you confirmed tallies with the GPS coordinates of that device at the time."

I look across at Mum, her face ghostly pale.

"This has to be a mistake," I bark at the phone. "Your information is incorrect."

"I'm not authorised to discuss the matter any further. I've just passed the details to our fraud investigation unit, and they'll be in contact with your mother within twenty-four hours. In the meantime, both accounts are now suspended."

With that, Rachel apologises and ends the call.

SIX WEEKS LATER

Chapter 5

Raymond George Jackson entered the world on the twenty-second of November 1939, just eighty days after Britain declared war on Germany. The youngest of six children, his earliest memories of life in London's East End involved the wail of air raid sirens and spending long, terrifying hours in a corrugated steel box while the Luftwaffe rained bombs on the city. His eldest brother, Frederick, lost his life fighting for King and country on a beach in Normandy, while his sister, Rose, was killed in a gas explosion on her way to school one cold February morning. She never got to celebrate her ninth birthday.

By anyone's standards, my granddad's childhood was traumatic, but he never let those early horrors define him. Quite the opposite, in fact. He left school at fourteen to work as an apprentice bricklayer and, although the work was hard and the conditions harder, he took immense pride in helping to rebuild our war-torn capital.

Ten years after he laid his first brick Ray spotted an opportunity while working on a building site in Whitechapel. He realised that there was good money to be made from restoring and selling ironmongery and doors destined for the scrapyard. After saving hard for a year, he managed to rent a small yard in Shoreditch — then an impoverished part of town and a far cry from the hip, desirable borough it is today — and he set himself up in business.

Then, in 1967, he met Dora Bingley, and a year later the couple married. The same landlord who owned the yard also happened to own a two-bedroom terrace house right next door, and that became home to the newlyweds. Three years later, their first daughter, Helen, came along, followed two years later by Lynn.

For the next few years, Ray worked night and day to build his business and provide for his young family. In 1975, Lady Luck paid him a visit when he won £9,000 on the Football Pools. It wasn't a fortune, but then Lady Luck paid a second visit. Desperate for cash due to a failed business venture, Ray's landlord offered to sell the yard and the house for £8,500. The deal done, Ray bought a second terraced house on the other side of the yard a few years later, which he converted into a shop with a flat above.

With their futures secured and a steady income, life in East London was comfortable but uneventful for the next decade. Eventually, his eldest daughter married and moved out, although the younger daughter's decision to abscond with the elder daughter's husband would never be forgotten.

Sadly, in 2008, Ray lost his wife, my gran, to a stroke. We'd only just celebrated her sixty-eighth birthday.

Granddad refused to move house despite his health issues and, although his business ceased trading, he spent most of his free time in his yard, mending, fixing, and making good just for the pleasure of it and to keep busy. Looking back, I guess it was his way of dealing with the loss of his wife, his one true love.

By 2015, it became clear that Granddad was struggling as the arthritis continued to undermine his mobility. An estate agent put the yard and the two freehold properties on the market and, six months later, a developer willingly dropped £5.2 million into Ray Jackson's bank account. Without even knowing it, the man born into poverty during the early months of World War II had become the most unlikely of multi-millionaires.

Granddad spent his last seven years living with Mum in the bungalow in Brentwood, and although his health continued to deteriorate, I like to think they were happy years — they certainly were for me. When he finally gave in and drifted off to be with Gran again, he left his entire estate to his two daughters, with a sizeable sum bequeathed to his only granddaughter. It was more than enough for me to buy my own home and provide financial security as I fulfilled my lifelong dream of creating art for a living.

Up until six weeks ago, my mother was also living a comfortable life. She had no financial worries and was looking forward to marrying a man she thought was her soul mate. Now, she's penniless and broken, all because of Bruce fucking Franklin or, specifically, the fraudster calling himself Bruce fucking Franklin.

On the day of Mum's wedding, everyone assumed that fate had inflicted two devastating blows to Helen Jackson. Firstly, she received that text from her fiancé. That was awful enough, knowing she wouldn't be getting married, and Bruce was likely injured. Then, someone hacked Mum's bank accounts and emptied them both.

We didn't realise at the time, but both events were connected.

While we waited for the bank's fraud prevention team to call, we continued our search for Bruce. In a final desperate act, we decided to see if anyone at Bruce's firm had heard from him. We found the website and called the number only to hear a recorded message: *This number is no longer in service*. We then sent an email, but that bounced back within seconds.

I can't say what it was, but something felt off about a big New York law firm having their phone lines terminated and email servers deactivated. I told Mum I needed some air and stepped out into the garden to make a call to the New York State Bar Association. An incredibly helpful chap by the name of Ethan tried his best to sound apologetic when he confirmed that the law firm where Bruce Franklin was supposedly a partner didn't exist. The website was merely a front, and within hours, it went down.

Looking back, the wedding was the perfect distraction to ensure Mum wouldn't be on her phone when Franklin emptied her accounts. And the message she received about the supposed accident was the perfect distraction, keeping us occupied in the hours after the money disappeared.

Another link in the chain of Franklin's deception was revealed within a week of the scam wedding. The expensive mobile phone he gifted to Mum was not an act of generosity but a Trojan horse — the tool he used to defraud her.

The police discovered a sophisticated malware program buried deep in the phone's operating system — impossible for the user to detect. That program allowed its master to remotely use every one of the phone's functions as if the actual owner had it in their hand. It recorded and stored every keystroke, every password, and even Mum's biometric details. The police suggested that maybe Franklin didn't immediately clear out Mum's accounts when she first used the phone because of her inability to properly operate the high-end device. They also theorised that maybe the eight-week period was purely to ascertain the extent of Mum's assets. What's eight weeks to a man who stands to steal £1.9 million?

Hard as it was, we had to accept that we might never know the full truth, but we knew enough — Bruce

Franklin had performed the ultimate long con, and not one of us suspected a thing.

To have her heart broken and to be humiliated in such a public way was almost enough to nudge Mum over the cliff of despair. Almost, but not quite. Then, she received a final catastrophic shove when the bank categorically refused to reimburse the money Franklin stole. In their view, Mum was either culpable for the loss because she used an insecure device or complicit with the fraud. Either way, when I called the bank and demanded to speak to a senior manager, they referred me to their lawyers. They ended that call with the usual reference to their terms of business.

It took a forty-minute meeting with a solicitor in Brentwood to confirm the bank's defence lay buried in their terms and conditions – the same terms and conditions everyone signs without ever reading.

As for the police, they've all but washed their hands of the case. In fairness, their forensic analyst thoroughly examined the mobile phone, but it failed to reveal any clues as to who planted the Trojan software. As for the man himself, Bruce Franklin is a ghost. To make matters worse, because he's not a British ghost, the police could do nothing but inform their counterparts in New York once they realised there were no leads to follow this side of The Pond. We did receive an apologetic letter from the deputy chief constable, but that letter also included several references to 'resources' and 'tough decisions'.

I now find myself temporarily occupying Granddad's old bedroom in the bungalow. Mum was so utterly broken that I had no choice but to move in with her. I think my presence has helped, and she's just about coping now, but the more time I spend with her, the more the rage builds inside of me. It's now so bad, I don't care if we never see a penny of that money again — it's justice I want.

The doorbell rings.

I open the front door to find Paula standing on the step with a suitcase by her side.

"You know I'm only away for ten days, right?" I say jokingly.

"I know, but I've never travelled light."

"Do you need a hand?"

"No, I'm good."

I stand back and let Paula wheel her designer suitcase into the hallway.

"Thank you for doing this," I say. "There's no way I'd be going if you hadn't offered to stay."

"Don't be daft," she replies, waving away my concern. "It's too good an opportunity for you to miss. And besides, it'll be nice to spend some quality time with Helen."

"Yes, and on the subject of quality time, I made sure the fridge is well stocked with wine."

"You know me so well, Gina Jackson," she chuckles.

As far as Paula and my mother are concerned, I've been offered the opportunity to attend a ten-day masterclass with a leading French art teacher in Paris. As once-in-a-lifetime opportunities go, I'd be a fool to turn it down. However, there is no opportunity, no leading French art teacher, and when I fly out of Heathrow Airport later today, I'll be heading west, not south-east.

"Which one is mine?" Paula asks, pointing towards the two doors to her right.

"This one," I reply, stepping across the hall and opening the door to the bedroom I've been temporarily occupying.

Paula follows me in, wheeling the huge suitcase behind her.

"There's fresh linen on the bed, and I did clear some space in the wardrobe but ..."

"It'll be fine. As long as I've got somewhere to rest my head at night, I'm a happy woman."

Paula is indeed a perpetually happy woman, and for that I'm glad. Mum needs her friend's positivity right now.

"Fancy a coffee?" I ask as Paula heaves her suitcase onto the bed.

"I'd love one. I'll unpack later."

She follows me through to the kitchen and leans up against the breakfast bar while I fill the kettle.

"Will your mum be back soon?" Paula asks.

"Her appointment was at one so she shouldn't be much longer."

One of the reasons Mum and Granddad chose this particular bungalow is its proximity to a doctor's surgery, just four hundred yards up the road. The assumption was that it would make Granddad's life easier, but Mum has had cause to visit the surgery twice in recent weeks.

"I offered to go with her," I add. "But she flatly refused."

"Maybe she's embarrassed. No one likes admitting that they're struggling let alone that they have to rely on anti-depressants."

"If only that were all Mum needs. She's not sleeping at all, hence the second visit to the surgery."

"Oh dear," Paula winces. "That's probably not helping."

"No, it's not. She's exhausted — mentally and physically."

The kettle comes to a boil and clicks off. As I'm about to open the cupboard, Paula steps over.

"She'll be okay, you know," she says softly, placing a hand on my arm. "Your mum is tougher than you think."

"I hope you're right."

"I am, and I'd never say this to her, but she'll eventually come to terms with losing the money."

"You think?" I snort. "I'm not sure I could."

"It's just money, Gina. She still has this place, and she has you, and me, obviously, plus Lynn and Stephen. She has people who love her and care about her — no amount of money can buy that, and no one can take it away."

Paula is right on one level. A few weeks ago, during one of her brief moments of positivity, Mum did say the money didn't matter. She's never had much throughout her life so being potless is hardly a new experience.

"Yeah," I sigh. "That's true."

I return Paula's smile but internally, I'm still a million miles away from accepting what happened to Mum. For me, the money in itself isn't the point of contention; it's what it represented. My granddad amassed it by working his hands to the bone for five decades, and for someone to swoop in and steal it away feels like an affront to his memory. It's not a point I'd raise with Mum because it'll only add to her already long list of reasons to feel awful.

I, however, cannot let it go, and that is why I simply have to do what I'm about to do.

Chapter 6

Saying goodbye to Mum was hard, but my cover story ensured she waved me off with a smile. When I first concocted the idea of travelling to New York and searching for Bruce Franklin, I knew Mum would do everything possible to talk me out of it if she even had an inkling of my plans, which is why I had to lie. The fact she seemed genuinely chuffed about my fictitious art workshop in Paris is a positive I hadn't factored in, but it's welcome.

"Attention, please," a disconnected female voice booms above my head. "Flight BA-189 to New York is now boarding. Please, could all passengers make their way to gate fifty-four. Thank you."

I tuck my tablet into a sleeve on the side of my cabin bag and set off towards the gate. The two double gin and tonics I gulped in the bar are keeping the worst of the pre-flight nerves at bay, but I now wish I'd had a third. I'm not a fan of flying at the best of times, but on this occasion, the purpose of my trip is reason enough to be apprehensive. There's no going back now, though.

With my bag over my shoulder, I keep one hand firmly pressed against the part where the tablet is stored. It's unlikely anyone will try to pilfer it on the way to the plane but losing the tablet would certainly compromise my quest. The hard drive contains every communication between my mum and the man who called himself Bruce Franklin: every WhatsApp message, every video call, every email and every photo they ever exchanged. Mum would be mortified if she knew I'd used her laptop to access all of her private messages, particularly as some of them were of a sexual nature, but I had to gather every crumb of information I could before deciding to book this trip.

There's not a lot to go on, and the police weren't that interested in any of it, but it could be enough to narrow my search for one man in a city of eight million people. If Bruce Franklin is still in New York, I intend to find him.

I hand my boarding card to a cheery woman at the gate and follow the walkway towards our aircraft. With every step, the nerves mount. Why didn't I have that third drink? I console myself with the knowledge that once we're in the air, I can order enough gin and tonic to knock myself out, hopefully for the entire eight-hour flight across the Atlantic.

After making my way to my seat, I keep my fingers crossed that the one next to mine won't be occupied by a chatterbox or, worse still, a middle-aged man with delusions of his own appeal. I'm not in the mood for conversation or a half-arsed attempt at flirting.

As it transpires, the seat is taken by a woman in her forties, wearing a business suit. She flashes me a thin smile before sitting down and plugging in a pair of earbuds. I spot the Audible logo on her phone screen, which hopefully means my fellow passenger will be immersed in an audiobook for hours. That suits me just fine.

All too soon the main cabin door closes and we begin taxiing towards the runway. The take-off is by far my greatest fear when it comes to flying, probably because I know it's when most aviation accidents occur. I really shouldn't watch those documentaries.

48

The plane comes to a stop. I take a few deep breaths, close my eyes, and grip the armrests because I know what comes next. Seconds pass, and then the engines suddenly roar into life. I'm pressed back in my seat as my mind latches onto a scene from one of the aviation disaster documentaries where a flock of birds are sucked into one of the plane's engines on take-off, and that engine then burst into flames. Did the plane crash? Did people die? I can't remember, nor do I want to.

At some point in the cacophony of screaming engines and seat-shaking vibrations, the tyres leave the runway. I don't know how high birds fly, or how quickly a plane ascends after take-off but surely, we'll be safe after a minute. I begin counting down from sixty, my eyes still firmly shut.

Finally, thankfully, I feel confident enough to assume we've passed the point of a likely bird strike. I open my eyes and check the view beyond the window to my right. I suspect we're now well above the height most birds fly, as I can just about make out the M25 motorway snaking off into the distance and an expanse of water, probably a reservoir, looks no bigger than a puddle. One of the cabin crew then announces the flight time and weather in New York. In my head, it's a sign that everything is as it should be, and there's no imminent risk of catastrophe.

Relaxing a fraction, I switch on my tablet and open a spreadsheet I've been working on for the last two weeks. It contains every lead I've pulled from the messages Bruce Franklin sent to Mum, listed in a vague order of significance. I'll start at the top with what I believe are the strongest clues to Franklin's whereabouts or places I might find someone who recognises him. I've already established that the apartment he claimed to own is actually a short-term rental property, as advertised on several vacation websites. The apartment, like his office in Manhattan, was nothing more than stage scenery for his act.

As the plane continues to climb towards its cruising altitude, I open the folder of photos that I pulled from Mum's laptop. There are thirty-one in total, but the vast majority are just pictures of Franklin smiling into the camera while standing against a door or a nondescript wall, offering no clues as to where or when they were taken. In each and every one of them, he oozes traits of the character he wanted to portray: solid, trustworthy, and dependable. Even now, knowing what he did, it's hard to look at his face and not see those traits.

Wanker.

Rekindling the inner rage helps to suppress the last remnants of my flying anxiety, but it won't help me sleep. I've already wasted so many hours lying awake during those dark, silent hours of the night, my guts churning and pulse racing as I imagine what hell I'd like to unleash upon Bruce Franklin. Mum has always been a passive, gentle character, always going out of her way to avoid conflict, whereas I've inherited my granddad's steely principles. As my first boyfriend will attest, I'm not one for forgiving and forgetting — I'm all about the karma.

Granddad once told me a tale about a guy called Freddy Milner, and how he tried to rip him off. Back in the late seventies, this Freddy character agreed to buy two pallets of reclaimed bricks from Granddad. The deal was cash on delivery, but when Granddad arrived and unloaded the pallets, Freddy couldn't find his wallet. Full of apologies, he agreed to drop the cash at the yard the next day. That day came and went, but Freddy failed to drop by. Nor did he drop by the following day or the next.

Granddad let the debt slide for almost two weeks and then visited Freddy's home. When he arrived, he found the bricks had been used to construct a lovely new porch at the front of the house. Unfortunately, no one was home, but a neighbour confirmed that Freddy and his wife had gone on holiday the previous day. When Granddad explained that Freddy owed him money, the neighbour offered a sympathetic smile and then explained that Freddy Milner had a reputation for welching on his debts.

The next day, Granddad returned to Freddy Milner's house and spent nine solid hours painstakingly de-constructing the porch brick by brick. He then loaded every single one of those bricks onto his truck, leaving a pile of tiles and timber blocking the door to the Milner homestead.

When Granddad first told me this tale, I asked why he went to so much trouble to get his bricks back. I pointed out that it probably cost him more in time than he stood to lose if Freddy Milner didn't pay up. Granddad then looked me in the eye and said that I should listen to him carefully. He said that if someone unfairly takes something from you, no matter how small or insignificant it might seem, letting them get away with it will cost you a hell of a lot more in the long term. To Ray Jackson, his principles were worth more than nine hours of unpaid labour.

As for Freddy Milner, he arrived home from his holiday to find a pile of building materials where his porch once stood. He did return to Granddad's yard to re-buy the two pallets of bricks he never paid for, but this time, Granddad insisted on cash up front and charged Freddy fifty per cent extra. He called it an inconvenience tax.

The moral of the story has stuck with me to this day — if someone takes from you, never let them get away with it. Never.

"Would you like a drink, Madam?" a steward asks.

I glance down at the photo of Bruce Franklin on the screen before replying.

"I'll take a gin and tonic. Larger the better, please."

It hasn't taken much, but I no longer want to calm my nerves. I want to stoke the rage. When I land in New York, I can't afford to be anything less than fired up for my mission. And when I finally track down Bruce Franklin, I will dismantle his world, but not in the same methodical way Granddad deconstructed Freddy Milner's porch — I want to take Franklin down with a fucking sledgehammer.

Chapter 7

My body clock is shot. There's only a five-hour time difference between London and New York, but long enough to mess with my sleep pattern. I was in my hotel room and fast asleep by nine o'clock yesterday evening and up this morning just before six.

Even though my eighth-floor hotel room offers a half-decent view north, and I'm currently watching the sun's early rays reflecting off the skyscrapers in the distance, it still feels surreal enough that I could be dreaming. It's not a dream, though, and even if it were, a nightmare would be a more fitting description — a £1.9 million nightmare, to be precise.

The last time I was in New York, Mum and I were typical tourists, but there won't be any time for sightseeing on this trip. I will, however, be visiting the same coffee shop where we first met Bruce Franklin after visiting the art gallery. It's a long shot, but his modus operandi might be to hang around in that coffee shop as many hundreds of tourists must pass through the gallery every day. The ideal hunting ground for his prey of choice: lonely, middle-aged women with a healthy bank balance.

It's also crossed my mind that Mum is unlikely to be Franklin's first and only victim. He was so convincing, his story so perfectly crafted, he has to be a career conman. And, like anyone who's worked decades in the same career, he's mastered the art of knowing how to utilise both his skills and time for maximum reward. If he's hitting two or three marks a year, and they're all losing amounts similar to Mum, Bruce Franklin is likely a very rich man.

It's all supposition on my part and meaningless at the end of the day, but if Franklin were a known conman with a string of convictions to his name, the police should have picked him up by now. Alas, they don't even have a file open because, besides the messages and photographs, they've nothing to go on. Not one lead.

I have asked myself if I'm being naive coming here, stupid even. Surely, if there were any actionable clues in the messages from Franklin, the police would have already followed them up. I'm just an artist from Essex, so what chance do I stand of finding Franklin if the legal authorities are convinced there's nothing to go on? It's a point I wrestled with for a few weeks, but then I realised I have what the New York Police Department will never have, and that's an unshakeable motivation. For them, it's a job; for me, it's deeply personal.

My stomach reminds me that, despite the early hour, it's past my regular breakfast time. Before I head out, I hop in the shower and put on appropriate clothes for the day. I'm reliably informed that September is the best month to visit New York as there's still plenty of sunshine without the oppressive heat of summer. Warm days and cool nights do appeal, not that it would have made one jot of difference if Franklin had stolen Mum's money in the height of summer or during the biting cold of winter — I'd still be here.

I'm about to leave the room when I catch sight of my reflection in a tall mirror near the door. I stop momentarily and stare at the woman looking back at me. She doesn't look happy, which is understandable considering the task she faces, but she doesn't look that different to the woman I saw in my bathroom mirror long before Bruce Franklin appeared on the scene. The aesthetics have altered a bit over the six months, primarily my shoulder-length auburn hair that's now dappled with honey-blonde highlights, but it's my green eyes that have changed the most. They haven't, of course, because eyes don't change colour, but they've lost a certain luminescence. Granddad used to say they sparkled like cut emeralds, but that lustre, like Granddad himself, is now noticeably absent.

I don't know how I'll restore that sparkle in the long term, but here and now, getting a solid lead on Bruce Franklin would certainly help the cause.

After a reassuring nod to the woman in the mirror, I leave the hotel room.

If there's one thing New York has no shortage of, it's hotels. When deciding which of the vast array to choose, I had three criteria: location, safety, and price. I spent probably too long whittling down my options and settled on a lesser-known chain hotel called The Avaro, just off Grand Street in Lower Manhattan.

With no idea where my search might lead me, the location is only important as far as it being fairly central and within a short walk of a subway station. As for the other two criteria, no major city is entirely safe, but I've spent enough time in central London to hone my threat instincts. The price is one I'm willing to pay, and I'm hoping it'll prove a sound investment rather than a straight-out loss.

I pass through the deserted hotel foyer, past a male receptionist who barely musters a smile, let alone a good morning. It's just gone seven, so I'll forgive him. Outside on the pavement I hesitate because even though the sun is up, there's a slight chill in the air. I briefly consider heading back to the room for a hoodie to slip over my

T-shirt, but I know I'll rue that decision by mid-morning. Besides, I'm only a minute away from the warm confines of a coffee shop.

With my bag slung over my shoulder, I set off.

I've not travelled widely, but I've been to at least half the capital cities in Europe, and one thing that links all of them is how similar they are. Strip away the monuments, the road signs, and all the tourist baubles, and you could be in any city. And although each will have plenty of independent businesses, most major streets are dominated by global brands. I've sipped coffee in a Starbucks in Paris, Rome, and Madrid, and this morning, I'm about to sample a branch in New York.

Knowing I'll be on my feet all day and covering a lot of ground, I don't feel so guilty about ordering a bacon and egg wrap plus a large Americano with three sugars. The high calorie jumpstart is much needed.

I take my order to a table next to an easterly-facing window to bask in the early morning sunshine while plotting my day. After demolishing the wrap, I pull the tablet from my bag and switch it on. I had considered bringing my laptop, as I prefer a physical keyboard, but it's too cumbersome to lug around with me. I could have just used my phone, but the small screen makes every task ten times harder. Being the Goldilocks character I am, I considered the tablet just right for my needs: large enough to view spreadsheets and trawl the internet but light enough to carry around.

The first row on the Bruce Franklin spreadsheet relates to the address he used and my starting point — the vacation rental he claimed to live in and own. I know he definitely stayed there because I have a copy of a video chat in which he walked around the apartment so Mum could see where he lived. I compared that video to the photos on the vacation home website, and although the police didn't agree it's the same apartment, I'm sure it is. What I don't know is how long he rented the place for, but it's where I'm heading as soon as I've finished my coffee.

I double-check the route to the Upper West Side of Manhattan and return the tablet to my bag. It's still a bit on the early side, but I'd rather head straight to my destination than linger. With that, I gulp back the coffee dregs and head outside.

Canal Street subway station is only a few hundred yards from Starbucks, and as I make my way in a westerly direction, the pavements are much busier than they were when I left the hotel: early birds in suits heading to the office, joggers in sweat-stained vest tops, and scores of anonymous souls heading somewhere or returning from nowhere. I study every face coming towards me, just in case a miracle occurs, and Bruce Franklin happens to be one of them. I know the chance of randomly spotting him within the first hour of my search is almost zero, but if you don't buy a ticket, you'll never win the lottery.

I arrive at the entrance to Canal Street subway and descend the stairs amongst the throng of commuters. I did toy with the idea of setting off after the rush hour, but I need to make the most of every minute I'm here. Besides, I've endured the morning crush on London's Underground more times than I care to recall, and it's hard to imagine worse.

After navigating the station concourse and escalators down to the platform, I join the stony-faced commuters waiting for the L train heading north. It's only a twenty-minute ride to 86th Street, but if the packed platform is any guide, it'll be standing room only for most of it.

The train comes into view and screeches to a standstill. The same protocol of allowing passengers to disembark is in force, but as soon as the doors are clear, there's a stampede to grab one of the few empty seats. I take my time and secure a spot in the corner beside the luggage compartment. It affords a good view down the carriage, and although I can't imagine for one second that Bruce Franklin ever takes the subway, there's no harm in keeping my eyes peeled.

The train sets off, and if I were to close my eyes, I could almost be on the Piccadilly Line back in London, heading somewhere I'd much rather be, like Leicester Square or Covent Garden. When I was a young teenager, I'd often stay at my grandparent's house in Shoreditch during the school holidays, and Granddad would occasionally give me a tenner to buy a travelcard so I could explore London on my own while he was working.

I once told an old school friend, Ella, about my adolescent sight-seeing trips across London, and she was horrified. Being a parent to two young girls, Ella said she couldn't imagine allowing her daughters to roam solo across the capital at any age, never mind at thirteen. Maybe she had a point, but from Granddad's perspective, he only granted me the same freedom he afforded Mum and Aunt Lynn when they were young, and no harm came to either of them. In Mum's case, the harm would come much later in life.

I stand in the corner, enduring the heat and the noise while watching the flow of passengers on and off the train at each of the thirteen stations. A handful of those stations have proper names, such as Houston Street and Christopher St-Sheridan Square, but most are named after the nearest street. American tourists in London must marvel at the names of our streets and tube stations over their utilitarian numbering system. Who wouldn't rather visit Mornington Crescent over 14th Street or Bromley-by-Bow over 72nd Street?

Finally, the train slows to a halt at another numbered station: 86th Street. I hurry out onto the platform before the flood of inbound passengers blocks my way.

After another escalator and another concourse, I finally emerge back into the sunlight on the corner of 86th Street and Broadway. My ultimate destination is only a few blocks away, and that knowledge tugs at an anxious knot in my stomach. I don't know why because there is every likelihood I'll return to 86th Street station within an hour, disappointed. Maybe that's the reason for the sudden pang of anxiety. Having spent weeks arranging this trip, all I had to focus on was mining leads and planning logistics, but now I have to face the stark reality — this might be the first step in the most foolish of fool's errands.

Chapter 8

As I stride purposefully along West End Avenue, I feel even smaller than my five-foot, two-inch frame. Both sides of the Avenue are dominated by imposing buildings that block the sun's rays and loom ominously over me. Even the smallest buildings are six storeys high, with the larger ones maybe eleven or twelve. Based solely upon the canopied front doors, most of them are there to provide a home, temporary or otherwise, for the wealthy.

I'm about to check my location against the map on my phone when it suddenly vibrates in my pocket. I pull it out and check the screen, but I don't recognise the number.

"Hello."

"Gina, it's Lynn."

I haven't spoken to my aunt since she dropped by the bungalow a few weeks ago, just as I was finalising this trip.

"Morning," I reply half-heartedly.

"It's afternoon, actually," she huffs. "Have you just got out of bed? I know what you creative types are like."

Overlooking her insult, I could kick myself for forgetting the five-hour time difference. As far as everyone back home is concerned, I should be enjoying the afternoon sunshine in Paris.

"Did you just call to have a dig, or was there something you wanted?"

"Yes, I want to know why you never told me you were going away."

"I didn't realise I had to run my plans by you."

"You don't unless those plans involve abandoning my sister. What were you thinking — running off to Paris when your poor mother is still so low?"

"For your information, Lynn, it was Mum who insisted I come here."

"But you didn't think to tell me? I could have moved in to look after her."

"I didn't see the point. Paula is more than capable, and she's less likely to do anything sketchy behind Mum's back."

"Get over yourself," Lynn snaps. "What happened between me and your no-good father happened a very long time ago. If your mother can get past it, so can you."

"Oh, I'm past it," I snap back. "But that doesn't mean I trust you, which is why I asked Paula to stay with Mum and not you."

"Your poor grandfather would be so disappointed if he knew what a vindictive mare you've become, Gina ... God rest his soul."

The mention of Granddad's name in such a disparaging manner raises my hackles. I bite back.

"I think he'd be more disappointed that you and your husband wasted a large chunk of his money on some insane business venture. How's that panning out for you?"

"Not that it's any of your business, but it's working out just fine, thank you."

While Mum squirrelled Granddad's inheritance money away in a supposedly safe savings account, Lynn invested her windfall on a madcap plan to buy a run-down hotel in Basildon, some ten miles from Brentwood. It was her husband, Stephen, who convinced Lynn that they could make a go of it, but after buying the building and blowing almost a million quid on the refurbishment, the hotel's occupancy levels are still below the break even point.

"If you say so, Lynn," I scoff. "But, unless you've got anything else you'd like to complain about, I'm due somewhere."

"There is something else, yes. I want you to call Paula and tell her that I'll take over."

"That's not going to happen. Mum is fine, and I trust Paula to keep her that way until I return."

"I'm her sister," Lynn protests.

"You were also her sister when you ran off with her husband."

"I've told you—"

"Sorry, I've got to go," I interject. "Bye."

I end the call knowing full well that Lynn will be fuming that I had the last word. It's not that I enjoy the constant bickering with Mum's sister, but I just can't seem to find the motivation to repair our fractured relationship. In life, there are some people you naturally get on with and others who just get under your skin. I'm sure Lynn feels exactly the same way, and that's about all we have in common.

Putting thoughts of Lynn to the back of my mind, I tap the phone screen to bring up the map of West End Avenue. The building I'm searching for is represented by a red pin, and it's just across the road. I walk on towards the nearest pedestrian crossing and hurry across to the opposite pavement.

One of the few buildings on West End Avenue to have a name rather than a number, Newton Heights is a ten-storey Art-Deco building with a plush, burgundy-coloured canopy protruding from its limestone façade. Although I've studied the building in photos, it's all the more impressive in real life, and the only way it might be considered more opulent would be the addition of a red carpet leading up to the front doors.

I approach those doors and place my right hand against the polished brass push plate, half expecting a uniformed doorman to appear.

The grandeur continues on the other side of the doors. I know from my cursory research that Newton Heights was originally constructed as a five-star hotel, but it welcomed its last guest in the late eighties, just before the parent company filed for bankruptcy. A developer purchased the building and, some years later, converted the old hotel into luxury apartments. From what I've seen thus far that developer went to great lengths to preserve the building's heritage.

The foyer, on first impression, is likely the same today as it was back in the thirties: polished marble floors, oak-panelled walls, and lighting provided by two impressive chandeliers hanging from a ceiling edged with decorative coving. The reception desk sits to the left, housing the only nod to modernity — a computer keyboard and monitor. That said, the young, dark-haired guy sitting upright in a chair behind the desk certainly wasn't around in the thirties, either. He flashes me a smile.

"Good morning," I say breezily as I approach the reception desk.

"Good morning, Miss," he replies.

I glance down at the gold-coloured badge attached to his jacket lapel. I really hope Enzo has a weakness for British damsels in distress because the bullshit story I've concocted is relying upon it.

"I'm in need of some help," I remark, pausing for effect.

I flutter my eyelids and offer a silent prayer that Enzo isn't gay.

"It's my father," I continue. "He's been missing for almost six months now, and we're at our wit's end."

"Oh dear," Enzo replies with a suitable level of concern,

"And we know that he was staying in an apartment here around the 12th of March this year."

Before the young man can respond, I pull out my phone and tap through to a photo of Bruce Franklin. I show the photo to Enzo.

"The reason we're so concerned," I continue. "Is that Dad suffers from schizophrenia."

"I'm so sorry," Enzo responds with an encouraging level of concern. "My grandma had mental health issues later in life. Is your father's condition serious?"

"I'm afraid it is," I reply solemnly.

I wrestled with my conscience about spinning such a twisted lie but, in the end, I figured that I had no choice because I've only got one shot at this. If I'm to make headway, I need to garner sympathy. Simply pitching up with a photo of some random guy isn't likely to prick anyone's conscience.

"How can I help?" Enzo asks.

"We've established that he rented an apartment in this building via one of those vacation websites, and knowing which specific apartment would be helpful. What we really need to know, though, is how he made the booking."

Enzo's attention remains fixed on the photo so I return the phone to my pocket so he can focus on my request.

"Is that something you can help me with?" I ask, although it almost sounds like I'm pleading.

"Have you spoken to the company that handled the booking?"

"I emailed them three times, begging for help, but they just ignored my emails. There's no phone number on the website, so I took the only remaining option and ... and here I am."

Enzo takes a moment and then runs a hand through his hair.

"There are twenty-three apartments in the building," he says in a low voice. "Most of them are owner-occupied or let to regular tenants, but three are available on a short-term rental basis. I guess your father rented one of those, right?"

"We know it's on the ninth floor if that's any help."

That seemingly inconsequential nugget of information came courtesy of Franklin during his video chat with Mum.

"That'll be apartment nineteen, then. It's the only one on that floor that's available on a short-term basis."

"Okay, great. Can you tell me who owns the apartment? Maybe they'll be able to find out how Dad made the booking."

"How will that help you find him?"

"Because we don't know how he paid for the apartment. There's no record on his bank account, so he must have another one we're not aware of. If we can establish which bank it is, we can ask them where he's been using his card."

It took me almost an entire weekend to put this tale together, and I've spent every day since trying to identify any holes in it. It's now about to get its final and most important test.

"Have you not asked the police to help?" Enzo responds.

"As you can likely tell from my accent, I'm from London. We spoke to the police there, but they said there's nothing they can do and we should contact NYPD. I don't know if you've ever had any dealings with your police department, but they're not what you'd call efficient."

"You can say that again," Enzo snorts.

"I reported Dad missing, but they haven't done a thing," I continue. "If he isn't taking his medication, and we're terrified he isn't, it's likely his condition will deteriorate rapidly."

The receptionist looks at his watch and then up towards the nearest chandelier.

"Please," I urge. "Help me."

"Listen, Miss," he says, returning his attention to the sorrowful English woman standing on the opposite side of his desk. "I've only been in this job for eight months, and I can't afford to lose it. The people who own the apartments here are rich, which means they're also powerful. If I get busted for sharing private information, I'll never work in Manhattan again."

"I completely understand," I reply, adding a little croak to my voice for extra effect. "But you have my word that I won't let on how I found out. If you help me, Enzo, no one will ever know. I promise."

What Enzo doesn't know is my true motive for finding out who owns the apartment. I'm one hundred per cent certain that Bruce Franklin is a fake name, and it's not beyond the realms of possibility that the scumbag who conned my mother used his real name to rent the apartment. I know from previous experience that landlords want to see proof of ID before they hand over the keys, and I can't see Franklin going to the trouble of obtaining a forged passport and bank account in his made-up name.

"I don't know who owns apartment nineteen," Enzo finally says. "But I do know the name of a man who might."

"Okay."

He reaches across his desk and opens a thick book. From my vantage point, I can see the row of handwritten text running down the page but not what that handwriting says.

"Every visitor has to sign in," Enzo confirms. "Doesn't matter if they're here to drop off a pizza or they're a Wall Street executive visiting a client — everyone has to sign in."

"I see."

"Every five or six weeks, a guy from the management company drops in to check on apartment nineteen. He's usually only here for ten minutes but he, like everyone else, has to sign in."

Enzo then flicks back a page and runs his finger down a column on the left.

"He was last here on the 27th of August."

Not that I want to interrupt, but replying would be tricky as I'm holding my breath. Enzo then looks up from the book.

"We've got a kid on the way, and if I lose my job because you ratted—"

"I made you a promise, Enzo, and I've never broken a promise, nor would I."

"The guy's name is Sean Hoffman, and the management company is called Pinhill Properties."

"I don't suppose you know if their offices are nearby?"

"Couldn't tell you," Enzo shrugs, slamming the book shut. "And I've already said too much."

I step closer to the desk and hold out my hand. "You're a good man, Enzo, and I know you'll make a wonderful father because you've helped me find mine. Thank you."

He shakes my hand while looking up at me with a strained smile. "Good luck."

"I appreciate it, and please don't worry — no one will ever know how I got Mr Hoffman's name."

Whilst I might have just spun Enzo a pack of lies, the promise I made was entirely genuine. I only hope that those lies still work when I spin them for a second time.

Chapter 9

My decision not to wear a hoodie is vindicated when I depart Newton Heights and stroll back up West End Avenue, the left-hand pavement now bathed in sunlight. As much as I welcome the warmth, I need to find somewhere to sit down and research both Sean Hoffman and Pinhill Properties.

It seems likely I'll need to take the subway again and being that there's always a coffee shop near a subway station, I head back in the direction of 86th Street.

Unsurprisingly, I don't have to walk far to find a suitable stop-off point. I enter the independent coffee shop, and rather than wait for a coffee, I grab a bottle of orange juice from the chiller, pay for it, and dash to the nearest empty table.

The juice bottle remains unopened as I pull out my phone and frantically tap the screen. The first and obvious point of call is Google, and I enter the name Pinhill Properties. The slow mobile connection adds a layer of frustration to my research, but eventually, the search engine returns the results. At the very top of the page is a listing that almost matches my search: Pinhill Property Management LLC. I quickly scroll down the page, but all the results seem to relate to the same company located in Flatbush, Brooklyn. I return to the top of the page and tap the first link.

Pinhill's website is as basic as it gets, offering just four options in the navigation menu. I'm not a landlord or a tenant, so I tap the link for the 'About Us' page. There's a paragraph of text about the company's history and values, but it's the title above the second paragraph that snares my attention. It confirms that Sean Hoffman is the owner of Pinhill Property Management.

I need a moment to consider my next move, so I sit back in the chair and crack open the orange juice.

When I was at art college, I took a job in a call centre, working six hours every Saturday for a double-glazing company. The role involved cold calling homeowners to try and book an appointment for a sales rep to visit, and I detested every minute of it. If I was lucky, maybe one in a hundred calls resulted in an appointment, but when I was talking to one of the sales reps in the staffroom, he gloated that for every four customers he visited, he made one sale. Arrogant as he was, he did admit that selling over the phone was considerably more difficult than selling in person. He then tried to convince me I should go out for dinner with him. He failed, and I left the job the following week.

As brief and soul-destroying as my telesales job proved, it did teach me a valuable lesson. When you're talking to someone on the phone, it's so easy for them to terminate the conversation. When you're standing in front of them, face to face, the chances of you being able to get your point across are massively increased. It's the reason why I decided to make this trip, and if my meeting with Enzo at Newton Heights is any barometer, it was the right decision.

With only a basic grasp of New York's geography, I return to my phone and search for Pinhill's address and the quickest method of getting there. It only takes a moment to establish that my next target is a forty-minute journey on the subway followed by a fifteen-minute walk. It's a relief but, before I set off, I need to make sure I'm not about to embark on a pointless journey. I turn my attention to how I can ensure that Sean Hoffman will be at his desk when I pitch up.

By the time the juice bottle is empty I'm ready to make a phone call. I plug Pinhill's number into my phone and tap the dial icon.

"Good morning," a female voice announces after the fifth ring. "Pinhill Property Management."

"Hi, there. I'm in a bit of a rush between appointments, but I was hoping I could book a slot to see Mr Hoffman later today."

"May I ask what it's in connection with?"

"I have an apartment on West End Avenue I'm looking to rent out."

"Okay, let me just pull up Sean's diary. One moment, Miss ..."

"Jackson."

"Thank you, Miss Jackson. Bear with me."

The sound of a mouse clicking is marginally louder than the quickening beat of my heart.

"I'm afraid today will be difficult," the woman then says. "How about tomorrow or Thursday?"

This is by far my best lead, but if it turns out to be a dead end, I need to know sooner rather than later.

"Neither work for me. I'm only in town today so it looks like I'll have to call another agent. Thanks for your—"

"Just give me one second," the woman interjects.

More mouse-clicking ensues before she returns to the line.

"I could squeeze you in today, but it won't be until early afternoon. Would two o'clock work?"

"Yes, I think it will. Book me in, please."

After requesting my email address and phone number, the woman confirms my appointment. I end the call and puff a sigh of relief. It's likely premature as the hard work is yet to come, but at least I've got a foot in the door.

A more immediate issue is how I spend the four hours before my appointment with Sean Hoffman. I pull out my tablet and reference the spreadsheet of leads. After the apartment, the next row relates to the coffee shop where Mum met Franklin. It was always likely to be the most time-intensive lead, so now is as good a time as any to follow it up. I check the journey details on an app and leave.

Much like London, tourists can view many of New York's tourist hotspots within a short subway journey. I take the L train south and, nine minutes later, hop off at 59th Street and Columbus Circle. It's a station I visited with Mum on our last trip as it's only a few minutes' walk to The Museum of Modern Art. I'm not sure Mum was quite as enthusiastic as I was about visiting the museum, but she seemed to enjoy browsing the headline pieces: Van Gogh's *Starry Night*, Dali's *Persistence of Memory*, and a painting I've never much liked, *Campbell's Soup Can* by Andy Warhol.

Alas, there won't be any time for art today, although my destination is temptingly close to The Museum of Modern Art. Maybe one day, I'll come back on my own and spend an entire week drifting around New York's art museums and galleries. Some might question which is sadder — spending an entire week staring at art or doing it alone.

Using the sat nav on my phone to guide me, I bypass the crowds loitering outside the museum and make my way to East 54th Street, passing the gallery and on towards the coffee shop we visited. It's only a minute's walk, and at the time, we didn't think anything of it, but if we'd walked a bit slower or maybe stumbled upon a different coffee shop, we might never have crossed paths with Bruce Franklin.

When I turn the corner onto East 54th Street, the scale of my task becomes obvious, to the point of overwhelming. This isn't some seldom-visited backstreet, and the pavements are busy, crowded even.

Trying to remain positive, I zigzag my way towards the coffee shop, but when I reach the infamous spot where we first met Bruce Franklin, my heart sinks. The coffee shop has gone, replaced by an upmarket jeweller. I should have considered that in a city as transient as New York, businesses must come and go all the time.

However, with time to kill, I decide that no matter how long the odds, I'll never know if I never try.

It takes just over two hours to visit every business within a minute's walk of the coffee shop. I repeat the lie about Franklin being a missing relative so many times that it becomes ingrained in my mind. I pose the question to scores of strangers, and their responses vary from mild sympathy to complete disinterest. What they all have in common, though, is that no one recognises the man in the photo.

Disappointed but not surprised by the outcome, I trudge back to the subway station.

The train heading to Flatbush isn't anywhere near as busy as the commuter train I journeyed on during rush hour, and mercifully, I'm able to secure a seat. With nothing else better to do, I pull out the tablet and delete one of the rows on the spreadsheet of leads. I was never optimistic that a member of staff in the coffee shop might recognise Franklin, but deleting the lead still smarts. Perhaps more worrying is that it wasn't even the most tenuous lead on the list. If my meeting with Sean Hoffman doesn't bear fruit, I'll be scraping the barrel of leads by tomorrow lunchtime.

I've enough self-awareness to realise when my optimism is flagging. I wonder if, in part, the creeping negativity is down to my environment. Being confined to an overly warm carriage with no natural light, surrounded by doleful faces, isn't likely to raise anyone's spirits. I put the tablet away, put my earbuds in, and open the Spotify app on my phone. At the very top of the screen is the playlist I listen to the most, although I'd die if anyone outside my circle of close friends discovered what a cheese-fest I've compiled.

The first track starts: *That Don't Impress Me Much* by Shania Twain. I'm immediately transported back in time to the late nineties, sitting next to Mum in the car on the way home from junior school. Whenever a song came on the radio she liked, up went the volume, and we'd sing along even if we didn't know all the words. The vast majority of the songs on my playlist are from that period, but there are also a few early seventies tracks that Granddad introduced me to, and I subsequently fell in love with: *Cracklin' Rosie* by Neil Diamond, *Life is a Minestrone* by 10cc, and David Bowie's *The Jean Genie*. If there's one abiding memory of my grandparents' house, it's the sound of music playing on a radio from morning till evening.

Shania Twain, still unimpressed, fades out, and another song begins. It has no connection to either Mum or my grandparents but someone else I cared deeply about. It's a song we heard on our first date, and although the memories of what followed are bittersweet, I wouldn't change them for the world. Now is not the time to lament what might have been, and I tap through to the next song.

If I wasn't concerned about my bag being stolen, I'd close my eyes and let the music carry me away. Instead, I stare at the floor and inwardly smile at the memories. I have my Mum and my grandparents to thank for ensuring I had a happy childhood, and now two of the three are gone, I've only got one opportunity left to demonstrate how grateful I am.

I owe it to my mum to find Franklin, and I can't let her down. I just can't.

Chapter 10

Flatbush isn't a part of New York commonly visited by tourists. That much is obvious as I make my way along the curiously named Cortelyou Road towards Flatbush Avenue. I know next to nothing about Brooklyn, but I do know the crime rate is higher here than in Manhattan, so I deliberately plotted my route to Pinhill's office along the main roads. I remind myself that the same rules for a lone woman apply here as they've always applied in London. Keep your chin up, eyes fixed on the road ahead, walk purposefully, and don't get your phone out unless absolutely necessary. In other words, don't do anything that might signal to an undesirable that you're a tourist, especially a lost tourist.

The other benefit of sticking to the main roads is that I don't have to memorise complex directions. Turn right out of the subway station, continue along Cortelyou Road until I reach Flatbush Avenue, and then turn left. Then, after a ten-minute walk, my ultimate destination, Farragut Road, will be on the right. Piece of cake.

After a minute or two on Flatbush Avenue, I start to relax a little. In a way, it reminds me of parts of London that have so far escaped gentrification. The shops lined up on both sides of the street cater to the needs of local residents rather than tourists, and the vibe is more communal than threatening. No one gives me a second glance as I stride along the pavement, but I suppose there's no reason they should. Unless I open my mouth, no one would know I'm a long way from home, and I deliberately dressed down so I wouldn't attract attention.

Halfway down Flatbush Avenue, I stop at a convenience store. The temperature must be in the mid-twenties, and with the sun directly ahead, I can feel dehydration setting in. I manage to buy a bottle of water without exposing my accent and then gulp it back outside the store.

Eventually, and with some relief, I reach the junction with Farragut Road and turn right. Not for the first time today, I go over my cover story again, ensuring that it's watertight. It worked once, so there's no reason it won't work again.

The offices of Pinhill Property Management come into view. It's not much to look at from the outside, but it blends into its surroundings perfectly. The main window has a vertical blind running from top to bottom, and the only way you'd know that there's a business inside is the prominent gold lettering on the glass, confirming the name of the business and its claimed position as the number one property management company in Brooklyn. American business owners love signs, it seems, and they like them to stand out, even at the cost of appearing tacky.

I cross the road and check the time. I'm five minutes early, but hopefully, Sean Hoffman appreciates his appointments running early rather than late. I push open the door and enter.

Inside, I can quite see why they had the vertical blinds installed. There are two desks stacked high with paperwork and a row of battered filing cabinets lined up against the back wall. If I were a prospective client, I'd likely turn around and leave on first impressions alone. The place is drab; as are each of the women at the desks.

"Can I help?" the one on the left says after finally looking up from her phone.

"I've got an appointment with Sean Hoffman at two," I reply, doing my utmost to sound like a woman who owns an apartment on one of Manhattan's swankiest avenues.

"Miss Jackson?" the woman confirms, peering at me over the top of her glasses.

"That's correct."

It did dawn on me that although I don't look like I own a swanky apartment, the British accent is considered authoritative to the American ear, so I've been told.

"Take a seat, and I'll see if Mr Hoffman is free yet."

As the woman reaches for a telephone on her desk, the mousey woman at the other desk stands up and, in a quiet voice, informs her colleague that she's heading out for ten minutes. She then leaves without so much as a glance in my direction.

"Your two o'clock is here," the now lone employee says into the phone receiver. "Shall I bring her through?"

She places the receiver down and stands up. "Come this way."

I follow her through a door and along a corridor towards the rear of the building. She stops at a door on the right, knocks twice, and then waits for a response. It strikes me as a bit unnecessary as she only spoke to Sean Hoffman twenty seconds ago.

"Come in," a male voice responds.

The woman opens the door and beckons me in. I take six paces forward until I'm standing in Sean Hoffman's office, and then the woman leaves us to it, pulling the door shut. The man himself is sitting behind a desk, his eyes still fixed on a computer monitor.

"Won't be a moment," he says without looking up.

I take the opportunity to survey my surroundings. The same size as the front office but a lot less cluttered, the space is split into two halves. Hoffman's desk, a well-stocked bookcase, and a couple of filing cabinets occupy the left side of the room, while an L-shaped sofa and coffee table fill the right-hand side. It's certainly more impressive than the front office where the two women work, and I presume this is where the boss entertains prospective clients.

"Sorry about that," Sean Hoffman says in a nasally Brooklyn accent. "Good to meet you, Miss Jackson."

He stands up and holds out a hand for me to shake. I step forward and oblige, and the moment my hand touches his, he adds his left hand and smothers mine, pumping it up and down with unnecessary enthusiasm. It's over the top, but he thinks I'm a potential client, and he's American, I remind myself.

"Nice to meet you too," I reply with a thin smile. "And call me Gina, please."

Hoffman finally releases my hand and invites me over to the sofa where we can talk in comfort, apparently. I let him lead and take the opportunity to appraise the man I'm about to lie to. I'd guess he's in his late forties or early fifties, but he's trying a little too hard to look younger. Rather than business attire, he's wearing inappropriately tight jeans and a black Hilfiger polo shirt designed for a man some two decades away from the curse of middle-aged spread.

He flops down on the sofa, and I join him, ensuring we're a comfortable distance apart.

"I understand you're looking to rent out your apartment on West End Avenue," he begins.

Time to confess my lie.

"I'm afraid that's not strictly correct, Mr Hoffman."

"Sean, please. And what part of it isn't correct?"

"All of it. I don't own an apartment ... well, not in Manhattan, anyway."

He replies with a confused frown.

"I lied because I'm desperate," I continue in a pleading tone. "And you're about the only man who can help me."

I can't risk letting him throw me out before I've had the chance to present the bullshit story about my missing schizophrenic father. I turn to face him, adopt my best puppy dog eyes, and go for it. It's a performance that a trained actor would be proud of, even if I say so myself.

"So, again, I apologise," I conclude. "But can you now understand why I'm so desperate?"

Hoffman leans back on the sofa and rests his arm along the top edge.

"What is it you want from me?" he then asks impassively.

"I need to know as much as you can tell me about Dad's booking. Your company handles all the bookings, right?"

"We do."

"Then, could you tell me? Please."

He drums his fingers on the back of the sofa for a long moment.

"If you tell me the real reason you want to know this dude's name, maybe I can help."

"I'm sorry?"

Hoffman stares back at me with a knowing smile.

"I've been around the block a few times, young lady ... enough times to know a lie when I hear one."

A warm glow begins blossoming across my cheeks.

"I, err ... I'm telling you the truth. Honest."

"I'm afraid I don't believe you. So, unless you're willing to be honest, I think we're done here."

I'm faced with a binary decision: reveal the truth about Bruce Franklin or get up and leave empty-handed. There's not really a decision to be made.

"Okay," I sigh. "I am trying to find someone, but not for the reasons I told you."

"Go on."

I relay the edited version of what happened to Mum, and it doesn't require any acting skills to let the anger carry on my words.

"Jeez," Hoffman responds once I've come clean. "Sounds like this dude took your mom to the cleaners."

"Yeah, he did, and I intend to make the arsehole pay."

"But you don't even know his real name."

"No, but you do ... or at least I hope you do."

The smile returns as he rubs his chin.

"I'm sure we have a name on file, and we do require ID from everyone who rents one of our properties, so maybe I can help you."

"That would be amazing," I gush.

"But this is New York, young lady, and no one does nothing for nothing in this city."

"I've got money if that's what you want. Not much, but some."

"Nah," he replies, shaking his head. "You've got something far more interesting than money."

"I have?"

He drops his arm off the top of the sofa and lets it land on his gut. Then, he reaches for his belt buckle.

"You know, Gina, I've never been sucked off by a British woman before. If you'd like the honour of being the first, I'll give you that name you're so keen to hear."

I stare back at him, open-mouthed. It then dawns on me that a gaping mouth might be a sign of what's to come. I snap it shut. Hoffman appears not to notice and continues unbuckling his belt. It's only then that I notice the wedding ring on his pudgy finger.

"Not a fucking chance," I eventually spit.

"Beg your pardon?"

"I am not sucking your dick."

"Guess a hand job will do, as long as you talk dirty to me in that cute accent of yours."

"I'm not ... no! Not in a million years."

"Seems you don't want that name as badly as you say."

"I do, but I'm not willing to prostitute myself to get it. And you're disgusting for even suggesting it ... what would your wife say if she knew?"

"She'd probably thank you. One less job for her."

Hoffman then checks his watch.

"You've got five seconds to make a choice," he says. "Indulge me or get the hell out of my office."

I consider his proposal for barely one of the five allotted seconds. Desperate as I am, there are limits to how far I'm prepared to go. I stand up.

"Here's a better offer," I say. "I'll give you a hundred bucks for that name, and then you can go pay someone else to suck your dick. How's that sound?"

"No deal. I want you to do it."

"Never going to happen."

"Your loss," he replies, refastening his belt. "Close the door on your way out."

Seething, I'd love nothing more than to tell the scumbag exactly what I think of him, but it'd likely be a waste of breath, not to mention time.

Settling on a glare and a shake of the head, I storm out.

Chapter 11

As I stride past Hoffman's receptionist, she doesn't even look up from the newspaper on her desk. I wonder if she knows that her boss is a pervy scumbag but chooses to turn a blind eye for the sake of a paycheque. It'd be easy to judge, but there are too many men like Hoffman. The receptionist could quit today and find herself working for another piece of shit tomorrow.

I slam the door shut and use the anger to propel my legs forward.

"Fuck!" I hiss.

Reaching the junction of Flatbush Avenue, I turn left and slow my pace a fraction. It's not possible that I could hate anyone as much as I hate Bruce Franklin, but Sean Hoffman comes a very close second. What kind of man sits and listens to a story about an innocent woman being conned for every penny and then, rather than help, chooses to leverage his knowledge for a minute or two of sordid sexual gratification?

Men. Bastard men.

As much as I could wallow in my disdain for Hoffman, there's a bigger issue in play than just his sick request. I've just walked away from the best hope I have of establishing Bruce Franklin's real name.

My anger soon turns to frustration. Somewhere in Hoffman's office, likely on a computer hard drive, is the key to my quest. I could return to my spreadsheet and continue chasing the other leads, but I can't deny that they're weak. The apartment booking was always going to be the best hope for unearthing Franklin's true identity, and it still is, but I need another way to unlock it — ideally, one that doesn't involve fellating a fat, middle-aged pervert.

Turning my thoughts to that challenge, I continue along Flatbush Avenue. As I walk, the traffic on the road begins to slow. Ahead, a queue has formed, although I can't see why because there's a big, brown UPS van blocking my view of the avenue. I stride on until I pass the van, and the reason why the traffic is crawling becomes apparent. A hundred yards ahead, two police cars are parked across the road, and a red-faced NYPD officer is waving the traffic towards a turning on his left.

I continue onwards until I reach the roadblock, but as soon as I draw level with the nearest police car, a female officer steps across my path.

"Sorry, Ma'am. I can't let you through."

"Why not?"

"There's been an incident at one of the stores. We're dealing with it, but the road will be shut for at least another hour."

"Great," I groan. "I need to get back to the subway station."

The officer turns and points towards the road where her colleague is currently funnelling the traffic.

"Head along Newkirk Avenue and take the second left. That'll lead you back towards the subway station."

As far as today goes, the minor detour is the least worthy reason to be agitated. I thank the officer and cross the avenue.

The traffic is no better on Newkirk Avenue as scores of drivers try to work out a new route to their destination without the benefit of diversion signs. The first turning on the left is already rammed with traffic, and several vehicles are blocking the way ahead while they wait to turn. I try to ignore the blaring horns and angry yelling and continue towards the second turn. However, as I approach the junction, a group of five unsavoury-looking youths approach from the opposite direction and make their way up the road I intend to enter. I pause for a moment and consider my options. With the luck I've had this afternoon, I'm not willing to take any chances.

I continue on and take the next turn on the left. From my earlier check on the map, the roads all run parallel, so I'll still end up in the same place, more or less, and it avoids even the remote possibility of encountering trouble with local gang members.

The other benefit of my new route is the lack of traffic. The quiet allows me to gather my thoughts but, as I walk, one thought dominates the rest — gaining access to the Pinhill computer system. I know a little about computers, but only enough to create a document or spreadsheet. What would be incredibly handy right now would be the ability to hack the computer in Hoffman's office. Not only would I have access to the rental records of the apartment on West End Avenue, but I could also teach Hoffman a lesson by sharing all his confidential files with the world.

It's a delicious thought, but that's all it will ever be unless I can find someone with the necessary skills and disregard for the law. Where do you even hire a hacker? I've heard of the dark web but I wouldn't know how to access it.

"You got spare change?" a voice suddenly crackles in my right ear.

Startled, I twist around while taking a step backwards. The voice belongs to a dishevelled man of indeterminable age. Based on his sweat-stained hoodie and rotting teeth, I'm amazed I didn't smell him before he crept up on me.

"No," I reply firmly. "I don't."

I turn and continue on my way, but the stinking skeleton doesn't give up. He matches my stride and draws level.

"C'mon, girl. Give a man a break, huh."

The absolute last thing a woman in my situation should do is show fear. Never one for half-measures, I come to a stop and confront the nuisance.

"Listen, mate," I say in the most Essex of voices. "I don't have any cash, and if you don't stop pestering me, you'll get a kick in the fucking balls for your trouble. Got it?"

The guy takes a step back and raises his hands, palms out. His eyes are so sunken into his skull that I can't tell if he's genuinely surprised, but his actions suggest he is.

"Shit, bitch," he mumbles. "No need for the attitude."

"Leave me alone, and you won't have to put up with my attitude."

I throw him a defiant glare, turn around, and walk briskly away. At some point, the adrenalin will lose its potency, and I'll probably regret fronting up to a man I suspect is a hard-core drug addict. For now, though, I'm relieved not to hear a second set of footsteps.

Fifty yards later, I risk a glance over my shoulder, but the druggie is nowhere to be seen. When I turn around, I realise why there aren't any vehicles using this street as a detour. Ahead, a dilapidated, five-storey building is wrapped in scaffolding, and two skips are blocking the road. A sign states that the road will be closed for five days. Fortunately, the pavement does continue, although on the other side of the street. Just as I'm about to cross, I hear a scuffing sound behind me. I don't even have time to turn my head before a hand lands on my shoulder and shoves hard.

There's a very good reason why Mum never insisted I attend ballet lessons as a little girl, and that's because I'm not blessed with perfect balance, never mind poise. The shove is enough to send me sprawling, and with nothing to arrest my fall, I know that a journey to the pavement is imminent. I land awkwardly, and it's enough to punch the air from my lungs. While I'm gasping for a breath, a familiar figure looms over me. Before I can react, he attacks the strap of my bag with a boxcutter.

I open my mouth to scream, but I can't suck in enough air. The druggie suddenly tugs at the now severed strap and snatches my bag before I've time to cling to it. His prize secured, he doesn't wait around to gloat.

I manage to clamber to my feet just as the druggie sprints towards the dilapidated building. Without looking back, he passes the first skip while I'm still struggling for breath. Everything important to me is in that bag, including my debit card and the tablet.

"Stop!" I manage to gasp, although it's a pointless waste of what little breath I have.

I've no other alternative. Still winded, I set off in pursuit.

I make it to the middle of the road and, trying my hardest to ignore the pain, run like my life depends on it. Drug addicts aren't renowned for their fitness levels, and when I check this particular drug addict's progress, I'm sure he's already slowing down. He passes the second skip and then darts towards the hoardings that surround the building at street level. He has an advantage in that he must know this area like the back of his hand whilst I'm already lost.

My central nervous system kindly delivers a second shot of adrenalin, and it's enough to up my pace.

"Stop!" I yell again.

The druggie momentarily glances over his shoulder, but as he refocuses on an escape route, a figure suddenly emerges from a gap in the hoardings. I'm still a good eighty yards away but close enough to hear the druggie's pained cry as his face makes contact with the figure's outstretched arm. The poleaxing happens so quickly that I'm almost as shocked as the mugger, but the shock soon gives way to relief.

I jog to a standstill, seven or eight feet from the figure who is now looming over the felled, motionless mugger. He then reaches down, snatches up my bag, and steps out of the shadow of the scaffolding.

My relief quickly turns to fear.

In the harsh afternoon sunlight, the man now clutching my bag is a significantly bigger threat than the emaciated drug addict. At least fifteen inches taller and a good foot broader than me, he looks powerful enough to pick me up with one hand and deposit my sorry arse in one of the skips.

He takes two steps forward while the glare of his ice-blue eyes bore into me.

I swallow hard and instinctively take a step backwards. The man then tilts his head to the left a fraction, almost as if he's weighing up how easy it would be to kill me.

Then, he slowly raises his right arm and holds out my bag. His jaw slackens as if he's about to speak. He duly does.

"You lose something, Doll?"

Chapter 12

I replay the words in my head. I expected a New York accent, but I'm sure what I heard was English, London-based, I think.

The interloper takes another step forward, my bag still hanging in the air, tantalisingly close but at the end of the same arm that possibly just killed a fleeing drug addict.

"You gonna take it, or what?" the man asks, his eyes briefly shifting to my bag. "I don't bite."

"You're ... you're from London," I manage to stammer.

"No flies on you, Doll."

I'm still weighing up whether or not to snatch my bag and run when the silence is broken by a low groan. It appears the drug addict isn't dead after all.

"Is he okay?" I ask, nodding towards the pile of skin and bone still lying in the shadow of the scaffolding.

"Dunno," the big Londoner replies with a shrug of his shoulders. "And I don't much give a shit."

On cue, the druggie slowly clambers to his feet and then staggers away without so much as a backward glance. My question answered, the big man puffs a long sigh.

"Have I gotta stand here all afternoon holding this?" he asks.

With suitable levels of trepidation, I step forward and reach out to take my bag.

"You're welcome," the man says as he releases it into my hand.

"I'm ... um, sorry. I mean, thank you."

"You from Essex?" the man then asks.

"Yes. Billericay and now Brentwood."

"Thought as much. You got a name?"

"Gina."

"What you doing around here then, Gina from Essex? You're a long way from home."

"I, um ... the police closed the road, so I had to take a detour."

"I meant, what are you doing in Brooklyn? Ain't many tourists in this neck of the woods."

He's nothing if not observant.

"It's a long story."

"Always is," he snorts. "But I ain't a patient man. What's the short version?"

"I'm searching for someone."

"How's that going?"

"Not great."

"Who you looking for?"

Now I have my bag, there seems little reason to hang around and answer the man's questions.

"Listen, um ... sorry, I didn't catch your name."

"Clement."

"Oh ... unusual name."

"I'm an unusual fella."

"Right, well, I'm genuinely grateful you retrieved my bag, but I need to get going."

Clement nods and then strokes the thick moustache draped around his mouth.

"Where you heading?" he asks.

"To the subway station."

"Want me to walk with you? That scrawny shit ain't likely to come back for more, but plenty of others will. They're like fucking rats round here."

"Um …"

"Before you answer," Clement continues. "There are two things you need to know about me."

"Okay."

"One, I ain't ever laid a finger on a bird, and that ain't gonna change. You've no reason to be scared of me, alright."

"Good to know."

"Two, my offer ain't a ruse to get inside your knickers."

"Wow. That's … also good to know."

"So? You want a chaperone or what?"

If he's as honest as he is frank, I shouldn't have any problems, and I can't deny that the prospect of meeting another crackhead is a concern.

"If you don't mind, I'd be grateful."

"No worries."

He digs his hands into the front pockets of his jeans and beckons me with a nod.

"Come on then."

Whether intentional or not, Clement keeps a safe distance away by walking on the road while I remain on the pavement.

"You gonna tell me who you're looking for, then?" he asks.

"A man."

"That narrows it down."

"Just someone who betrayed my mother."

"Ahh, right. Shag another woman, did he?"

"If only," I huff. "Broken hearts mend eventually."

"What'd he do, then?"

Faced with the choice of walking in silence or venting to a stranger, the latter is just about preferable. I relay the basic details of what Franklin did.

"How is she?" Clement asks once I've finished my sorry tale. "Your mum."

It's not the question I expected, but there's a simple answer.

"Broken."

"Then why aren't you back in Essex, keeping tabs on her?"

"Because ... because the anger is eating me alive. I couldn't just sit around and do nothing."

"So you thought you'd come over here and play detective?"

"That's the plan."

"But it ain't working out?"

"One step forward, one back."

"You're standing still, then?"

As I no longer have to contend with the threat of being mugged, I can refocus my anger on the incident in Sean Hoffman's office. I wouldn't necessarily be so candid with a stranger, but I decide to share the experience with Clement in the hope he offers to visit Hoffman. I'd love to see that.

Alas, all I get for my candour is a tut and a slight scowl.

"I don't suppose you know how to hack a computer system?" I ask, more in hope than expectation.

"Hack? As in, take a meat cleaver to it?"

"Err, no. Hack, as in remotely access a computer."

"Can't help you there, Doll. All this modern computer stuff goes right over my head."

I'm not surprised, but I keep that thought to myself.

"But," Clement continues. "I can think of a few other ways to get that name."

"Really?" I respond, my voice an octave higher. "How?"

"You really wanna know?"

"I wouldn't have asked if I didn't."

We reach the end of the street, and Clement steps onto the pavement, where he comes to a sudden stop.

"You fancy a cuppa?" he asks. "There's a diner on the next block, and I convinced the bloke who owns it to stock Tetley."

"Tetley?" I snort. "You know how to woo a girl."

"As I said, I ain't trying to woo no one, particularly you."

"A woman with thinner skin might take offence at that statement."

"None intended, Doll, but there's nothing of you. I've picked bigger scraps of meat from my teeth after a steak dinner."

His response, brutally frank as it is, at least sounds sincere.

"Well, seeing as we're being frank with one another, you're not my type either," I say in retaliation.

"Why's that? Too good-looking?"

"Too old, more like."

"Cheeky cow," he chuckles. "I'm in the prime of my ... life."

Overlooking the peculiar intonation in his bass-heavy voice, at least he seems to have a sense of humour — he must have, considering his retro sideburns and old-school attire. I'm not exactly on top of the latest fashions, so maybe bell-bottom jeans are all the rage again.

"So, a cup of Tetley, then?" I say. "And I'm buying. I owe you that much."

"Not gonna argue," he says, turning away from me. "This way."

I don't follow him because I have a savage yearning for a cup of tea, but solely because I'm dying to know what methods he might have up his sleeve for extracting that name from Sean Hoffman. If one of those methods involves low-key violence, all the better.

"What brings you to New York?" I ask as we stroll along the pavement side by side.

"I had a bit of business down south, and I'm now trying to get back home."

"Home as in London?"

"Home as in Camden."

"There are plenty of flights back to London most days. What do you mean by trying?"

"I ain't got a passport, so I need to find another way back."

"Can't you just go to the British Embassy and tell them you've lost your passport?"

"I ain't lost it. Never had one."

"Then how did you get to America in the first place?"

"That, Doll, is a bloody good question."

"Does it have a bloody good answer?"

"If it does, I ain't worked it out yet."

We reach the diner, and Clement enters first, holding the door open for me.

The place is deserted, but it's no great surprise considering the dated décor and faint whiff of cigarette smoke lingering in the air.

"Alright, Dex," Clement calls out to a middle-aged black guy behind the counter.

"Be with you in a tick," he replies.

My chaperone falls onto a booth seat near the window. I briefly inspect the seat opposite and then sit down.

"You don't like it in here?" Clement asks.

"I never said that."

"Your face did."

"It has its charms, I suppose."

"Closest thing I've found to a proper greasy spoon like you get back home. Just don't ask for grits."

"Why not?"

"Pure fucking filth, Doll. That's why."

I stifle a chuckle and sit back in the seat.

"What's with your use of the word doll?"

"You one of those feminists who finds it offensive?"

"I never said that. I'm just curious because you rarely hear it these days."

"It's just a habit I picked up a long time ago."

"I like it, actually. My granddad used to call my nan Doll now and then."

"Used to?" Clement replies, his left eyebrow raised.

"They're both gone now."

"Sorry to hear that."

I respond with a nod because I don't want to dwell on a subject that still feels so raw, even now.

"Can I ask you a question?" I say, switching the conversation away from my past.

"You can ask."

"What did you do in London before you ended up here?"

"Do?"

"Yeah, for a job."

"Bit of this, bit of that, but mainly folk paid me to fix their problems."

"What kind of problems?"

"The type that requires a certain kind of solution. Let's leave it at that."

"And is that what you were doing down south?"

"Kind of."

Our conversation is interrupted when the black guy, Dex, ambles over.

"You found yourself a friend, Clem?" he says with a broad smile. "And a pretty one, too."

"We're just getting acquainted, ain't we, Doll?"

"Err, I suppose."

"Another Brit?" Dex asks, turning to me.

"Yep."

"That'll be two cups of Tetley tea, then?" he chuckles.

"Fine by me," I reply because I'm more interested in sating my curiosity rather than my thirst.

94

Dex returns to the counter, and I throw another question at Clement.

"How much do you charge for your problem-solving service?"

"Depends who's asking."

"Me, obviously. You said you had a couple of ideas on how I might get hold of that name I need, and I'm willing to pay for those ideas."

"I ain't gonna charge you."

"That's not what I hoped to hear. In my experience, when men say they're willing to do a favour for a woman, there's almost always an underlying motive."

"Yeah, you're probably right, but not in this case. I wouldn't charge you because I'm not in that game these days. I don't need the money."

"If it's not money, what is your motive?"

Clement stares back at me, his eyes narrowing slightly.

"It seems that I've finally found my calling."

"Your calling?"

"Dishing out just deserts."

"What does that mean?"

"There are some real wrong'uns in this world, and I make it my business to find 'em and administer my own brand of justice."

"Like a vigilante, you mean?"

"It's more complicated than that."

"How so?"

"You only have to walk a hundred yards up the road, and you'll bump into someone up to no good, like that streak of piss who snatched your bag. People break the law every day, sometimes 'cos they ain't got a choice, sometimes 'cos they're just thick as shit. I'm only interested in the real evil fuckers who are beyond salvation. The kind of scum who'll never change, never see the error of their ways."

"That's an interesting ... what would you call it? A hobby? A pastime?"

"As I said, it's a calling."

"Who's doing the calling?"

Before I get an answer, Dex returns to the table.

"Two cups of finest Tetley tea served in a cup and saucer just for my British customers."

"Cheers, Dex," Clement says with a nod.

"Did you want anything to eat?"

"I'm good, ta. I'll nip back later."

"The tea is fine, thanks," I reply, although I definitely won't be returning later.

As Dex wanders off, Clement begins spooning an obscene amount of sugar into his cup. I'm tempted to pass judgement, but I'm more interested in hearing an answer to my question.

"Well?" I continue. "You said that your current occupation is a calling, so who's doing the calling?"

Clement picks up a teaspoon and stirs his tea. He leaves me waiting for several seconds before replying.

"You're not interested in my motives, are you? The only reason you're sitting here sipping tea with me is because you want to get your own back on this Franklin fella, right?"

There's patently a lot more to Clement than just his crude vocabulary and significant brawn. He's observant.

"Yes," I reply.

"And you want something from me?"

"You said you had ideas, and I'd like to hear them."

"Thing is, Doll, is that they ain't ideas you could run with on your own."

"Why not?"

"'Cos you ain't me."

"Never a truer word spoken, but what are you saying exactly?"

"If it's revenge you want, there ain't no one better in this city to help you get it."

It's a bold claim, and if any man other than the significant unit sitting opposite had made it, I'd have grave reservations about their sincerity. However, life has taught me that there's a world of difference between best intentions and happy endings.

"Can I just clarify what it is you're offering here?"

"Go for it."

"You want to help me find Bruce Franklin and exact revenge without any payment or with any expectation of reward?"

"Just about sums it up, yeah."

"And you genuinely have ideas on how we can establish his real name?"

"That's what I said."

I reach for my cup and take a slow sip of tea. The prospect of securing an ally to aid in my quest is certainly appealing, but I haven't entirely taken leave of my senses ... yet.

"Can I think about it?" I ask.

"If you like, but I ain't gonna beg. There's plenty more folk out there with tales as sorry as yours."

"I know."

"I'll be here tomorrow at ten in the morning having breakfast. If you want my help, be here. If you don't, good luck."

"Understood."

I reach into my bag and take a ten-dollar bill from my purse.

"That's for the tea," I say, placing it on the table. "I should get going."

"Lots to think about, eh?"

"Plenty."

I take a final gulp of tea and get to my feet.

"Thanks again for stepping in and rescuing my bag," I say. "Whether we meet again or not, I am grateful."

Clement sits back and looks up at me.

"Yeah, seeya tomorrow," he says with a wink.

Chapter 13

I fell asleep at half-eight last night, mentally and physically drained. To say yesterday was a long day would be an understatement, but it didn't end when I left a run-down diner in Brooklyn. For the entire journey back to my hotel and several hours after, my mind chewed itself up while trying to make sense of events.

Of all the decisions I made yesterday, deciding to eat a four-cheese pizza two hours before I fell asleep proved a mistake. At some point during the night, I experienced a dream as surreal as it was vivid. I recall standing on top of the Empire State Building with Clement, although, in my dream, he was even bigger than he is in reality, almost King Kong-like. His monstrous arms outstretched, he dangled a man in each hand: Bruce Franklin and Sean Hoffman, both held upside down by an ankle. This morning, I can still picture the horror on their faces as I instructed Clement to let them drop one hundred and two storeys to their respective deaths.

Satisfying as such a reality might be, it won't get Mum's money back, and that's as important as seeing Franklin get his comeuppance.

Lying in bed with the television on, I finish the last gulp of the awful instant coffee the hotel provides and stare down at my tablet. It's hard not to feel pessimistic.

I've put a lot of paint on a lot of canvas over the years, and occasionally, I might step back from a piece of work, satisfied that it's complete, only to return the next day and stare at it in disgust. I now accept that when it comes to art, my perspective will shift from day to day, and so too will my emotional state. I didn't expect to experience the same shift when looking at a spreadsheet.

Tossing the tablet onto the bed, I lie back and close my eyes.

The chance meeting with my fellow Brit yesterday has played on my mind since I woke up. If he hadn't intervened and stopped that druggie, I'd have lost my bag, its contents and, more than likely, any appetite to continue the search for Franklin.

Perhaps it was written in the stars that Clement and I would bump into one another. Or perhaps I'm deluded for considering his offer of assistance. Would it be any more deluded or foolhardy than making this trip in the first place?

The same ifs, buts, and maybes continue to swirl around my mind like scraps of litter in a windswept alley. My phone suddenly rings, offering a welcome distraction.

"Hi, Paula," I say after accepting the call. "Everything okay?"

"No need to panic," she replies calmly. "I'm only calling to see how you are and to put your mind at rest in case you were worried about your mum."

"That's very sweet of you, and I'm good, thanks."

"Are you enjoying the course?"

I'm about to confirm I am and that I'm just getting ready for the second day when I remember the time difference. It's lunchtime in Essex, so early afternoon in Paris.

"Yeah, it's fantastic. We're just about to restart after lunch, so good timing on your part."

"Any good-looking French lads caught your eye?" Paula asks in a playful tone.

"I'm here to learn, not to flirt."

"There's always time for flirting, Gina."

"There is in your world," I chuckle. "Particularly after a few cocktails."

"That is true, as every barman in Brentwood will attest."

We laugh along together, and then Paula's tone changes.

"Listen, we had a visitor yesterday evening. It's nothing to worry about, but I thought you should know."

"A visitor? Who?"

"Your Aunt Lynn and her henpecked husband."

My mind returns to the call I received yesterday morning and Lynn's spiky attitude.

"I'm sorry, Paula. She called me yesterday morning to complain that I never asked her to watch Mum, but I thought she got the message."

"Obviously, I don't know her as well as you do, but I get the impression that Lynn doesn't like being told what to do."

"You're not far wrong. What happened?"

"They spent a good hour in the kitchen chatting to your mum, but I wasn't invited to join in, so I watched TV in the lounge. Then, they just upped and left without even saying goodbye."

"Did Mum shed any light on what Lynn wanted?"

"You know your mum never has a bad word to say about anyone, so she didn't say much. Reading between the lines, though, I think Lynn was a bit miffed that Helen didn't ask her to stay and me to leave."

"That bloody woman," I huff. "I'd already told her that you have everything under control."

"You shouldn't let yourself get het up about your aunt. I'm sure she only has your mum's best interests at heart."

"Maybe, but she just gets under my skin."

"I think that much is obvious, but you should try and look at the situation from her perspective."

"Should I?" I snort.

"Helen is her sister, and there's no stronger bond than blood, whereas I've only known your mum for a few years. I do understand why Lynn feels so aggrieved."

It's true that Mum and Paula have only been friends for a couple of years after they met at a yoga class at the local gym, but, in my view, Paula Webster has been a more positive influence on my mother than Lynn ever has. The fact she's never slept with Mum's partner is also another reason why I have all the time in the world for Paula but very little for Lynn.

"I wish I could be so understanding," I reply. "But I just don't trust her."

"I know, sweetheart, and I understand why, but I'm sure she's only doing what she believes is for the best."

"What's for the best is you keeping an eye on Mum."

"I'm chuffed that you have so much faith, and trust me, I'm doing my best to keep her occupied."

"I do, and on that note, have you got anything planned this afternoon?"

"Nothing exciting. Your mum wants to have a clear out before the bungalow goes on the market, so I'm helping her sort through mounds of old paperwork."

"I told her that there's no rush to sell the place, and there's no sense doing anything until early next year."

"She's just trying to be organised, and anything that helps keep her busy is a good thing, right? It's better than sitting around and dwelling on what that bastard did to her."

"Yeah," I sigh. "You're right."

I end the call with a promise that I'll try to ring Mum later. Paula, being Paula, tells me not to worry and to focus on having a good time. Little does she know that my chances of having a good time on this trip are close to negligible if I don't find Bruce Franklin.

The distraction over, my thoughts immediately switch back to a diner in Brooklyn. Clement said he'd be there at ten o'clock, which is a little under two hours away. I need to make a decision while I still have time to make one. Whatever I decide, I need to get up and take a shower, and maybe it'll help bring a little clarity to my thoughts.

The shower does indeed help, only inasmuch as I have a slightly clearer idea of a plan. If I do meet Clement, there's nothing to stop me from walking away if I don't like what he has to say. I might waste an hour or two of my morning, but it's not as though I've got a long list of prime leads to follow.

Decision made, I set off for the subway with my phone and debit card in my pocket, but my bag safely stashed away back in the hotel room. Not knowing where the day might take me, I'm not willing to risk another mugging.

The journey to Brooklyn passes without incident; not least because I missed the crush of the morning commuters. I then take a slow walk along the same route I covered yesterday afternoon, albeit in reverse. The journey, although incident-free, did allow me time to dwell on alternative methods I might employ to get that name from Sean Hoffman. Having already spent a chunk of yesterday evening going over the same question, I have to concede that I'm out of ideas. It's the only reason I'm now approaching Dexter's Diner.

I push the door open and enter.

Five of the tables are occupied, as are two of the booths running up the left-hand wall. Sitting in the exact same spot as yesterday is the reason I'm here.

"Mornin', Doll," he says as he notices my approach.

"Good morning."

"Sit your arse down. You eaten yet?"

I slide onto the bench seat, glancing at the grease and ketchup-smeared plate in front of Clement.

"Err, not yet."

"What do you fancy? Dex does a half-decent fry up."

"I might just have coffee and toast."

Clement twists around and calls out my order to Dex at the counter. There's no enquiry about whether I want white bread or brown. I'm not sure I'll eat it either way, but I don't want to start acting like a diva.

"Thanks, Clement."

"Don't thank me, Doll — you're paying for your breakfast and mine."

"Eh? Am I?"

"You still owe me for yesterday."

"I bought you a cup of tea."

"You think that's all my efforts were worth?"

"No, of course I don't. I'll pay for breakfast as well."

"Good girl," he grins back at me. "See, we already have an understanding."

He then nudges his plate to the side, sits back, and rests his hands on the table. They're as rough as his voice, and each one the size of pork knuckle.

"It's a bad habit," he then says.

"What is?"

"Biting my nails."

"Sorry?"

"You were looking at my hands."

"Um, yes. Sorry."

"Not my worst habit, though."

"I'm sure it's not. Is that a packet of cigarettes in your breast pocket?"

"It is, but I'm down to one pack a day now."

"Good for you, but that's probably one pack too many."

He shrugs his shoulders.

"Anyway," I say, switching the subject. "You said you had a couple of ideas on how I might get that name I'm after. I was hoping you'd share them with me this morning."

"Three, as it goes."

"Okay, three is better than two."

Dex arrives at the table with a mug and pot of coffee.

"Your toast will just be a few minutes," he confirms before filling the mug.

"Thank you."

"You're welcome, Miss. Anything else for you, Clem?"

"I'll have another brew, seeing as my friend here is picking up the tab."

Friend is a stretch, but I don't correct him. Dex returns to the counter, and I return to our conversation.

"So, Clement, these ideas."

"Yeah."

"Can I hear them?"

"Alright."

He stretches out his arms and then folds them across his chest. Even if we weren't sitting directly opposite one another, it'd be hard not to feel intimidated by his sheer bulk. Every part of him is oversized.

"Your first choice is to do what the bloke asked you to do," Clement then says. "But there are a few problems with that."

"A few? I've only thought of one, and that's more than enough for me, thanks."

"And, who's to say he'd give you the name, anyway? Once he's shot his load, what you gonna do if he refuses? Spit it back at him?"

"Ewww!" I grimace. "That's disgusting."

"Just putting it out there, Doll. You gotta consider all options."

"That's not an option," I reply, rolling my eyes. "Never was, never will be."

"Can't say I blame you. The next option is a bit of a punt, but it's simple."

"Go on."

"You and me pay this Hoffman bloke a visit, and I twist his bollocks until he talks."

"Ooh, yes. I like that idea."

Too late, I realise my response sounded a little on the enthusiastic side.

"However, on reflection," I cough. "Maybe just *threaten* to twist his bollocks. I'm sure that would be enough."

"It's an option, but it ain't ideal, Doll."

"Why not?"

"'Cos a bloke will say anything when he's scared. He could give us any old name, and then you're on a wild goose chase for the next week."

"I don't have time for that."

"Then, your best bet is option three."

"Which is?"

Dex returns to the table with my toast, leaving me in suspense as he swaps small talk with Clement. I chew on a slice whilst waiting patiently for Dex to depart. Finally, he does.

"Where was I?" Clement asks.

"You said your third option is the best one."

"Yeah, it is."

Rather than elaborate, he strokes his moustache a couple of times.

106

"Well?" I prompt. "Are you going to tell me?"

"I ain't sure you've got the balls to go through with it," he replies with a glint in his eye. "Metaphorically, of course."

I lean forward and fix Clement with a hard stare.

"I want that name from Hoffman, and I'll do anything to get it."

"Not quite anything, eh?"

"No, not *that*, but almost anything else."

"Alright. Here's what we do."

Chapter 14

I stare at Clement, speechless, and then my gaze slowly falls to my plate and the remaining slice of toast. I've suddenly lost my appetite.

"What do you think?" he asks. "You reckon you can pull it off ... so to speak?"

I take a sip of coffee before answering.

"To be frank, Clement, I much prefer the bollock-wrenching option."

"Your call, Doll, but you know the risk. If you wanna avoid wasting time, the third option is your best bet."

"That's as maybe, but you're asking me to put an awful lot of trust in you, and I know nothing about you."

"What do you wanna know?"

"Um ..."

I run through a list of possible questions, but all I can think of are the pointlessly banal questions likely asked during a job interview. Knowing where Clement sees himself in five years' time is of no interest or help.

"Let me tell you a little story," he says, filling the dead air. "It's about a bird who flies all the way from Essex to New York in the hope of finding a needle in a bleedin' haystack. Then, she bumps into a bloke, and although she don't trust him, that bloke couldn't give less of a shit. The end."

"Not exactly a happy ending," I respond.

"We'll have to wait and see about that, but the only way you're gonna trust me is to give my plan a go. There ain't anything I can say that's gonna make a difference here and now."

"No, but—"

"Listen, Doll. The way I see it, you can finish your toast, fuck off, and carry on doing whatever it was you were doing, or you can take a punt on a stranger. I ain't gonna sit here and sob into my Tetley either way."

As blunt as his analysis is, it's wholly accurate.

"Do you really think your plan will work?"

"Dunno, but as I see it, what else you gonna do?"

It's a good question, and the truth is that my alternative options range from weak to none.

"Okay. I'm up for it."

"You wanna make the call, then?"

"Now?"

"No sense sitting on your arse thinking about it. You want something done, just bleedin' do it."

I heed Clement's advice and tell him I'm heading outside to make the call. If I were to think about his plan for any length of time, I'd likely talk myself out of it.

Out on the pavement, I pull out my phone and tap a number still fresh in my call history.

"Pinhill Property Management. How can I help you?"

"May I speak to Sean Hoffman, please?"

"Who's calling?"

"Gina Jackson. Tell him I'm interested in taking up his offer — he'll know what I'm referring to."

"One moment."

I begin a slow pace up and down the pavement while I wait for Hoffman.

"Hello again, Miss Jackson," comes a nasally voice down the line. "I didn't think I'd hear from you again."

"Trust me, if I had any other option, I wouldn't be making this call."

"But you don't?"

"No," I sigh. "Which is why I've decided to take up your offer if it still stands."

"As it happens, your luck is in. My receptionist has a dental appointment at eleven-thirty this morning, so she'll be out of the office for an hour, and my clerk doesn't work Wednesdays. We'll have the place all to ourselves."

"And to be clear, this is a business transaction, right? I provide a service, and you give me the information I need. Agreed?"

"I know what you want, and you know what I want. Seems pretty straightforward to me."

"How do I know you won't just give me dud information?"

"You don't, but there's no reason for me to lie to you, Miss Jackson."

"Fair enough. I'll be there at eleven-thirty."

"I'm already looking forward to it."

I end the call and inwardly shudder. If there's any consolation, it's that I've only completed the first step of Clement's plan, and there's still time to bail if I change my mind. I return to the diner.

"All done," I announce as I retake my seat in the booth.

"How'd it go?" Clement asks.

"As well as could be expected. He'll be alone in the office at eleven-thirty — forty minutes from now."

"That's better than expected, Doll. If he's on his own, it makes the job that bit easier."

"Your part, maybe," I snort.

"My part, your part, it's all for the same cause."

"True, but I can't say I'm looking forward to it."

"It'll be fine, but if it all goes tits-up, there's always the fall-back option."

"His bollocks?"

"Yeah," Clement nods.

110

I never thought I'd feel reassured by the thought of a man having his bollocks aggressively manhandled, but I'll take it.

We go over the plan again, ensuring that every detail and every eventuality is covered. Despite his somewhat shabby appearance, I'm surprised at just how methodical Clement is. By the time we're ready to leave, I'm feeling slightly more optimistic about our chances of success, but I wouldn't go as far as saying I'm confident.

I pay the bill and follow Clement out the door.

"Which way?" he asks, pulling a pack of cigarettes from his pocket.

"Back towards Flatbush Avenue," I reply, pointing up the road. "And then it's about a ten-minute walk from there."

Clement lights his cigarette, and we set off along the pavement, walking side by side. I quickly realise it's an opportunity for me to quiz the big man without it sounding like an interrogation or a job interview.

"Where are you staying while you're here?" I ask nonchalantly.

"You know that building near where you lost your bag?"

"The one covered in scaffolding?"

"Yeah, that one. It used to be a hotel, and I bagged myself the penthouse suite."

"It looks like it's about to fall down."

"It's a bit rough around the edges, but they're turning the place into luxury flats, I'm told."

"If it's no longer a hotel, how did you end up staying there?"

"I bumped into the site foreman in a bar, and we got chatting. He told me they were having problems with druggies breaking in and using the place to do whatever the fuck druggies do. I needed somewhere to kip, so we came to a gentleman's agreement. I get somewhere to

111

stay for free, and in return, I deal with the druggies if they try breaking in."

"Define *deal with*."

"They're druggies. Don't take much to scare 'em off."

We cross the street, and I try another question.

"I take it that you're still working on a plan to get back to London?"

"I know how I'm gonna get back."

"How?"

"There's only one way, and it ain't a way I'm keen on, but beggars can't be choosers."

"And that is?"

"A bleedin' ship, and I hate ships."

"That's a long journey for someone who doesn't like being at sea."

"Six bastard days," Clement spits. "And I ain't looking forward to it, I can tell you."

"If you've already worked out your passage, what are you still doing in New York?"

"The ship I've sorted only sails once a month, and I didn't have the five grand fare sorted the last time it set off."

"Five grand?" I wince. "Not cheap."

"Not legit, either, but without a passport, it'll have to do."

"You don't fancy staying in America, then? It's a big country, and there are plenty of places worth visiting."

"I ain't no tourist, Doll, and I wanna be back in the Smoke."

"I take it by your accent that you've always lived in London?"

"Born and bred. It's home."

"You sound like my granddad. He grew up in Bow and then moved to Shoreditch, but when it came to moving to Essex, he really wasn't keen. He said London had always been his home, and he wouldn't feel right living anywhere else. It took us months to convince him it was for the best."

"It gets under your skin. I couldn't live anywhere else."

"Which is why you're willing to suffer six days as a paid stowaway?"

"About sums it up, yeah."

We enter Flatbush Avenue, and I'm hit by a sense of déjà vu — not surprising as I walked the same route yesterday. There is one key difference though, and that's the reaction of people on the pavement as we walk towards them. Yesterday, I felt anonymous, but it's almost impossible to fly under the radar when you're walking next to a man as imposing as Clement. For all the glances he receives, I notice how no one, particularly the men, want to risk making inadvertent eye contact. I should be perturbed but surprisingly I find the reaction to my companion reassuring. No one is likely to mess with me with Clement by my side.

The further we progress along Flatbush Avenue, the fewer pedestrians there are. I'm about to pose another question when Clement asks one of his own.

"What do you do when you're not hunting conmen, then?"

"For a job?"

"Yeah."

"I wouldn't call it a job as such, but I'm an artist."

"What kind of artist? Paint? Music? Piss?"

"Mainly paint," I snigger. "But I've been known to drink too much on occasion."

"Bet it don't take much for you to get wasted."

"You'd be surprised. I've got hollow legs."

"If we find this bloke you're after, maybe we'll get a chance to test that claim."

His use of the word 'we' comes as a surprise. I agreed to his help with Hoffman, but I never suggested what might happen should I get the name I want. I remind myself that I need to take one step at a time. There's no sense fretting about something that might never happen.

"I hope you're right, Clement ... on both counts."

As we approach the final few hundred yards before the final turn, I catch sight of a familiar figure on the opposite pavement, striding purposefully back up Flatbush Avenue.

"That's the receptionist from Pinhill Properties," I remark. "At least we know that Hoffman wasn't lying on that front."

"So far, so good."

We reach the junction with Farragut Road and turn right.

"How much further is it?" Clement asks.

"It's just up on the right."

"This is where we part ways, then. You gonna be alright?"

"As long as you play your part, I will."

"It'll be fine, Doll. I know what I'm doing."

I take a deep breath and mentally prepare myself.

"I bloody hope so, Clement, because I don't."

Chapter 15

I push open the door to Pinhill Properties and enter. Unlike yesterday, it's silent and both desks are vacant. I clear my throat to announce my arrival. Within a few seconds, the sound of footsteps thump from the corridor, followed by a sight I'm already dreading — Sean Hoffman.

"You came," he says with a grin.

"I said I would."

"And so will I soon enough," he laughs.

It takes every ounce of willpower not to let the disgust reach my face. Hoffman then steps over to the front door and flicks the lock.

"We don't want to be disturbed, do we?"

"Not really, no. I'd like this over and done with."

He stares at my chest and licks his lips.

"I don't think that'll be a problem, Missy. I'm all fired up and ready to go."

With epic levels of reluctance, I follow him back along the corridor to his office. He shuts the door, and for a second, I panic until I realise there's no lock.

"I was thinking," I say. "I'd like that name before we get down to business."

"That ain't happening," Hoffman replies. "I get my reward, you get yours."

I had a feeling he'd say that, but it was worth a try.

"Right, well, let's get on with it," I say in my most strait-laced tone of voice. "Drop your trousers and sit on the sofa."

I've never been into role-play, and this is about as close as I've ever had to venture. I'm not looking forward to it, but it's necessary.

"Ohh, I like a woman who takes control," he purrs while unbuckling his belt. "And it sounds so hot in that accent."

"Just do as you're told."

"Yes, Ma'am."

As he's about to unzip his trousers, he stops and stares back at me.

"You know, I think I'd love to look at those cute British titties while you're doing your thing."

"What? That wasn't part of the deal."

"I'm renegotiating the deal."

There's no way I'm getting my tits out, but it does dawn on me that removing my t-shirt might play to our advantage.

"I'll take my t-shirt off, but the bra stays on. If you're not happy with that, the deal is off."

"I can live with that, but before you take it off, I want to see your cell."

It takes a moment to realise he means my phone.

"Why?"

"I want to be sure you're not recording our ... interaction."

I pull out my phone, unlock the screen, and show it to Hoffman.

"Happy now?"

"I will be when you put it in my desk drawer."

"Fine," I huff. "If it satisfies your paranoia."

I step over to his desk and, while I'm there, take a glance out of the large window behind it. The vertical blinds, thankfully, are set at an angle to allow maximum light in.

My phone stashed, I turn around to find Hoffman tugging down his trousers and crumpled boxer shorts. That sight alone is enough to summon bile to the back of my throat. I step closer, swallow hard, and slip off my t-shirt. In the three seconds it takes to remove it, Hoffman has stripped off his trousers and shorts but not his black socks. As sights go, it's without doubt the least sexually arousing I've ever had the misfortune to lay eyes on.

"Sit down," I demand.

He does as he's told. Now I'm at the mercy of a virtual stranger.

"You just gonna stand there?" Hoffman asks, noting my hesitancy.

Slowly, I take two steps forward, keeping my eyes fixed on the floor rather than the semi-flaccid penis awaiting my arrival. I get within leaning distance and then drop to my knees. Never in my entire life have I felt so cheap, so tawdry. Why the hell did I let Clement talk me into this?

"Say something hot," Hoffman purrs.

If I open my mouth, I'll likely vomit into his lap. Even if I felt like whispering sweet nothings, my mind is otherwise occupied, frantically repeating a single word over and over: *abort!*

Just as I'm about to give in to my mind's demand, the sound of a knuckle rapping on a window changes everything. I dare to look up, and judging by the frown on his face, Hoffman isn't happy with the unexpected interruption. It's all the opportunity I need to retreat from the sofa.

"I thought you said we wouldn't be disturbed," I say.

"Just wait right there," he replies, getting to his feet.

117

He puts his trousers back on, waddles over to the window behind his desk, and sweeps the vertical blinds aside. To my eternal relief, there's a big guy in a denim waistcoat standing on the opposite side of the glass. He points at the window and mouths two words: open it.

"What the hell?" Hoffman groans before opening the window.

"About bloody time," Clement grunts. "The office door is locked, and I've got a delivery out front for a Mr Hoffman."

"What delivery?"

"I'm paid to deliver packages, mate, not answer questions. If the front door ain't open in the next twenty seconds, I'm off."

Threat delivered, Clement turns around and walks towards the alleyway at the rear of the building.

"Jesus H Christ," Hoffman mumbles before closing the blinds.

"Are you going to be long?" I ask. "I haven't got all day, you know."

"I'll be back in a sec. Wait there."

I have no intention of waiting anywhere. As soon as Hoffman steps through the doorway, I slip my t-shirt on and retrieve my phone from the desk drawer. Then, I silently peek around the door. Once I've confirmed the coast is clear, I sneak back up the corridor so I can witness the final part of Clement's plan unfold.

By the time I take my first glance across the main office, Hoffman is already unlocking the front door. On the opposite side is Clement, holding a mobile phone to his ear.

"Where's the delivery?" Hoffman snaps.

"Just wait up," Clement replies. "I'm trying to get hold of your wife, but she ain't picking up at the moment."

I can't see Hoffman's face, but I'd bet he's sporting a confused scowl. Clement then clarifies the position.

"Look behind you."

Instinctively and without thinking, Hoffman looks back over his shoulder. He sees me standing in the doorway, but it doesn't matter now. I return a smile as Clement shoves Hoffman from behind. He stumbles backwards, just about managing to stay on his feet. My accomplice steps into the office, locking the door behind him.

"What the fuck is going on here?" Hoffman blasts once he's steadied himself. "Get out of my office!"

"Not before we've had a chat," Clement replies with a menacing snarl. "If your arse ain't on a chair in the next three seconds, you'll be carrying your teeth home in your pocket."

Only an absolute fool would think twice about arguing with a man the size of Clement. Hoffman proves he's no fool by scurrying to the nearest chair and falling onto it.

"What do you want from me?" he gulps. "We don't keep cash on the premises."

"I don't want your money. I wanna show you a photo I just snapped."

Clement reaches into his pocket and plucks out a basic mobile phone. It takes him a few seconds to navigate the menu, but then he leans forward and holds the phone out so Hoffman can clearly see the screen. The perverted business owner squints, and then the colour drains from his face.

"It don't look good, does it?" Clement remarks. "You sitting on a sofa with your cock and balls on full display, and a young woman in a bra kneeling in front of you. No way of talking yourself out of this one, Sunshine."

Realising he's been set up, Hoffman visibly deflates. It's now my turn to take control. I stride across the office and stand next to Clement, glaring down at the pitiful excuse for a man.

"You're going to show me the file for Apartment 19, Newton Heights, West End Avenue, and every last detail you have on record for the man who rented that apartment on a specific date. Clear?"

"You bitch," he sneers. "I should have known—"

"Shut your mouth," Clement growls. "If you wanna keep your marriage and your face intact, I suggest you do exactly as she asks without any lip. Got it?"

It's been a long time since any man has stood up for me, and even though the man in question is still a stranger, his words are reassuring. They're also effective, as Hoffman eventually nods in response.

"I need to use the computer in my office."

"I'll be watching every keystroke," I say. "And remember, Sean, divorce is expensive — can you afford to give your wife half of everything you own, including this business?"

His expression provides an answer without him even uttering a word. Hoffman then reluctantly gets to his feet and traipses back toward his office, with Clement following close behind.

True to my word, I stand behind the office chair as Hoffman nudges a mouse around a mat. He clicks it at least half a dozen times while navigating to the record I want to see. Eventually, he spits a question over his shoulder.

"What date was it?"

"The 12th of March this year."

After scrolling down the page, he clicks on a link.

"That apartment was rented to a man named David Smith."

My heart beating ten to the dozen, I lean forward to double-check the name on the screen.

"Did you check his ID?"

"We check the ID of every guest on every booking."

"Do you keep a copy?"

"No, because people don't like copies of their personal documents kept with a private company. They show us ID, and we check it's legit. That's all."

To ensure I have a copy of David Smith's booking, I pull out my phone and take a photo of the computer screen. My interest initially peaks when I notice the file contains a phone number and an email address but that interest quickly wanes. I must have left a dozen messages on Franklin's voicemail, plus I sent at least fifty text messages. Unsurprisingly, he never responded to any of them. As for the email address, it's just the name 'Franklin' followed by an underscore and a series of random numbers. It's not the kind of address anyone would actually use for their main email account. Then, I notice his address — the sneaky shit used Mum's address back in Brentwood. I'll double-check the phone number later, but for now it would be prudent to issue a warning to Hoffman just in case Bruce Franklin is still checking his text messages and emails. I step to the other side of his desk.

"I know what you're thinking," I say in a level voice.

"Doubt it," he snorts.

"You're contemplating revenge by contacting the man whose record you just accessed. If you're thinking of warning him that we're on his tail, that would be a mistake."

"A bleedin' big mistake," Clement adds from the doorway.

"We're now off to find David Smith, but if you tip him off, I will send that photo to your wife ... along with an apology for sleeping with her husband."

"And I might pop back and kick ten shades of shit out of you," Clement warns.

"So, Sean, keep your mouth shut. Understood?"

Hoffman puffs a resigned sigh and then nods. I look across at Clement and he signals we should leave. I concur, but I want to leave with a parting shot.

"And just for the record," I sneer at Hoffman. "You have by far the smallest penis I've ever had the misfortune of clapping eyes on. Well done."

Without waiting for a reaction, I follow Clement back along the corridor, through the front office, and out onto the pavement. We continue walking in silence until we're back on Flatbush Avenue, clear of Hoffman's office.

"Could you have left it any later?" I remark after puffing a sigh of relief. "I was about two seconds away from bolting when you finally knocked on the window."

"I couldn't get the bastard camera thing to work," Clement replies. "But no matter. You got what you wanted, and that fat piece of shit didn't. I'd call that a result."

"Yes, you're right," I concede. "I can't believe your plan actually worked."

"Never in doubt, Doll," he grins down at me. "What you gonna do next?"

"I need to sit down and research the name David Smith."

"There's a bar not far from here. I think I deserve a pint, don't you?"

With my nerves still jangling, Clement isn't the only one who could do with a stiff drink.

"You lead me there, and I'll get them in."

Chapter 16

The Pegasus is exactly the kind of dive bar I imagined Clement might frequent: dark, dated, and a second home to a handful of misfits already well-oiled by lunchtime. The landlord would do well to invest in a decent air conditioning system to negate the whiff of damp brickwork and musky body odour.

We step up to the bar, and a gum-chewing redhead with no sense of style or shame ambles over.

"Hey, Clem," she coos. "What can I get you?"

I don't recall putting on an invisibility cloak this morning, but patently I did.

"What do you want?" Clement asks me.

There's no way I'm willing to risk the glassware in this place touching my lips.

"Bottle of lager, please."

"Two beers," Clement says to the redhead.

"Coming up."

My cloak continues to function as two bottles of Budweiser are placed on the bar in front of Clement. Using just his left hand, he grabs both by the neck and ushers me to a corner away from the nearest misfits.

"I think we've earned this," he remarks, handing me one of the bottles. "Cheers, Doll."

"Cheers."

I take a quick glug and try to overlook the frothy, hoppy fizz that follows.

"Listen," Clement then says. "I don't wanna piss on your fireworks before you've checked, but David Smith ain't exactly an uncommon name."

"That thought had crossed my mind," I reply, pulling out my phone. "But let's see."

I begin my search on Google, using a filtering method that only lists results containing the exact name I'm looking for. I also include 'New York' to wheedle out every David Smith beyond this city.

"Not a great start," I groan. "My search returned over fourteen thousand results."

More in hope than expectation, I tap the first link on the page. It takes me to a profile on the networking website LinkedIn, but it belongs to a financial analyst of East Asian descent. The next link leads me to a page on an insurance company's website and the profile of a man some ten to fifteen years younger than the one I'm looking for.

"This bloke is a conman, right?" Clement remarks before taking another gulp of lager.

"That's exactly what he is."

"And he spent months priming your mum before he cleared out her bank accounts?"

"Eleven months, give or take a few weeks."

"That's a long time to invest in one mark, don't you reckon?"

"He must have known the payoff would be worthwhile."

"Stands to reason then that bloke is a pro. You don't go all in if there's a chance someone knows what you've got in your hand."

"I don't follow."

Clement shifts in his seat, trying to find a few extra inches of legroom.

"What I'm saying, Doll, is that you ain't gonna find him in the phone book or anywhere else that obvious. In his line of work, he'd have to be a fucking idiot to leave a trail on the interweb thing for the Old Bill or anyone else to follow."

I don't want to hear this, but that doesn't make it any less true. Another glance at the phone screen only reinforces Clement's point.

"What am I supposed to do, then?"

"You got anything else to go on?"

"Not really," I sigh. "I did put together a list of leads but … the more I look at them, the weaker they seem."

In my head, I'd imagined a scene where I discover Bruce Franklin's true identity, and the police swooped in to arrest him within hours, but not before I'd confronted the scumbag. I've played out that scene so many times it's almost become a reality. The actual reality couldn't be more of a disappointment.

"You want me to take a look?" Clement says. "Fresh set of eyes and all that."

"I wouldn't want to waste any more of your time."

"You sound like you've given up already. Didn't have you pegged as a quitter."

"I'm not, but I'm not delusional either."

"You'd be amazed how many times I've heard that word over the last few years. It ain't easy to keep believing when there's a voice screaming in your ear that you've lost the plot, but that voice ain't you, Doll."

"Sorry?"

"That voice in your head telling you that you're on a hiding to nothing. It ain't you."

"Don't take this the wrong way, but you don't know me."

Clement leans back in his seat and puts his hands behind his head.

"No, I don't know you," he says. "But, from what I've seen, you kinda remind me of someone."

"Who?"

"Nelly was her name. She used to come in the pub with an old mate of mine, Jaffa Rigby."

"Jaffa?"

"Poor bastard had ginger hair."

"Oh."

"Anyway," he continues. "Jaffa always bought pork scratchings for Nelly, but if he gave her the packet, she'd demolish every last scratching in seconds. Instead, he left the packet on the table, and he'd throw one Nelly's way every now and then. The packet would last all evening that way."

"Sorry? He threw pork scratchings at his partner?"

"She weren't his partner — Nelly was a Jack Russell Terrier."

"Lovely," I snort. "You're comparing me to a dog?"

"Let me finish."

"Go on."

"One night, some drunken dickhead wanders in and stops by Jaffa's table for a word. He then decides to help himself to a pork scratching. Big mistake."

"Why?"

"Nelly weren't happy sharing. That cute little hound went mad, sinking her teeth into the bloke's leg, and she wouldn't let go for love nor money. Took two of us to get her off him."

"So now you're comparing me to a bad-tempered Jack Russell. This just gets better and better."

Clement rolls his eyes. "Don't get it, do you?"

"Get what?"

"I got the impression you were like Nelly 'cos when you get your teeth stuck into something and that something matters to you, there ain't no one who's gonna make you let go."

126

He takes a quick gulp of lager while I sit silently, trying to unpick his assessment.

"Have I got that wrong, Doll?"

"Well, um ... no, I suppose it's a fair assessment, but how could you possibly know that? We only met yesterday."

"We all have a voice screaming in our ear and sometimes mine is on the money."

"Like an instinct, you mean?"

"Call it that if you like."

"And this instinct of yours believes I'm ready to give up?"

"That ain't what I said. The opposite, in fact."

"Good," I huff. "Because I'm not ready to give up."

Clement smiles back at me, almost as if he knows there's one surefire way to rekindle my resolve, and that's to test it.

"You gonna let me see what leads you've got, then?"

"They're on my tablet, back at the hotel."

"You carved 'em in stone? Bit much."

"No, I mean ... are you taking the piss?"

He shrugs and reaches for his bottle.

"If you want to see them, we'll have to go to the hotel."

"I ain't got much on for the rest of the day, so we'll finish these and head over there."

A sense of unease suddenly engulfs me. It's partly because I don't know if it's a good idea to invite Clement back to my hotel room, but mainly because I don't want to be ridiculed when I reveal how tenuous the reasons for my trip really are.

"Right ... um ..."

"Don't shit your knickers," he interjects. "I ain't gonna whip my jeans off and ask you to get on your knees — I told you I ain't offering my help in the hope of a shag, alright."

"I know."

"So, we gonna get going?"

With the lesser concern covered I'm out of excuses.

"Sure."

I empty my bottle and then head to the bar to settle the bill. It kills me to leave the redhead a tip, but she only receives one solitary dollar.

As anyone who has ever travelled on an underground train will attest, engaging in conversation is almost impossible. For that reason, I don't speak to Clement until we emerge from the subway station around the corner from my hotel.

"It's this way. Not far."

Again, I'm taken by the reaction of pedestrians as my companion strides along the pavement. Then, I remember my instinctive reaction the first time I clapped eyes on him. That fear is still there, like owning a pet pitbull that wags his tail most of the time yet could rip your face off without warning, but I'm less wary than I was yesterday. Granddad always pointed out that trust is built gradually, and if you want to build anything that lasts, you do it brick by careful brick.

We bowl through the hotel foyer and hop into one of the two lifts. As the doors close, Clement makes an observation.

"You know they don't call 'em lifts," he says. "The Yanks."

"Elevators, I believe."

"Stupid, if you ask me. Why use four syllables when you can use one?"

"Err, I've no idea."

"And while we're on the subject, a word of warning — never ask for beans while you're over here. You ain't getting Heinz."

"Noted," I chuckle.

He doesn't realise it, but Clement's throwaway remark goes some way to extinguishing the last of my concerns

128

about inviting him into my hotel room. However, it doesn't remove any doubts about him seeing my woeful list of leads.

Too late now.

I unlock the room and invite my guest in first. After ducking under the door frame, he walks slowly forward, looking left and right as if inspecting the room.

"It's the best I could get for my budget," I say, closing the door. "It's not exactly The Ritz, but it'll do."

"You should see my room," he replies as he makes for the window. "It's twice the size of this."

"Lucky you."

"Yeah, but you've got carpet, and I ain't seen any rats yet, either."

"You have rats where you're staying? That's grim."

"They're a bit like the druggies, Doll. They stay out of my way."

"I can imagine, but it does beg the question: why not stay in a proper hotel?"

"'Cos, I'm a ghost over here."

"A ghost?"

He flashes me a strange kind of look but then returns his attention to the window.

"I ain't got a passport, or bank account, or a driving licence," he then says. "Basically, I ain't got nothing they want when you try checking into a hotel in this neck of the woods."

"Oh, I see."

Clement then takes a long, final gaze out of the window before unceremoniously lowering himself into one of the two tub chairs beside the room's desk-cum-dressing table. He's an ill fit.

"I'll just grab my tablet," I say before opening the wardrobe door and fishing out my bag.

It takes a good thirty seconds for the tablet to boot up, so I use the time to make myself comfortable in the second tub chair. Clement appears fascinated by the device on my lap.

"That's a tablet, is it?" he asks.

"Yes. Surely, you've seen one before?"

"Can't say I have. What's it do?"

"Pretty much the same functionality as a smartphone, but it's bigger, obviously. I find it easier to use when I'm working on documents, and it has a stylus so I can sketch ideas down whenever inspiration strikes."

"Can I have a butcher's?"

"Sure."

I pass the tablet to Clement, and in his huge hands, it almost looks like a smartphone. He stares down at the screen as it sparks into life, but his fascination is short-lived. After a final cursory inspection, he hands the device back to me.

"I'll stick to a pen and paper," he grunts.

"I get the impression you're very much a traditionalist."

"Yeah, you could say that. Newer don't always mean better."

I'm about to tease him about being a dinosaur, but it occurs to me that if it wasn't for the internet and smartphones, David Smith couldn't have accessed Mum's bank account. Maybe Clement has a point.

"Right," I puff. "Let me show you what I've got."

I open the spreadsheet and grimace.

"That bad, eh, Doll?"

"See for yourself."

I pass the tablet back to Clement, and he holds it up, directly in front of his face like a child reading a book. He clearly wasn't lying about never seeing a tablet before. I then watch his eyes flick across the screen while I wait for the snorts of derision.

Long seconds pass, and then, without comment, he passes the tablet back to me.

"Well?" I prompt. "Anything you think could be worthwhile?"

"I ain't gonna lie to you — there's more chance of me winning Miss Great Britain than there is of you finding your man with those leads."

"Oh," I sigh.

"And don't go imagining me in a swimsuit — it ain't pretty."

"Thanks for putting that thought in my head. I'll never sleep soundly again."

"You're welcome."

Frustrated, I'm about to shut the tablet down when Clement's body language shifts. He sits up and strokes his moustache.

"You got a photo of this bloke?" he then asks.

"I've got plenty of photos of him. Why?"

"I wanna see what the geezer looks like — see the whites of his eyes."

I don't push any further and turn back to the tablet. After a few taps on the screen, I open the folder containing every photo of Smith I harvested from Mum's laptop.

"Here you go," I say, holding the tablet up. "That's him."

Clement takes a long, hard stare at the digital rendition of David Smith's face.

"Smug-looking prick, ain't he?"

"Yes, but he's also charming, which is what drew Mum in."

"Met plenty of blokes just like him — here today, gone tomorrow types. I wouldn't trust 'em as far as I could boot 'em, and that's some distance."

"Sadly, Mum did trust him. We all did."

"That why you're here? You feel bad 'cos you didn't spot the viper in the nest?"

131

"Partly, yes, but really, I want justice for Mum, and no one else is going to get it for her."

Clement nods slowly as if digesting my words.

"You said you've got other photos?" he then says. "Can I see 'em?"

"If you like."

I lean forward and demonstrate how to swipe through the rogues' gallery.

"Swipe?" Clement comments. "That meant to nick something in my day."

"Jesus, how old are you?"

"Too bleedin' old, Doll."

He doesn't elaborate any further and focuses on the screen. I sit back in my seat as Clement spends a good thirty seconds inspecting each photo before moving on to the next. At his rate of progress, it'll be dinner time before he's finished.

"How do I go back?" he asks. "I wanna check another photo."

"Swipe the screen in the opposite direction."

"Gotcha."

"Do you want a cup of tea while you're doing that?"

"Yeah, go on," he replies without looking up.

I get up and fill the crappy plastic kettle with enough water for two cups. The teabags the hotel provides are produced by a company I've never heard of, but the tea can't be any worse than the coffee.

While I wait for the kettle to boil, I check Facebook on my phone purely to kill time. There's little to pique my interest, but I continue scrolling down the page.

"Come here a sec," Clement suddenly calls over.

"What is it?" I reply flatly as the kettle clicks off.

"Just get your arse over here, and I'll show you."

I traipse back across the room and plonk myself down in the chair.

"I've been over those photos a thousand times," I say. "So, whatever you think you've found, it's likely something I've already dismissed."

"Look at this photo," Clement says, ignoring my comment.

"What about it?"

"He's wearing a ring on his left hand, right?"

"So?"

"In two of the other photos, he ain't wearing it at all."

"Your point being?"

"Can you zoom with this thing? Make it bigger?"

"Just pinch the screen."

Clement quite literally pinches the edge of the tablet. I cough back a snort of laughter.

"No, like this," I say, demonstrating how to zoom in and out.

"Just zoom in on the bleedin' ring, will you," he huffs.

I zoom in as far as I can before the image blurs too much. The gold ring is garishly chunky and set with a circular aquamarine stone in the centre.

"I've seen a ring like that before," Clement then declares. "I only noticed 'cos it's stupidly big and fucking ugly."

"Each to their own, but so what? There are probably tens of thousands of similar rings out there, so I don't see the significance."

"Look closer."

I lean in and study the ring. Only then do I notice there are four letters etched into the design below the stone, almost invisible against the gold: *B.C.N.Y.*

Chapter 17

"Shit," I gasp. "How did I miss that?"

"Don't get too excited," Clement warns. "We've gotta decipher those letters first, and they don't mean fuck all to me. You?"

"No, but I presume the N.Y. part is New York, right?"

"Makes sense."

Clement passes the tablet back to me, and I immediately open up a web browser.

"I'll google it."

The letters could well turn out to be meaningless, but at least we've got a lead worth pursuing.

"Bugger," I groan as the results page loads, and I scan the first few links.

"What?"

"The only organisation that officially uses the letters B.C.N.Y. is The Boys' Club of New York."

"What's that when it's at home?"

"Give me a moment, and I'll check."

I tap through to the website and read the introductory paragraph on the home page.

"It's a youth organisation that provides after-school and weekend activities for underprivileged kids."

"Why would a kids' youth club issue fuck-ugly gold rings?"

"They wouldn't. I think we can assume this isn't the same acronym as the one on the ring."

"Any others?"

I tap the back button and scour the list of results.

"Baptist Convention of New York?"

"Don't seem likely."

"No, I concur. What about the Building Code of New York?"

"That don't even warrant an answer."

"Brazilian Center of New York?"

Clement returns a blank stare.

"I'll look it up."

It takes less than ten seconds to confirm that the Brazilian Center of New York is an arts organisation focussing on Brazilian culture.

"It's not that, either."

I continue on to the second page of results, each link more tenuous than the last. The third page is enough for me to give up.

"Nothing," I remark, placing the tablet on the desk. "Whatever B.C.N.Y. stands for, it's not widely used."

"That don't leave us with much choice then. I'm gonna have to get hold of the bloke who had a similar ring."

"Similar, or the same?"

"I caught a glimpse of it for maybe two seconds, so I can't say for sure. Unless you've got any other bright ideas, it's gotta be worth checking."

"Fair enough. How do we go about doing that?"

"I need to make a call. I'll nip out on the balcony."

"I'm not going to eavesdrop if that's your concern."

"Couldn't give a shit if you listen in — I want a smoke."

"Oh, right."

"And what happened to that cuppa?"

"I'll finish it now."

Clement squeezes out of the tub chair and then fiddles with the lock on the balcony door. I don't like heights, so I've had no reason to mess with the door.

I return to tea-making duties, and while it's brewing, I use the time to nip to the loo. As I close the door to the bathroom, my hand instinctively moves towards the lock. I'm alone in a hotel room with a man I know next to nothing about, so common sense suggests I should lock it.

"Brick by careful brick," I whisper to myself while engaging the door lock.

Bladder emptied, I return to the room just as Clement is closing the door to the balcony.

"Any luck?" I ask while removing the teabags from the cups.

"I got a name ... and a warning."

"A warning about what?"

"Not to piss off the bloke we're going to see."

"You might need to elaborate. Who exactly did you call?"

"The bloke who hired me to keep the druggies at bay. Pete."

"So, who are we going to see?"

"Blair Ealy. He's an architect."

"The guy with the ring?"

"Yeah, I bumped into him last week when Pete was showing him around the building. Poor bugger almost shit himself when I appeared at the end of the hallway. Probably 'cos I was only wearing my pants."

"Why were you walking around in your pants?"

"Why not?" he shrugs. "It was a warm day."

I roll my eyes and reach for one of the cups of tea.

"Forget the tea. Let's make a move."

"And where exactly are we going?"

"West Eleventh Avenue, near Union Square. Ain't far on the tube."

"The subway, you mean."

"You say *tomato*, I say tomato."

"Pardon."

He frowns down at me. "The song?"

"What song?"

"Ella Fitzgerald? Louis Armstrong?"

"Nope. Still none the wiser."

"Youth of today," he mutters while making for the door. "No bleedin' clue."

There's no further mention of tomato-themed songs on the way down to the hotel foyer, but the moment we step out onto the pavement, Clement clears his throat.

"Listen, Doll," he says. "You might have to tell a few porkies to get us in to see this Blair fella."

"Why?"

"I don't think we got off on the right foot."

"Would that have anything to do with you introducing yourself in nothing but your underpants?"

"Probably didn't help, but that wasn't what pissed him off."

"What did?"

"The first thing I said to him."

"Which was?"

"I said: Fuck me, it's Errol Brown."

"Who is Errol Brown?"

"Lead singer of Hot Chocolate."

"*You Sexy Thing*, right?"

"Amongst others, yeah, but Mr Ealy didn't take too kindly to the comparison. Last time a bloke glared at me like that, he'd just found out I knobbed his missus ... once or twice. He weren't happy."

"Oh dear."

"Anyway, I didn't wanna piss Pete off, so I just buggered off back to my room."

We reach the subway station, and if Clement has any plan for bringing the disgruntled architect back on side,

137

it'll have to wait until we get close to where we're going. The journey is brief, though, and within ten minutes, we're on a different street but with the same issue.

"His office is just up here, I think," Clement says as we turn into West Eleventh Avenue.

"What am I supposed to say to him?"

"If there's a reception, tell them you've got a message for Blair Ealy, but you need to give it to him in person. Hopefully, they'll call him down."

"And if they don't?"

"One step at a time, Doll. No point wasting energy on a problem that ain't a problem yet."

"What do I say to him when he comes down?"

"Just tell him Clement says sorry, and then I'll come join you."

"Where are you going to be?"

"Watching from outside because you look harmless — I don't."

"No argument on that front."

We reach the entrance of an office building with a revolving door and a modest reception area beyond. To me, it looks like every other generic office building in Manhattan. If you ignored the sign above the door — Dalton & Associates Architects — it could be home to just about any white-collar company.

"You sure you're up for this?" Clement asks.

"Actually, I walked into another building yesterday and spun a tale to the receptionist, so I'm sure I'll be okay."

"Nice one. I'll be waiting and watching."

With a parting nod, I step into the revolving door and shuffle out the other side into the air-conditioned reception area. Alas, there's no gullible young man of Italian descent behind the desk but a woman roughly my age, although that's where the similarities end. Her stiff posture suggests there might actually be a rod up her arse.

"Good afternoon," she says dryly as I approach the desk. "How may I help you?"

"Can you ask Blair Ealy to come down, please?" I say in a middle-class variation of my English accent.

The woman reaches out her left hand to a mouse on the desk, leaving it to rest there. Her bright yellow nails are as false as her smile, but interestingly, I notice there's a band of white skin on the fourth finger. A ring obviously resided there at some point recently, but no more.

"May I ask the purpose of your request?" she asks.

I can hardly tell her the truth, but if I just say it's private, she'll pull up the drawbridge. Thinking on my feet, the missing ring provides a potential way in.

"What's your name?" I ask, softening my voice a touch.

"Chelsea."

I glance over my shoulder and then lean my arms on the top edge of the desk.

"As one woman to another," I say in a hushed voice. "I can't lie to you ... I've had enough lies myself of late. The reason I need to see Blair is private, but seeing as he's never told me his home address, I had no option but to pay him a visit at work."

I follow up my bullshit with a doleful pout, hoping it triggers Chelsea's empathy switch.

"Men," she snorts. "They're all the same."

"Amen, sister."

The receptionist then clicks the mouse a couple of times and adjusts the microphone of her headset.

"Let me see what I can do for you," she says with a thin smile. "Your name?"

"Tell him ... tell him, Megan Essex."

"Is that your actual name?"

"If he knows I'm here, he won't come down."

"I understand."

It might be that Chelsea sees me as a fellow woman scorned, but it could be that she wants some drama to liven up what must be the dullest of jobs. Either way, she waits a moment and then reactivates her fake smile.

"Mr Ealy, it's Chelsea in reception. You have a visitor — a Miss Essex."

There's a worrying spell of silence before Chelsea speaks again.

"Miss Essex did apologise for calling by unannounced, but she just needs a one-minute conversation relating to one of your projects."

I try to read Chelsea's face to gauge what she's hearing, but she then speaks again.

"I'll tell her you're on your way."

I wait a moment before mouthing a thank you.

"No problem. I hope you get what you came here for."

"So do I, Chelsea. So do I."

The receptionist looks set to say something, but then her attention switches to the monitor.

"I need to answer a call. Good luck."

After thanking her again, I retreat to the far side of the reception area, close to the revolving door and only feet from the lifts. A sudden bong sound and the door of the nearest lift sweeps open to reveal a forty-something black guy. As he steps out of the lift, into the bright lights of the foyer, I can see why Clement drew a comparison to the lead singer of Hot Chocolate.

"Mr Ealy?" I enquire, stepping forward so I'm directly in his path.

"That's me. And you are?"

"I'm the reason you're not at your desk. I have a message for you."

"A message from whom?"

"Clement. He said he's sorry."

140

I study the architect's soft brown eyes for a hint of emotion but all I see is mild confusion.

"Clement?" he replies.

"Yeah, me," comes a voice from behind. "We met last week at the hotel site in Brooklyn, with Pete."

The big man steps up beside me and offers his hand to Blair Ealy.

"I didn't mean to offend," he says, sounding almost genuine. "So, I hope you'll accept my apology."

Blair Ealy's eyes flick towards Clement's hand and then his face adopts the last expression I expected as a broad smile forms.

"I think it's me who owes you an apology," he says, shaking Clement's hand. "There might have been a misunderstanding on my part, which is why I was a little frosty when we met."

"I'd say Clement is easily misunderstood," I remark in an attempt to further thaw the ice.

Blair nods and then turns his eyes back to Clement.

"In my defence, I thought the term *Errol Brown* was some kind of colonial British slur. I've never heard the name before, but when I got back to the office, I looked it up."

"What do you reckon, then?" Clement asks. "Bit of a likeness, right?"

"When I showed her a photo, my wife certainly thought so," Blair chuckles. "And I feel a bit foolish not knowing who you were referring to. I've heard of the band Hot Chocolate, but I didn't know the lead singer's name."

"We're good, then?" Clement asks.

"Of course, although you really didn't have to drop by and explain. I fully intended to speak to Pete again this week and ask him to pass on my apology."

"There might be another reason we dropped by," I then interject, glancing down at Blair's left hand. "That ring on your finger."

Chapter 18

A glance is a glance, no more than a second or two, but time enough to conclude that the ring on Blair Ealy's finger appears almost identical to the one Clement and I studied in a photo back in the hotel room.

"My ring?" Blair responds, automatically looking down at his left hand. "What about it?"

"It's very distinctive," I reply. "And almost identical to one I'm researching."

It occurs to me that I'm about to question a guy who doesn't even know who I am.

"Sorry," I add. "My name isn't Megan; it's Gina, and I'm trying to track down a man who owns a ring that looks similar to yours. May I take a closer look?"

Adopting a bemused expression, the architect raises his hand and holds it twenty inches from my face. I lean in and double-check I'm not mistaken. Below the aquamarine stone, the same four letters are etched into the gold.

"B.C.N.Y.," I murmur.

"That's right," Blair responds. "Berkeley College, New York. It's my grad ring."

"Your what?" Clement asks.

"Graduation ring."

A raft of potent emotions hit me in quick succession. Not only do I have Bruce Franklin's real name, but I now know the college he attended. There are, however, still significant gaps in my knowledge.

"Sorry for the barrage of questions I'm about to pose, Blair, but do all students receive a ring like yours when they graduate?"

"You had to buy one, and they weren't cheap. My grandparents paid for mine."

"What year did you graduate?"

"2001."

"Which means you're ..."

"I'm forty-four."

That makes Blair a few years younger than the man I'm hunting, assuming David Smith didn't lie about his age — he lied about everything else, so I need to be wary.

"I don't suppose the name David Smith strikes a chord?" I ask. "He has a ring exactly like yours, and he's a similar age, give or take a couple of years."

After a moment of silent consideration, Blair shakes his head. "Sorry, no. It's not the kind of name that sticks in the memory. He might have been at Berkeley while I was there, but we're talking more than two decades back."

It's a long shot, but I then pull out my phone and show Blair a photo of David Smith. It receives the same apologetic response.

"If I wanted to research former students at Berkeley, where would I go?"

"Besides the university itself?"

"As you said, it was a long time ago. I'm interested in where David Smith is today."

Blair falls silent for a moment and then suddenly clicks his fingers.

"There was a reunion during the fall of 2021 to mark the twentieth anniversary of our graduation. I couldn't attend because I was out of state at the time, but the guy who organised it, Bryson Renwick, set up a Facebook group. If you can join that group, someone might know the whereabouts of your guy."

I've only known Blair Ealy for a few minutes, but that doesn't quell my desire to hug the man.

"You have no idea how grateful I am," I gush. "Thank you so much, Blair."

"It's no bother, and you know you could have just picked up the phone. Why the subterfuge?"

"My fault," Clement replies. "I thought you had the hump with me."

"I did briefly, but we're good now, right?"

"Yeah, we're all good, mate."

Blair then looks at his watch. "I need to get back to my desk. I hope you find who you're looking for."

"So do I," I reply. "And thanks again."

He turns and takes a couple of steps towards the lift but then pauses.

"Oh, one final point, Clement."

"Yeah?"

"Thanks for wearing clothes this time."

"No worries," the big man grins back.

As the lift doors close on Blair, I head for the exit, deliberately avoiding eye contact with Chelsea at the reception desk. I'd like to say I feel bad for the white lie, but it's for the greater good. Besides, I might not have been wronged by Blair Ealy, but Mum was sure as hell wronged by David Smith.

Out on the pavement, I pull out my phone and ask Clement to wait.

"What you doing?" he asks.

"I'm searching for the Facebook group Blair mentioned."

It doesn't take long to find, but then I hit a major hurdle.

"Bollocks," I groan. "It's a private group."

"Meaning?"

"I have to request access, and then it's up to the group admin to approve my request."

I tap the button to join the group and duly receive a notification to say it's awaiting approval.

"How long does it take?"

"Could be minutes, hours, days, or never. It's a dormant group for an event that happened two years ago, so I don't know how often the admin checks it."

"That ain't ideal, Doll."

"Let me see if I can find the guy Blair mentioned. What was it? Bryson Renwick?"

"Yeah, something like that, and there can't be many blokes with that name. Not like David bleedin' Smith."

"Fingers crossed," I reply while typing Bryson Renwick's distinctive name into the text field.

I tap the search icon and wait for Facebook to tell me some good news. It doesn't take long.

"Wow," I gasp. "There are only two people named Bryson Renwick on Facebook, and one of them lives in Perth, Australia."

"And the other?"

I tap the link to the other Bryson's profile page. Based on his photo, he appears middle-aged, but he certainly hasn't looked after himself as well as Blair Ealy patently has: his greying hair, sallow complexion, and jowly chops add years. For a second, I wonder if I've found the right man, but then I notice his location below the photo.

"He lives in New Jersey. It has to be the same man who organised the reunion."

"Can you give the bloke a bell?"

"We're not Facebook friends, so I can't get his number. I can message him, though."

"Ain't that the same problem? You've gotta sit on your hands and wait for him to reply."

"What do you suggest?"

"There's something over here called the White Pages. It's a bit like the phone directory we have back home. You can get his number from there."

"Oh, okay. Dare I ask how you know about the White Pages?"

"When I was down in Georgia, the bloke I helped out used it. He was looking for his old man."

"Did he find him ... his dad?"

"Yeah, he did."

"And you helped him?"

"Amongst other things. I sorted out a few wrong'uns in the process."

"The Devil went down to Georgia," I mumble under my breath.

"What's that?"

"Oh, nothing," I say dismissively. "It's just a song my mum loves. She played it all the time when I was a kid."

"Despite appearances, Doll, I ain't the Devil — quite the opposite."

He fixes me with a stare that somehow conveys both reassurance and menace. In the few seconds I have to unpick the mixed messaging, I reach a conclusion. Clement has proven a great help already, which is what I'd expect from a friend, but he'd make a truly terrifying foe.

"Anyway," I cough, turning away from the big man. "Let me see if Bryson Renwick is listed in the White Pages."

It only takes ninety seconds and one modest payment to secure the information I need.

"I have a phone number," I say. "Two, in fact."

"Nice one. You gonna give the bloke a bell, then?"

"I need a minute to plan what I'm going to say."

Clement looks up and down the street and then reaches into his breast pocket.

"Ain't nowhere to sit down and have a cuppa so I'll make do with a smoke."

"Okay. I'm calling him now."

The listing in the White Pages included both Bryson Renwick's landline and mobile numbers, and I decide to try his mobile first. After a brief moment of dead air, it rings.

"Hello," a voice answers.

"Hi. Mr Renwick?"

"This is he. Who's calling?"

"Sorry, my name is Gina Jackson. Blair Ealy gave me your details."

I wait a few seconds for the name to register.

"Ahh, yes," Bryson Renwick says brightly. "I haven't seen Blair in years. How is he?"

"He's, um ... doing really well. We were just talking about the Berkeley Reunion, which is why your name came up."

"Oh?"

"I understand you organised the reunion in 2021?"

"That's correct."

"I'm calling because I'm desperately trying to track down a guy who attended Berkeley in the late nineties, early noughties. The name didn't register with Blair, but he suggested you'd be the man most likely to remember, seeing as you organised the reunion."

"Who is it you're looking for?"

"David Smith."

"Hmm ..."

Silent seconds tick by before Bryson Renwick replies with actual words.

"I'm sorry," he says. "I can say with some certainty that if David Smith graduated from Berkeley, it wasn't the class of 2001."

My shoulders slump.

"Oh ... right. That's one graduation year I can scratch from our list of contenders, I suppose."

"Why are you so keen to find him? Are you a reporter?"

"Lord, no," I splutter. "I'm ... it's a private family matter, but basically, David was once good friends with my mother. She'd love nothing more than to see him again."

It's true that she would, but only to kick the arsehole squarely in the nuts.

"I'm sorry I can't help, but I do know someone who likely can."

"Really? I'll take any help I can get."

"An old friend of mine, Joseph, is on the Alumni Association committee, and they have a database of every class graduate going back some fifty or sixty years."

"And do you think Joseph might check that database for me?"

"I'm sure he will, but bear in mind that he won't give out personal information. At best, he'll be able to confirm the year that David Smith graduated, and if you're lucky, he might confirm if he's still living in New York."

Considering there's likely an address on that database record, it's a poor offer. It's the only offer on the table, though.

"Anything would be useful, Bryson. Anything at all."

"I'll see what I can do. Is this the best number to contact you?"

"It is, yes."

"I probably won't be able to speak to Joseph until this evening, so bear with me. If you haven't heard back within twenty-four hours, it'll be because he hasn't had a chance to look up your guy."

"I understand, but I would be eternally grateful if you could explain that I'm desperate to find David. I've travelled all the way from London, and I'm only here until next week."

"I guessed from your accent that you're not local, and you have my word I'll plead your case to Joseph."

"Thank you, Bryson."

I end the call and turn to Clement.

"He said there wasn't a David Smith in his graduation year, but a friend has access to a database of graduates going back decades. He'll speak to him this evening."

"Ain't much else we can do till then."

I'm not sure when Clement and I became a *we*, but without his assistance, I'd likely be back in the hotel room staring at a list of hopeless leads. Irrespective of what happens next, I do owe him more than a shitty breakfast.

"No, there isn't, but do you fancy grabbing a bite to eat later? My treat ... a thank you."

"Sure."

"And, if you don't mind, I'll choose the venue. No offence, but I'm not eating at Dex's Diner or, God forbid, the Pegasus."

"Alright, but nothing too fancy."

"I'm thinking a steakhouse. There's one called Gallards opposite my hotel."

"That'll do."

"Great. Shall we meet up at say ... seven?"

"Works for me."

"I doubt I'll hear from Bryson before then but let me grab your number just in case."

Clement reaches into his pocket and hands me his phone.

"Dunno my number. These things ain't my bag."

I take the phone and find his number in the empty contact list. I add my number and then call my phone so Clement's number flashes up on the screen.

"Okay, got it. Do you want to know your number?"

"Not really," he grunts.

I hand the phone back and ask if he's heading to the subway station.

"Nah, I hear there's a record shop a few blocks away. I'm gonna go check it out."

"Are you into vinyl?"

"What do you reckon?" he replies with a smirk.

"Sorry. Stupid question," I snigger. "Enjoy."

We part ways and I head back along the street towards the subway station. As I stroll along, I dare to hope that maybe, just maybe, my target is within touching distance. I have a name, and I know which university he attended. It's more than I expected, and if my luck holds out, maybe Bryson Renwick will call with good news while I'm tucking into a rib-eye this evening.

If I can establish that David Smith is living in New York, it'll only be a matter of time before I find an address. Then, I might need to consider whether I want a big man in double denim with me when I knock on Smith's door.

Having seen how he dealt with one scumbag, Sean Hoffman, it's a tempting prospect.

Very tempting indeed.

Chapter 19

When I arrive back at the hotel, I've already decided how I'll utilise the few hours before I meet up with Clement — searching online for David Smith. I didn't have much luck earlier, but that was before I established the connection to Berkeley College.

Before I make myself comfortable on the bed with the tablet, there's a phone call I need to make. I dial Mum's number. To my surprise, she picks up on the first ring.

"Wow, that was quick," I remark. "It's me, Mum."

"Oh. Hello, darlin'," she replies, her tone a little downbeat.

"Are you okay? You sound a bit ... a little tired."

"I'm alright, but I've just this second put the phone down after a long call with your Aunt Lynn."

Just the mention of Lynn's name is enough to raise my hackles.

"What did she want?" I ask flatly, making no effort to mask my disdain for the woman.

"Nothing, really. She just called for a natter, and to see how I'm holding up."

"Did Paula tell you I called yesterday? She said that Lynn came over with Stephen on Monday evening."

"Yes, she did."

"What did they want?"

"Nothing. They're just concerned about me."

There's something in Mum's voice that doesn't inspire confidence. However, I don't want my call to become an interrogation.

"As long as Lynn isn't being her usual interfering self. That's all I'll say on the matter."

"Good. Now, why don't you tell me all about Paris."

Knowing full well that Mum would welcome the distraction from her own thoughts, I did take the precaution of researching a few titbits about my supposed trip. I don't like lying to my mum, but if it makes her happy to know that at least one of us isn't on the brink of a nervous breakdown, it's a price I'm willing to pay.

After spinning a few tales about my fictitious day in Paris, I nudge the conversation towards the reason for my call: Mum's state of mind.

"Have you been managing to sleep any better?" I ask.

"No, not really."

Not what I wanted to hear.

"Have you been getting out? An hour's walk in the fresh air would do you the world of good."

"That's what Paula suggested. It's been raining today, but we'll probably go out tomorrow."

"How are you finding it, living under the same roof as Paula?"

"She's been so lovely, but ..."

Mum draws in a deep breath.

"But she can be a bit too much at times. She's obsessed with keeping busy, and I understand what she's trying to do, but maybe I just want to be alone sometimes."

My mother might well want to be alone, but that's the last thing I want. Paula is there to push back against Mum's depressive thoughts because I know from experience that they'll take root if left unchecked.

"It's good to keep yourself busy, right?"

"So I'm constantly told," she grumbles.

"Because it's true."

"I know, and I am trying. Paula helped me sort out the mess with my paperwork, and we're going to de-clutter the bungalow before it goes on the market."

"There's no urgency to put it on the market. You know that."

"There is. I can't afford to pay the council tax."

"I told you I've sorted that."

"Did you?"

"Yes, it's paid up until April, so there's no need to fret."

"And what about all the other bills: gas, electric, water, and the rest?"

"Mum, it's all under control."

"Is it? When I was going through the paperwork with Paula, she found some bills from last month — hundreds of pounds I don't have."

I make a mental note to text Paula later and ask her not to let Mum look at her disorganised filing system again.

"I've spoken to all your utility companies and set up a direct debit from my account. I did tell you I had it all in hand. There's nothing for you to worry about."

"Apart from the fact I'm bankrupting my daughter."

"I'm far from bankrupt," I respond, trying not to let my frustration show. "I've still got a large chunk of Granddad's inheritance money squirrelled away, and I've got several commission pieces to work on when I get back. It's all good, okay?"

"Alright," she sighs. "If you say so."

"I do."

There's a moment of silence. I can imagine Mum on the other end of the phone, crumpled in the armchair in the hallway: mentally, emotionally, and physically exhausted. For a moment, I consider giving up my search for the man who instigated Mum's spiralling mental health issues and jumping on the next plane back to London, but I won't. The only way I'll drag Mum out

154

of her pit is to reset the clock, financially and legally at least. Alas, there's nothing I can do to take away the emotional pain David Smith inflicted.

"It'll be alright, Mum," I say quietly. "I know it will."

"Will it?" she replies in barely a whisper.

"Yes, and I need you to remain strong until ... until things get better. Can you do that for me?"

Another moment of silence is finally punctuated by a sharp intake of breath.

"I'll be fine, darlin'," Mum says. "Trust me."

I wouldn't go as far as to say her words reassure me, but maybe all she needs is a good night's sleep. And at least Paula is there to watch over her.

"I'll let you get on with your evening," I say. "And try to get some sleep."

"I will."

"Okay. I love you, Mum."

"And I love you too."

It feels like an appropriate note to end the call. I promise to phone again tomorrow, but Mum tells me not to worry, and to enjoy myself. I don't say it, obviously, but neither is likely.

Trying not to let my thoughts linger on Mum, I switch the tablet on and focus on the only way I can make myself useful. Once the tablet is ready for action, I get comfortable on the bed, propping both pillows behind my back, and then type the name David Smith into the Google search field.

Two hours later, I toss the tablet across the bed and get up. If I never see the name David Smith again, it'll be too soon. Not only have I clicked on hundreds of links to dead ends, but I've looked at countless men of every age and ethnicity, but not the one I'm after. It crosses my mind that maybe David Smith is another alias, but I don't dwell on that possibility for long. He must have shown a passport to Pinhill Properties when

155

he rented the apartment on West End Avenue, and for now, I'm willing to bet all my chips on that passport being genuine. I have no other choice, really.

My stomach rumbles, reminding me that I'm due to meet Clement for dinner soon. I hop in the shower and throw on the first sweatshirt and pair of jeans I drag from the suitcase. I then take a quick glance in the mirror to see if I can get away without makeup.

"Fuck it," I snort.

I can't be bothered, and I doubt that my dining companion will care.

When I pass through the hotel foyer and exit onto the pavement, I'm surprised to see Clement waiting outside the restaurant across the street. I don't know why I'm surprised because, for all I know, he's the obsessively punctual type.

I cross the street.

"Evening, Doll," Clement says before taking a long draw on his cigarette.

"Hey. How long have you been waiting here?"

"Few minutes. Any news from that Bryson fella?"

"Nothing yet."

He nods and then flicks his cigarette butt towards the gutter. It doesn't quite make it.

"We going in, then?" he asks, gesturing towards the door to Gallards Steakhouse.

He then steps forward and opens the door for me.

"Thank you."

It didn't dawn on me to book, so seeing that only a quarter of the tables are occupied is a relief. A waiter bustles over and introduces himself as Jordan.

"Welcome to Gallards," he says. "Have you booked a table?"

"We haven't," I confirm. "Did we need to?"

"No, it's not a problem at all. For two, is it?"

"Please."

156

"Come this way," he says, turning up the brilliance of his plastic smile.

I don't know if the waiter thinks we're on a date, but the fact neither of us has made any effort to dress up should be evidence enough that we're not. Looking around at the décor, it's not really the kind of restaurant you'd choose for a date night, anyway. It has the same kind of relaxed vibe as the Beefeater restaurants back home. I should have probably checked first, but I hope the prices are comparable, too.

We order a couple of beers, and Jordan leaves us with a menu each. Clement inspects it for mere seconds before slapping it down on the table.

"Sixteen-ounce rib-eye," he says. "With all the trimmings."

My eyes flick towards my own menu, and the price of Clement's choice. Forty bucks for a main is a lot, but I can hardly complain after inviting him out and choosing the restaurant.

"Sure," I reply with a strained smile.

Jordan returns with our beers and asks if we're ready to order.

"We'll have the sixteen-ounce rib-eye, please," I confirm. "And the seared chicken."

"How would you like the rib-eye?" he asks me.

It should be fairly obvious from looking at us that I'm not the one who wants an enormous slab of dead cow. I nod towards Clement.

"I want it torched, mate," he says to the waiter.

"Um, torched?" Jordan enquires with obvious trepidation.

"Yeah, black as the ace of spades."

"I think he means well done," I interject. "Very well done."

"No problem."

Jordan scuttles away, and I turn the conversation to our respective afternoons.

"Did you buy anything at the record store?"

"Not much point seeing as I ain't got a record player. I just like nosing through the old albums."

"Any favourites?"

"Nothin' you've likely heard of. All before your time."

"Like, how far before?"

"Sixties. Seventies."

"You're into that era I presume?"

It might explain his attire, although I decide not to enquire.

"Yeah, I am."

He doesn't expand any further, choosing to take a slug of beer instead. I switch the conversation to my afternoon.

"Well, while you were browsing vintage records, I was holed up in my room, searching the internet for David Smith."

"Didn't you do that earlier?"

"That was nothing more than a quick check. I wanted to have a proper deep dive to see if I could find anything online referencing David Smith, New York, and Berkeley College."

"I take it you didn't?"

"Nothing ... actually, not nothing. There are more than enough David Smiths out there but it's impossible to say, without a photo, if any of them are the one I'm looking for."

"Trouble is, you don't even know if he lives in New York. America's a bleedin' big place, Doll, and your man could be anywhere from here to San Jose."

"Don't say that," I sigh. "I'm only just about clinging on to hope as it is."

"Good job you bumped into me then," Clement smiles back.

158

"Why's that?"

"Obvious, ain't it? You need me."

"Do I?"

"Yeah, but you probably ain't worked that out yet. You will, though."

I'm about to dig into Clement's statement when a sudden vibration in my pocket distracts me. I tug out my phone and check the caller's name on the screen. With my pulse quickening, I look across the table to Clement.

"It's Bryson Renwick," I gulp. "I guess I'm about to find out if I need your help ... or not."

I snatch a quick gulp of lager before accepting the call, just to lubricate my suddenly dry mouth.

"Hi, Bryson," I then breathe heavily into the phone.

"Evening, Gina," he says in a level tone. "Have I caught you at a good time?"

"Yes, yes. I'm in a restaurant, but we've only just ordered, so I've got time to speak."

"Okay, great."

"Um, do you mind if I put you on speakerphone? My, um ... friend is sitting opposite, and he's been helping me with the search for David."

"Not at all."

I remove the phone from my ear, tap the speaker icon, and place it in the centre of the table.

"Can you hear me, Bryson?"

"Loud and clear."

"Great. So, I hope you don't mind if I cut to the chase — did you have any luck with your friend?"

"Yes, and no."

"Oh."

"I explained your situation to Joseph, and whilst he was sympathetic, he did stress the point I made. He can't disclose personal information about anyone on the association's database of former students."

"That's ... disappointing."

"However, I convinced him that it wouldn't be a breach of confidence to simply check if there's a David Smith on the database, and what year he graduated. After a bit of umming and erring, Joseph agreed."

"So, you can tell me that much?"

"No."

"Pardon? I thought you said—"

"I'm afraid the news isn't good," Bryson interrupts. "Because Joseph did a check on every Caucasian male named David Smith who graduated Berkeley between 1995 and 2005, and the computer returned zero results."

I glance at Clement. His forehead is scoured with the same confused frown lines as mine likely is.

"Are you saying that no one called David Smith graduated Berkeley in that decade?"

"No, there are two men on the database with that name, but they're both black."

"That doesn't make sense. The man I'm looking for wears a Berkeley graduation ring — I checked it against Blair Ealy's and his is identical."

"Is that all you're going on? He wears a Berkeley grad ring?"

"Err, yes."

Bryson conveys his feelings by sucking air across his teeth.

"Just because he wears a grad ring doesn't mean he attended Berkeley."

"Why else would he wear it?"

"It's a fair question, but people do all kinds of crazy things for reasons most of us wouldn't understand. Only last week, I read about a guy who was removed from a recent veteran's parade because he turned up with a chest full of medals that weren't his. The guy bought them on eBay and got some kick out of pretending to be a war hero."

"That's awful, but we're talking about a college graduation ring. Who would pretend to ..."

I don't have to finish my question or wait for Bryson to reply because I know exactly who would pretend — a conman.

"Pretend is an interesting choice of word," Bryson continues, his tone noticeably harder. "How well does your mother know this man you're looking for?"

I close my eyes for a second. When I open them, Clement is staring straight at me.

"Tell him the truth," he mouths.

Resigned to my fate, I puff a long breath and deliver an apology to Bryson Renwick. I then explain the sorry tale of my hunt for Bruce Franklin and how it led me to New York, and the discovery that his real name is David Smith.

"Man, that's just awful," Bryson says once I've explained. "But I wish you'd been honest with me from the start. It might have saved us both some time."

"I know, and all I can do is apologise again. It was never my intention to deceive you or waste your time."

"You certainly deceived me, but under the circumstances, I can forgive you. As for the time-wasting, if you'd told me the truth about your mom, I could have helped you earlier, and I wouldn't have needed to call in a favour with Joseph."

"You could have helped me, how?"

"I could have told you about Evelyn Conroy."

"Who's Evelyn Conroy?"

"She's the widow of Roger Conroy, and in January of this year, she met a guy on one of those dating websites. On their third date, he went back to Evelyn's house and spiked her drink with a sedative. While she was unconscious, he emptied her jewellery box and hightailed into the night, never to be seen again."

"That's terrible, but I don't understand the relevance."

"Roger Conroy graduated Berkeley a year before Blair and me. His grad ring was stolen that night along with Evelyn's jewellery."

"With respect, Bryson, I very much doubt the ring on David Smith's finger is likely to be the one stolen from that poor woman's jewellery box."

"I'd say there's a higher-than-average chance it's the same ring."

"I really don't see how. There must be hundreds, if not thousands, of those rings out there."

"You're probably right, and I'd agree with you if it wasn't for one detail."

"Namely?"

"The asshole who conned poor Evelyn went by the name of Franklin Bruce."

Chapter 20

I don't like wasting money, particularly on food. Call me risk-averse, but I'm more than willing to chance an upset tummy by eating a sandwich a few days past its sell-by date rather than throw it away.

Last night, I paid an eighty-dollar bill in Gallards Steakhouse even though I left half the food on my plate. The only consolation was that my dinner companion polished off the chicken, so all that remained was a portion of sweet potato fries and a pile of chargrilled vegetables.

That was, of course, after I ended the call with Bryson Renwick, but I called him again after the waiter cleared our plates. I had to hear the full story of what happened to Evelyn Conroy.

Although they graduated from Berkeley within a year of one another, Bryson and Roger Conroy were strangers. The former only learned of the latter's tragic death in a boating accident when he read Roger Conroy's obituary in the Alumni quarterly newsletter three years ago. Bryson was so shocked that he organised a fundraiser for Roger's widow, Evelyn, and her fifteen-year-old daughter. Just one former Berkeley grad helping out the family of another, as Bryson put it.

A month after Roger Conroy's death, Bryson and his wife, Sarah, attended a memorial service in Bridgeport,

Connecticut. Afterwards, he presented Evelyn Conroy with a cheque for twenty-thousand dollars; every cent donated by former Berkeley graduates. The Conroys were not a wealthy family, so the money was a huge help to Evelyn and her daughter. Over the ensuing months, her gratitude slowly morphed into friendship, mainly with Sarah, and the two women stayed in touch. They also met up whenever Evelyn and her daughter visited New York.

It was during one of their regular conversations via email that Evelyn confessed she'd met someone on a dating website. Sarah actively encouraged her to pursue the initial attraction, reassuring Evelyn that after three years of mourning, no one would resent her trying to find love again.

It wasn't love that Evelyn Conroy found, though; it was the complete opposite. She met a conman by the name of Franklin Bruce.

Just before nine o'clock this morning, while I was impatiently wearing out the carpet in my hotel room, I received a text message from Bryson Renwick. During our second call yesterday, I pleaded with him to contact Evelyn and ask if she would be willing to meet with me today. Bryson's text message confirmed an address in Bridgeport, Connecticut and Evelyn Conroy's phone number. Roger Conroy's widow, and perhaps a victim of that same man who conned my mother, had agreed I could pay her a visit.

That's why I'm now standing on a platform at New York's famous Grand Central Station. Why there's a slightly uncouth man-mountain standing next to me is less obvious.

"You really don't have to come," I remark for the second time since we met at the station entrance fifteen minutes ago. "I can catch up with you as soon as I get back to New York."

"Anyone would think you don't want me tagging along," Clement replies after stifling a yawn.

"No, it's not that. It's just ... it's just that I don't know if you meeting Evelyn is a good idea. She's more likely to open up to me. You're ... well, a bit intimidating."

"Plenty of birds have opened up to me, Doll," he replies with a wink. "Can't resist my charms, you see."

"Jesus," I groan. "That's not what I meant, and definitely not a topic of conversation I want to continue, thank you very much."

"Don't get your knickers in a twist. I was kidding, alright."

"This isn't a laughing matter, Clement. This is important."

"Yeah, I know, which is why I'm coming with you."

"And, as I've already implied, twice, I don't need a chaperone."

He turns to me and shakes his head. "Your trouble, Doll, is you don't know what you need."

"Right," I snort. "As if you know anything about me."

"Not you, maybe, but I've met chicks like you before. Tough as nails on the outside but inside, that's a different matter."

"Oh, really?" I reply, defiantly putting my hands on my hips. "And what is it about *chicks like me* that you're so certain of?"

He stares down at me and blinks slowly, almost cat-like. "You're lost."

"Lost?" I scoff. "Hardly."

"Maybe lost ain't the right word but it ain't far from the right one. How old are you? Thirty?"

"Thirty-three."

"No rings on your fingers, no kids I'm guessing?"

"Not yet, no. So what?"

Before he can answer, the doors of the train carriage we've been waiting to enter suddenly hiss open. I look back at Clement to see if he's going to answer my question but he just waves towards the open carriage doors, inviting me to enter first. I accept the invite, but not before throwing him a frosty scowl.

In the time it takes to find a seat and settle into it, I realise that the one hour and thirty-seven-minute journey to Bridgeport will likely feel a lot longer if I'm at loggerheads with my travel companion. I wait for him to squeeze his bulk into the seat opposite before offering an olive branch.

"If I seem a bit testy this morning, it's because I barely slept a wink last night."

"Is that an apology?"

"No."

"Thought not," he snorts, the hint of a smile grazing the edges of his moustache. "Not your style, eh?"

"I was going to let it lie, but seeing as you want to keep poking, you know fuck-all about me, my style, or my life, so keep your observations to yourself, please."

We haven't even left the station yet, and I've already broken my vow to stay calm. I wait for a reaction, but Clement just sits there, arms resting on the table, impassive.

"Sorry," I mumble. "I really didn't sleep well last night."

"It's all good, Doll."

"It's not. I hate being so narky, but ..."

There's a line I don't want to cross, but my words have led me right to the edge of it.

"But?" Clement prompts.

"It's nothing. Forget it."

"You know what they say: confession is good for the soul."

"Is it, though?"

"Fucked if I know," he shrugs. "But it ain't good to keep shit bottled up. That'll mess with your head in the long run."

166

I reply with a semi-smile and then stare out of the window at nothing in particular.

"I ain't all about the brawn," Clement then says, pulling my attention back from the window.

"No?" I respond.

"There's a brain up here, you know," he says, tapping a finger against his temple. "And that brain has processed some fucked-up stuff in recent years, but you know what?"

"What?"

"It ain't fucked no more. I ain't lost."

Unsure how to react to what sounds like an earnest statement, I reply with a simple nod.

"You gonna tell me what kept you awake last night, then?"

"Um, I ..."

"Let me guess. You're worried about your mum?"

"I'm struggling to remember the last time I wasn't worried about her."

"Those worries keep you awake every night?"

"No, not every night."

"What was so different about last night?"

I lock eyes with Clement, searching for the signs I saw in someone else's eyes not so long ago — someone I desperately wanted to trust but inevitably couldn't. For all the looking, though, there's nothing in Clement's eyes to suggest he isn't being entirely sincere.

Brick by careful brick, Gina.

"I did something I'm not proud of," I reply, fiddling with the cuffs of my sweatshirt.

The man opposite doesn't say a word. Intentional or otherwise, I feel compelled to continue.

"Mum has had real problems sleeping since ... since that wanker left her at the altar. It got so bad that she went to the doctor, and he prescribed sleeping pills."

"Okay," Clement nods.

"I'm terrified that she'll do something stupid, so I emptied her bottle of sleeping pills before I left for New York and replaced them with aspirin. When I spoke to her yesterday, she sounded dreadful, and the fact she can't sleep is down to me. I took her pills away, knowing full well that she'd suffer as a consequence."

I stop fiddling with my cuffs and slump back in the seat.

"There you have it," I sigh. "That's why I couldn't sleep."

Clement strokes his moustache a couple of times and then clears his throat.

"Maybe you'll feel better if I tell you about Terry Turban."

"Err, right. Who the hell is Terry Turban?"

"Terry used to run the newsagents on the corner of the street where I lived for a while. I nipped in there most days to buy fags and a paper. Nice bloke, Terry — salt of the earth type."

"God, I'm not sure I want to know the answer, but was his actual name Terry Turban?"

"Nah, course it weren't, but it was that or Punjab Pete. He came over from India with his family, you see, and no one could get their mouth around his proper name, so we gave him the choice of Pete or Terry. He went with Terry."

"I presume you didn't mention the suffix element of his new name?"

"Yeah, I did."

"Seriously? And he still let you in his shop?"

"He loved the name — even got his missus to use it, but her English weren't great, so it never sounded quite right. Anyway, Terry had a problem with some of the local kids giving him lip and the like. He gave them lip back, and things started getting a bit out of hand. One night, the little shits sprayed the front of his shop with graffiti. Proper vile stuff, too, not just your usual drawing of a cock and balls."

"That's awful."

"It pissed me off enough that I tracked down the ringleader and gave him a sharp lesson in race relations."

"What did you say?"

"He was a teenager, so I went easy on him. I only hung him upside down from a railway bridge for a few seconds — long enough for him to get the message that Terry's shop was off limits."

"I presume that worked?"

"Sort of. The kids didn't go anywhere near the shop again, but I shot myself in the foot by getting involved. As it turned out, the kid I dangled from a bridge happened to belong to the bird I'd just started seeing. She weren't too happy about it and that was the end of that."

"This is all very interesting, Clement, but I'm struggling to see the relevance."

"You've gotta do what your gut tells you, 'cos if you don't, you'll suffer a lot more than the odd sleepless night. Yeah, your mum ain't sleeping well, but imagine how you'd feel if she did something stupid and you hadn't switched those pills."

I've already imagined that horrific scenario too many times, which is what led me to a chemist and a packet of aspirin.

"And, in my case," Clement continues. "I lost out on a guaranteed shag, but if I hadn't given that kid a talking to, who knows what might have happened to Terry and his family. One day, it's graffiti, the next is a petrol-soaked rag through the letterbox. Don't bear thinking about."

I'm still not entirely sure I'd compare my situation to the characters in Clement's tale, but that doesn't mean I'm not grateful for him trying to make me feel a little better.

"You're right — I took the least-worse option, and I shouldn't keep beating myself up about it."

"Nah, you shouldn't, but you know what you *should* do?"

"No."

"Get some bleedin' kip. Anyone ever told you that you're a right stroppy madam when you're tired?"

Despite myself, my lips curl into a smile.

"Yes, one or two people."

I heed Clement's advice and close my eyes.

Chapter 21

I don't sleep, as such, but drift in and out of consciousness. At some point, my attempt to drift back into unconsciousness is thwarted when Clement taps his knuckle on the table.

"Wakey, wakey," he says in a low voice, although it comes out more like a growl.

I open my eyes, blink away the mist, and then squint at the harsh light in the carriage.

"Feeling any better, Doll?"

"A bit," I yawn before stretching my arms. "But, God, I'd willingly commit murder in return for a large mug of coffee."

"We ain't got much further to go so don't go killing anyone just yet."

"I'll try not to."

Through still-bleary eyes, I check the time. Clement wasn't far wrong in his estimation as we're only seven minutes from our destination.

"You ever been to Connecticut?" I ask.

"Nope. You?"

"No, but spending three months in New England is definitely on my bucket list."

"Three months? Long time for a holiday."

"I know, which is why it'll probably stay on my bucket list for a while. I really want to rent a house and see what it's like living here from October until Christmas."

"Cold and wet."

"Probably," I snort. "But I have this romantic notion of experiencing the autumnal colours, then Halloween, Thanksgiving, and the run-up to Christmas. Maybe it's just a rose-tinted interpretation but I'd love to experience all of it for real, rather than through a TV screen."

"Not like this, then?"

"No. Not like this at all."

I turn and look out of the window at the urban outskirts of Bridgeport. There's nothing remarkable about it, but it's a far cry from the grimy, claustrophobic landscape of New York. Reason enough for me to draw a positive first impression. I can't help but wonder if I'll feel quite so positive on the return journey.

Eventually, the train comes to a standstill, and a disembodied voice from a speaker above our heads confirms we've arrived at Bridgeport. Clement stands up and rolls his neck a couple of times while I go through my usual routine whenever disembarking a train and check three times that I haven't left anything behind.

We quickly clear the platform and enter the ticket hall. There's no coffee shop, but there is a vending machine.

"I need something to drink," I say to Clement while fishing my purse from my bag. "Do you want anything?"

"I'm good, ta."

In need of a caffeine shot, I decide on a can of Coke. I wasn't counting, but I'd guess barely ten seconds elapsed between the can dropping into the chute and the last drop of Coke passing my lips.

"Thirsty, were we?"

"Parched," I reply.

We head outside to the street and a short line of taxis queued up against the kerb. As soon as Bryson Renwick's text landed this morning, I checked Evelyn Conroy's address on a map, and it's less than two miles away from the station.

"Where we heading?" Clement asks as he steps towards the first taxi in the line.

"1211 Howard Avenue."

"Gotcha."

He bends down and confirms the address with the driver before opening the passenger's door.

"You alright with me sitting in the front?" he asks.

"I doubt you'd fit in the back, so your question is academic. Just get in."

I hop into the back seat and then get to witness the driver's stunned expression as Clement slowly shoehorns himself into the passenger seat. If the driver is frustrated at the delay while the big man tries to buckle his seat belt, he does a good job of hiding it.

Eventually, the driver shifts the gearstick and pulls away. We've barely covered a hundred yards when the first question arrives.

"You guys from out of town?" the driver asks.

"Yeah," Clement replies. "What gave us away?"

"That would be your accent," the driver replies gleefully, Clement's sarcasm going straight over his head.

"No flies on you, is there, Sherlock?"

"No-siree," the driver replies, looking pleased with himself.

I can't see Clement's face, but I can almost hear his eyeballs rolling in their sockets. He then turns his head to the right and stares out of the window — the universal sign for don't say another word to me.

After five minutes of silence, the driver takes a right turn into Howard Avenue. I scan the first house for a number: 732. Only a few hundred houses to go.

By the time we pull up outside number 1211, I've got a pretty good impression of the neighbourhood. All of the houses are of the traditional New England design with slatted wooden planks to the front and most benefiting from a full-width covered veranda. The key difference between each of the houses is the condition. Some are pristine, with neat lawns and freshly painted woodwork, while others are tired and tatty. None of them are what you might call grand.

I pay the taxi fare, plus the obligatory tip, and we get out of the car.

Standing next to Clement on the pavement, I take a moment to appraise Evelyn Conroy's home. I wouldn't describe it as pristine, but neither would I say it's tatty. At some point, the wooden planks were stripped of paint and stained a shade of burnt-umber. I don't enquire, but I'd bet Clement would refer to it as turd-brown.

"Ready, Doll?" he asks.

"I guess so."

Clement steps towards the low chain-link gate and opens it. I then follow him up three brick steps to the wooden veranda and a solid-looking front door, unimaginatively stained the same shade as the wooden planks on either side of it.

With my stomach in knots, I press the doorbell and take a step back. Clement takes three, maybe to counter the significant difference in our bulk. I'm still not entirely convinced that his presence is a good idea, but after our chat on the train, I feel less concerned about Evelyn opening the door, screaming, and slamming it shut.

A scuffing noise breaks the silence, followed by the sound of a solid bolt sliding from its saddle. The door opens and a woman peers around the edge, a brass security chain running horizontally a few inches below her chin. In her early fifties, I'd guess, her sandy-grey hair is tied back, and her hazel eyes are almost cartoonishly large.

"Hi, Evelyn?" I say so warmly it almost drips out of my mouth.

"You are?" she replies in a low voice.

"I'm Gina ... Gina Jackson, and this is my ... err, friend, Clement. Bryson said he called you about us paying a visit."

"You're the Brit whose mom lost a small fortune?"

"Sadly, that's me."

She then looks up at Clement.

"Alright, darlin'," he says. "Nice to meet you."

There's a distinct and obvious hesitancy in Evelyn's eyes, enough to cause a sudden pang of regret in my chest.

"You got a kettle?" Clement then asks in the same tone as a curious child. "They ain't so much a thing over here, are they?"

"Yes, I have a kettle."

"Don't suppose you've got tea as well? I'm dying for a brew."

"You remind me of someone," Evelyn responds, ignoring Clement's cheeky request.

"Charles Bronson?" he retorts with a Cheshire cat grin. "We're both good-looking blokes, so I get it."

To my amazement, a slight smile reaches Evelyn's lips. She then turns to me.

"Is he for real?" she asks.

"I'm afraid he is," I chuckle. "I know he looks like a grizzly bear in denim, but he's harmless enough. I promise."

After another glance at Clement, the woman who is yet to confirm she is Evelyn Conroy unfastens the security chain and swings the door open.

175

"Come in," she says before retreating into the hallway.

I enter first and wipe my feet on the mat.

"Would you mind taking your shoes off?" our host asks. "I've just cleaned all the floors."

"No problem."

I untie the laces of my trainers and kick them off. Clement leans up against the door frame and grabs the heel of a battered Chelsea boot. He then switches position and tugs off his left boot to reveal a gnarly looking big toe protruding from the end of his sock. He notices my horrified face.

"Couldn't find a darning needle," he whispers by way of explanation.

Fortunately, our host doesn't seem overly perturbed by the sight of Clement's toe and invites us to follow her through to the kitchen.

Like the exterior of the house itself, the kitchen is tidy and functional but eminently bland. Evelyn invites us to sit at a large oak table while she fills a stove-top kettle.

"How do you know Bryson?" she calls over.

"We don't really. A guy who attended Berkeley put us on to him."

There's no follow-up question as Evelyn arranges three cups on a tray before stepping over to the table. The only way I'll loosen the knot in my stomach is to get straight down to business.

"Did Bryson go into detail about what happened to my mum?"

"He told me enough," Evelyn replies, taking a seat in the chair next to mine. "Your mom lost a lot of money to a conman, correct?"

"She lost money, yes, but that man took so much more from her."

Evelyn purses her lips like she's suddenly got a sour taste in her mouth.

"I know that feeling," she says flatly. "I suppose Bryson explained what happened to me?"

"Not in any detail, but enough for me to think it could be the same man who conned my mum."

"Franklin Bruce?"

"The man who conned my mum used the name Bruce Franklin. Now, that could be just a coincidence, but he met Mum while we were visiting New York, so it's not beyond the realms of possibility that it's the same man."

"I could show you a photo if you want to check?"

"Great minds," I reply with a tepid smile. "I've got photos of him on my phone. Would you mind taking a look?"

"Sure."

Ever since Bryson Renwick told me the name of the man who stole Evelyn's jewellery, I've churned it over in my mind so many times that I've almost convinced myself that it is a coincidence. Granddad used to warn me about overthinking things and I should have heeded his advice on this occasion.

With almost crippling levels of trepidation, I pull out my phone and tap through to the clearest photo of Bruce Franklin, or Franklin Bruce, or David bloody Smith. In it, he's wearing a navy blazer over a crisp white shirt and smiling into the camera with all the sincerity and faux warmth of an election candidate.

I hold the phone out for Evelyn to look, my lungs holding on to the last breath.

"Is it him?" I gulp.

Evelyn leans forward and squints hard, but there's no obvious sign of recognition in her eyes as she stares at the screen for the longest seconds of my life.

"What do you think?" I ask. "Is it him?"

Rather than answer my question, Evelyn reaches into her cardigan pocket and removes a mobile phone. She then taps the screen several times, concentrating hard at every step.

"You tell me," Evelyn then says, placing the phone on the table in front of me.

Almost in unison, Clement and I lean forward to look at the photo displayed on the screen. The face smiling up at us doesn't have neatly trimmed hair or a clean-shaven jawline — quite the opposite. This man's hair is darker, collar length, and likely styled with a relaxed hand rather than a brush. His mouth is framed with a goatee beard, setting an overall impression of a man who might work in the arts: theatre, comedy, or, most likely, music.

As I stare down at the photo, focussing harder, I look past the dark, collar-length hair and the goatee beard. That's when I let out an inadvertent gasp.

The eyes are a giveaway.

The same smoky-grey eyes that deceived my mother. It's him.

Chapter 22

I watch Clement's face as he takes the first sip. His left cheek twitches slightly, but it's enough to confirm his first thoughts of Evelyn Conroy's tea. I hope he's better at faking sympathy than hiding his disdain for milky-weak tea.

Evelyn sits back in her chair and takes a moment to compose herself.

"You don't have to do this," I say. "I know from experience how hard it must be."

"No, I need to," Evelyn replies in a weak voice. "It's about time I exorcised a few demons."

She then straightens her shoulders and puffs out a long breath.

"I used to love Christmas," she begins. "But not as much as Roger. He'd spend a whole weekend out in the front yard, putting up lights and decorating the house until you could barely see an inch of timber. He always said it was for Lauren, our daughter, but he was like a goofy kid as soon as December rolled around."

Evelyn's lips form a slight smile, likely prompted by the memory of her late husband, but it dissolves as quickly as it appeared.

"Last Christmas was the third one without my Roger, though," she continues. "And by far the loneliest. Lauren is at college now, and she's going steady with a lovely boy she met in her first year. They decided to go south for Christmas, to get some sun and party with their friends."

"That must have been hard."

"It was, but that girl has been through so much. It pained me to do it, but when she first mentioned the idea, I positively encouraged her to go ... said it was a relief as Sarah and Bryson had invited me to stay with them over Christmas. I was lying, obviously, but I didn't want Lauren to miss out just because she felt obligated to stay home with her widowed mother for another year."

I don't know what to say, but Evelyn, seemingly keen to unload, continues.

"On Christmas Eve, I opened a bottle of wine, and I was checking Facebook on my computer, seeing if Lauren had posted any photos of her trip. Then, an advert for a dating website popped up. I can't say if it was the wine or just the feeling of loneliness, but the thought of spending another Christmas on my own just killed me, so I clicked the advert and spent an hour creating a profile."

Evelyn then looks at her cup, perhaps wishing it contained wine rather than insipid tea.

"My neighbours, Ethan and Libby, invited me to spend Christmas Day with them and their family. It was sweet of them but seeing them so happy together just made me feel ... it's horrible to say it but I felt so envious of what they had, and it made me realise how much I missed having someone special in my life."

"If it's any consolation," I reply. "I've felt like that myself of late, and I know Mum did too, before ..."

"Before *him*?"

"Yes."

"Well, honey, that's obviously what he preys upon — loneliness. If memory serves, he mentioned that word in the first sentence of the first message he sent through the dating website."

"When was that?"

"The day after Christmas Day, and I'm not going to lie to you — when I read his message and looked at his profile photo, my heart skipped a beat."

"The photo on your phone?"

"Yes, that one. I only keep it to remind myself of how stupid I was, and how I should never let my guard down again."

"I do understand how difficult it must be, raking over all of this, but what happened after he messaged you?"

"We continued swapping messages for a couple of weeks and then he asked me out for dinner. I already felt like I knew him by then, so I didn't hesitate. He booked a table at a lovely bistro in town, and we met for the first time outside. I was running late because my car wouldn't start but he couldn't have been nicer about it, even though he'd been waiting out in the cold for fifteen minutes."

"Was that the night he came back here?"

"No, it was not," Evelyn replies, somewhat defensively. "I might have been lonely, but I wasn't about to invite a man I'd just met back to my house for a nightcap."

"Sorry, I didn't mean to ... sorry."

"Anyway," she continues. "We met up again the following weekend and had dinner before he took me to see a show at the theatre. The only difference was, he picked me up and dropped me back home, which I thought was a lovely gesture, considering my damn car had been the reason why our first date almost never happened."

"Bet you wish the bleedin' motor hadn't started that first night," Clement interjects, unhelpfully.

"Not a day goes by," Evelyn replies. "But you can't turn back the clock, more's the pity."

"So, you had a second date?" I say, flashing a glare in Clement's direction.

"Yes, and at the end of the evening, he drove me home and walked me to the front gate. He then kissed me on the cheek and thanked me for being such wonderful company. And that was that. I couldn't quite work out if he was just a gentleman or if he wasn't interested in me … you know, physically."

"Or maybe he was just lulling you into a false sense of security," I suggest. "He's nothing if not patient."

"That's exactly what he was up to," Evelyn replies bitterly. "Because on our third date, we went to the cinema and then to a bar afterwards. He didn't touch a drop of alcohol because he'd offered to pick me up and drop me home. I had two glasses of wine, though, which was enough for me to lower my defences."

"How so?"

"He drove me home again, but on the way, there was a problem with his car — the engine kept cutting out. We made it back to Howard Avenue, just, but the engine cut out again halfway down the street. Of course, he insisted on walking me all the way to my front door, and then he said he'd return to the car and call Triple-A."

"I'm guessing that never happened?"

Evelyn visibly winces at my question, maybe because I'm asking her to recollect the moment she let a fox into her coop.

"No, it never," she eventually replies, keeping her eyes trained on her cup. "I wanted him to want me, and the wine gave me the courage to suggest he could call Triple-A and wait for them in my sitting room … maybe even open a bottle of wine while we were waiting. I wasn't thinking straight, but I thought that once we were alone, he might … you know … show me some affection."

I wish I knew Evelyn well enough to reach across the table and give her hand a squeeze. Instead, I remain silent and let her continue in her own time.

"He kissed me on the cheek," she continues. "And said he knew I had a kind heart the moment he first met me, and that was enough to blow away any lingering doubts. He then followed me inside and made his call to Triple-A — an act for my benefit, obviously — before we made ourselves comfortable on the couch."

"Is that when he spiked your drink?"

"Did Bryson tell you that?"

"He did, yes."

"It's just a guess because I really couldn't say. After about twenty minutes, he noticed I'd emptied my glass and offered to refill it. I told him that I couldn't allow a guest to pour me a drink, but he was so charming and said that I deserved to be waited on. He was in the kitchen for no more than a minute, so I had no reason to suspect anything until ..."

"Until?"

"Halfway through my second glass of wine, I began to feel tired, like overwhelmingly tired. At first, I thought maybe I'd just had one glass too many, but I can usually drink a couple of bottles before I get too giddy. No, this was different — this wave of tiredness just knocked me for six. It was like ... the only way I can explain it is it was like having an anaesthetic before an operation. One minute, you're fully aware of your surroundings, the next, the world is fading to black."

Evelyn takes a sip of tea before continuing.

"I woke up on the couch just after ten the following morning, feeling like death and still in my outfit from the night before. At first, I couldn't work out why I was there, but slowly the memories drifted in. I had no reason to be concerned at that point, so I headed upstairs for a shower. That's when I noticed it.

183

"Noticed what?"

"I keep my jewellery box in a drawer, but when I entered the bedroom, it was sitting on top of the dressing table. I might have put it down to forgetfulness, but then I noticed the bottom drawer on the left-hand nightstand was slightly open. That was Roger's side of the bed, and I hadn't touched those drawers in months. In that second, I just knew something wasn't right. I dashed over to the dressing table and opened the jewellery box, fearing the worst but hoping that maybe I was just being paranoid. It was empty — not so much as an ear stud left."

"Or your husband's college ring, obviously."

"I didn't have a lot of expensive jewellery, maybe a few thousand bucks in total, but that ring was a piece of Roger. Losing that broke my heart, and because I invited the thief into our home, I'll never forgive myself."

Evelyn appears visibly upset by her own admission, and once again, I consider reaching out and taking her hand. That is until Clement clears his throat.

"We'll get it back," he suddenly declares. "When we find him."

I don't remember setting up a detective agency with Clement or agreeing to be his partner, but now is not the right time to discuss his assumptions. Now is the time to mine our host for useful information.

"Did the police dust the jewellery box for fingerprints?" I ask.

Evelyn shakes her head.

"Why not? Isn't it standard procedure in a robbery?"

"I didn't report it to the police."

"I don't understand. Surely you want your husband's ring back ... and the man who conned you to face justice?"

Without saying a word, our host slowly gets to her feet, crosses the kitchen, and opens a drawer. I shoot Clement a confused frown, but he doesn't respond in any discernible way. Finally, Evelyn returns to the table, clutching a scrappy piece of white paper in her right hand.

"This is why I never contacted the police," she says, retaking her seat.

I lean forward as Evelyn turns the scrap of paper over and lays it flat on the table. Scrawled in black ink are eight words. Those words barely form a sentence, but the message couldn't be any clearer: *Call the police, and I'll cut Lauren's throat.*

"Christ," I gulp.

"See why I never called the police?" Evelyn responds. "He left the note on top of my phone in the kitchen where he knew I'd find it."

"You reckon he meant it?" Clement asks.

"I don't know, but I wasn't willing to risk my daughter's life to find out. I only kept the note in case ... in case anything did happen."

His question answered, Clement gets to his feet while reaching for his breast pocket.

"You mind if I nip outside for a smoke?"

"Go ahead," Evelyn replies, nodding to a door on the far side of the kitchen. "You'll have to unbolt it first. I keep all the doors bolted these days."

The big man nods an acknowledgement and strides over to the door. After unbolting it, he disappears outside, closing the door behind him.

"Filthy habit," I remark, purely to break the silence.

"I can think of worse," Evelyn replies. "And far worse men than your friend. He strikes me as a no-nonsense kind of guy."

"He's certainly that."

There's a moment of silence as Evelyn sits back in her chair and stares down at the note.

"I'm sorry for what happened with your mom," she then says. "Maybe if I had called the police, they'd have caught him before he had a chance to do what he did."

"You've nothing to be sorry for. The man is a piece of shit, excuse my language, but he's also exceptionally good at covering his tracks. Even if you had called the police, it's highly unlikely they'd have found him."

"Have you had any luck in your search?"

I explain what we've uncovered thus far and reveal the name David Smith.

"I wish it meant something to me," Evelyn says apologetically. "But honestly, it doesn't."

"It's okay. It's just our luck that he's got such a common name."

The door to the backyard then opens, and Clement re-enters the kitchen, trailing the stench of cigarette smoke. After bolting the door, he returns to the table and announces that he's had a thought.

"This prick didn't leave a note for your mum, did he?" he asks me.

"No."

"So, why leave one here?"

I look at Evelyn just as she looks at me. We both reply to Clement's question with a shrug of the shoulders.

"I reckon," Clement continues. "He let something slip that he didn't want you revealing to the Old Bill?"

"Old Bill?" Evelyn questions.

"The police," I reply, acting as interpreter.

"What could he have possibly told me that might be of help?"

"Dunno," Clement replies. "But why leave the note? He nicked the best part of two million quid from his last mark and didn't bother with a threat, so why threaten you?"

Evelyn's brow furrows as she appears to dredge her memory. It's frustrating for me to watch, and no doubt just as frustrating for her.

"I honestly don't know," she eventually admits.

"Tell you what," Clement says. "After we've gone, why don't you sit down with a pad and pen, and write down every detail you can remember about those evenings out you had: where you went, how you got there, people you talked to ... anything and everything you can remember."

"Do you think it'll help find him?"

"Yeah, I do."

"Then I'll do it the moment you leave. What do you want me to do once I've finished."

"You could take a photo of whatever you write down and send it to me via WhatsApp," I suggest. "Or, if anything significant comes to mind, just call me."

"Okay. I can do that," Evelyn says with maybe the slightest hint of hope in her voice. "Anything to help catch that man."

Mission set, our host politely asks if we'd like another cup of tea before we leave. I decline on account that we've got a long journey back to New York ahead of us. Clement doesn't argue.

"How did you get here from the train station?" Evelyn then asks.

"We hopped in a taxi. I got their number, so I'll call them and arrange a ride back."

"No, you won't. I'll drive you back."

"That's very kind of you, but there's really no need."

"Every minute you spend waiting for a taxi is a minute that could be spent looking for that man, so I insist."

Evelyn grabs her car keys from a hook and slips on a pair of black Crocs sitting next to the doormat. No further debate, it seems.

Five minutes later, we're making the return journey in almost the same fashion we made the first: Clement sitting in the front passenger's seat, staring out of the side window, and me sitting behind Evelyn. There's little in the way of conversation, and, brief as the journey will be, it's uncomfortable.

"I wouldn't trust myself to drive over here," I say, purely to break the silence. "I'm not the best driver when I'm on the right side of the road."

"I'm not a great driver myself," Evelyn replies. "I only got my licence two years ago, and I rarely drive anywhere other than the short journey to work and to pick up groceries."

"Oh, right."

I wonder if Evelyn's reason for leaving it so late in life to obtain a driving license is down to the fact she no longer has a husband to do the driving. I don't ask.

We take a series of turns and I recognise the route. There's only one final turn before we're back on the street where the station is situated. Evelyn eases off the accelerator and takes the final turn.

"Goddammit," she mutters while simultaneously reaching for the sun visor and straightening the steering wheel. With the sun directly ahead and nothing to block its rays on their journey, I sympathise with Evelyn — being so vertically challenged, the sun visors in my car are next to useless. Clement has no such issue, as his head is virtually touching the roof of the car.

We reach the drop-off zone outside the station, and I undo my seatbelt. Just as I'm about to get out, Evelyn holds up her right hand.

"One second," she says, her hand returning to the gear selector.

"Everything okay?" I ask.

"I've just remembered something that happened on that last night ... oh, forget it. It's not likely to be of any significance."

"Go on. Please."

188

Evelyn turns in her seat while I shuffle to my right so I'm not trying to talk to her through a headrest.

"On the way to the cinema, he stopped to get gas. After filling up, he went inside to pay, and I pulled down the sun visor to check my make-up. Most cars have a little vanity mirror, don't they?"

"Most, yes."

"This car didn't, but it did have a no-smoking sticker on the underside of the visor."

"Can't smoke anywhere these days," Clement complains. "Dunno why you'd slap a sticker up in your own car, though ... unless it weren't his car."

"A hire car?" I suggest. "Or maybe it—"

"Shush a second," Evelyn interjects, pinching the bridge of her nose. "I need to think."

For what feels like an eternity, the only sound in the car is the engine ticking over.

"There was a sticker in the back window," she eventually splutters. "I just thought it was advertising the name of the dealership, Now, what was that name ..."

More bridge pinching follows, but this time it's accompanied by a series of pained groans and sighs. Then, Evelyn suddenly sits bolt upright.

"Munson!" she announces. "That was it!"

"I'll google it," I respond. "One second."

I frantically type Munson car hire into Google and tap the search icon. The search engine then spits out a list of results with the most relevant right at the top.

"Munson Car Hire, 134th Street, Queens."

"Is that the nearest branch?" Evelyn asks.

"I'll check."

I tap through to the website and on first impressions alone, it's clear the Munson Car Hire is not a nationwide company. It's as basic as any website I've ever visited, with just three pages and a few poorly written lines of text.

"Based on the website I think Queens is their only branch. They're not exactly Avis or Hertz."

I look up and expect to see some flicker of hope in Evelyn's eyes because her throwaway thought has provided us with a solid lead. Instead, her mouth is slightly agape, and all the colour has drained from her face.

"Are you okay?" I ask.

"Sweet Lord," she gulps. "How could I have been so stupid?"

"Sorry?"

"Triple-A," Evelyn says in a low voice. "Why would you call Triple-A for a hire car? You wouldn't — if you had a problem, you'd call the hire company."

"You didn't know it was a hire car."

"I should have realised."

Looking at a woman I barely know, there's an all-too-familiar expression etched across her face. It's like looking at Mum in the days after her aborted wedding.

I reach forward and place a reassuring hand on Evelyn's arm.

"I'll tell you what I've told my mum a hundred times — what happened to you was not your fault. That man was a professional con artist, and he fooled all of us, including me."

Evelyn responds with a slight nod before turning her attention to Clement.

"If you find him, will you do me a favour?"

"Name it," the big man replies.

"Get my Roger's ring back ... then, make that asshole pay for what he's done."

Chapter 23

After saying goodbye to Evelyn, and Clement offering his assurance that a thorough beating will be administered when he catches up with David Smith, we get out of the car and watch her drive away.

"What do we do now?" I ask, more to myself than Clement.

"We should check out the car hire place."

"To what end?"

"You know I said I couldn't get a bank account 'cos I ain't got any ID, well, I couldn't hire a car either 'cos I ain't got a driving licence."

"So?"

"If they wanna see a driving licence, stands to reason they'll copy all the details from it: full name, date of birth ... and an address."

A sense of déjà vu strikes.

"You're probably right, but unless the owner of Munson Car Hire is a married man who gets his kicks by swapping information for sexual favours, how do you propose we get to see a copy of David Smith's driving licence?"

"One step at a time. Let's check the place out first, see what we're dealing with."

"You want to head there now?"

"Unless you've got any better ideas?"

I don't have any ideas, better or worse.

"No, I don't."

"We gonna go get the train, then, or what?"

I turn and traipse towards the main doors of the station. Once we're inside, I pull out my phone and check the route.

"We get the train to Penn Station and then the Long Beach branch to Jamaica. From there, it'll be quicker to hop in a taxi."

"How long?"

"Two and a half hours. The train to Penn leaves in fourteen minutes."

"Time for a quick piss and a smoke, then. You gonna wait here?"

"Well, I'm not joining you in the gents, that's for sure."

Clement saunters off, and I'm glad for a few minutes of peace to process the conversation with Evelyn. Fortunately, there's a bench near the vending machine where I can sit, wait, and ponder. I sit down, but I've barely had the chance to summon a single thought when my phone rings. I don't recognise the number, but I do recognise the area code as Brentwood, so I accept the call.

"Gina Jackson."

"Oh, um … hi, Gina. This is Eric from Regency Cars. Have I caught you at a good time?"

It takes a few seconds to process the name. Eric drove Mum and me to the registry office.

"Hi, Eric. Yes, I'm okay to talk for a moment, but I'm waiting for a train."

"No problem, I'll keep it brief. It's … um, a bit awkward, really. I'm so sorry to hassle you but there's still an amount owing on your invoice."

I don't like being in debt to anyone, but I'm willing to excuse myself on this one occasion because settling the bill for Mum's wedding car wasn't high on my list of priorities six weeks ago. Even so, I do feel bad for Eric.

"I'm so sorry — it completely slipped my mind. How much is outstanding?"

"The balance is £110. I've not chased payment because ... err, I know the day didn't quite go according to plan, and I wanted to let the dust settle."

"No, it didn't, but that's not your problem. I should have sorted the invoice."

"These things happen."

"Still, it's no excuse. If you can bear with me, I'll make the payment when I'm back in the country next week. I'm currently in ... Paris."

"I'm sorry. I knew you were away, but I didn't realise you were overseas."

"It's okay ... wait, how did you know I'm away?"

"I called round your place earlier. I just happened to be passing and thought I'd try my luck."

"You mean my mum's place in Windsor Gardens?"

"I thought you lived there."

"No, I don't. Who did you speak to?"

"A man and a woman were walking down the driveway as I got out of my car."

"How old were they, roughly?"

"Middle-aged."

"And they told you I was away?"

"It was the woman who told me, to be specific. I wouldn't swear on it, but I'm sure I've met the chap before. I couldn't say where I'm afraid."

It doesn't take Hercule Poirot to work out who that couple were — my interfering aunt and her husband. Eric likely saw them in the aftermath of Mum's wedding, although I'd have thought he'd recognise Lynn more than Stephen.

I end the call with another apology, and I promise Eric that I'll transfer the outstanding money to his account next week. My first instinct is to call Lynn and demand to know why she was visiting Mum, but after a moment's reflection, I conclude it would be a waste of time. She'll get defensive and insist she has every right to visit her sister.

"You need the loo?" Clement says, suddenly appearing from beyond the vending machine.

"Eh? No, I'm fine."

"You sure? You've got a face like someone in need of a good shit."

I realise I'm still frowning at the thought of Lynn's visit and relax my facial muscles.

"I just received a call and … it's not important. Family stuff."

"Not a problem I've ever had."

"You get on with your family?"

"I ain't got no family, Doll."

"Oh, right. I'm sorry to hear that."

He just shrugs and then looks up at a giant clock on the wall.

"Better head out to the platform," he says.

I get up and follow Clement through the ticket barrier to the platform. With a few minutes to kill before our train arrives, and my travel companion unwilling to discuss his family, or lack of one, I pose a question relative to the reason we're here.

"What did you think of Evelyn?"

"How'd you mean?"

"Her demeanour."

"I think she still ain't over what that tosser did to her. Didn't you clock her hands when she was talking about him — shaking like a leaf?"

"She's likely still traumatised by the experience, and us pitching up to ask her questions probably didn't help."

194

"I reckon our chat made her realise what kind of bloke she invited in for a drink that night … if she didn't already know."

"A devious, heartless scumbag."

"Yeah, that, but he's pure wicked with it, which is why we've gotta find him."

"That's why I'm here, but when did *I* become *we*?"

"It's always been *we*, Doll, from the moment we met. You just ain't worked out why yet."

"Eh?"

Clement turns and stares up the tracks. I'm about to press him on his cryptic statement when he speaks again. "I get the feeling your mum and Evelyn what's-her-face ain't the only women this bloke has done over."

"That thought certainly crossed my mind."

"There's gotta be more. What are the chances that we happened to stumble on his only other victim?"

"Low, I suppose."

"Bleedin' low, I'd say. If he's conning women here and back in Blighty, stands to reason that he's moving around to cover his arse. And if he's moving around, that likely means he's leaving a trail of victims behind him."

"You think so?"

"Yeah, once your average conman has ripped off his intended, they don't hang around. Move on, find another mark, do the deed, and move on again. They're like fucking sharks — never stop swimmin', never stop looking for their next meal ticket."

"Only a handful of shark species swim continuously, but I take your point. Maybe there are other women out there who've fallen prey to his charms."

"That's what I reckon."

"I could set up a Facebook group and post the photos Mum collected. If I spread the word, it might encourage other victims to get in touch, and we might collectively piece enough information together to catch the bastard."

"That ain't a good idea."

"Why not?"

"This bloke ain't an amateur, Doll. The minute he smells trouble brewing, he'll go to ground. He's got plenty of money, so he can go anywhere in the bleedin' world."

"He could be anywhere in the world already. For all we know, he might be lying on a beach in Thailand and funding his retirement with Mum's money."

"Maybe, maybe not, but what if he ain't in it just for the money."

"I don't understand. What other motive could there be besides money?"

"Take your pick," Clement snorts. "People do all sorts of fucked-up things for all manner of reasons — always have, always will."

Most days, merely watching ten minutes of the news on TV would be enough to validate Clement's assertion.

"Take that ring," he then continues. "Why's he wearing it in those photos he sent your mum?"

"Err, I don't know."

"Feels like ego to me — a trophy from one of his victims."

"Seriously?"

"Can you think of any other reason he's wearing it? A pawnbroker would probably pay five hundred quid for a ring like that, so why not sell it?"

It's actually a valid question, and Clement's theory sets off a troubling series of thoughts. What kind of twisted nutjob keeps mementoes from his previous crimes?

"You get my point now, Doll?"

"Your point?"

"This ain't just some cheeky chancer you're trying to track down. This bloke's got a screw loose, and he needs stopping."

"You've deduced all that on the evidence of Evelyn's shaking hand and a stolen ring in a photo?"

"That, and I've been around long enough to know that when something smells off, it's usually 'cos it's rotten. And when I say rotten, I mean rotten to the fucking core."

The sun — an ever-present feature of our time on the platform — slips behind a cloud. The sudden drop in temperature could be the reason a chill dances its way down my back, or it could be Clement's assessment of the man I'm trying to find. For the first time since I clapped eyes on him in that backstreet in Flatbush, I can see the logic in having a guardian close at hand.

"Can I ask you a question?"

"No law against it, Doll."

"Why *are* you helping me?"

"I told you — it's my calling."

"That's so vague," I protest. "Don't get me wrong, I am grateful, but I would like to know why you're getting involved ... specifically."

"Specifically," he huffs. "I ain't got a choice. This is what I do, why I'm here."

"What are you then? Some kind of charitable bounty hunter?"

"If that's what you wanna call it, suits me."

It's not an answer that makes much sense, but in my current position, it's one I have no choice but to swallow.

In the distance, a train comes into view while a high-pitched voice announces the arrival of the one-twenty train to Pennsylvania Station, New York.

"Guess this is us," I remark. "Another leg of the wildest goose chase."

"Or another step closer to finding this fucker."

With the fast-approaching train drowning out our conversation, all I can do is look up at Clement with a half-hearted smile and hope that he's right and I'm wrong.

Chapter 24

Clement instructs the taxi driver to continue past Munson Car Hire and stop one hundred yards further along the road. When we eventually pull over, he hands the driver a twenty-dollar bill and tells him to keep the change. It's as much as the big man has said since we left Bridgeport, although he napped for most of the journey.

As the taxi driver speeds off in search of his next fare, I'm left standing on the pavement with no idea why we're a good hundred yards from where we need to be.

"Is there a reason we didn't stop outside the car hire place?"

"Yeah. I wanna get a proper butcher's before we go in. See how the land lies."

"I presume you have a plan, then?"

"Of sorts. Come on."

Clement beckons me to cross the road with him. I'm not sure what he's up to, but I follow.

"When we're opposite the car hire place," he says in a low voice, "we stop, and I want you to get your phone thing out. Look at it like we're lost, and you're checking a map."

"Why?"

"So I can have a smoke and do what I need to do."

"Fair enough. I'm no actress but considering I don't have a clue where we are, it's not much of a stretch to pretend we're lost."

Like so many American streets, 134th Street seems to run forever in both directions, although I doubt the scenery changes much. We're relatively close to JFK Airport but based on the number of empty lots and tired buildings, I get the impression we're not in prime real estate territory.

We draw level with Munson Car Hire. Clement stops, turns to face me, and pulls out his cigarette pack.

"Turn around a bit," he orders as I stare down at a blank phone screen. "So your back is to the road."

I do as I'm asked, and it becomes apparent why he asked me to turn around. With the chasm in our respective heights, Clement can stare straight over my head towards the car hire premises without rousing suspicion.

"Don't look like much of a set-up," he says after a few seconds. "There's just a portacabin and an area where they park the cars."

"Right," I reply, unsure what else to say.

"Cheapest hire cars in New York, so the sign says."

"I don't care how cheap they are. I wouldn't drive around this city if you paid me."

I glance up, expecting a reply, but Clement's eyes are trained straight ahead. I've no idea how old he is, but I have noticed a few grey hairs sprouting from his temples, so maybe he needs glasses. It would explain the crow's feet and slight squint. I turn my attention back to the phone I'm holding at chest height and consider checking Facebook while I wait for Clement to finish his observations. It would be marginally more interesting than staring at a blank screen, but only just.

"How much longer?" I ask. "It's getting chilly out here."

"I wanna check there's just one bloke in the portacabin."

"Wouldn't it be easier to go in and check?"

Rather than answer, he takes a step to his left and cranes his neck. After a puff on his cigarette, he relaxes his stance and steps back towards me.

"Best I can tell, there's only one bloke in there. Time to go in and have a chat."

"What exactly are you going to say to him?"

"I'm gonna check he's got what we want, and then I'll make the bloke an offer."

"Of?"

"His choice: cold hard cash ... or violence."

Before I can argue, Clement strides past me and steps into the road. I jam my phone back into my pocket and hurry after him.

"Clement, I never agreed to violence," I hiss while trying to keep up with him. "And even if this guy can be bribed, I don't have any cash on me."

"Don't sweat it, Doll. It's all in hand."

It's as much as I can do to scurry along in his wake, but as concerned as I might be for what Clement has planned, I remind myself that if we don't get an address for David Smith, this is the end of the road.

We pass through the open gates and the weather-beaten sign Clement quoted. The portacabin has also seen better days, and whoever fixed the sign to the door, confirming it houses the reception, didn't quite fit it straight. There's a grimy window to the left of the door, covered with a wire grill, presumably to stop heavy objects from breaking the glass.

Clement tugs the door open and steps inside. I hesitate for a moment, still concerned that once I cross the threshold, there's a risk I'll become an accomplice to a crime.

"In for a penny," I mumble under my breath.

I step through the portacabin door and screw my face up when I'm hit with the overwhelming stench of cheap coffee and stale farts. My attention then quickly switches to the desk on our left and the pale-faced guy sitting behind it. With ferret-like eyes and lank hair, I'd wager a decent sum that there's material on his hard drive that could land him in jail for a year or two.

"You the boss?" Clement asks as the man sits back in his chair.

"Yeah, how can I help?"

"If I want to hire a car, what do you need from me?"

"When do you want it for?"

"Don't matter. I just wanna know what I need."

"A credit card for your payment and a security deposit. I also need to take a photo of your driving licence."

"What for?"

"Insurance and legal. If a customer has an accident or commits a crime using one of our cars, we need to know who was driving it."

"And what do you do with that photo?"

"I upload it to our booking system."

"How long does it stay there?"

"A year, maybe eighteen months."

Clement steps forward and casually sits down on one of the two chairs on our side of the desk. Whatever he's got planned, I suspect I'm about to see it actioned.

"What's your name, mate?" he asks the man.

"Brian. Brian Munson."

"This your set-up, then?"

Brian Munson shifts uncomfortably in his chair as if he's finally cottoned on that the hulking man opposite might not be in the market for a cheap rental car.

"Are you looking to hire a car?" he asks.

"Nah, I'm not. But I do have a proposition for you."

"A proposition?" Munson gulps.

"Yeah, and it's a straightforward one. See, we're looking for a toerag who stole a few million quid from her mum."

Clement thrusts a thumb over his left shoulder, should Munson be in any doubt about who *her* is.

"And we know he hired a car from you ... when was it, Doll?"

"Err ... January," I splutter, not expecting to be part of this, whatever this is.

"We need to know where he lives, and that's where you, Sunshine, come in. You're gonna let us see a copy of that bloke's driving licence."

"That ... no, I can't do that," Munson responds. "Customer data is confidential."

"Thought you might say that, which is why I'm gonna make you a one-time offer."

Clement then unbuttons the right-hand pocket of his denim waistcoat and pulls out a wad of bank notes. He then slaps the wad on the desk.

"Five hundred notes for a copy of a driving licence. Not a bad deal, eh?"

Munson looks at the money and then at Clement. The big man sits back and folds his arms while I look on, dumbfounded. Why is he willing to sacrifice so much cash for a cause that isn't even his?

"Well, mate? You gonna take the cash ... or the alternative?"

"What's the alternative?"

"I knock you spark out, we find that bloke's details ourselves, and you wake up in a few hours with a broken jaw. How's that sound?"

"I ... I'll take the cash."

"Thought you might."

Munson tentatively stretches out his right arm and then snatches up the cash. He deposits it in a drawer before turning to face his computer monitor.

"What's the guy's name?" he asks.

"David Smith."

"And he hired a car in January, you say?"

"Yeah, this year."

With the prospect of violence no longer imminent and Munson already tapping away at his keyboard, I step over to the second chair. Rather than sit down, I choose to stand so I can partially see the computer monitor.

"I've found a record for a David Smith," Munson says. "He hired a Toyota Corolla on three occasions: twice in January and once in early February."

"And you've got a copy of his driving licence?" I ask.

He clicks the mouse twice. "Yes."

"Print us a copy. Please."

"Sure, but it'll take a few minutes for the printer to warm up."

"That's alright," Clement says. "It'll give you a chance to tell us about the three times that bloke hired a car from you."

"What do you want to know?"

"How long, and the mileage he clocked up."

Munson turns back to the screen without argument. More mouse clicking ensues while a whirring sound emanates from a decade-old printer in the corner.

"Both the first and second time, he racked up around one hundred and forty miles."

"How far is it to Bridgeport?" Clement asks.

"Connecticut?"

"Yeah."

"At a guess, sixty or seventy miles."

"What about the final time he hired a car?" I ask.

"Just shy of three hundred miles."

Whether this information is relevant or not remains to be seen, but as we know so little about David Smith's movements both here and back home, every scrap is worth gathering.

"Do you remember him?" I ask, more in hope than expectation.

"Lady, I hire out a dozen cars a day, every day of the week. I can barely remember my customers from yesterday, let alone nine months ago."

The printer suddenly makes a series of clunking sounds, and the pitch of the whirring changes.

"It's printing now," Munson confirms, getting to his feet.

Despite the two-minute wait, he still has to loiter by the machine while it decides if it feels like carrying out its job. Eventually, it spits out a single sheet of paper. Munson checks it and then places it on the desk in front of Clement.

"You never got that from me," he says. "Whatever this guy did, and whatever you plan to do to him, I want no part of it."

Clement ignores Munson and leans forward. I mirror his action as we both stare down at the black and white copy of a New York driving licence. Even though it's in shades of grey, and his hair is styled differently, the photograph of the holder is unmistakably the man we're looking for. The name at the top of the licence confirms it: *Smith, David.*

All that matters to us, though, are the two lines of capitalised text beneath Smith's name: *Apartment 2D, 956 Blake Avenue, Brooklyn, NY 11212.*

I continue to stare down at the grainy, black-and-white photo, scarcely able to believe that I'm looking at David Smith's address — his actual address, less than ten miles from where I'm standing.

"Job's a good'un," Clement then remarks before grabbing the sheet of paper, folding it twice, and tucking it into his pocket. "Now, just one more thing."

He gets to his feet and takes a couple of steps around the right-hand side of the desk.

"That five hundred I gave you," he growls at Munson. "I forgot to tell you ... there's a condition attached."

Munson sinks into his chair, clutching the armrests as if he's on a rollercoaster.

"C-c-condition?"

"Yeah. You're gonna give us a lift to the station in Jamaica."

Chapter 25

After a silent and nervy ten-minute drive, Brian Munson pulls over to the kerb. Perhaps keen to get Clement out of his car, he doesn't even apply the parking brake.

"Nice doing business with you," the big man says before opening the passenger's door.

"Um, thanks," Munson says hesitantly. "You too."

When I think about how he might spend his ill-gotten cash, it makes my skin crawl. I get out of the car and thank my lucky stars I'll never have to see Brian Munson's face again.

Clement joins me.

"I'm hungry," he says. "Let's go find somewhere to eat, and we can talk about what we do next."

"Next? That's obvious, isn't it? We head straight for Brooklyn and David Smith's home address."

My suggestion is initially met with a grunt.

"You ain't thought this through, have you, Doll?"

"I've thought of nothing else since the day that wanker crushed my mum's soul. For that alone, I intend to kick him in the nuts ... repeatedly."

"I like your style," Clement replies with a snort of laughter. "But there's a flaw to your plan."

"It seems pretty sound to me."

"Think about it. He was living in this flat in January, months before he ripped off your mum. Now, if you had a few million quid in your bank account, would you still be living in a flat in the arse end of Brooklyn?"

Clement's question feels like a punch to the gut, not least because it's such an obvious assumption — why would Smith remain in a Brooklyn flat when he could be living in the lap of luxury wherever he fancies?

"Your point is valid," I respond. "So, do you think it's still worth checking the place out?"

"I said he probably ain't gonna be living there, but that don't mean the trail's stone cold. As I said, we'll head over there and see what's what."

"Okay."

"For now, though, I'm bleedin' famished. Let's eat."

With my emotions running high, I don't have much of an appetite. I do, however, need to pay attention to Clement's advice.

We don't have to walk too far before he stops outside a pizzeria.

"You like pizza?" he asks.

"I neither like nor dislike it. It'll do."

We head inside.

Once we're seated, and the waiter has taken our order, I finally get the opportunity to say what I should have said the moment we stepped out of Brian Munson's car.

"Thank you for ... for dealing with that Munson creep and getting what I need."

"It's alright. Money usually talks, but in his case, I was tempted to give him a slap just for the sake of it."

"That would have been the icing on the cake, but thank you, anyway. As soon as we pass a cash machine, I'll make a withdrawal."

"What for?"

"To pay you back, obviously."

"Don't be daft," he says, waving my offer away. "It weren't my money so it ain't like I'm out of pocket."

"Eh? Whose money was it?"

"Just some piece-of-shit drug dealer. Don't think he told me his name."

"I'm confused. Why did a drug dealer give ... wait. You're not involved in the drug trade, are you?"

"Like fuck I am," he replies with enough force to make his point. "Just so happens that there's a lot of young blokes wandering around my neighbourhood every night, and most of 'em with large amounts of cash on 'em. Easy pickings."

"Are you telling me that you mug drug dealers?"

"I wouldn't call it mugging. I'd say I'm doing my civic duty."

"I doubt the drug dealers see it that way."

"Couldn't give a shit how they see it. If I take cash off 'em, they can't re-stock their poison, and it ain't as if they're gonna go crying to the Old Bill, is it?"

"Probably not, but it strikes me as a bit ... well, foolhardy. Surely most of them are armed over here?"

"Probably. Makes no odds to me."

"You're not worried about being shot?"

"Nothing worries me these days," he says, leaning back in his seat and locking his spade-like hands behind his head. "I just do what I've gotta do."

"Your calling?"

"Yeah, that."

The waiter returns with two bottles of Bud and confirms our pizzas won't be long. I'm still mildly intrigued about Clement's reckless hobby, but there are more important matters to discuss.

"Shall we talk about a plan?" I ask.

"We'll head over there once we've eaten and check the place out."

"And then what?"

"Depends on what we find."

"And that won't be David Smith."

"Probably not, but a lead is a lead, Doll."

"I hope you're right. It feels like I'm chasing shadows."

Clement takes a long pull from the bottle of Bud and then gives his moustache a now-customary stroke.

"You ever heard of the Great Train Robbery?" he asks.

"Kind of. Some gang robbed a train back in the seventies, right?"

"It was 1963, but yeah, a gang held up a Royal Mail train north of London. Got away with more than two and a half million quid."

"A lot of money now, but a fortune back then."

"Yeah, it was, and you've gotta give that gang credit. They knew how much money was on that train and planned every last detail to make sure they got their hands on it. Ballsy, and brilliant."

"I doubt Royal Mail were so impressed."

"Probably not, but despite all that planning and pulling off one of the greatest-ever heists, they got caught. Do you know how?"

"No idea."

"Monopoly."

"As in, the board game?"

"Yeah."

"You'll have to elaborate."

"After they'd done the job, they hid out in a remote farmhouse twenty-odd miles from the scene. With Old Bill swarming around the place, it made sense not to hang around anywhere too close while they divvied up the cash. Then, they got wind that the Old Bill had decided to search further afield for the gang's hideout, and they'd likely get a knock on the door if they hung around."

"I presume they hung around too long, and that's how they were caught?"

"Nope, they all got away from the farmhouse in time, but they relied on one bloke to torch the drum as soon as they'd gone so there wouldn't be any evidence left. I dunno what went down, but that didn't happen, and when the Old Bill came knocking, they found a Monopoly set on the dining table. From that, they got the whole gang's dabs, and most of 'em were picked up pretty sharpish after that."

"Ouch. I bet whoever failed to torch the place was popular."

"Yeah, I don't reckon he stayed on anyone's Christmas card list, but it goes to show one thing, Doll."

"What's that?"

"Don't matter how thorough the plan, how well it's executed; it only takes one little mistake to trip you up."

I don't want to query the point of Clement's tale because, whether he intended to or not, the moral is enough for me to cling to. David Smith probably didn't think he was making a mistake by renting a flash apartment on West End Avenue under his real name. Nor is it likely he considered it a mistake to wear a grad ring he stole from a Bridgeport widow. Maybe he thought that offering that same widow a lift in a hire car was inconsequential until he realised it wasn't and left a threatening note to cover himself.

David Smith *has* made mistakes, but for all I know, they're just breadcrumbs leading us up a blind alley. It remains to be seen if any of them will be as catastrophic as that one mistake made by a gang of men who robbed a Royal Mail train and then played Monopoly to while away the hours.

Our pizzas arrive at the table. I chose the smallest option, only ten inches across, but Clement's is the size of a manhole cover.

"You know that's a pizza for a family of four?" I remark as he rips into it.

"I ain't got a wife, and if I do have any kids, they sure as hell ain't here, so I suppose it's all mine."

211

He proceeds to roll up an entire slice and, with a single bite, bolts down half of it. The fact that his pizza is loaded with mushrooms contributes to my disgust.

I manage four slices before my stomach shuts up shop for the day. Clement, however, continues to process his pizza with all the efficiency of an industrial compactor. He reminds me of a dog my grandparents once owned, Barney. He was a loveable, black and tan mongrel with lopsided ears and a propensity to hoover up anything dropped on the floor more efficiently than any Dyson. I remember one time, not long after I started my periods, I was rummaging through my bag in my grandparent's kitchen. I inadvertently dropped a tampon on the floor, and within a split second, Barney snapped it up and swallowed it whole. He then looked up at me expectantly, perhaps hoping I might toss him another tampon treat.

With no desire to watch Clement eat, I nip to the toilet and, whilst sitting on the loo, take the opportunity to plot our route across town to Brooklyn. When I return after barely five minutes, my dining companion is sitting back in his chair, his plate empty.

"You havin' pudding?" he asks as I retake my seat.

"I couldn't even finish my pizza, so no."

He then picks up a menu and studies it for a few seconds before returning it to the table.

"Nothin' I fancy," he remarks. "You mind if I finish yours?"

He nods down at the two remaining slices of pizza on my plate.

"Help yourself. I'll get the bill."

In the time it takes me to hail a waiter, and for that waiter to reach our table, Clement wolfs back both slices of pizza.

"Did you enjoy your meal?" the young man asks, noticing our empty plates.

212

"Pizza was good," Clement replies after sucking tomato sauce from his finger. "But a bit of spotted dick and custard on the dessert menu would've been nice."

"I'll, um, mention that to the manager."

He won't, but as the likelihood of us ever returning is nil, I'm not sure it matters.

Once the bill is settled, we leave the pizzeria and make our way back towards the subway station. Being the end of the working day, the streets are busy, and it's likely the train will be rammed.

"How many trains we gotta get?" Clement asks as we walk.

"Three. It'll take fifty minutes or thereabouts."

"Fuck me," he groans. "Why is gettin' anywhere in this city such a pain in the arse?"

"We could get a taxi."

"At this time of day?" he retorts, giving me the side eye. "It'll take all bleedin' evening to get there."

"Subway it is, then."

Discussion over, we pass through the main entrance to the subway station. Part of me is dreading the rush hour journey because I suffer from low-key claustrophobia, but a much larger part is concerned about what we'll find once we reach our destination.

Deep down, I know that Clement is right about the likelihood of David Smith still living in a Brooklyn apartment. What isn't so clear is whether or not I'm about to follow the final breadcrumb, and all that awaits us is the brick wall at the end of that blind alley.

An hour from now, I'll know for sure, and that thought is enough to set my stomach in a spin again.

Chapter 26

When we emerge from the Sutter Avenue-Rutland Road subway station, the sky that greets us is noticeably darker than when we left Jamaica. It isn't just dusk approaching but a coalition of thundery grey clouds blotting out all but the odd sliver of blue sky.

Some might call it ominous. A bad omen, even.

After checking the final leg of our journey on my phone, we set off in an easterly direction. Within the first few hundred yards, it's obvious that we're not in a part of the city frequented by either tourists or the well-heeled. I thought Flatbush was a rough borough, but if my early impressions of this neck of Brooklyn are anything to go by, we're unlikely to pass an artisan deli or organic coffee shop on the way to our destination.

"It's grim, isn't it?" I remark as we pass a shuttered shop popular with graffiti artists. "It's not the kind of area I thought David Smith would choose to reside."

"Seen better," Clement grunts. "Seen worse."

It's another dozen steps before he adds to his statement.

"Don't think we'll find any public bogs. I should have taken a shit before we left the pizza place."

"Thanks for sharing."

"Just sayin', Doll."

The navigation app confirms we need to take a left turn, leading us into the mid-section of Blake Avenue as it intersects with Van Sinderen Avenue. After our turn, the property we're looking for should be just over half a mile further on.

There are no shops on Blake Avenue, just a mishmash of residential homes from austere apartment blocks to tired townhouses and the odd single-storey detached box behind a chain-link fence. It's a street that's likely home to folk who commute into the city for their daily toil in the thousands of shops, restaurants, and hotels. A lot of hours, not much pay.

We cross two intersections before the navigation app confirms our destination is just ahead.

"Should we cross over?" I ask.

"In a sec."

We come to a stop directly opposite 956 Blake Avenue. I know very little about architecture, but I can't imagine that the man or woman who designed 956 was top of their class in architectural college. The L-shaped structure is eight storeys high and constructed with dark-brown bricks, but beyond those three features, it's just a characterless monolith of a building.

"It looks like something the council would build back home," I remark.

"Yeah, in the sixties," Clement retorts. "Build 'em high, build 'em cheap."

We continue to stand and stare up at the building, although I'm unsure why.

"Seen enough?" I ask.

He nods, and then looks up and down the street.

"Let's go see if anyone's home."

We get as far as the main doors, and Clement grabs the handle. After giving it a thorough shake, he states the obvious.

"It's bleedin' locked."

215

"Great," I groan. "Now what?"

"Fuck all we can do but wait. Block this size, someone's bound to come or go before long."

Before I can object on the ground of freezing my tits off, a black guy with a low baseball cap and denim jacket with the collar turned up appears on the other side of the door. He pushes it open and strides away without so much as a glance in our direction.

"Told you," Clement remarks, grabbing the door before it closes. "Ladies first."

I step into the hallway and grimace at the state of the flaking paint on the walls and cracked tiles beneath my feet, not to mention a strange odour hanging in the air. There's a lift straight ahead, but two lengths of red and white tape stretched diagonally across confirm it's out of order. The gloomy stairwell to the left looks as inviting as a dentist's chair.

"Guess we're taking the stairs," Clement says. "Floor D, ain't it?"

"Yep, and assuming this is A, we've got three flights to climb."

We begin the climb, and by the time we reach floor C, I rethink my plan to kick David Smith in the nuts, not that we're likely to find him waiting for us.

"You're out of shape, Doll."

"That obvious?" I pant. "I shouldn't have cancelled my gym membership."

It's a relief when we reach floor D, and Clement opens the door from the stairwell to the landing.

"What flat number is it?" he asks.

"Two," I reply, stepping through the doorway.

The landing isn't in a much better state than the ground-floor entrance hall. There are no cracked floor tiles but there is a carpet in a suspect shade of brown. God knows what horrors it's hiding — I'm just glad that it is.

"I don't get it," I remark. "Why would Smith choose to live here?"

"Maybe he likes shitholes," Clement replies unhelpfully.

Not knowing which way to go, I instinctively turn left. There are two doors on either side of the hallway but the first one is number five and the one opposite, six.

"Other way."

We turn around and pad across the sticky carpet to the far end of the landing. The door to apartment two is the last one on our left, conveniently positioned next to the fire escape.

"Do we knock?" I ask, looking up at Clement.

"They ain't gonna come to the door through the power of prayer, are they, Doll?"

"Alright, smartarse."

I turn around, take a deep breath, and knock.

As unlikely as it is that David Smith is behind the door, my hands instinctively ball into fists as a vision of his face floats into my mind. As the seconds pass by and the door remains unanswered, the hatred sets my jaw rigid.

The sudden sound of a lock turning triggers my brain to release a shot of adrenalin. I no longer want to punch David Smith — I want to leap at him like a feral tomcat and dig my nails into his face. I want to scratch and spit and claw at his flesh ...

"Yes?"

The man in the doorway is not David Smith. Bleary-eyed, balding, and not much taller than me, he's wearing suit trousers and an off-white shirt, the top three buttons unfastened.

"Oh, err ... hello," I splutter while swallowing back the still-present rage. "Sorry to disturb you."

"If you're from the Mormon Church," the man replies in a Texan accent, "I'm not interested."

"No, we're not. I'm trying to find someone who used to live at this address. Desperately."

"Right."

"So, can I ask: have you lived here long?"

"I don't live here," the man replies, scratching the top of his chest. "I'm attending a three-day conference in the city, and this is an Airbnb."

My heart sinks. At best, this guy's revelation creates another long line of hurdles to overcome, with no guarantee I'll ever reach the finish tape.

"I don't suppose you happen to know who owns the apartment?"

"Couldn't tell you. Sorry."

The man shoots a tired smile in my direction and goes to close the door. Metaphorically, it's likely also the door closing on any chance I have of finding David fucking Smith.

"How'd you get in?" Clement then suddenly asks.

"Pardon?"

"There ain't no reception desk downstairs, so how did you get in the flat?"

"With a set of keys, obviously."

"Don't be clever with me, Sunshine — I ain't in the mood. Where did you get the keys from?"

The man swallows hard and then nods over my shoulder.

"Airbnb emailed me with instructions to collect the keys from a guy named Joe in apartment eight."

"See," Clement says. "Weren't that hard, was it?"

The man nods and then quickly closes the door. We're left standing at the end of the landing.

"Suppose we'd better go see Joe at number eight," I puff.

We head back along the filthy carpet, past the stairwell, and stop outside the last door. I knock on the door, and with zero chance of David Smith opening it, I manage to keep my emotions in check this time.

"Someone's home," Clement remarks. "You hear the TV?"

"Hard not to."

I'm about to knock again when the door creaks open.

"What?" snaps a gangly figure with pockmarked skin and stubble for hair.

"I understand you handle the Airbnb bookings for apartment two. Is that correct?"

"Dunno what you're talking about, and I'm busy."

"We literally just spoke to the man renting the apartment, and he told us—"

"I don't care who you spoke to. Whatever it is you're after, it ain't here. Capiche?"

Point made, he slams the door in my face.

I look up to the ceiling and groan. If I thought it'd help repair my now shattered hopes, I might be tempted to cry for a bit.

"Doll," Clement then says in a low voice.

"Yes?" I puff, still looking up at the ceiling.

"I need you to do something for me."

I slowly lower my gaze and focus on the big man. "What?"

He points at a patch of carpet four or five feet back along the landing.

"I want you to stand in that exact spot and stay there until you hear me call your name."

"Why?"

"Don't ask, just do it."

If his gruff tone of voice wasn't enough to strongly suggest I comply, his icy stare certainly is. I take four steps to my left and stand roughly where instructed.

"Dare I ask what you're doing, Clement?"

"What I do best," he replies while adjusting his feet until he's standing directly in front of the door to apartment eight. He then takes two steps back, so his shoulder blades are almost touching the door of the apartment opposite. Then, he draws a deep breath.

He slowly turns to me. "Do. Not. Move."

Before I've time to confirm I won't, Clement raises his right leg, crane-like, and strikes out at the door to apartment eight. The second his huge boot comes into contact with the wood, an ear-splitting crack reverberates up the hallway. It's followed by the sound of the now-open door clattering against the inner wall of the apartment's hallway.

I open my mouth to ask what the hell he's playing at, but by the time the first word reaches my lips, Clement is already through the doorway and gone. Every muscle in my body primes for a pursuit until my brain reminds those muscles of the instruction I received only seconds ago.

Rather than move, I listen intently. I hear muffled noises and something that sounds like a yelp, but it's impossible to isolate sounds above the blare of the TV.

My instructions were to do nothing, but Clement never clarified how long I need to stand here. How long has it been? Ten seconds? Twenty? Thirty? I should have kept track for no other reason than to calm a sudden spike in my anxiety levels.

"What the fuck, Clement?" I whimper.

Heeding my own advice and keen to avoid a panic attack, I start counting in my head. Slow, measured breaths and the mindless task of counting settles my heart rate a fraction, but it's unlikely to drop below ninety beats per minute as long as I'm standing here alone.

Then, a sudden creaking noise undoes my good work. I let out a gasp and focus on the source of the sound — the apartment hallway. A figure steps into view.

"You alright, Doll? You look a bit peaky."

Chapter 27

It says a lot about the residents of 956 Blake Avenue that the sound of a door being kicked almost clean from its hinges isn't worthy of investigation. Maybe if Clement had used a shotgun, one of the neighbours might have shown an interest.

"You coming in?" he asks, standing in the doorway.

"What ... what did you do to him?"

"Nothin' much."

"Is he okay?"

"He's just having a quick nap, but he won't be out for long. Get your backside in here if you wanna ask him questions."

Clement turns and steps back into the hallway of apartment eight. I've been dying to move for the last few minutes, but my legs suddenly don't want to cooperate.

I remind myself why I'm here.

The hallway is dark and stinks of weed, but as I follow Clement through another doorway, the smell becomes almost overpowering. The cause is a still smouldering spliff in an ashtray, sitting on top of a small table next to an armchair. From my position, I can just about see the top of a closely shaved head, silhouetted against a TV screen fixed on the opposite wall.

With a degree of trepidation, I enter the lounge and slowly take a wide berth around the side of the armchair.

The apartment's resident, Joe, is slumped back against the cracked leather, his head lolled to the left slightly, eyes flickering.

"I just gave him a quick tap," Clement says as he silences the TV by pulling out the plug. "But he'll live."

If Joe were slightly less of an arsehole, I might have some sympathy. Even when I notice the leather belt strapping his wrists together, I can't find much in the way of pity.

"He was very rude to me," I reply. "It's his fault ... in a way."

"Yeah, that's what I thought."

Clement then steps towards the armchair and delivers two sharp slaps to Joe's left cheek.

"Wakey, wakey, Sunshine."

The gangly pothead emits a groan and rolls his head left and right. His eyes then flicker open, and when he finally focuses on the significant bulk of his assailant's frame, those same eyes widen dramatically.

"You shout, scream, or raise your voice," Clement growls, leaning over the armchair. "And I'll drown you in the bathtub. Got it?"

Joe nods. It's a painful gesture, if his wincing is any gauge.

"What ... what do you want from me, Man?" he just about spits.

"Nothing much. Just some answers."

"About what?"

"I'll let my friend ask the questions. Word of warning, though, lie to her or piss us around, and I'll drag your arse to the bathroom, and we'll see how long you can hold your breath."

"Alright, alright," Joe pleads. "Just don't hurt me, Man."

Clement backs away and stands in front of the TV, arms folded. It's my cue to ask the questions I hoped to ask before Joe slammed the door in my face. I step

222

towards the armchair and consider my first question. I can't help myself.

"Are you always so rude to people who knock on your door?"

He sneers up at me but then his eyes briefly flick past my right shoulder, towards the real threat in the room.

"Sorry," Joe mumbles.

"So you should be. Now, who owns apartment two?"

"A guy called Dylan Schultz."

"And how long has he owned it?"

"I dunno ... few years, I guess, but he moved out last summer. Met some fat-ass bitch from Florida and moved down there."

"Which is why he now rents it as an Airbnb, presumably?"

"Yeah."

"Do you handle all the bookings?"

"No," he spits. "Dylan pays me two hundred bucks a month to look after the place ... hand out the keys, let the cleaner in, but that's about it."

"What does he look like? Dylan?"

"Short, stocky ... bit older than me."

"I don't know how old you are."

"Thirty-one."

After seeing the photo on Evelyn Conroy's phone, it's clear that David Smith alters his appearance from one target to the next. However, there's no way he'd ever pass as a short, stocky guy in his mid-thirties. Obviously, he never owned apartment two when he lived there.

"Have you got a phone number for Dylan Schultz?"

"Yeah, but what do you want it for?"

"I'm going to call him and ask for the details of a man who rented the apartment back in January, possibly for a few weeks ... unless you can help me if I give you his name and show you a photo?"

223

"Fat chance," Joe snorts. "I can't even remember the name of the dude staying there tonight. They knock on my door, show me some ID, and I hand them the keys. That's it."

I could press him further, but his obvious appetite for pot and the fact he's probably seen scores of renters over the last nine months would suggest it'd be a waste of time.

"So, Dylan's number?"

"It's on my phone, but you won't be able to get hold of him for a few weeks."

"Why not?"

"Because he's probably in the middle of the Caribbean Sea or wherever the fuck they go. Dylan's a chef on one of those cruise ships."

Brilliant. The only person who might be able to reveal anything worthwhile about David Smith is incommunicado, and I'll be back in Essex by the time he returns to dry land.

"I'll take his email address."

"Whatever," Joe shrugs. "It's dylan.schultz86@gmail.com."

I pull out my phone and record the email address in a notes app. Dylan Schultz might not be able to receive phone calls, but he must have access to email. Whether he replies to mine remains to be seen, but it looks like it's the last remaining breadcrumb.

I turn to Clement. "I think I'm done."

"What about the driving licence?" he replies.

"What about it?"

"How'd that Smith bloke get a New York driver's licence registered in this building if he weren't living here?"

We both turn to Joe. He shrugs.

"How long does it take to get a driver's licence?" Clement asks me. "Days? Weeks? Months?"

"In New York, I've no idea, but back home, it can take three or four weeks ... sometimes longer."

"And you don't know how long it's gonna take, right?"

"No."

"So, Smith applies for a driving licence, saying he lives here, and then he happens to rent the flat on the same day it arrives in the post. Don't seem likely, does it?"

"It seems very *un*likely."

Again, we both turn to face Joe, and Clement directs a question this time.

"You got any idea how a bloke who don't live here managed to get his hands on a letter from the driver's licence department or whatever the fuck they're called?"

"How would I know, Man?"

"You got the keys to that flat, and no one else has."

"Anyone could have the keys. Someone rents the place for a night, and they just get a spare cut."

"But how would they know their letter had arrived?" I ask.

"I dunno."

"You don't know a lot, do you, Sunshine," Clement growls. "Show him the photo, Doll — see if that jogs his memory."

I pull out my phone again, tap through to the photo of David Smith, and hold the device at arm's length.

"He might have had longer hair and a goatee beard when he stayed here."

Joe looks at the photo for barely a second. "I don't remember him."

Without warning, Clement suddenly jumps forward and clamps his hand around Joe's neck.

"I warned you, didn't I?" he snarls, his face no more than eighteen inches away from the terrified pothead. "I said, you lie to us, and you're a dead man."

I wish I knew Clement well enough to tell if his threat is a bluff. In Joe's shoes, however, I wouldn't want to take that risk. If he is lying, I only hope he spills the truth before Clement is finished strangling him.

"Last chance, Dickhead," the big man says, and I'm inclined to believe him.

Clement releases his hand perhaps seconds before Joe's eyes pop out of his skull.

"You recognise him, don't you?"

In amongst the coughs and the splutters and the gasps for air, there are two slight nods of the head.

"How'd you know him?" Clement asks.

"I ... I ..."

Joe coughs again, but one quick glance at the man who almost throttled him seems to bring clarity to his thoughts.

"I met him at JFK."

"That's more like it," Clement responds. "And now you're gonna tell us every last detail. How you met, what was said, and how he ended up getting a driver's licence sent here."

Resigned to his fate, Joe's shoulders slump and he swallows hard.

"I work at JFK," he begins. "I'm a baggage handler."

I'm surprised to learn he has a job, but that doesn't mean I've misjudged him.

"I was getting towards the end of my shift when this guy comes to the counter, saying his bag hadn't landed on the carousel."

"When was this?" I ask.

"Last year. December. It's always crazy in the run-up to Christmas."

"Go on."

"Sometimes a bag gets missed so I asked one of our crew to check the cage. While the guy was waiting, he took a call. I wasn't listening but it was hard not to

226

overhear because he was yelling down the phone. There was some mix-up with his hotel booking and they didn't have a room."

"And let me guess," I interject. "You offered him apartment two?"

"Yeah, I was doing us both a favour. It was getting on for midnight so I said he could stay for a hundred bucks. He agreed, and by the time we found his bag, my shift was over. I drove him back here, he gave me the hundred bucks, and I handed him the keys to the apartment."

"So, how did you go from that one-off deal to him using this address to obtain a driving licence?"

"He knocked on my door the following morning to give me the keys and to say thank you for helping him out of a hole. He then asked if I was interested in making some easy money."

"How?"

"He said he was going through a rocky divorce and his wife was trying to fleece him for every penny. What he needed was a temporary address so he could set up a new bank account and move some of his money. I felt sorry for the guy ... my ex fucked me over which is how I ended up living here."

"You let him use the address for your friend's apartment?"

"The deal was one hundred bucks for every letter. All I had to do was make sure I picked them up from downstairs and keep hold of them until he was next in town. He said it was easy money, and it was, but I didn't know he was gonna get a driver's licence sent here. I swear."

"How many letters are we talking about?" I ask.

"Since January, maybe seven or eight. I can't remember exactly."

"And how many times has he dropped by to collect his mail?"

"Four."

"The last time being?"

"I dunno ... weeks ago."

I take a moment to parse what we've just discovered.

"Let me get this right," I say. "Whenever an item of post arrives for David Smith, you contact him and let him know."

"Yeah. I send him a text message."

"And, then he comes to collect it?"

"Eventually."

I turn to Clement.

"We could send him a message, saying a letter has arrived."

"And when he turns up to collect, we make sure we're waiting, right?"

"That's what I'm thinking."

I return my attention to Joe.

"Where's your phone?"

There's a moment's hesitation before he cusses under his breath. I'm sure he's pissed that we're about to terminate his arrangement, and any further cash payments, but he's in no position to argue.

"In my pocket," he eventually huffs.

Clement steps forward and does the honours, fortunately. He then hands the device to me.

"What's the pin?" I ask Joe.

"1111."

I unlock the phone and tap on the icon to open the messaging app. There aren't many, but I presume it's because Joe, like most people under fifty, prefers an app-based messaging service. I scroll down until I find a message from someone called DS.

"Is DS David Smith?"

Joe nods, and I open the string of messages between the two men. The last message received from Smith was on the eighth of August — only three or so weeks after

228

he emptied Mum's bank accounts. It states that he'll collect on Tuesday. I scroll back to the last message Joe sent to ensure consistency, copy it, and then paste the text into a new message: *You got a letter.*

I tap the send icon.

"Done," I say to Clement. "Now we just have to wait for Smith to reply."

"We gonna piss off, then? No point hanging around now you've got his phone."

"Hey!" Joe protests. "You can't take my phone — I need it for work."

I consider our options. Joe might be an obnoxious pothead, and he did slam the door in my face, but it seems unfair to take his phone.

"We'll give it ten minutes," I suggest.

Not that I want to discuss it in front of Joe, but there's another good reason for waiting. If someone stole my phone, the first thing I'd do is activate the remote lock so it can't be used. I've no idea whether he's that smart, but I'd rather not take the risk.

"You got any beer in the fridge?" Clement asks Joe, seemingly resigned to a wait.

"Couple of cans."

"Want one?"

"Gee, thanks," Joe snorts. "So kind of you to offer me one of my own beers."

"I was talking to her, Dickhead," Clement replies, jabbing his thumb in my direction.

"I'm okay, thanks."

The phone vibrates in my hand. My pulse quickening, I unlock the screen to read what I hope is a new message.

"He's replied."

"What's he say?"

I open the message. It's not quite what I expected: *What colour is the envelope?*

After relaying the message to Clement, I consider my reply.

"Why does he wanna know that?" the big man asks.

"Your guess is as good as mine. What do I say to him?"

"Pick a colour and reply."

Most of the junk mail I receive tends to come in coloured envelopes, and I don't want him to think it's junk, which leaves two options. For no real reason, I go with white over brown and send a reply.

"Sent," I confirm.

Clement remains where he is, as do Joe's beers, while I pace up and down the eight feet of threadbare carpet in front of the TV. The seconds seem to stretch on forever until the phone finally vibrates again. I come to a stop and check the incoming message: *It's probably junk. Do me a favour and shred it.*

"Fuck!" I snap.

"What's the matter?" Clement asks.

I hold the phone up so he can read the message for himself. I then watch his face as his eyes lock on the screen. However, as I wait for a similar reaction to mine, Clement continues to stare at the screen, frowning hard.

"It's over," I say, lowering the phone. "This was our last chance."

"Somethin' odd about those messages, Doll."

"What?"

"Check 'em."

With minimal enthusiasm, I humour Clement and do as he asks. Two messages, fifteen words in total, and as far as I can see, there's nothing odd about them at all.

"I'm not in the mood for games, Clement," I groan after reading both messages for the third time. "What's odd about them?"

Clement turns to Joe. "How do you spell colour?"

"What?"

"Just spell it."

230

"C-O-L-O-R."

"And favour?"

"F-A-V-O-R."

It takes a second to realise the significance of Clement's ad-hoc spelling test, but the moment I do, I look at the message again.

"Smith used British English," I gasp. "Why would he do that?"

There's an obvious reason, and fortunately, there's someone in the room who can confirm it. I spin around and face the armchair.

"David Smith — is he British?"

"Err, yeah," Joe replies as if I'm asking the most obvious of questions.

"Are you sure?"

"I didn't ask to see his birth certificate, but his accent is the same as yours, and he flew in from Heathrow that day he lost his bag."

"How do you know he wasn't faking his accent?"

"I don't, but when I asked him for ID to prove the lost bag was his, he showed me a British passport."

I stare down at the gobby pothead, open-mouthed. I don't know what to say, but he does.

"And ... and some of his letters were from England," he splutters, keen to reinforce his claim. "The stamps had pictures of the Queen on 'em."

If he's lying, and I can't for the life of me think of any reason why he would, this changes everything.

"I need to call Evelyn Conroy," I say.

"To check if the arsehole who conned her had a British or Yank accent?"

"Exactly."

"What you wanna do with matey here? We done with him?"

"I want to get the number for Smith and compare it to the one we got from Pinhill's rental records, but after that, we can leave him be."

I hurry through to the hallway and tap the call icon for the most recent entry on my contact list. Evelyn picks up on the fourth ring.

"Hi, it's Gina Jackson. Can you talk for a minute?"

"Sure."

"This might sound like an odd question, but what accent did the man who called himself Franklin Bruce have?"

"He was English."

"Are you certain?"

"Of course I'm certain. One of Brian's colleagues grew up in England and he and his wife came over for dinner plenty of times. The bastard who stole from me had the same accent — as English as yours."

"I wish you'd mentioned that earlier," I sigh. "It's not an insignificant detail."

"You're English, your friend Clement is English, and I presume your mother is English. Why would I presume you didn't know he was too?"

It's a fair point.

"Sorry, Evelyn. I didn't mean to sound so snippy. It's just ... I won't bore you with the details, but I've only just discovered his nationality. We all thought he was American: me, Mum, our family ... everyone."

"Does that change anything?"

I pause and give Evelyn's question due consideration.

"It changes everything," I reply in a low voice. "How, though, I'm not yet sure."

Chapter 28

I awake to my fourth full day in New York and the fourth night in the hotel. If I had to pay for the room based on the hours of sleep I've accumulated, I'd be paying a lot less than the number on my receipt. I flopped into bed just after nine last night and spent the first two hours staring up at the ceiling, my mind ablaze with questions.

The most fundamental of those questions, and the one that's plagued me ever since Mum's aborted wedding, remains unanswered: where the fuck is the man who ruined her life? If my task was difficult before, it now feels almost impossible. I don't know the specifics, other than he's conned my mum and Evelyn Conroy, but David Smith patently operates on both sides of the Atlantic.

That in itself makes him twice as hard to catch. If it wasn't for the fact I detest the man with every fibre of my being, I might almost admire his work ethic. While he was ripping off Evelyn and probably countless other lonely middle-aged women, he was wooing Mum and preparing his plans to empty her bank accounts. David Smith is a transatlantic parasite and a cunning one at that.

I grab the tablet from the nightstand and unlock the screen. The same page of notes I fell asleep to greets me. Unlike my spreadsheet of leads, at least this document contains more than mere speculation. Now, I have certainties and strong possibilities to work with. I know that the man who proposed to my mother is not Bruce Franklin but David Smith, and I know that, in all likelihood, he isn't American but British.

Looking back, we didn't have a clue about his true nationality, but why would we? Smith's con was nothing if not meticulous, and perhaps his deftest sleight of hand was convincing us he was American. His New York accent wouldn't pass muster here but, in suburban Essex, it was convincing enough. Then, there were the photos of his supposed home on West End Avenue — again, convincing. And the graduation ring he stole from Evelyn Conroy added a touch of authenticity. It's now easy to see why he didn't immediately pawn what would prove to be a useful prop in his act.

Then, there's the most obvious reason for his subterfuge — minimising the risk of being caught. A US citizen committing a crime on UK soil muddied the waters when it came to the police and which force might take responsibility for solving it. As it transpired, neither did, and Smith must have known he'd have a significantly better chance of getting away with his con if everyone involved, including the authorities, believed he was American.

I switch off the tablet and return it to the nightstand. I've studied the facts long enough to realise I might have reached the end of the line. Maybe now it's time to return home and show Essex Police what I've unearthed. There's another reason why returning home ahead of plan makes sense. For all the time I've been chasing across New York, I've been able to keep the sense of guilt at bay. It's the quiet moments alone when it returns, and the little voice in my head continually reminds me that I should be at home, looking after Mum.

234

There is, however, a short-term solution to silencing the voice. I snatch up my phone and call home. With every unanswered ring, concern adds fuel to the guilt, although I know there could be a dozen perfectly innocent reasons why no one is home to take my call. Just as I prepare for the answering machine to cut in, the ringtone abruptly ends.

"Hello," Paula says breathlessly.

"Hi, it's only me," I reply. "Are you okay?"

"Yes, yes. I was in the garden putting the washing out."

"Oh, sorry. Is there a reason Mum didn't answer?"

"She's upstairs asleep."

I glance at my watch. Nearly nine here, so early afternoon in Brentwood.

"Why is Mum asleep at lunchtime?"

"She didn't sleep well at all last night, and by mid-morning, she looked exhausted. So, I made her a mug of warm malted milk and insisted she tried to get her head down for a few hours."

"That's good of you, Paula. Thank you."

"It's what I'm here for, sweetheart — to look after her until you're back."

"On that note, there's a chance I might cut short the trip."

"Oh, why's that?"

"The last few days of the course aren't really relevant to my discipline, and if I'm being honest, I'm still feeling guilty for abandoning Mum."

"Don't be silly," Paula chides. "Helen would be feeling a damn sight worse if she thought you missed out on a once-in-a-lifetime opportunity on her account. You know that."

"Maybe," I sigh. "But my point about the course is still valid. I'll let you know as soon as I've made a decision."

"Make sure you do, and we'll meet you at the airport."

Having Paula and Mum waiting for a flight from Paris that I'm not on is a problem, but I don't currently have the mental bandwidth to think of a plausible reason to decline the offer. I'll have to think of an excuse before I depart.

"That's kind of you."

There's a moment of silence before Paula speaks again.

"How's the weather over there?" she asks brightly. "It's been lovely here the last few days."

Shit. There could be a hurricane tearing through Paris as we speak, but without a way to quickly check, I need to move the conversation along. As it happens, there is a topic I'd like to bring up.

"Um, I've not had much chance to get outside. On another note, do you know what Lynn and Stephen were doing at the bungalow yesterday?"

"Lynn and Stephen? Yesterday?"

"Yes, I ... someone I know popped by, and they said they saw Lynn and Stephen coming down the driveway."

"Ohh, right. What time was that?"

"I don't know exactly. In the afternoon."

"Your mum and I popped to the garden centre for a few hours, so they must have called by when we were there."

It's a consolation that they never got to see Mum, but that doesn't mean they won't try again.

"Would you do me a favour, Paula?"

"Sure. Anything."

"If Lynn and Stephen drop by again, can you let me know?"

"Of course. In fact ... forget it."

"What is it, Paula?"

"It's nothing, sweetheart. Ignore me."

"Please, tell me. If it's anything to do with Lynn and Stephen, I want to know. I don't trust either of them, but particularly Lynn."

"If I tell you, will you promise me not to say anything?"

"That depends on what you tell me."

"It'd mean breaking your mum's trust, and that's not something I'd do lightly."

"I wouldn't want to put you in an awkward position, so you have my word I won't say anything to Mum."

Paula draws a deep breath as I wait to hear if she's willing to break a confidence.

"While we were at the garden centre," she then says, "we had a cup of tea and a sit down for twenty minutes. I could tell that something was bothering Helen as she seemed anxious, fidgety."

"And did you ask her what was bothering her?"

"It was like getting blood out of a stone, but she eventually told me. Before all the hoo-ha with Bruce Franklin, your mum had agreed to lend Lynn some money. Apparently, the hotel had a temporary cash-flow problem, and they needed a hundred grand to tide them over for a few months."

My grip on the phone tightens, as do my jaw muscles.

"A hundred grand?" I just about manage to spit.

"Yes, but you never heard that from me, okay?"

Angry as I am, there's no sense venting at the messenger, particularly as Paula didn't have to tell me.

"I'm grateful you told me, and rest assured, I won't breathe a word to Mum."

"Are you going to say anything to Lynn?"

"Too bloody right I am."

"Can I give you some advice before you do?"

"I'm listening."

"Wait until you're back home and you've calmed down. Nothing is going to happen while you're away, and you have my word that I'll call you if Lynn and Stephen drop by again."

I consider Paula's advice for a moment.

"You're right," I concede. "And besides, I want to look Lynn in the eye when I confront her."

"Good girl," Paula replies in a maternal tone. "You know it makes sense. Act in haste, repent at leisure, eh?"

"I know. As it happens, that was one of Granddad's favourite sayings."

"He was a wise bloke, your granddad, and I'm sure he'd be very proud that you're taking such good care of your mum."

He wouldn't be so proud of his youngest daughter if he knew how she'd frittered away the money he left her and is now harassing his other daughter for a loan. Supposition, sadly.

I thank Paula again, and she reiterates that I should confirm when I'm coming home so they can meet me at the airport. I ask her to pass on my love to Mum and end the call.

Tossing the phone on the bed, I consider getting up for a shower, but the revelation about David Smith's nationality has dampened my sense of urgency. Specifically, it's dampened it by fifty per cent because although my foe could be in New York, there's just as much chance he's in the UK. Not for the first time, I also have to concede he could be anywhere on the planet with almost two million quid in his bank account.

My phone rings. I reach over and check who's calling before answering.

"Morning, Clement," I say with limited enthusiasm.

"Alright, Doll. You had breakfast yet?"

"No, I'm still in bed."

"Get your arse up and meet me in the reception in half hour."

"Why?"

238

"I'll buy breakfast, and then we need a little chat."

"About what?"

"The price of chopped liver," he snorts. "What do you think it's about?"

"David Smith, presumably."

"Yeah, him."

"I've been thinking about nothing else since I got back to the hotel last night. Maybe it's time to give up and head home; tell the police what I've unearthed."

"Before you do anything, we need to talk. Downstairs, half-hour, alright."

"But—"

Clement cuts the call before I can argue.

Reluctantly, I clamber out of bed and wander through to the bathroom, hitting the light switch en route. Whoever designed the lighting scheme in this particular bathroom clearly got a full ten hours of sleep every night and likely lived a stress-free life. I've not managed either of late, and the harsh white lighting only emphasises the physical symptoms: sallow skin, a trio of spots dotted across my forehead, and both eyes ringed with dark circles. The baggy, shapeless grey T-shirt I wore to bed does little to enhance the look.

"What are you doing?" I ask the woman in the mirror.

She doesn't answer, but if I were to give her any advice, it would be to go home and forget all about David Smith. He's already taken so much from Mum, but if my reflection is any barometer, he's still taking from me, even now.

Chapter 29

Feeling marginally better post-shower, I take the lift down to the reception. I did consider calling Clement and cancelling, but there are two reasons I decided against it. Firstly, I'm starving, and secondly, if it weren't for his intervention earlier in the week, I would likely have flown home days ago, with nothing new to tell Essex Police apart from the fact I was mugged in New York. The very least I can do is join him for breakfast before we go our separate ways.

When the lift doors open, I step into the reception area and scan the space. There's a happy-looking couple at the desk talking to the male receptionist, but no sign of Clement. I check my watch — exactly ten o'clock. I'll give him five minutes and then call, but if he's not here soon, I'll head out and eat alone.

I make my way towards a sofa to wait, but the automatic doors whoosh open before I get there.

"Mornin'," Clement says, ambling towards me with a brown paper bag in his right hand.

"Good morning. What's in the bag?"

"Breakfast. You can eat it in your room."

"That's not quite what I had in mind when you suggested breakfast."

"Change of plans, Doll. Lots to talk about, and I don't wanna do it with people around us, earwigging."

240

I eye the bag. Whatever's inside, it's unlikely to be a large Americano with two sugars.

"It's sweet of you to bring breakfast, but I desperately need a coffee."

"Go and grab one, then, and I'll meet you in the room." He then holds out his left hand. "Key?"

I'm intrigued enough to comply, and hand over the key card.

"Fifth floor," I confirm. "Room 505, in case you've forgotten."

"Alright. Don't be long."

"I won't, but this chat better be worthwhile if I'm missing out on a proper breakfast. Do you want anything from the coffee shop?"

"Nah," he replies before turning his back on me and striding away.

The queue in Starbucks is mercifully short, and five minutes later, I'm back in the lift. I've already sipped a third of the Americano by the time I reach the door to my room. Without a key, I have to knock.

Clement opens the door without a word and steps back into the room. He then lowers his oversized frame into one of the tub chairs.

"Chop, chop, Doll. I ain't got all morning."

I roll my eyes and deliberately dawdle over to the other chair.

"What's for breakfast?" I ask.

"Didn't know what you like," he replies, digging a hand into the bag. "But seeing as you're from Essex, I thought I'd keep it simple."

Clement passes me a bun-shaped object wrapped in greasy paper. I choose to ignore his veiled insult.

"Bacon and egg muffin," he confirms. "Enjoy."

"Are you not eating?"

"I had my breakfast two hours ago. I've been up since the crack of bleedin' dawn."

241

I unwrap the muffin and, as unappetising as it looks, take a bite. It's barely lukewarm but edible.

"So, what is it you so urgently need to chat about?" I ask after swallowing the first mouthful.

"Our little trip out to Brooklyn yesterday evening, and a few things our new friend had to say."

"Specifically?"

"I was lying on my bed last night, thinking what was said and ... and somethin' he mentioned kept playing over and over like a needle stuck on a record."

"And that was?"

"Stamps."

"Stamps?"

"Yeah, he said one of the letters matey received had stamps on it, 'cos he remembered the picture of the Queen."

"Am I missing something here, Clement? If you want to send a letter, you need to put a stamp on it."

"Exactly. You and me would use stamps, but companies don't. They have those machines that print straight onto the envelope, right?"

"A franking machine."

"Yeah, one of them. Anyway, that's why I got up so early."

"Because of a letter with stamps on it?"

"There was something else I wanted to check, so I paid our pal another visit. He weren't too chuffed to see me at his door again, but I used the carrot rather than the stick this time."

"You didn't punch him in the face, you mean?"

"Nah, I gave him two hundred bucks on condition he made me a coffee. He was chatty enough after that."

"And what did he reveal that we didn't learn last night?"

I take another bite of the muffin while I wait for Clement's answer.

"That envelope from Blighty — the one with the stamps — definitely weren't sent by a company. The address was hand-written with a biro."

Chewing on a cremated piece of bacon, I stare back at Clement, waiting for an explanation as to why this information is relevant. He, in turn, stares back at me.

"Fuck me," he eventually grunts. "You ain't exactly the brightest button in the tin at this hour, are you?"

"Patently not," I manage to reply, swallowing a semi-masticated mouthful of muffin. "Enlighten me, O wise one."

"Unless he was sending letters to himself, someone back in Blighty must have known about his dodgy address."

I stop eating.

"Who?"

"Your guess is as good as mine, but that Joe reckons the envelope had documents in it."

"How'd he know that?"

"The size and the weight. He said he got a load of similar-sized envelopes from the court when his ex divorced him. Legal documents and shit, you know?"

I drop the rest of the muffin on the wrapper and sit back. This is potentially significant information, but I've yet to consume enough caffeine to work out how significant.

"There's something else," Clement continues. "About your mum."

"What about her?"

"I've been thinking about how she and that tosser first met. A coffee shop near an art gallery, right?"

"Yes."

"Bit of a coincidence, that," he says, stroking his moustache. "Him just bumping into a lonely woman with a few million quid in the bank."

243

"David Smith is a conman, Clement, and he must meet potential targets all the time. It's a numbers game, and Mum was just unlucky."

"Yeah, but what if she weren't?"

"Pardon?"

"I bet she's asked herself a thousand times how things might have panned out if you'd wandered into a different coffee shop, or five minutes later, or not at all. I bet she blames fate or destiny or some other bullshit."

"What exactly are you saying?"

"I'm sayin', Doll, that there's a chance that none of that mattered. If you hadn't wandered into that coffee shop, he'd have bumped into your mum somewhere else that day. Bottom line — I reckon he knew she was minted, and he targeted her because of it."

"How could he know? We'd never met the man before, and Mum sure as hell didn't advertise the fact she had money."

Clement fixes me with a look that could be sympathetic, but it doesn't fit his face.

"Maybe our bloke didn't know your mum had money," he says in a low voice. "Until someone told him ... maybe that same someone who sent a letter across The Pond."

"Eh? You mean someone Mum knows?"

"It's just guesswork, but it makes a lot of sense. You were a few thousand miles from home, and he pretended to be a Yank. Why'd he do that?"

That's one question I've already given thought to.

"To throw the police off the scent after he stole Mum's money."

"Yeah, there's that, but there's another reason. If he were a Brit, it'd be a lot easier to check his backstory and dig out any skeletons in his closet. It'd also mean he'd have to spend more time with your mum, which he probably didn't wanna do as it bumped up the chances of him being found out. Saying he lives in New York gave him a bloody convenient cover story, don't you reckon?"

As Clement's theory sinks in, along with the implications, my stomach seems to shrink.

"If you're right, and Smith had help, it means ... it means that there could be someone back in Brentwood who knows Mum, and knows that she's still vulnerable."

"As I said: it's just guesswork, Doll, so don't go into panic mode."

I stare back at Clement, unable to say anything because my mind is too busy turning over the possibilities of what could happen back in Brentwood while I'm on the other side of the Atlantic.

"Jesus," I gulp. "In hindsight, I don't think I should have come here."

"If you hadn't, your mum would still feel like shit, and you'd be none the wiser about that bloke. And trust me, Doll, there really ain't no bliss in ignorance. I can tell you that for nothin'."

There's a slightly bitter edge to Clement's statement, but I've got too much going on in my head to press for further details. I take a deep breath and, feeling fractionally less panicked, get to my feet.

"There's nothing else I can do here," I declare. "And whether your theory is right or not, I need to get back to Essex. I can't take any risks."

"Yeah, I hear you," Clement replies. "When you gonna head home?"

"As soon as I can get a flight."

"Thought you might, and it's time I headed home, too. I should be back in Blighty over the weekend."

"Right, okay. Wait ... you said you don't have a passport, and I'm pretty sure a ship will take at least five or six days to cross the Atlantic."

"There's a reason I bunged that Joe a few hundred bucks — I needed a favour."

"What favour?"

"I heard a rumour that you can buy a seat on a freight plane, but I ain't got any connections at the airport, so it weren't an option ... until Joe gave me a name and a number."

"That sounds dodgy as hell."

"A bit," Clement shrugs. "I spoke to the bloke earlier and all I've gotta do is be at the airport when he messages me, and he'll sort the rest. He does it a couple of times a month, so he says."

"And how are you going to get through customs?"

"It's a freight plane. I dunno how it works, but it ain't like they're gonna be checking pallets for passports, is it? No, matey gets me on the plane, I hide out somewhere until take off, and then bunk out the other end. Piece of piss."

"I guess that partially answers my question but why the urgency to jump on a dodgy flight this weekend?"

"Obvious, ain't it?"

"No, not really."

"This fucker has gotta be found, Doll, and the clock is ticking. Makes sense to pick this up back home as soon as I can get there, right?"

As Clement waits for an answer, I take a moment to try and arrange my emotions into some sort of order. Even before this conversation, I was racked with guilt and worry, but now there's another emotion to contend with — low-key fear.

"I don't know if I can keep searching for Smith," I say in a low voice. "I just ... I just want to keep Mum safe. She's my priority."

"I know, but you being back in Essex ain't gonna change anything, is it?"

"How'd you mean?"

"That tosser still has her money, and no one gets over losing the kind of money she lost ... unless they get it back."

Clement doesn't know it, but it's the same argument I had with myself weeks ago and the reason I jumped on a plane. Was I naive or stupid? Determined or deluded? Maybe I was a little of everything, but the real driving force behind my decision is still here, still burning hot in my chest.

"Maybe you're right," I say wearily. "But do you *honestly* think we can find him?"

"He's already made mistakes, so yeah, I do."

I still have my doubts, but there's no denying that Clement at least sounds sincere. On reflection, perhaps those doubts relate to his motive rather than his resolve.

"I know you said this was a calling, but I never expected you to follow me three thousand miles to help. It's a lot to ask."

"It's what I do," he says dismissively. "Ain't got no other purpose these days."

"And if we find David Smith?"

"He'll get what's coming to him — a bit of divine justice, I reckon."

I hold Clement's gaze for a few seconds. For the first time since he crashed into my life, I look beyond his cold eyes, his grizzled features, and the frankly ridiculous facial hair.

"Brick by careful brick," I murmur.

A slight smile reaches his lips.

"Trust, eh?" he replies. "Takes time to build."

My mouth bobs open.

"How'd you know I was referring to trust?"

"Don't matter," he says, getting to his feet. "You wouldn't believe me if I told you."

"I might."

247

"Maybe we'll talk about it once you've got what you need?"

"And what is it you think I need?"

Clement bows his head a couple of inches and looks me straight in the eye.

"Vengeance, Doll. Vengeance."

Chapter 30

As the plane taxis towards the terminal, I stare out across the rain-slicked tarmac. In the distance, a band of lush green grass contrasts against the grey backdrop courtesy of our schizophrenic British weather. Still, it's a relief to be back, not least because the flight was awful. Somehow, the pilot managed to find every pocket of turbulence on the way, killing any chance of sleep.

My options for an earlier flight were limited, so I took what's known as the red-eye. It's a term I'd never heard until the middle-aged businessman in the seat next to me complained about his company being so tight, they'd booked him on our red-eye flight from JFK to London Heathrow. We departed at nine o'clock last night and, with the time difference, we've just landed a little after nine in the morning. I haven't checked a mirror, but I suspect the term for our overnight flight is appropriate.

I feel like shit, but I'd rather feel like shit here than back in a New York hotel.

The plane finally reaches the terminal and, after a few minutes, one steward opens the door while another confirms we're able to depart the aircraft, but not before checking we've all got our belongings. It's not a reminder I need.

It takes almost an hour to pass through customs and collect my suitcase from baggage reclaim. My ordeal isn't over, though. I still face a fifteen-minute journey on the Heathrow Express to Paddington, and from there, another fifty minutes for a second train to reach Brentwood. Even then, there's still a taxi ride to Mum's.

As I trudge towards the rail platform, wheeling a three-ton suitcase behind me, I almost regret not informing Paula about my return. I could have asked her to pick me up outside, but knowing Paula's nature, she'd have likely planned a surprise by waiting in the arrivals hall with Mum for a tearful reunion. For them, the surprise would have been discovering I arrived in a different terminal, and from a different country.

It's a measure of how exhausted I am that both the train legs of my journey pass by in a haze. I eventually emerge from Brentwood station and mumble an address to a taxi driver. He deposits my suitcase in the boot while I flop into the back seat and close my eyes to avoid conversation. It works.

Over twelve hours of travelling, queuing, and waiting mercifully ends with the eighty-yard walk up Mum's driveway. Her car is parked by the garage, but Paula's is noticeable by its absence. Maybe they've gone out, which would be a minor blessing as I can leave a note to say I'm back and then nap for an hour or two.

I unlock the front door and drag the suitcase into the hallway.

"Mum?" I call out, not expecting a response.

A figure then appears in the kitchen doorway.

"Gina!" Mum cries. "What are you doing back here?"

Rather than wait for an answer, she rushes forward and throws her arms around me. In that one moment, the tension that's been threatening to cramp every muscle in my body suddenly eases. It's like lying in a hot bath after hours of vigorous activity.

I can finally breathe. Mum is okay. For now, anyway.

"I have missed you," she says, stepping back but keeping her hands on my shoulders. "But why are you back already?"

It seems Paula didn't tell Mum there's a chance I might return ahead of schedule. She probably didn't want to get Mum's hopes up until I'd confirmed.

"The rest of the course isn't that relevant to me," I reply. "And I ... I'm keen to get back to work."

"You're just like your granddad — he hated being idle for too long."

Mum's mind seems to drift off before she snaps back to reality.

"I'll put the kettle on, and you can tell me all about Paris over a nice cup of tea. How's that sound?"

"Sure, but let me dump the suitcase in my room first."

"Go ahead. Paula's out at the moment."

"Ah, right. Where's she gone?"

"An old school friend invited her to lunch at that flashy brasserie in town. The silly woman was going to decline because she didn't want to leave me alone for a few hours, but I said I wouldn't talk to her for the entire weekend if she did that."

"Nicely done," I chuckle. "Give me a minute, and I'll join you in the kitchen."

I open the door to the bedroom that has been my temporary home for almost two months, and Paula's temporary home for five days. She'll be returning to her own home later, but it's impossible to see a point in my immediate future where I leave Mum living alone.

"Bloody hell," I groan, surveying the mess.

I love Paula to bits, but I didn't know she was such an untidy mare. There are clothes scattered across the bed, a soggy towel on the floor by the wardrobe, and it appears our guest brought enough beauty products to stock a salon. Most of those products are haphazardly distributed across the entire width of the dressing table.

No wonder she wanted me to let her know when I'd be returning — it'll take an hour to tidy up her mess.

I wheel the suitcase over to the wardrobe, then pick up the towel and deposit it in the wash basket. My thoughts then turn to a more concerning issue than Paula's untidiness: Lynn and Stephen. As much as I want to quiz Mum about them scrounging money for their stupid bloody hotel, a promise is a promise. The best I can do is drop Lynn's name into the conversation and see what comes of it. Before that, though, I need to spin a few white lies about my supposed time in Paris.

When I wander into the kitchen, Mum is stirring one of two mugs on the side. She turns and smiles at me over her shoulder. "Sit yourself down. Tea's ready."

"That was quick," I reply, pulling out a chair at the table.

"I was about to make myself a brew when you came in. You must have heard the kettle."

Mum chuckles to herself and then joins me at the table, placing one of the mugs on a coaster in front of me.

"Come on then," she says, taking a seat opposite. "Tell me all about Paris."

"I'd love to say I spent my days strolling along the banks of the Seine in the autumn sunshine and my evenings enjoying the finest French cuisine, but it wasn't like that."

"No?"

"The course was intense, so at the end of each day, I just wanted to veg out in the hotel room and sleep."

"Oh, that's a shame. I bet Paris is lovely this time of year."

The moment the words leave her mouth, there's a distinct change in Mum's expression. It's almost as if a dark cloud has cast a shadow across her face. The trigger, I fear, is because she made a similar statement last year about how lovely New York would be in the summer. It *was* lovely, but it was also the place where Mum first met the man she still thinks is called Bruce Franklin.

"Are you okay, Mum?"

"I'm ... yes, I'm fine."

I know better than to press her. The ten minutes of normality were no more than a reminder of the woman she once was. I don't know if that woman will ever permanently return, or if this broken imposter is now my mother for life. One thing is certain, though — she is not fine, not by a long chalk.

I'm about to reach across the table when my phone rings. Mum's eyes have now glazed over so I might as well take the call.

"Hello?"

"Alright, Doll. It's me."

"Hi, Clement."

"Just a quick one," he says gruffly. "I'm gonna be on a flight this evening, leaving about ten o'clock."

"Okay."

There's a pause while Clement clears his throat.

"Between you and me, I might be shitting myself a bit."

"Why?"

"Ain't ever been on a plane before. Don't like 'em ... or boats. Fucking hate boats."

I'm about to ask how a man who routinely mugs armed drugged dealers could possibly be afraid of flying, or boats, but that's not a question I want Mum to overhear.

"You'll be fine. Once you're up, it's like being on a bus."

"You reckon?"

"Honestly, there's nothing to worry about."

"Good ... cool. You back home yet?"

"Just arrived."

"How's your mum?"

"We're just having a cup of tea."

"Christ, I could murder a cuppa. Anyhow, I'll let you get on, and I'll give you a bell when I'm at Heathrow."

"Great. Sounds like a plan."

"Assuming the bastard wings don't fall off the plane halfway across the Atlantic."

If the circumstances were different, I might have laughed at his paranoia, but one glance at Mum reminds me they're not.

"I'll see you soon, Clement."

"Yeah. Bye."

I put my phone on the table and retake my seat.

"Who's Clement?" Mum asks, looking up from her mug.

"He's um ... just some guy I met in Paris."

"Oh," she replies, her eyebrows arching slightly. "Just a friend, or ..."

"He's just a friend," I reply firmly.

It's hard to say whether Mum is pleased or disappointed by my answer. There was a time, before her world imploded, that she'd relentlessly nag me about finding someone and settling down. Now, though, I wonder if that's the last thing she wants. After her first husband ran off with her sister and the man who asked to be her second robbed her financially and emotionally, a degree of parental concern would be understandable. I'm not my mum, though, and I'm certainly not in the market for a relationship at the moment. The scars are still raw from the last one.

"Anyway," I say brightly. "What have you been up to while I've been away?"

"Trying to get things sorted with the bungalow."

"What do you mean?"

"I need to sell it, Gina. I told you I can't afford to live here much longer."

"And I told you not to worry about it. Let's see how things pan out between now and Christmas, and you can decide in the New Year."

Mum takes a slow sip of tea before replying.

"Paula said the same thing — I should wait."

"There you go, then. We both want what's best for you, and I think it would be sensible to hang on for a while."

"I just don't see the point. The police have all but given up on catching ... on catching *him*. The money has gone, and I can't live on fresh air for the rest of my days."

We're not covering virgin ground with this conversation, and in some respects, Mum's argument is as sound now as it was the last time we discussed it. Selling the bungalow does make sense, but I know she doesn't want to. This place was meant to be her forever home, and it also happens to be the place where Granddad lived out his final years. It's far more than just bricks and mortar to Mum.

I reach across the table and take her hand.

"Let's just have one last Christmas here, eh? Try to make it one to remember ... for all the right reasons."

Mum returns a thin smile, but it's obvious she's far from convinced that this coming Christmas, or any Christmas for the foreseeable future, will be worth remembering.

"We'll see," she says, quietly.

I don't push back or question her stance, but then I spent seven hours on a plane wondering what other motive Mum might have to rush through the sale of her home. There's an obvious one, and I intend to deal with her tomorrow. Today, after I've enjoyed a few hours' sleep, there are other priorities I need to address.

"Anyway," I say, stifling a yawn. "I suppose I'd better unpack."

"You should have a nap first. You look exhausted."

"To be honest, I was thinking the same. Do you mind?"

"Of course—"

Mum doesn't end her sentence as the sound of the front door slamming shut snares her attention. Seconds later, Paula saunters into the kitchen.

"Gina!" she cries out. "What ... what a lovely surprise."

Paula crosses the floor, her arms open. I stand up, and she pulls me into a hug.

"I thought you were going to let me know when you were coming home," she whispers as we embrace.

"Sorry," I whisper back. "Spur of the moment thing."

Hug administered, Paula releases me and then turns to Mum.

"I bet you're glad to see this one back."

"I've missed her, yes."

"I'm also glad you're back," Paula then says with a grin, returning her attention to me. "I can now pop to the shops this afternoon. You don't mind, do you?"

"Don't be silly. You've already done more than enough, and besides, I'm going to grab a nap for an hour."

Her smiley expression changes in a heartbeat.

"Oh, my God," she blusters. "Your room!"

"Too late," I chuckle. "I've already seen the devastation."

Paula appears genuinely mortified.

"I'll go tidy it now," she says apologetically.

"Don't worry about it. I'm too tired to care."

"No, I insist. If I'd have known you were coming back, I'd have tidied it sooner."

"Honestly, Paula—"

"I'll be five minutes, tops. You carry on chatting to your mum. I'm sure you've still got plenty to tell her about Paris."

Without waiting to hear my objection, Paula hurries away to clean up her chaos.

"I don't know where she gets her energy," Mum remarks. "That woman never seems to stop."

"How's it been, having her stay with you?"

I retake my seat so we can talk without fear of Paula overhearing.

"She's been amazing, but ..."

"But?"

"Between you and me," Mum says in a low voice. "She wears me out."

"How so?"

"Since you left for Paris, we've been shopping in town, to the garden centre twice, the cinema, dinner at a restaurant, and we've been out for a walk on the common every day."

"Um, you'll have to blame me for that. I might have suggested that keeping busy would help ... you know, keep your mind occupied."

"It did, but when you're trying to function on a few hours' sleep, just getting dressed is a drag, never mind anything else."

"Her heart's in the right place."

"I know it is, bless her."

"Maybe you can put your feet up this afternoon. Watch a bit of telly."

"I think I'd like that."

"That's settled then."

I give Mum's hand a quick squeeze and then transfer our mugs to the already full dishwasher. True to her word, Paula breezes in while I'm rooting around the cupboard for a dishwasher tablet.

"All spick and span," she announces. "Well, spick at least."

Both Mum and I thank Paula again, and then I see her and her suitcase out to her car.

"You didn't say anything to your mum about what we discussed, did you?" she asks.

"About Lynn trying to borrow money? No, I gave you my word I wouldn't."

"Thank you."

Paula shuts the car boot and then seems to stall for a moment.

"Are you going to say anything to Lynn?"

"I was planning to pay her a visit tomorrow."

"If you think it'll do any good. You're back now, so it's not as though she can pop over and harass Helen again, is it?"

"No, true."

"Sleeping dogs, Gina."

She gives me another hug and then suggests the three of us go out for cocktails soon. With a promise I'll try to convince Mum, I wave Paula off.

That one physical action drains the last ounce of energy. I need some bloody sleep.

Chapter 31

"For crying out loud," I groan, kicking off the duvet.

It's half seven on a Sunday morning, and I should be fast asleep. My body clock, however, has other ideas. Grabbing a nap yesterday afternoon didn't help. I slept for two hours, and then when I went to bed just after ten, I couldn't sleep. Instead, I put on my detective's hat and tried to fill the time constructively.

Tried, being the operative word.

The duvet discarded, I yawn and then swing my legs out of the bed. Even though I changed the linen yesterday afternoon, the room still carries the faintest hint of Paula's perfume. It's quite sweet, almost sickly so, and I'm not a fan.

Bleary-eyed, I stagger through to the bathroom and park my backside on the toilet. As my bladder empties, I unlock my phone and stare at the web browser tab I left open last night. Seeing it now, in the cold light of day, I'm no more enthusiastic about the data it displays.

The genealogy website confirmed that in the years 1970 to 1979, 4,193 UK birth certificates included the name David Smith. Even if twenty per cent of those David Smiths never made it to their fortieth birthday, it still leaves a pool of 3,354 contenders.

If I researched one of those David Smiths a day, it'd take over nine years to complete the list. Beyond just time, I dread to think what that search would cost, both financially and emotionally.

Before I stumbled upon the genealogy website, I went through the motions of checking the usual sources people turn to when trying to find an individual: Google, Facebook, Twitter, and LinkedIn. Much like my search in New York, I found scores of men named David Smith, but not the actual David Smith who conned my mother. In the end, I had to concede that I face the same problem here I did three thousand miles away — without a way of narrowing down the search parameters, it's futile. So too, is scouring social media platforms, I concluded. Smith isn't stupid, so why publish his personal details online for the authorities or his victims to find?

Frustrated by a lack of progress, and in desperation, I then pulled up the photo of a computer screen I captured in Flatbush. The rental page from the Pinhill Properties website listed a phone number for David Smith, but it didn't tally with the number he gave to pothead Joe. It seems obvious now, but Smith probably has a pocket full of SIM cards he can use and then discard — all random, all untraceable.

With no leads left to follow up, tenuous or otherwise, I'm now inclined to question the suggestion Clement made in the hotel room. I've turned my mind inside out, trying to think of anyone who might fit the bill as David Smith's accomplice, and I cannot think of anyone who would be so cruel. It's so unlikely that there's only one logical conclusion: the theory is just simply wrong. We don't know what was in that envelope, nor do we know who sent it, but it could have contained something as innocuous as a holiday brochure or an auction catalogue. As far as jigsaw pieces go, I can't make the idea of an accomplice fit.

My only remaining hope is to do what I originally planned and contact Essex Police. I can tell them about

Clement's theory regarding an accomplice and let them decide if it's credible or not. As for the man himself, I haven't heard from him since our brief chat on the phone yesterday, so maybe the wings did indeed fall off his plane.

I wash my hands and wander through to the kitchen in need of caffeine.

"Morning."

"Christ, Mum," I pant. "You scared the life out of me."

With my focus on reaching the kettle, I didn't even notice Mum sitting at the table.

"Sorry."

"It's okay. How long have you been up?"

"I lose track," she replies wearily. "An hour or two, maybe."

"You must be exhausted."

"I'm past that stage. If there's a word for how tired I feel, I can't think of it."

After checking there's enough water in the still-warm kettle, I flick the power switch.

"I'll make us both a strong coffee. It might help."

Mum nods, although I wonder how many times she's already filled the empty mug in front of her. It then dawns on me that I'm responsible for Mum's lack of sleep. I meant to return her sleeping pills to the container in the bathroom yesterday but clean forgot.

"Maybe now I'm back, you'll sleep a bit better," I say over my shoulder while ladling an obscene amount of coffee granules into mugs.

"Fat chance," she says so quietly I only just catch it.

I turn around, intent on offering Mum some reassurance, but the sight of her is enough to steal my words. Her elbows resting on the table, head buried in her hands, she looks utterly broken. I swallow back the lump of guilt, but it remains lodged in my chest. I shouldn't have left her.

As much as I need coffee, I step across the kitchen and pull out the chair next to Mum's. I then place my hand on her back.

"It'll all be okay," I say gently, rubbing my hand across her back. "I promise."

"When, though?" she croaks. "It's been two months and ... and I feel as sick today as I did the day it happened."

Now I remember why I went to New York. I went to find the wanker who did this and, quite possibly, kill him.

"It takes time," I say, trying not to let the anger reach my voice. "I know you've been through a traumatic experience, but they say that time is a healer, right? You've got to believe that, Mum."

The kettle rumbles loudly and then turns itself off with a click.

"I'll get that coffee. Then, I was thinking, maybe—"

The doorbell interrupts my suggestion that we pop out for breakfast.

"Who's that at this hour?" Mum sighs, getting to her feet.

"Do you want me to get it?"

"No, it's probably Amazon. I ordered some earplugs yesterday."

Mum wanders towards the hallway, and I return my attention to the much-needed coffee. As I pour water into the mugs and stir, I can just about hear Mum in conversation with someone, although her voice is too distant to hear what's being said. It's unlike the Amazon drivers to stop for a chat, but I suppose the benefit of starting early is they don't have to drop the parcel on the front step, ring the bell, and then dash off back to the van.

I take a sip of coffee and close my eyes to savour the bittersweet taste of morning fuel. Besides the first mouthful of wine at the end of a long day, there are few pleasures in life so quick to impact my mood.

"Gina, you have a guest," Mum suddenly says.

Confused, I put the mug down and turn around.

"Mornin'," Clement booms from the opposite end of the kitchen. "Kettle just boiled, has it?"

I open my mouth, but words fail me. I then glance at my mother, who is staring up at our uninvited guest. Fortunately, her expression is one of mild curiosity rather than abject terror. My expression, on the other hand, is likely similar to that of an inflatable sex doll.

"Wh-what ..." I just about stammer.

"I said, has the kettle just boiled?" Clement casually replies. "I'm gasping for a brew."

I intended to say, what the fuck are you doing here? In hindsight, that would have immediately put Mum on edge, and the last thing I want to do is cause a scene in her kitchen.

"Where are my manners?" Mum then says to herself, suddenly forgetting her woes and switching into hostess mode. "Take a seat, Clement."

Seething, and primed with questions — many, many questions — I reach up into the cupboard for another mug. I've no choice but to sit and smile politely until I can get Clement alone.

I pour the last of the boiling water into the mug and throw a teabag in.

"Sugar?" I bark over my shoulder.

"Three, cheers."

When I turn around, Clement is sitting at the end of the table, and Mum has retaken her seat. Before I get the chance to say anything, she turns to our guest.

"So, how do you two know each other?"

"We bumped into one another in—"

"Paris!" I interject a little too strongly. "Sorry. Paris."

263

I place the mug of tea in front of Clement and glare at him, wide-eyed.

"Yeah, Paris," he then says, casting a sly wink in my direction. "We were queueing up for a baguette by the Eiffel Tower, weren't we?"

"Yes," I reply through gritted teeth.

"Turns out that we've got a lot in common, what with me being an art dealer and all that."

Sweet Jesus.

"Oh, you're an art dealer," Mum coos. "I hope you don't mind me saying, but you don't look like an art dealer."

"You make a good point ... Helen, ain't it?"

"Yes, that's right."

"As I was sayin', Helen, I work with fringe artists. You know, those who don't fit in with the mainstream. I'm like the Screaming Lord Sutch of the London art world."

I've no idea who Screaming Lord Sutch is, but it's a relief that Clement is clearly a seasoned bullshitter.

I sit down and try to steer the conversation towards safer waters.

"Clement's from Camden, aren't you?"

"Yeah, born and bred. You originally from Essex?" he asks Mum.

"No, I was born in Shoreditch and lived there up until my late teens."

"London girl, then," Clement beams. "You and me are gonna get on like a house on fire."

Mum smiles coyly as her cheeks flush pink. If Clement starts flirting with my mother, I will not be held responsible for my actions.

"What brings you to Brentwood at this hour?" she asks.

"That's a good question," I add with just enough scorn to get my point across. "What *does* bring you to Brentwood at this hour?"

"I've got a bit of business to sort out in town later, and I thought to myself, wouldn't it be nice to drop in on Gina? Maybe she'll knock me up a full English?"

Clement fixes me with a stare, accompanied by a defiant smile.

"That's so thoughtful of you," I respond dryly. "What a shame we don't have any sausages or bacon, or even eggs in the fridge."

"Now you've mentioned it," Mum interjects. "I quite fancy a full English."

"There we have it," Clement says, clapping his hands together. "I'll nip out and grab some bacon, sausages, and what have you."

I don't appreciate being railroaded, but maybe this is the ideal opportunity to question Clement without Mum present.

"You don't know where the nearest shop is, so I'll tag along," I announce, getting to my feet. "Give me two minutes to get ready."

It's testament to how little I want to leave Clement alone with my mother, that it takes less than sixty seconds to change. As I hurry back towards the kitchen doorway, I catch the end of Mum's sentence.

"... very proud of her."

"Yeah, she's a feisty little thing, no mistake."

"Ready?" I cough, entering the kitchen.

They both turn to face me. Clement nods.

"We'll only be twenty minutes, Mum. Will you be okay?"

"I'm sure I'll be fine for twenty minutes," she replies, rolling her eyes.

I usher Clement out of the kitchen and through the front door, waiting until we're at the end of the driveway before letting loose.

"What the hell are you playing at?" I snap. "Turning up here unannounced."

"That's some welcome," Clement huffs before jamming a cigarette in his mouth.

"Do you blame me for being irritated? How the hell did you even find Mum's address?"

"Ain't that many people called Helen Jackson living in Brentwood, Doll."

"That doesn't answer my question."

"Seeing as there ain't no phone books these days, or even bleedin' phone boxes, I told the cab driver I'd give him a hundred bucks if he could find your mum's address. It only took him a minute to find it on his phone."

"What? Why bribe him in dollars?"

"It's all I had on me. The cabby didn't seem to care."

It appears Mum forgot to opt out of having her phone number and address publicly listed when she moved into the bungalow. It might explain why she receives so much junk mail.

"And what did you intend to do if that cabby had drawn a blank?"

"I'd have given you a bell, but I thought you'd enjoy the surprise."

"Well, you got that wrong."

"Did I wake you up or somethin'?"

"No, we were both awake. I'm annoyed because ... because you don't understand the situation with Mum."

"You told me most of it."

"What I didn't tell you is how she's coping. Or not coping, to be precise."

"That why you told her you've been in Paris, eh?"

"Exactly."

"Why lie to her?"

"I could hardly tell her I was heading to New York to search for the man who destroyed her life. She'd have done everything possible to talk me out of it."

266

"Don't she wanna find the bloke who robbed her blind?"

"Of course she does, but not so badly she'd let her only child hunt him down. Mum would have told me it was too risky, too dangerous."

"And now?"

"And now, what?"

"Now you're back safe and sound, you gonna fess up? Tell her where you've been, what you know?"

"Absolutely not."

"That's a pity."

"Why is it?"

"I was gonna have a chat with her."

"About what, exactly?"

"Your mum knows more about that Smith bloke than anyone, and if we're gonna find him, she's the one who'll put us on the right path."

I come to a stop, partly because we have to cross the road, but mainly to reinforce the point I'm about to make.

"I've already decided to pass on what we now know to the police. I don't want Mum getting involved."

"Bit late for that, ain't it?"

"I mean, I don't want to put her through any more torment."

"And you reckon she'll be just fine, eh? Give it a few months, and she'll forget all about it?"

"No, I just—"

"And what about David bleedin' Smith? How many more women is he gonna rip off? Don't that bother you?"

"Of course it does, which is why I said I'll speak to the police."

"I didn't have you down as a quitter, Doll, and you ain't gonna want to hear this, but your mum won't ever get over what he did ... unless she gets justice."

"Did you hear me? I'm not quitting — I'm letting the police take the reins."

"Right," Clement huffs. "Fat lot of use that'll do. Even if they get off their arses and look for him, they won't find the bloke. And, if by some miracle they do, what do you reckon will happen? I doubt it'll even reach court, and it won't matter anyway, as he'll have stashed your mum's money away. She won't see a penny of it."

We cross the road in silence, although Clement's sermon continues ringing in my ears.

"I'll say one more thing," he then adds. "Do you know what your mum needs more than anything?"

"Time to heal."

"Nah, that's bullshit, and you know it. She needs hope."

"Hope for what, exactly?"

"That the world ain't as shit as she currently thinks it is. You ain't even gonna tell her that you're passing the buck to the Old Bill."

"I ... no, I'm not passing the buck. I'm protecting my mother."

"From what? That ship has sailed, Doll."

Clement suddenly stops and puts his hand on my shoulder — not forcibly, but with enough pressure to halt my stride.

"Tell me something," he then says. "If your granddad were still around, what would he do?"

"Not much. He was crippled with arthritis."

"Don't be a smartarse. It ain't your style."

"I don't know what Granddad would do," I sigh.

"Yeah, you do. He'd fight for his family until he had nothing left to give. That's what blokes of his generation did. They sure as fuck didn't give up or go whining to the Old Bill."

I take a moment to actually consider Clement's question, rather than his assumption.

"He'd spend every waking hour trying to find Smith. And when he found him — and he *would* find him — he'd probably beat the living daylights out of him."

"It was your granddad's money he took, weren't it?"

"Yes," I gulp. "Everything he worked his entire life for."

"Then don't let this go. It ain't just your mum who's gotta live with what that tosser did. You've gotta live with it, too."

I look up at the ashen sky and close my eyes for a moment. A picture floats into my mind of Granddad in his yard, toiling away day after day, week after week, for more years than I've lived. I then picture his face on the day he proudly told us how much he'd sold that yard for. He wasn't proud because he'd made an unwittingly astute investment — he was proud because he knew his girls would never have to worry about money ever again. He gave us that security, and for that very reason, I know he died a contented man.

No one is content now, and Granddad's legacy is in tatters.

Chapter 32

Clement offers to carry the bag. I don't object.

We leave the mini-mart and wander back up the road. Besides a brief debate about sausages as we stood in front of the chiller cabinet, we've both had little to say since our previous conversation. On my part, it's because I'm still trying to make sense of a dilemma I thought I'd resolved. On Clement's part, I have a theory. Now he's said his piece he doesn't have to say anything else. It's an effective strategy and one I wouldn't have credited to a man like Clement. Then again, I can safely say I've never met a man like him before, so maybe I'm doing him a disservice.

"I can't tell her I went to New York," I say as we amble along.

"I know."

"She'll be so upset I lied and—"

"I get it, Doll. You don't wanna make a bad situation worse."

"So, how do I let her know what we've unearthed if I can't tell her the truth?"

"Looks like I'll have to admit a small white lie. I'll tell her I ain't an art dealer."

"I don't think she'll take much convincing. Of all the professions you could have chosen, art dealer would be the last I'd have gone for."

"It was that," Clement chuckles. "Or I tell her I'm your gynaecologist."

"Err, overlooking the question of why my gynaecologist would pop by on a Sunday morning, you look even less like a gynaecologist than you do an art dealer."

"I've seen my fair share of fannies over the years, so I reckon I could wing it."

"That's ... nice," I cringe. "Can we get back to the problem at hand, please?"

"It ain't a problem. We just tell your mum you hired me to look for Smith, and I've just got back from New York. It ain't far from the truth, so she won't suspect anything."

I chew Clement's idea over for a few seconds.

"You know, that's actually not a bad plan."

"Told you that problem solving is my speciality."

"Don't get too cocky. I'm still not entirely convinced it's a good idea to involve Mum, but if we do tell her what we've discovered, you cannot mention your accomplice theory."

"Why not?"

"Because Mum's a trusting soul, maybe too trusting, and she'd be distraught to think someone close to her might be involved."

"Fair enough. I won't mention it."

"Good, and I have to say that I'm not convinced it's a plausible theory, anyway. I went through a list of everyone Mum knows yesterday, and I can't imagine anyone on that list being callous enough to aid a conman. It's just too much of a stretch."

"You might be right, but don't discount it."

"I won't. Just don't even hint at it to Mum, okay?"

"Yeah, yeah. I hear you."

We cross the road again, retracing our steps back toward the bungalow.

"How you wanna play this?" Clement then asks.

"What do you mean?"

"You gonna sit your mum down and tell her everything, or do you want me to tell her?"

"Um, I don't know yet. Let me think about it."

"We'll have breakfast first, right? I'm starving."

"Yes, we'll have breakfast first."

"Nice one."

"Oh, and one other point. When you're talking to Mum, be patient and be gentle with her."

"Course."

"I mean it. Over the last week, I've seen you use blackmail, bribery, and casual violence to get information. You be on your best behaviour with my mother, or it won't be just David Smith receiving a swift kick in the nuts."

"Understood," Clement says with a snort of laughter. "And that's more like it."

"What is?"

"You, remembering why this matters and getting riled up again. It's good to see."

"Well, I am a feisty little thing," I reply with a wry smile.

"Yeah, that you are."

We arrive back at the bungalow in a better position than we left. My primary concern is no longer Clement turning up unannounced but the impending difficult conversation with Mum. As I unpack the groceries, I reassure myself with the knowledge that she's already at rock bottom, so whatever I say, it's unlikely to make matters worse. Unlikely, but not impossible.

"Do you need a hand, Love?" Mum asks as I place a pan on the hob.

"Yes, please."

I don't need a hand, but Mum seems happier when she's busy. By happier, I mean less likely to break down in tears.

"Want me to do anything, Doll?" Clement calls across from the table where he's reading a newspaper.

"It's all in hand, thanks."

The benefit of a full English breakfast is that it doesn't take long to throw together. Mum deals with the eggs and beans while I fry up the sausages and bacon. I don't know if you'd call it a *full* full English, but it's close enough.

We transfer the plates to the table and settle down to eat.

"When was the last time you visited Shoreditch?" Clement asks Mum while ruthlessly stabbing a sausage with his fork.

"I haven't been there since my dad moved out, seven or eight years ago now."

"Bet it ain't like the place you remember as a kid."

"Far from it. Now it's full of young, trendy types with silly hair and no sense of humour."

"Not a place for the working class these days, eh?"

"Sadly not, but that's progress, I suppose. What people with money want, people with money get."

"You ain't wrong, Doll," Clement replies before biting into his sausage.

The small talk continues until all three plates are empty. I don't know if it was the hearty breakfast or Clement's talk of old London Town, but Mum seems less subdued than when I first stumbled into the kitchen this morning. It's as good a time as any to roll the dice.

"Mum," I say in a cautious tone. "I don't want you to overthink this, but there's something I need to tell you."

"What is it?" she replies, swallowing hard.

"It's nothing to worry about, but I might have told you a teeny white lie about Clement's profession, and why he dropped by this morning."

Mum looks quizzically at Clement.

273

"Truth is, Doll," the big man says before I can continue. "I ain't an art dealer — I'm a private investigator."

"A what?"

"You know, like Columbo, but without the badge ... or the rain mac."

"I don't understand," Mum says, and by her tone of voice, she really doesn't.

"I asked Clement to help me find Bruce Franklin."

The fuse lit, I pause for a moment and await the potential explosion. There's no immediate reaction other than my mother's puzzled frown.

"Why?" she eventually asks. "The police said there aren't any leads to follow."

"The police couldn't find their own arses in the dark," Clement responds. "And we — I mean, I've — unearthed a few interesting facts about the man who stole your money."

Mum turns to me. "You told Clement about what happened?"

"I had to. I needed his help."

"Don't you think I've suffered enough humiliation without you discussing what that man did with complete strangers?"

"It's not like that, Mum. Clement is our best chance of finding David Smith."

"That's hardly the point," she snaps. "And who the hell is David Smith?"

"He's the man who ripped you off," Clement replies. "That's his real name, and he ain't a Yank. He's as British as you and me."

Mum sits back in her seat and stares into space. Helen Jackson is the woman who gave birth to me, nurtured me through infancy, witnessed my first words and my first steps, and guided me through school. She is my mother,

274

and yet, looking at her now, I couldn't hazard a guess at what she's thinking.

"Mum? Are you okay?"

She doesn't respond to my question, but ever so slowly, she turns her head in Clement's direction.

"What else did you find out?" she asks.

"Cold comfort, Doll, but you ain't the only one he's ripped off. He's been at it across The Pond, but thankfully for us, he made a few mistakes along the way."

"There are others? Women like me?"

"There are, and I met one, so yeah. He's a serial conman, and that's why I intend to find the fucker and put a stop to him."

"What did he do to the woman you met?"

Clement relays the lowlights of Evelyn Conroy's encounter with David Smith. When he's finished, Mum shakes her head.

"That poor woman."

"And you can bet your last farthing there are plenty more," Clement says.

There's a slight change in Mum's demeanour, almost as if she's just remembered where she left a misplaced pair of gloves or her car keys. It is, perhaps, relief.

"I thought it was just me," she then murmurs. "Silly old Helen Jackson — the only woman stupid and desperate enough to marry a conman."

"Oi, enough of that," Clement chides. "You ain't done nothing wrong, and you ain't stupid."

"Am I not?" Mum bites back. "No offence, Clement, but you don't know me."

"No, I don't, but that's the point of me being here. I need your help."

"With what?"

"Finding David Smith. I was hoping we could have a chat to see if there's anything you remember that might point us in the right direction."

275

"Hasn't Gina already told you everything?"

"Yeah, but it ain't the same as hearing it from you. If we're gonna find this bloke, I bet it'll be down to some small detail he overlooked. It always is."

"Do you really think that?"

"Wouldn't be wasting my time if I didn't, Doll."

"What about the police? Shouldn't we tell them what you've found?"

Clement gives his moustache a quick stroke and then rests his meaty forearms on the table.

"Could do, but let me ask you a question. What would your old man do?"

Mentioning Granddad is a risky strategy that I wish Clement had discussed with me. It might have stoked my determination, but it could have the opposite effect on Mum.

"I've never told anyone before," she then says, straightening her shoulders. "But my dad kept an old World War II revolver in one of his tool chests. I only know this because, back in the day, we had some bother with a lad who kept pestering my kid sister, Lynn. That lad didn't heed Dad's first warning, and he showed up at the house one evening, drunk as a skunk and making all kinds of threats. Dad collared him and stuck that pistol in his mouth — said he'd save the bullet for the next time that lad showed up. We never saw sight nor sound of him again."

I'm slightly taken aback by Mum's anecdote. The man she described doesn't correspond with the sweet-natured gent I knew, but then I guess it shows how far a man will go to protect those he loves.

"Does that answer your question?" Mum continues.

"Yeah, it does."

Mum then turns to me.

"Put the kettle on, please, Love. Clement and I need to talk."

Chapter 33

After performing my tea-making duties, I return to the table with three steaming mugs.

"Cheers," Clement grunts.

"Thank you," Mum says. "You can leave us now."

Having not retaken my seat, I stare down at my mother.

"Pardon?"

"I'd rather do this without you here."

"Charming."

"No, you don't understand, Love. If I'm to relive every awful moment of what that man did, I don't want you suffering with me."

"I've been there from the beginning, Mum. I know better than anyone what he's done to you."

"Which is why I don't want you to go through it again. It's about time I did what a mum is supposed to do and protect her daughter."

"I'm touched, but ... well, you don't even know Clement."

"You're worried about leaving me alone with him?"

"No, but ... um, it's just—"

"Do you trust this man, Gina?" Mum asks, nodding across at Clement.

Her question throws me, and internally, at least, I flounder for an answer. I can't deny that the big man has given me every reason to trust him, and the bricks are certainly mounting up, but I'm still wary. It's not his fault — that would be the last person I placed my faith in. The person I entrusted with my heart, only for them to crush it.

Clement isn't that person, though, and it's unfair to judge him on another's actions.

"Yes, Mum. I trust him."

"Then that's good enough for me. Why don't you go and watch TV or have a nice soak in the bath while we talk?"

I glance across the table at Clement, hoping he'll put to bed the last of my lingering doubts.

"If you're gonna have a bath, don't be in there too long," he says with a faint grin. "I'm gonna need a turf out in about half an hour. It's the beans, you see."

"You are truly disgusting, Clement," I groan. "But I think I'll watch TV, anyway."

I throw Mum a parting smile, hoping it provides some assurance that the man she's about to unburden to isn't totally obsessed with his toilet schedule.

Once I've made myself comfortable on the sofa, I switch the TV on and scan the guide for something worth watching. Who knows if Clement's conversation with Mum will prove worthwhile, but fretting about it won't change the outcome. I need a distraction.

Twenty minutes into a show about unruly dogs and their frankly idiotic owners, my eyelids begin to droop. The solitary coffee hasn't helped ease my tiredness, and I'm not inclined to fight the sudden urge to sleep.

At some point, the sound of the lounge door opening snaps me back to reality. Blinking hard, I glance up at Clement, leaning against the door frame.

"Must have nodded off," I rasp. "Are you done?"

"Yeah."

I sit up and cough a couple of times to clear my throat. Then, I notice the time.

"You've been chatting for over an hour," I remark. "Is Mum okay?"

"She's fine. Just putting some washing on or something."

"Did you get anywhere?"

"Dunno. Maybe."

"What does that mean?"

"It means, Doll, I ain't sure."

"Nothing obvious, then?"

"If it were obvious, I wouldn't be standing here scratching my arse."

His remark is figurative rather than literal, thankfully.

"Right. So, what do we do next?"

Clement looks over his shoulder, craning his neck to see up the hallway before turning to face me again.

"You need to have another think," he says in a low voice.

"About what?"

"Who helped Smith, 'cos I'm pretty bleedin' sure someone did."

"I told you, I can't think of anyone who'd stoop so low."

"He had help. I'm sure of it."

"I know you think that, but it's just a theory based on a single envelope sent to Smith from the UK. It's a heck of a stretch to assume he had an accomplice, let alone someone Mum knows."

"It ain't just the envelope. Do you know how that arsehole got your mum to fall for his con?"

"As much as it kills me to admit it, he was a charmer. We all fell for his act."

"Yeah, but you didn't get the soul mate treatment, did you?"

"The what?"

"Your mum ever tell you she thought she'd met her soul mate?"

"Err, a few times, yes."

"Why'd she think that?"

"It's just something people say when they're in love, isn't it?"

Clement snorts what might be a laugh but could be derision. "I take it you ain't ever met your soul mate?"

I shrink into the sofa. "This isn't about me. What's your point?"

"The first time they went out together in London, they went to a Greek restaurant that Smith booked in advance, right?"

"Um, yes."

"What's your mum's favourite film?"

"Uh?"

"Just answer the question, Doll."

"Her favourite film is *Mamma Mia*. She must have watched it dozens of times."

"Smith took her to that Greek restaurant and told her he'd chosen it because he loved Greek food and dreamed of spending a summer on a Greek island one day... just like the island featured in his favourite film, *Mamma Mia*."

"Bloody hell, Clement," I scoff. "That film was massively popular, particularly with middle-aged women. Christ, he might as well have said he liked prosecco and Michael Bublé."

"Dunno who that is, but how about Disaronno? Is that massively popular 'cos I ain't ever heard of it?"

"Pardon?"

"Disaronno. It's your mum's favourite tipple, ain't it?"

Personally, I can't stand the sweet, almond-flavoured amaretto, but Mum adores it.

"Yes, it is."

"Bit odd that Smith was also a fan of the stuff. He ordered a glass at the end of their meal."

"Okay, I concede that's less of a coincidence, but it's not beyond the realm of possibility that Smith just struck lucky."

"No, it ain't, but then the next day, he booked tickets for a West End show. Don't suppose you remember which one?"

"*Moulin Rouge*. Mum's wanted to see it for years."

"I know — she told me. She never told Smith, though."

I sit up, my attention suddenly piqued.

"Didn't she?"

"Nope, and I could go on if you like, but we'd be here all day. The bottom line, Doll, is that Smith convinced your mum that they were soul mates. And she believed him 'cos they had so much in common. Too bleedin' much when you think about it."

I cast my mind back to the time Mum spent with the man she thought was called Bruce Franklin, and all I can remember is how happy she was. And there was never any reason to question that happiness. She was in love, simple as that.

"I know it makes sense, but ..."

I'm unable to finish my sentence because what Clement is suggesting still seems so improbable.

"The bloke is good-looking, right?"

"If you like that kind of thing, yes, I suppose."

"And a charmer?"

"As I said, yes."

"I've met plenty of good-looking charmers over the years, but what Smith had in mind needed more than just a square jawline and the gift of the gab. If you're gonna convince a woman you've only met half a dozen times to trust you beyond all doubt, you need 'em to fall quick and fall hard."

"I guess."

"Best way to do that is to prove you're soul mates — destined to be together."

Clement then glances up the hallway again.

"You sure you can't think of anyone who might have told Smith all this stuff about your mum? A friend she only sees now and then, or a family member she's not on good terms with ... or an ex?"

The mention of an ex sends my thoughts spinning towards one man. My estranged father is certainly a grade-A arsehole, but we've had nothing to do with him for years. I doubt he even remembers Mum's middle name, let alone her favourite alcoholic beverage.

"Mum doesn't have a huge circle of friends," I confirm. "She has plenty of friendly acquaintances, but she met most of them through classes at the gym. None of them know Mum that well, though."

"What about family?"

"I haven't seen my dad in decades or anyone on his side of the family. Since my grandparents passed, there's just me, Mum, and my Aunt Lynn."

"Any issues with your aunt?"

"You could say that," I huff. "She had an affair with Mum's husband — my dad — when she was in her late teens. They then pissed off up north and moved in together."

"You ain't a fan, I take it?"

"I can't stand her, but that doesn't mean ..."

I let my words hang, allowing a few seconds for my thoughts to catch up.

"What?" Clement prompts.

"I can't stand Lynn, but, as Mum keeps reminding me, what she did happened a long time ago."

"Yeah, but?"

"Who said there's a but?"

"Your boat did."

"Oh, it's just ... no, she wouldn't do that to her own sister."

"She shagged her brother-in-law and then set up home with the bloke. That's not exactly sisterly, is it?"

"Well, no."

"Was there any beef with your granddad's will? Did she get less than your mum?"

"No, they both got the exact same amount. Mum put hers in a savings account, but Lynn and her sucker of a husband blew their share on ..."

Two thoughts land simultaneously. That money pit of a hotel and Paula's revelation that Lynn asked Mum for a hundred-grand loan.

"What is it, Doll?"

I clamber up off the sofa and usher Clement into the lounge before closing the door.

"What you got your knickers in a twist about?"

"It's more than likely nothing," I reply, keeping my voice to barely a whisper. "But I found out that before Smith robbed Mum, she'd agreed to lend Lynn a hundred grand. And it's just a suspicion, but I also think she's been harassing Mum to sell the bungalow. No prizes for guessing why."

"What does she want the money for?"

"They bought a hotel with Granddad's money and then spent hundreds of thousands on repairs. I think the money ran out, and now the business is floundering."

Before he even does it, I know what Clement is about to do. He raises his hand towards his mouth.

"Could be something," he says.

"It's a terrible ... no, wait. We can cross Lynn from the list of suspects."

"Why?"

"Because she asked to borrow money *before* Smith emptied Mum's bank accounts?"

"You know that for sure, do you?"

"No, but what does it matter? If she was helping Smith, it's safe to assume that her motive was a cut of his ill-gotten gains. In which case, why would she ask to borrow that hundred grand?"

"You've answered your own question, Doll."

"Eh? How?"

"You've dismissed your aunt as a suspect because she asked to borrow money. If she was involved with Smith, just asking to borrow money shifts suspicion, don't it?"

"Christ," I mutter. "I thought I had trust issues, but you're on a different level."

"All I'm saying is that her asking to borrow money might have been a smokescreen. And it worked, didn't it?"

I puff a long sigh and fold my arms.

"Alright, let's run with your theory that Smith had an accomplice, and although I'm a long way from convinced it could be her, Lynn is our chief suspect. How do we prove it one way or the other?"

"Dunno about proving it, but it'd be good to have a chat with the woman, eyeball to eyeball."

"I was actually thinking about talking to her myself at some point today."

"Leave it. We'll see her tomorrow."

"Why wait?"

"Don't you wanna spend some time with your mum?"

"Um, yes ... obviously."

"Then we'll go tomorrow. Besides, I've already got plans for today."

"What are you up to?"

"Sorting out somewhere to stay for the night. I passed a B&B on the way here, so I'll likely check in there."

"And that's the extent of your plans?"

"Nope. I'm gonna find a proper British pub, enjoy a few pints of proper British beer, and tuck into a proper British roast dinner."

284

"I almost envy you."

"I'd invite you along, but to be honest, Doll, I just wanna sit on my arse and savour being back home. I ain't 'alf missed being here."

"Fair enough," I reply with a thin smile. "I'll see you tomorrow."

"Yeah, you will. I'll give you a bell in the morning, alright?"

"Sure."

With a parting nod, Clement steps over to the door and opens it. He then pauses a second.

"Oh, yeah," he says over his shoulder. "Look after your mum, and remember what I said."

"Err, remind me."

"She don't need pity. She needs hope."

Don't we all, Clement. Don't we all.

Chapter 34

It proves quite the boon to get eight hours of solid sleep. Even though it's a Monday morning, and pissing down outside, I feel pretty good. Mum is still in bed, enjoying a lie-in, which I hope is in part because of yesterday's events but also because I returned her sleeping pills to the bottle in the bathroom.

Although she didn't say much about her chat with Clement, there was a slight but noticeable upturn in her mood for the rest of the day. We watched a movie together in the afternoon and then ordered a Chinese takeaway for dinner, accompanied by a bottle of wine. As much as I wanted to ask how she felt about the big man, I didn't want to tempt fate. For me, it was enough just to spend a quiet, relaxing day in Mum's company, without any drama or emotional turbulence.

As Mum said before heading to bed, it was a good day. That said, her bar for a good day is set pretty low. She didn't cry or, to the best of my knowledge, drift off to that dark space she's inhabited all too frequently in the last few months.

She is, as I had to remind myself this morning, still £1.9 million poorer, though. I've told her countless times that it's only money, and money alone is no guarantee of happiness, but we both know I'm side-stepping the point. It's not that Mum doesn't have the money — it's that David Smith does.

That's my motivation for continuing the search, even though I'm concerned we're now clutching at straws. Actually, we might even be clutching at thin air, but I've decided to place my trust in Clement until he gives up. It should probably be the other way around, but for reasons I still can't understand, he has the tenacity of a bull terrier with a stick. He just won't let it go, even though the stick isn't his.

"Morning, Love," Mum says with a yawn as she shuffles into the kitchen.

"Eight-thirty?" I reply with a chuckle. "What time do you call this?"

"I could sleep for a week, and I'd still need to catch up."

I get up and guide Mum to my still-warm chair.

"Sit down, and I'll make you a coffee. The kettle hasn't long boiled."

"Thank you."

I quickly make Mum a large mug of coffee and return to the table.

"Do you have any plans today?" she asks.

"Err, yes. I'm heading out with Clement later. I shouldn't be more than a couple of hours."

"What are you up to?"

"It's um ... nothing, really."

"You don't want to tell me, do you?"

"No, it's not that. It's just—"

"You're worried I might get my hopes up. Is that it?"

"A bit. Maybe."

Mum reaches across the table and clasps her hand around mine.

"The fact you're even trying means a lot to me. As for Clement, I don't know where you found him, or how you're paying for his time, but I am grateful."

I don't want to suggest that her gratitude might be premature, and I certainly don't want to get into a conversation about Clement's involvement. I settle on a wan smile, and Mum turns her attention to the steaming mug of coffee.

"Anyway," I announce, brightly. "I'm starving. Fancy some breakfast?"

"I'll do it."

"How about I cook, and you clean up?"

"Go on then."

Craving normality, I knock up scrambled eggs on toast, and we swap small talk until our plates are empty. Mum then fulfils her part of the deal, leaving me to focus on the practicalities of my mission this morning.

"Oh, do you mind if I borrow your car?" I ask.

My car failed its MOT a few weeks ago, and I haven't had time to organise the repairs, so it's sitting in a parking bay back at my flat.

"You don't have to ask."

"Thanks. I'm just going to grab a quick shower."

"Okay, Love."

Mum swaps my conversation for the radio, tuned to a station dedicated to seventies music. I exit the kitchen with the Bay City Rollers bidding me *Bye, Bye, Baby*.

After I've finished in the bathroom and thrown on a pair of jeans and a sweatshirt, I make a quick call to Clement.

"Hello," he answers gruffly.

"Morning. It's me ... Gina."

"Alright, Doll. What's up?"

"Nothing. I was just double-checking you're still up for visiting Lynn."

"Yeah. What time?"

"I can pick you up in half an hour?"

"Should be alright. I'm just cleaning my pants in the sink at the moment."

"Thanks for the share," I groan. "What's the address of the B&B?"

"It's called Mugford House. Queens Road, I think."

"Don't worry, I'll find it. I'll see you soon."

"Alright."

I end the call with the simple tap of an icon on the screen. If only it were so easy to dismiss the mental image of Clement scrubbing the gusset of his underpants. I inwardly shudder.

After double-checking the contents of my bag, I slip on a jacket. I'm about to inspect my appearance in the dressing table mirror when the doorbell rings.

"I'll get it," I call out while hurrying through to the hallway.

When I open the front door, I'm mildly surprised to see Paula on the doorstep.

"Oh, hi."

"Morning, sweetheart."

She then hands me a couple of letters.

"You're moonlighting as a postwoman now, are you?"

"Work isn't that tight, yet," she chuckles. "No, I arrived just as your postman was heading up the drive. Thought I'd do my good deed for the day and save him the walk."

"Ahh, right."

"I actually dropped by because I seem to have lost my laptop cable. I don't suppose you've come across it, have you?"

"No, but that doesn't mean it's not in the bedroom."

I stand back and wave Paula in. "Feel free to have a look."

She joins me in the hallway, wiping her feet on the mat.

"How's your mum today?" she asks in a low voice.

"She's not too bad. We had a nice day yesterday, just relaxing."

"That's good. Any plans for today?"

"I'm heading out soon for an hour or two, and I think Mum planned on catching up on the soaps."

"Would you like me to hang around until you get back?"

"I can't ask you to do that, Paula. You've already done more than enough."

"Don't be daft," she replies, placing her hand on my upper arm. "It's hardly a chore, is it? And besides, I don't have anything in my diary until this afternoon, so I'm happy to have a coffee and a natter."

"If you're sure?"

"Positive."

"I'll go let Mum know while you hunt for your cable."

Mum, as it turns out, is indifferent about having company, but she's too polite to decline the offer.

"I'll be back before noon," I confirm, pecking a kiss on Mum's cheek. "Do you need anything while I'm out?"

"No, thanks."

Having completed her search, Paula returns from the bedroom.

"Any luck?" I ask.

"It's not in there," she sighs. "Guess I'll have to pop into town later and buy a new one."

"It'll probably cost as much to park as it will to buy a new cable," Mum remarks.

I leave them in the lounge, discussing the exorbitant cost of parking in the town centre.

Once I've moved the seat in Mum's car, I double-check the exact location of Clement's B&B on Queens Road. It's only a five-minute drive, but long enough for the doubts to creep back in. As much as I dislike Lynn, what I'm about to do could hammer an insurmountable wedge into what's left of our family. That assumes she had nothing to do with David Smith's plot, and I'm still struggling to believe Lynn is capable of destroying her own sister's life. If it wasn't for the fact she already double-crossed Mum once, I doubt very much I'd be willing to take such a risk.

Still, as they say on every TV police drama, at least I can eliminate Lynn from our enquiries.

I don't have to look too hard for Mugford House, as there's a distinctive and imposing figure leaning up against a lamppost outside. I pull over and lower the passenger's window.

"Morning," I shout.

Clement ambles over and gets in.

"Alright?" he grunts.

"I'm okay. What's the B&B like?" I ask, looking up at the tatty sign fixed to the front gate.

"Not bad. The landlady cooks a decent breakfast ... and she's easy on the eye."

"Easy on the eye?" I parrot.

"You know: nice arse, great set of knockers."

I turn to my passenger, mouth agape.

"What?" he says innocently. "You asked."

"I know what easy on the eye means, Clement. I didn't need the 1970s-style translation."

"Women," he groans, shaking his head. "Moan when you don't get compliments, moan when you do."

"I don't think your landlady will see your objectification as a compliment."

"We'll see about that tonight, won't we?"

"Will we?"

"You won't, but I will. She promised me a slap-up meal later, and I can have whatever I fancy for afters."

"Bloody hell. Are you staying in a B&B or the set of a *Carry On* film?"

"Wouldn't have thought you'd know what a *Carry On* film is, Doll."

"My granddad was a fan. I watched one or two when I was a kid."

"I quite fancied Babs Windsor," Clement remarks, putting his seatbelt on. "Even though she was a short-arse, like you, and just as gobby."

"I ... is that an insult or a compliment?"

"Neither. We gonna get going, or what?"

I roll my eyes, check the mirror, and pull away. A few hundred yards on, at a junction, I glance left and catch my passenger stroking his moustache.

"Something on your mind?" I ask.

"Just wondering how you wanna play this?"

"I confront Lynn about the hundred grand, gauge her reaction, and then go from there."

"And how are you gonna explain me being there?"

"I haven't thought that far."

"Want my advice? Just tell her I'm an old friend from out of town."

"Hmm, okay."

"It's that, or you tell her I'm your new fella."

"Jesus Christ," I cough. "Lynn might be a lot of things, but she isn't stupid. You could not be less my type, Clement."

"And you ain't mine."

"No, I mean, you *really* aren't my type."

"Fuck me, Doll," he huffs. "I get it, alright."

"Good."

Clement doesn't strike me as the type to be easily offended, but he doesn't say another word until we reach the A127 dual carriageway that leads all the way to Basildon.

"What is your type?" he asks, deciding to resurrect the conversation.

"I don't know if I have a type, as such."

"What was your last fella like?"

"He was a dick."

"How long ago did he dump you?"

292

"I beg your pardon," I reply indignantly. "It was me who dumped him, actually ... and it was five years ago."

"Bleedin' hell," Clement snorts. "You ain't had nookie in five years? No wonder you're a bit tetchy."

"I'm not ... what? Nookie? Who the hell calls it that?"

"I do, and you didn't answer my question."

"Did you ask me a question? I just heard a thinly veiled insult."

"Five years?"

"You asked when I split up with my *last fella*. That was five years ago."

"Yeah, I heard that part."

"I've had another relationship since. We were together, kind of, for a little over two years."

If Clement is as intuitive as I think he is, there's nothing left for me to explain. The prolonged silence suggests he either didn't understand or he's wisely decided not to comment further.

"What happened, then?" he asks after a minute or so. "With the bird you were seeing?"

"It's complicated," I reply, almost on autopilot.

"Wanna tell me the non-complicated version?"

"Not really. It's still ... it didn't end well."

"So, I weren't far off then? *She* dumped you."

"Has anyone ever told you, Clement, that sometimes it's best to leave your thoughts in your head, unspoken?"

"Yeah, granted — tact ain't my strong point."

"Really?" I gush with mock surprise. "I'd never have guessed."

"But she did dump you, right?"

"You can also add empathy to the list of social skills you're lacking. I don't want to talk about it."

"Alright," he says, holding his hands up. "I get the message."

"Good."

I begin a count in my head. By my reckoning, if he doesn't say anything before I reach ten, there's a good chance he did get the message. I reach six, and he clears his throat.

"I knew a few lezzas back in the day. None of 'em looked like you, mind."

"Lezza?" I reply scornfully. "Seriously, Clement?"

"Lesbian, then."

"Who said I was a lesbian?"

"I hate to break it to you, Doll, but if you're a bird and you're partial to a bit of fanny, that makes you a lezz ... a lesbian."

"You've never heard the term bisexual before? And did you not hear me say I don't want to talk about it?"

"You said you didn't wanna talk about the bird who dumped you. You never said we couldn't talk about you batting for both teams."

"How would you feel if I asked you about your sexual preferences? Actually, don't answer that."

"I'm just curious, that's all."

I turn and fix him with a suitably frosty glare. "Do you remember what curiosity did for the cat?"

"Fair dos. Won't say another word."

Almost at the exact moment Clement finishes his sentence, we pass a sign indicating Basildon is three miles away.

"We'll be there in less than ten minutes," I remark, drawing an indelible line under the prior conversation.

"Righto."

As I indicate to exit the dual-carriageway, I do what I've tried to do for months and compartmentalise thoughts of *her*. The heartache I suffered was insignificant when compared to what David bloody Smith put Mum through. And, whilst my broken heart might be beyond repair, I'll do anything I can to patch up Mum's, even if it means pissing off her sister in the process.

Chapter 35

I pull into one of the many empty parking bays and kill the engine. The Haywain Hotel is directly ahead.

"Looks like the Crossroads Motel," Clement remarks, slipping off his seatbelt.

"The what?"

"You never heard of *Crossroads*?"

"No. Should I?"

"It was a TV soap set in a motel ... Birmingham way, if memory serves."

I know nothing about the Crossroads Motel, but I do know that the characterless building across the car park is fifty-odd years old, and it was known as the Haywain Motel until Lynn and Stephen purchased it last year and swapped the M for an H. I remember them telling Mum that they decided to buy it because they wanted to avoid the usual problems associated with an older building. What they hadn't factored in was the liberal use of asbestos in the construction industry during the sixties and seventies, including, as they later discovered, all thirty-six bedrooms of the Haywain Hotel.

That was the start of their problems and if the scaffolding covering one-third of the building is any barometer, not the last.

"You sure she'll be there?" Clement asks as we make our way across the car park.

"They can't afford staff, so there's no one else to work on reception."

"I see," he replies thoughtfully.

We enter the double doors to the reception area. Besides the low-key classical music piped from speakers in the ceiling, it's eerily quiet for a hotel. A figure appears through a doorway behind the reception desk.

"Gina," Stephen blurts. "Lovely to see you."

I've often wondered how Stephen ended up with Lynn because they have such different personalities. She's hard-nosed, cold, and controlling, while her husband is a nervy, people pleaser. A doormat, some might say.

"Hi, Stephen," I say, approaching the desk. "Is Lynn around?"

"Um, she's ... yes. Would you like to speak to her?"

"Please."

Stephen's eyes momentarily shift towards Clement, but that's as far as his interest in the big man goes.

"I'll go find her. Bear with me a mo."

He disappears back through the doorway. I'm about to nose at their bar menu when Clement taps me on the shoulder. With a nod, he beckons me to the corner of the reception area, away from the desk.

"You said they're skint, right?" he asks in a low voice.

"Yes, hence Lynn hassling Mum for money."

"Who's paying *their* wages, then?"

Clement points over my shoulder towards a large picture window and the car park beyond. I turn around and follow his finger towards a blue van parked near the far end of the building. The silver-coloured writing on the side confirms the van belongs to Ashman & Son, Roofing Contractors.

"Whatever they're doing," Clement adds. "It ain't gonna be a small job; not with all that scaffolding."

"Hmm ... interesting."

The sound of footsteps draws my attention away from the window. Stephen is back behind the reception desk.

"Lynn is just doing some paperwork in the bar. Go on through."

He gestures towards a set of double doors below a prominent sign confirming the location of the bar and dining room. From memory, they're one and the same space.

"Thanks, Stephen."

Clement trails behind as I cross the floor and push open the right-hand door. The cocktail of odours that greet me confirms the dual purpose of the room: a top note of burnt toast and a base note of stale lager. And there, sitting at one of the dozen or so tables, is Lynn. She looks up from an open folder but doesn't stand.

"To what do I owe this pleasure?" she asks, replacing the lid on her fountain pen.

I half expected a question about Paris, but Lynn has never been one for small talk with her least favourite niece. Mind you, I'm her only niece, so, technically, that also makes me her favourite.

"I was hoping we could have a chat," I reply impassively.

"Why?" Lynn gulps, her eyes widening as if it's just dawned on her that there might be a worrying reason for my visit. "It's not your mum, is it? Has something happened?"

"Mum's fine. She's at home with Paula."

"Right ... well, I wish you'd called ahead, Gina. We have a lot to do on a Monday morning, so I don't have time to sit around and natter."

"I'll keep it brief. Mind if I take a seat?"

I don't wait for an invite, but Lynn doesn't object as her focus has switched to my companion.

"Are you not going to introduce us?" she asks, staring up at Clement.

298

"Sorry. Clement, this is my Aunt Lynn. Lynn, this is Clement — an old friend."

"Alright," the big man says.

"It's nice to meet you," Lynn replies, although her eyes betray the sentiment.

"He's staying in the area for a while," I say, just to add a little context. "And we're heading off somewhere straight after."

Lynn replies with a sour semi-smile and then makes a show of looking at her watch.

"So, what's the reason for your ... unexpected visit?"

"I'll get straight to the point. Why did you ask to borrow £100,000 from Mum?"

Lynn recoils at my question, the prominent muscles in her neck tensing. I expected an immediate response, but she puffs a slight sigh and then quickly glances towards Clement, standing a few feet back from my chair.

"This is a family matter, Gina," she eventually says. "Not something I wish to discuss in front of strangers."

"Clement isn't a stranger."

"He is to me."

"I don't care. He's here to serve as my witness."

"Witness?" Lynn spits. "What is this? A trial?"

"Not at the moment, no, but there are questions to be answered."

"Does your mother know you're here?"

"No, she doesn't, and I think it's best she doesn't know anything about this conversation. Agreed?"

"Fine," Lynn huffs, folding her arms. "I don't know why you've got a bee in your bonnet about it, but yes, I did ask Helen if we could borrow some money, and I stress *borrow*. It was all above board ... we had a contract drawn up and even insisted on paying interest."

"So, you must have been gutted when Bruce Franklin waltzed off with every last penny in Mum's bank account."

"I *was* gutted, yes, but for my sister. No one deserves what that despicable man did, least of all Helen."

"No, she didn't, but it must have put you in a difficult position, right? What was the hundred grand earmarked for?"

"That's … that's none of your business."

"It wasn't, but it became my business the moment you started harassing Mum about selling the bungalow."

"I beg your pardon?" Lynn blasts. "I don't know where you got that idea from, but I have not been harassing Helen about anything, least of all selling her home."

"I don't believe you."

"Believe what you like, Gina. I really don't care."

"That much I know."

She sits back in her seat and removes the lid from her fountain pen.

"This conversation is over," she says. "You've asked your questions, and I've answered them. If you don't believe me, tough. I don't have time to sit here listening to your nonsense."

I've one last question I need to ask.

"Who's paying for the roofing contractor? Judging by all that scaffolding, it must be a major job and an expensive one."

"How we fund repairs is none of your business," she replies defiantly.

"Does Mr Ashman and his son know you're skint, or are you hoping that when Mum sells the bungalow, she'll lend you that hundred grand?"

"I told you, I haven't said anything to your mum about selling the bloody bungalow."

"Then why did you and Stephen wait until I was in Paris before dropping in to see Mum?"

"We were in the area, so we thought we'd drop in to say hello. That's the only reason."

"And the second time? On Thursday?"

My question is met with a fierce scowl and a shake of the head.

"Just go, Gina. I can't be doing with your attitude this morning."

"Are you going to answer my questions? Why did you go back to the bungalow on Thursday, and how are you funding your roofing project?"

"I didn't see your mum on Thursday, and ... actually, I'm done."

She gets to her feet and points towards the door. "Leave. Now."

Lynn might not have answered my questions, but both her body language and heated reaction are telling.

"Fine," I snap back. "But don't think you've heard the last of this."

I get up, throw a nod towards Clement, and stride back towards the doors. Stephen chirps a goodbye as I steam through the reception area towards the exit, but it goes unacknowledged.

Halfway across the car park, I slow my pace and glance across at my strangely silent companion.

"Told you she was a cow," I remark.

"Yeah, you did."

He doesn't say another word until we're back in the car.

"Dunno what to make of that," he says. "She's a narky one, your aunt."

"Narky, yes, but I can't say if she was lying or not."

"What's your gut telling you?"

"That people who are overly defensive usually have something to hide."

"If you knew for sure that she lied, that'd give you something to work with."

"How am I supposed to do that? Even if I could climb up on the roof and ask him, I doubt the contractor will discuss his customer's payment terms with me."

"Probably not. How did you find out that your aunt visited your mum on Thursday?"

"Long story short, I owe some money to a guy who runs a wedding car company, and he dropped by on Thursday to collect. He bumped into Lynn and Stephen coming down the driveway, and they told him I wasn't at home, so he called me."

"And he was sure it was them?"

"No, but I assumed it was them because they're the obvious contenders."

"I reckon you need to ask the bloke to be sure. If it turns out to be your aunt, you've gotta ask yourself why she lied."

I sit and ponder Clement's suggestion and quickly determine that it's the only practical way I'm likely to catch Lynn out.

"I still owe him that money, so I'll give him a call and offer to drop it off. I can then ask him to confirm it was Lynn and Stephen he bumped into."

"How you gonna do that? I don't think they're gonna come along for an ID parade, do you?"

"I'm sure there are photos of Lynn and Stephen on Mum's Facebook page. I'll show him one of those."

"Sounds like a plan. You wanna do it now?"

"Seeing as Paula is at home with Mum, I'm not in a desperate hurry to get back."

I pull out my phone and scroll through the recent contacts until I find Eric's number. After tapping the call icon, I don't have to wait long for him to pick up.

"Hi, Eric. It's Gina Jackson."

"Oh, hello. You're back, are you?"

"I am, and you're top of my to-do list. I was hoping I could drop by and give you the balance of my outstanding invoice."

"There's no hurry," he replies. "A bank transfer in the next few days will be fine."

"I'd prefer to get it out of the way if you don't mind. Will you be at home in about half an hour or so?"

"I'm in all day. Do you know my address?"

"No, I don't."

Eric relays his address, and with our destination confirmed, I end the call.

"Right," I say. "Back to Brentwood."

"That where he lives?"

"Yep, about a mile from Mum's place."

"Time enough to work out what you're gonna do about your aunt ... if it turns out she was bullshitting you."

"We'll have to see. I still can't believe that she'd have anything to do with what happened to Mum."

"But she's got enough money to hire a roofer."

"Has she, though? And if she was there on Thursday, why would she be hassling Mum about selling the bungalow if she was involved with David Smith? To ask for money once might be a ruse to cover her involvement, but twice? That doesn't make sense."

"Unless he stiffed her too."

"How'd you mean?"

"The bloke's a conman — they ain't renowned for their honesty. He could have promised your aunt half the money and then fucked off the moment it landed in his account."

I consider Clement's suggestion for no more than the few seconds it takes to put on my seatbelt. Not for the first time this morning, the doubts creep back into play.

"That's plausible, I suppose, but it could also be irrelevant if Eric doesn't recognise Lynn and Stephen. To be frank, it feels like we're chasing our tails."

"It's a lead, and every lead is worth checking out."

"Hmm, you reckon?"

"What I reckon," Clement says, perhaps picking up on the scepticism in my tone. "Is that the only reason we're sitting here is because you pushed past all those

303

ifs, buts, and maybes. They've got you this far, Doll, and I wouldn't be sitting here now if I thought you were wasting your time."

The big man's pep talk is as welcome as it is unexpected.

"Thank you. I appreciate the positive vibes."

"Any time," he replies with a grin. "Although, if I weren't sitting here, I'd likely be bouncing up and down on my landlady, so let's get a move on, eh."

Chapter 36

Although I've never had cause to drive along Durden Avenue, I could easily have predicted what the road might look like, solely because I've met one of the residents, and journeyed in the back of his vintage Jaguar. It's the very picture of middle England with its post-war detached houses, privet hedges, and neatly trimmed front lawns.

Crawling along in first gear, I reach number fourteen and turn the wheel towards the kerb, careful not to put a tyre on the manicured grass verge.

"I'll wait here," Clement announces, settling into his seat. "Nothing I can bring to the party."

"I won't be more than a few minutes."

Having stopped at a cash machine on the way, I double-check the notes are still in my jacket pocket before getting out of the car.

When Eric opens the front door, he greets me like an old friend, to the point he insists I pop inside rather than stand on the doorstep. The hallway décor is in keeping with the exterior of the house, and if I were asked to place a bet, my money would be on Eric being responsible for the impeccably papered walls and gloss-white bannisters.

"You really didn't have to drop this off," he says as I hand him the cash.

"It's the least I can do, and I wanted to apologise in person for not paying the invoice sooner."

"I'm grateful, but you didn't have to."

"Cards on the table, Eric, I do have an ulterior motive."

"Oh?"

"When we spoke on the phone last week, you said you bumped into a couple coming down the driveway when you dropped by to see me."

"Yes, that's right."

"This might sound a strange request, but if I show you a photo, would you mind confirming it's the same couple?"

Eric appears puzzled but agrees. I pull out my phone and tap through to Mum's Facebook profile. From there, I don't have to scroll far to find a post featuring a photo of Lynn and Stephen, captured last Christmas Day when the four of us had lunch together. I suffered it for Mum's sake, although seven glasses of Buck's Fizz certainly helped.

I show Eric the photo. "Is that the same couple?"

He leans forward and squints hard at the screen for a few seconds.

"The woman looks vaguely similar, but I'm pretty sure that's not her," he then declares.

I'm so taken aback by Eric's response that I double-check the screen to confirm it's displaying a photo of Lynn and Stephen. It is.

"Are you absolutely certain?"

"The woman I met had shoulder-length auburn hair."

As Lynn has a severe bob and dyes her hair a deep chestnut colour, Eric's observation is likely correct.

"What about the man?"

"He was mid-forties, with dark-brown hair, and he wore a sharp suit. Distinguished looking — handsome, you might say. At the time, I thought there was something familiar about him, and he smiled at me as if we'd met before."

"So it's possible he knew you?"

"Maybe," Eric replies with a slight shrug of the shoulders.

"Sorry to press you, but I really need to know who they were. Can you do better than maybe?"

It takes several seconds of pained memory dredging before I get an answer.

"I wouldn't swear on it," Eric says. "But I attend a business networking breakfast at the Holiday Inn, and he looked a lot like a chap who did a talk last month ... or maybe the month before."

"Do you have a name?"

"Mike, or it might have been Mark. I remember his surname, though: Goodwin. It happens to be my wife's maiden name."

"How certain are you that it was him?"

"Hmm, that's a tough one," Eric muses. "Fifty per cent, perhaps. You have to understand that I've been attending networking events for more than a decade, and I've met an awful lot of middle-aged men in suits over the years."

"I understand. I don't suppose you remember what he does for a living?"

"I'm not sure, but I think the talk was about retirement planning or something along those lines. To be honest, I arrived late so I only caught the last five minutes of his presentation."

Notwithstanding the mystery woman who isn't Lynn, I'm curious why these characters were at Mum's home. It would be easy to assume that they intended to visit one of the neighbours and simply got the wrong address, if not for the fact they told Eric I wasn't home.

"One more question, if I may?"

"Sure."

307

"This Mr Goodwin — do you know the name of the company he works for?"

I wait a few seconds until Eric flashes an apologetic smile. "I'm afraid not. Sorry."

"That's okay. Thanks again for your patience, and the next time I need a man with a Jag, you'll obviously be top of my call list."

"Glad to hear it."

I leave Eric in peace and return to the car.

"How'd you get on?" Clement asks as I close the driver's door.

"It wasn't Lynn and Stephen."

"She was telling the truth, then?"

"About not being there on Thursday? It seems so."

"Who were the couple, then?"

"That's a very good question. I've no idea who the woman was, but Eric thinks he recognised the man. He's given me a name ... well, part of a name."

"Why don't you just ask your mum who they were?"

"Because Mum wasn't home when they called by. She and Paula went to the garden centre on Thursday afternoon."

"You've lost me then, Doll. Why does it matter who they were?"

"It matters because they knew my name. And it's a mad theory, but ..."

It's so mad, I can't bring myself to say it.

"I'm listening," Clement prompts. "Go on."

"Eric's description perfectly matches David Smith's: mid-forties, brown hair, distinguished-looking."

Clement reaches for his moustache, which in itself is a good sign. In his shoes, my immediate response would be to scoff at such a crazy suggestion.

"It ain't completely mad," he eventually says. "But you've gotta ask yourself two questions. One: how do you confirm if it was him? Two: what the fuck is he doing back at the scene of the crime?"

"I don't know the answer to the second question but regarding the first, I might be able to rule Smith out."

"How?"

"Eric had a hunch he recognised the guy from some networking event. If I can find out where he works, we can pay him a visit. If it turns out it was him with that woman last Thursday, I'd like to ask who she was and what the hell they were doing at Mum's place. If it wasn't him ... well, my theory might be a little less mad than I first thought."

"Alright. We gonna go chat to this bloke now?"

"Give me a minute. I need to do a little googling first."

I enter the name Mark Goodwin into the search field, and then add 'retirement planning' and 'Brentwood' to narrow the search. After a deep breath, I cross my fingers and tap the search icon.

"Bingo!"

"You got him?"

"Yes, although I didn't get his name quite right. Mike Goodwin is a partner at Geras Financial Planning, and their office is less than a mile away."

"Let's go talk to Mikey Boy, then."

I double-check the address on a map and confirm their office is located in a small business park on the outskirts of town.

We set off, and a few minutes into the journey, Clement poses a question.

"Who's this Paula woman at home with your mum?"

"She's a friend — a good friend. Paula stayed with Mum while I was in New York."

"Wouldn't have been her or your mum with this bloke, then?"

"If it were Mum, Eric would have recognised her. He drove us to the registry office for the wedding that

309

never happened. As for Paula, she's a blonde in every sense of the word and the woman on the driveway had shoulder-length auburn hair, apparently."

"Right. Suppose we'll find out for sure soon enough."

"Only if Mike Goodwin was the man with her. If it wasn't him ..."

I don't need to finish the sentence, and judging by his silence, neither does Clement.

A few minutes later, we arrive at St George's Business Park and stop in one of the dozen bays earmarked for visitors. Once we're out of the car, I scan the identikit buildings for Geras Financial Services.

"I think it's at the far end," I remark, squinting to read the small sign on the last building.

"Lead on, then."

We pass a firm of solicitors, an accountant, and a web marketing agency before we reach the double doors to the business we're here to visit. I enter first and Clement follows close behind.

I half-expected an open-plan office but there are just two desks facing one another with a door to the side leading, presumably, to the rest of the building. One of the desks is unoccupied but there's a twenty-something woman behind the other.

"Can I help?" she says, with one eye still on her computer monitor.

"Yes, I'd like to speak with Mike Goodwin, please."

The woman glances up at the clock on the wall behind my left shoulder.

"He's not here at the moment but we're expecting him back shortly. Would you like to make an appointment?"

"Nah, you're alright," Clement replies. "We'll catch up with him another time."

He then nods towards the door but after three steps, he throws a parting question at the woman.

"Is that old sod still driving a Merc?" he asks in a jokey manner. "Or has he got himself something a bit less German?"

"Err, Mike drives a Range Rover."

"Nice. Business must be good."

With that, Clement puts his hand on my shoulder and guides me back outside. He doesn't stop walking until we're standing outside the web marketing agency.

"Why didn't we make an appointment?" I ask. "And what's with the question about Mike Goodwin's car?"

"Better to talk to the bloke out here and, if he's due back soon, we need to know what motor he drives."

"Why?"

"You want answers, don't you, Doll?"

"Obviously."

"Then trust me. Better to have a chat out here."

"Fair enough. Shall we wait in the car?"

Before Clement can answer, the roar of a high-powered engine causes us both to turn towards the car park. A dove-grey Range Rover approaches at speed and pulls into an empty parking bay just beyond the entrance to Geras Financial Services.

"Looks like that might be him," Clement remarks. "Come on."

I can barely keep up as the big man strides purposely back in the direction we just came from. We reach the Range Rover just as the driver is getting out.

"You Mike Goodwin?" Clement asks.

"Who wants to know?"

"She does."

I come to a stop by Clement's side. The man in front of us matches the description Eric gave me, although calling him handsome is a stretch.

"Mr Goodwin?"

"Yes."

"I'm Gina Jackson. You visited my mum, Helen Jackson, last Thursday."

I wait for some flicker of acknowledgement, but Mike Goodwin just stares back at me, impassively.

"I'd like to know why you were there?" I add, stepping forward so we're within five feet of one another.

"I'm afraid I'm not at liberty to discuss my diary with you, Miss Jackson. Client confidentiality."

"All I need to know is if you were there. Number four, Windsor Gardens."

"As I said, I can't discuss any matters relating to clients."

He then turns and opens the back door of the Range Rover, presumably to retrieve a suit jacket draped on a hanger.

"You can tell her if you were there or not," Clement says. "It ain't that hard."

"I'm afraid, I can't," Goodwin replies, reaching for his jacket. "Now, if you don't mind, I've got a meeting in fifteen minutes."

To signify his reluctance to continue the conversation, he turns his back on us. Clement then steps towards the Range Rover.

"Nice motor," he says.

Mike Goodwin turns around and straightens up, his jacket in his left hand. He opens his mouth to say something, but Clement suddenly lurches forward, clamping his right hand on Goodwin's crotch while pinning the financial planner to the rear flank of the car with his forearm.

"Keep your gob shut till I say otherwise," Clement growls, only inches from Goodwin's face.

I'm not sure which of us is most taken aback by the big man's assault but judging by the look of abject terror on Goodwin's face, it's probably him.

312

"Now, my friend asked you a question," Clement says in a low rumbling tone. "Answer it and you keep your plums."

"What ... what do you want to know?" Goodwin stammers, his eyes wide and pleading.

I'm not entirely comfortable with Clement's interrogation tactics but needs must.

"Were you at number four Windsor Gardens last Thursday ... in the afternoon?"

"Yes."

It's an admission that immediately destroys my theory about David Smith. I'm not sure whether to be frustrated or relieved but, for now, there are other questions to be answered.

"Who were you with?"

"I ... I ... I wasn't with anyone."

"You were seen on the driveway with a woman. Who was she?"

Goodwin tries to turn his head towards the office, perhaps in hope that one of his colleagues might rush to his rescue. He's bang out of luck.

"Who was the woman?" I ask again, more forcibly.

"Helen Jackson ... your mother."

His reply throws me for a moment.

"My mother?"

"Yes," he whimpers.

"You're lying."

"I'm not. I swear."

Considering Clement has a tight grip on Goodwin's family jewels, it seems unlikely he'd lie.

"Why were you there?"

"To ... to discuss a retirement planning matter."

"Specifically?"

Another glance towards the office doors does little to boost Goodwin's resolve.

"I was there to finalise the details of your mother's equity release plan."

"Her what?"

"Equity release. It's a … it's a scheme to release equity in a property."

"Exactly how much of my mother's equity are we talking about?"

"Five hundred."

"Pounds?"

"Five hundred thousand."

My mouth opens but only as a reaction to Goodwin's revelation. I'm sure there are plenty of other questions I should ask him, but I'm struggling to get past the five hundred grand mental block he's just dumped in my way.

"Let him go," I mumble.

Clement removes his hand from Goodwin's crotch, but the forearm remains pressed across his chest.

"Remember, Sunshine, I know where you work. You tell anyone about this little chat and you'll be seeing me again. Got it?"

Mike Goodwin nods enthusiastically and Clement removes his arm. The big man then takes a couple of steps back and it's all the invitation Goodwin needs to nervously flee the scene.

"We should get out of here, Doll, just in case he decides to call the Old Bill."

"Um … right."

We move quickly and silently back to the car but I'm more concerned about my mother's decision to release a huge chunk of equity from her home than the police turning up. Nevertheless, once I'm back behind the wheel, I don't hang around.

"Why does your mum need half a million quid?" Clement asks once we're clear of the business park.

"She doesn't, and I've no idea why she'd set up an equity release loan. The last time we talked about her finances, she was set on selling the bungalow."

"And she's never mentioned a meeting with that Goodwin fella?"

"No, and there's no way Mum would make such a huge financial decision in her current state of mind. She'd talk to me about it first, without doubt."

"You're sure?"

"One hundred per cent certain."

"And that bloke you spoke to half an hour ago — the one who drove the wedding car — he was just as certain it wasn't your mum he bumped into when he called round?"

"Yes, he seemed pretty certain. It doesn't make any sense."

"Oh, it does. Doll."

"Eh? How?"

"It makes perfect sense ... if someone is pretending to be your mum."

Chapter 37

I don't so much as pull over as veer towards the kerb and screech to a sudden halt. Mercifully, there aren't any pedestrians around.

With the engine still running, I turn to Clement.

"What did you say?" I gulp.

"Think about it, Doll. It's the only explanation that makes any sense."

"You mean ... identity theft?"

"Dunno what you'd call it but look at the facts. Your mum gets rinsed by a conman, and then he fucks off, but he knows that your mum still has money, although it's tied up in her home, right?"

"Yes."

"Now, we know that Smith received letters sent to that address in Brooklyn, and maybe one of those letters had something to do with a second bite of the cherry. If he's got an accomplice, she could have posed as your mum, and between them, they could have set up this loan. It's a risky play, but half a million quid is enough dough to tempt anyone."

Despite my scrambled mind, Clement's theory does resolve a fair number of my unanswered questions. But who would be so audacious they'd not only con a woman once but risk everything for a second shot at whatever she had left? And what kind of heartless bitch would partner up with such a man?

"We need to go back to see Mike Goodwin. He might not even know he's part of a con."

"Maybe he does, maybe he don't, but there's only one place we need to go, and that's back to your mum's place."

"But ... once that money is released ... it's all Mum has."

"You go back and see that bloke, what happens? At best, the Old Bill get involved, and they'll want to interview your mum. You reckon she'll be up for that?"

It's not a question I have to think too long or hard about. I shake my head.

"And while the Old Bill are filling out forms and badgering your mum, David Smith gets wind that the game's up, and he disappears again. We'll never find the bloke ... or that first pot of money he took from your mum."

"What do we do then?"

"If I'm right, whoever is helping Smith must know your mum reasonably well. Chances are, they probably don't look too different either."

"We've been through this. I can't think of anyone who'd stoop so low."

"You're gonna have to think a bit harder, Doll. If I'm right about this, *someone* is helping Smith."

"I suppose ... I could ask Paula. She might know of mutual friends that I haven't thought of. I'll have to be discreet, though. If you are right and Smith is trying to scam Mum for a second time, it'll push her over the edge."

Clement nods, and I take a deep breath to slow my racing heart. I need to stay calm, not least because I don't want to crash the car on the way back to Windsor Gardens.

The journey is thankfully short and flashes by in a blur. With one final turn of the wheel, I enter Mum's driveway and come to a stop in the exact same spot Paula's car occupied when we left.

"Paula isn't here," I confirm for Clement's benefit. "She might have popped to the shop for Mum."

The big man grunts and gets out of the car. I hurry up to the front door, unlock it, and step into the hallway.

"Only me, Mum," I call out.

I follow the sound of the television through to the lounge. Mum is sitting in her preferred armchair.

"You've been a while," she remarks.

"Sorry, yes. Um, when did Paula leave?"

"Don't panic," Mum replies in a slightly defensive tone. "She's barely been gone ten minutes. I'm not a child, you know — I can be trusted to be in my own home alone."

"I know. It's just ... I was hoping to have a word with Paula and thought she'd still be here, that's all."

"She received a phone call, and whatever it was about, she got a bit flustered and said she had to shoot off. Something to do with work, apparently."

"And she got that call ten minutes ago?" Clement asks from the doorway.

"Yes. Maybe fifteen at the most."

"Right. Do you mind if I make myself a cuppa?"

"No, of course not."

"Cheers. Do you fancy one?"

"I'm fine, thanks," Mum says with a tepid smile.

Clement subtly nods his head to suggest I should follow him through to the kitchen.

"I'll give you a hand."

Mum returns her attention to the screen while I lead Clement to the kitchen. He quietly closes the door behind us.

"This Paula, bird," he says in a low voice.

"What about her?"

"Bit of a coincidence that she received a phone call almost the same time we left Goodwin, don't you think?"

"Pardon me," I hiss. "I hope you're not suggesting what I think you're suggesting."

"I ain't suggesting nothin'."

"Good. And just for your info, Paula has short blonde hair whereas the woman Eric met had hair similar to Mum's."

"Fuck me," Clement snorts. "Not like she might have worn a wig, is it?"

"It's not Paula, okay. She's a good friend and a loyal one."

"Where was she last Thursday afternoon?"

"I don't ... hold on, I think she was at the garden centre with Mum. Yes, I'm sure that's what she said when I called her last week."

"And you believe her?"

"Of course, I believe her."

"No harm asking your mum, then, is there?"

"Why?"

"Process of elimination. That work for you?"

"If it gets that stupid idea out of your head, I'll ask her now. Wait here."

I spin around and open the kitchen door. When I return to the lounge, Mum is engrossed in some awful daytime quiz show.

"Um, Mum."

"Yes."

"This might sound like a strange question, but how long were you at the garden centre on Thursday?"

Mum picks up the remote control and pauses her programme.

"Thursday?" she says, almost as if she doesn't understand the meaning of the word.

"Yes, Thursday. Paula said you went to the garden centre. You had a cup of tea in the cafe."

"That was Wednesday."

"Are you sure?"

"I didn't go anywhere on Thursday afternoon ... apart from my bedroom."

"Your bedroom?"

"I think we were planning to go out for a walk in the afternoon, and Paula made lunch. I was about to get ready, but I had a funny turn."

"In what way?"

"It was a bit like being drunk: lightheaded at first, but then I felt dreadful. I think it must have been one of those twenty-four-hour bugs."

"So, you didn't go to the garden centre?"

"I could barely get out of my armchair, never mind browse border plants. Paula suggested I have a lie down and she helped me to bed. That was the last thing I remember until I woke up just before *Eastenders*. To be honest, it was the best sleep I've had in ages."

"Sorry to labour the point, but you're certain you visited the garden centre on Wednesday rather than Thursday?"

"*Eastenders* is on Thursdays, so yes. It definitely wasn't Thursday."

"Right ... um, sorry. I'll let you get back to your programme."

"Is something wrong?"

"No, no. It's ... I'm just trying to ... it's not important."

When I return to the kitchen, Clement is leaning up against the fridge freezer, arms folded.

"Well?" he says.

"Mum was in bed asleep on Thursday afternoon. She wasn't feeling well."

"All afternoon?"

"Apparently so."

320

Clement takes a moment to stroke his moustache before he responds to my update.

"She lied, then, this Paula."

"Paula isn't a liar. Maybe she just got her days mixed up."

"Do you know where she lives?"

"Of course I do."

"Is it far?"

"A ten-minute drive."

"Right, why don't we pop over and ask her, just to satisfy my curiosity?"

"Fine," I huff. "I'll ask her if she can think of anyone I haven't already considered, but if you think I'm going to accuse her of being David Smith's accomplice, you're deluded."

"You ain't the first to suggest that, Doll. Probably won't be the last, either."

"You're certainly off the mark with Paula, and once you meet her, you'll understand why. She's one of the loveliest people you could wish to meet."

"Let's hope I'm wrong, then. Shall we get going?"

"Alright," I respond with a frown. "But I'm sure there's an innocent explanation, and it'll prove a waste of time."

I pop my head around the lounge door and let Mum know we're nipping out for half an hour. Fortunately, she's so engrossed in the quiz show that she doesn't question where we're going or why. She'd be mortified if she knew that Clement has suspicions about her best friend, no matter how tenuous.

We return to the car and, once I've put my seatbelt on, I confirm the rules of engagement.

"Just to be clear, Clement, I'm only doing this to eliminate any unfounded suspicions you have. If you upset Paula in any way, we're done. Understood?"

"I'll be the model of discretion, Doll. Scout's honour."

If there's one word I'd never use to describe the man next to me, it would be discreet. I start the car and reverse back down the driveway. Once we're heading back up Windsor Gardens, I pose a question to Clement.

"Once we've wasted half an hour on this fool's errand, where do we go?"

"What do you mean?"

"I mean, do you think we should speak to Mike Goodwin and tell him that he's now embroiled in a fraud case?"

"Let's take one step at a time. For all we know, he might be involved, and there's a chance that it was him who called Paula."

"And there's a much more likely chance it really was just a phone call about work."

"Come to think of it, where does she work? If that phone call was genuine, she's more likely to head there than home."

"Paula works from home. She's a freelance copywriter."

"Guess we're heading in the right direction, then."

That direction is towards a village on the southern outskirts of Brentwood. Paula lives in a beautiful little cottage that she purchased after her parents passed away a few years back. It's the kind of home I can imagine living in at some point in the future once the urban lifestyle starts to grind.

A few minutes into the journey, I happen to glance at the speedometer. Without consciously realising, I'm the wrong side of the speed limit. That urgency is tied to my need to get this over with so we can deal with the more important issue of Mike Goodwin's fraudulent equity release loan. Somehow, I've got to deal with that without Mum finding out.

I arrive at a bend a little faster than I anticipated and have to press hard on the brake pedal.

"Bleedin' hell," Clement groans. "Take it easy, eh."

"Sorry. I'm just a bit anxious and lost concentration for a second."

"It'll be alright. We'll get this sorted."

"God, I hope you're right. I just want my normal, boring life back ... and Mum's."

"Wouldn't mind a boring life myself, truth be told."

"I don't know why, but I get the feeling you've never had a boring life."

"Maybe not boring, but normal."

"What's stopping you from living a normal life?"

Clement chuckles away to himself but doesn't answer my question.

"Well?" I urge.

"I can't even remember what normal feels like and I sure as hell don't see it returning to my life any time soon."

"It's your life. Surely it's up to you?"

"Yeah, you'd think, but we can't always have what we want, can we?"

"No," I sigh. "We can't."

Whether Clement did it intentionally or not, his comment nudges my thoughts towards the day when all this will be just a memory, and I'll be forced to look forward again, rather than back. I made plans once before and that didn't end well, so Christ knows what the alternative is. Living in a constant state of pessimism or ambivalence?

We pass a sign for the village, dragging my attention back to the here and now, and a visit to a dear family friend I'm less than happy about.

"Much further?" Clement asks.

"She lives on a lane about five hundred yards further on, just past the village green."

Seconds later, I indicate right and take the final turn. We pass a meadow and a thicket of trees, and then, after

I slow down for a sharp bend in the road, we reach the row of four cottages.

Being they were built long before parking was an issue, the only place to park is a layby some fifty yards past the last cottage. There are only two cars in the layby and neither belongs to Paula.

"I don't think she's here," I remark while tugging the handbrake. "Her car certainly isn't."

"Which of those houses is hers?"

"The first one we passed. Number one."

"Maybe she stopped off to get her curtains dry-cleaned."

"Eh?"

"That first house didn't have any curtains. I could see straight into the lounge and the front bedroom."

"Well, maybe she's got blinds."

"In an old place like that? Wouldn't look right, would they?"

"I don't know. I'm not an expert on interior design. Anyway, Paula isn't here which leads me to suspect she's gone to see a client on an urgent work-related matter."

Rather than reply, Clement leans forward and studies the nearside wing mirror for several seconds.

"What's so fascinating?" I ask.

"The old boy pruning his roses."

"You don't strike me as the horticultural type."

"I ain't, but I'm gonna go have a word with him. I might have a quick butcher's through the window of number one while I'm there."

"For what reason?"

"To see if there are blinds."

Seemingly set on his pointless plan, he removes his seatbelt and opens the passenger's door.

"Hang on. I don't want you upsetting Paula's neighbours so I'll come with you."

324

I scramble out of my seat and follow Clement as he strides purposefully towards the row of cottages.

"I don't know what you're hoping to achieve," I say in a low voice as we approach the cottages.

"Neither do I," comes the reply. "But you don't ask, you don't get."

Paula's neighbour shifts his attention from the rosebush as we step towards the low stone wall separating his garden from the lane.

"Afternoon," Clement says in a moderately friendly tone.

"Good afternoon," the neighbour replies.

"We're trying to find Paula. Lives at number one."

I glance towards the lounge of Paula's cottage. There definitely aren't any curtains and I can't see any evidence of blinds, either.

"I'm sorry," the neighbour says. "You've missed her."

"When will she be back?" Clement asks. "Do you know?"

"Back? You misunderstand — Paula moved out just a few days ago."

Chapter 38

Confused, I step right up to the stone wall.

"Paula has moved out?"

"That's what happens when you sell your property, yes."

"Wait ... she's sold her cottage?"

The old guy's eyes narrow, as if he's suspicious of my question.

"Are you friends of hers?" he asks.

"Yes, we are," I reply defiantly. "Paula was the maid of honour at my mum's wedding in the summer."

"And you didn't know she was selling up?"

"Obviously not."

"You're not the only one," the old guy huffs. "We weren't close, but I thought it was a bit rude that she put her house up for sale without warning us, and she didn't even knock on the door to say goodbye."

"How do you know she's sold the house, then?"

"My wife happened to overhear the estate agent talking to a young couple in the back garden last month. I can only assume Paula wanted to keep it low-key because the estate agent didn't put up a for-sale sign, and it wasn't listed on Rightmove, either. We had a quick nose, hoping to get an idea of what our place might be worth, you know. Then, on Saturday afternoon, a van parked up outside and two burly men spent an hour loading furniture and boxes into it. Does that answer your question?"

The old guy is clearly irritated by my questioning and returns to his roses. In any other circumstance, I'd apologise for my tone, but here and now, he'll just have to assume I'm rude.

I turn and look up at Clement. "What the hell is going on?" I ask, trying to retain some semblance of composure. "Where is Paula?"

"Let's get out of here," he replies, throwing a nod to the old guy.

Still confused, I follow Clement back up the lane.

"Why wouldn't Paula tell me or Mum that she intended to sell up and move?"

"She obviously didn't want you to know. What you've gotta ask yourself is: why?"

"I ... I don't know."

"Maybe it's because she was helping Smith, and once they got their hands on that loan money, she intended to fuck off sharpish, with no loose ends left behind."

"No way," I snort. "Not Paula. There has to be another explanation."

"Simplest one is usually the right one, Doll. Sorry."

"She wouldn't be so cruel to Mum, and ... and she's the last person you'd suspect of being involved with a con artist."

"That's the point — you're not supposed to suspect 'em."

"Even so, I just can't see Paula being involved."

"Where is she then?"

We reach the car, and I turn around to look back at the cottage that is apparently no longer Paula's. Now Clement has seeded the question, I have to ask myself why she never mentioned what is a significant change in her circumstances. She loves that cottage and if she had to sell it, there's no way she'd keep that news from us.

327

But she did.

"Maybe I should call the police."

"You can call the Old Bill, but before you do, I wanna take a look inside the house."

"Paula's?"

"Yeah."

"Why? Didn't you hear what her neighbour said? She's moved out and taken everything with her."

"No one takes everything with them. You'd be amazed what folk chuck in the bin before they go."

"I don't understand, Clement. What's the point?"

"If she is bent, and found out that we've rumbled her plot, she'll be panicking. And people who panic make mistakes."

"Assuming she *is* involved with Smith, and I'm still struggling with that notion."

"If we get inside the house, we might find some actual evidence. You wanna come with me?"

"How are you going to get in there?"

"There's only trees and bushes behind the houses. We'll cut around and go in through the back door."

I still don't see the point, but if I've learned anything about Clement, it's that following his logic usually pays off. Besides, I need to determine beyond all reasonable doubt that we haven't spectacularly misjudged Mum's best friend.

"I need to make a call first."

"To who?"

"Just give me two minutes."

I pull out my phone and call the Haywain Hotel. Stephen answers on the third ring, announcing the hotel name.

"Stephen, it's Gina. Can I speak to Lynn. It's urgent."

"I don't think that's a good idea, Gina. She's still upset about your visit earlier."

"I'm sorry, but ... please, let me just speak to her."

"She told me what you said and just for the record, I borrowed the money for the roof repairs from my brother. You've no idea—"

"Please," I interject. "It's about Mum."

Stephen puffs a sigh before asking me to hold. I'm then treated to the most inappropriately happy hold music before Lynn finally says my name.

"What's happened?" she asks, her tone frantic.

"Nothing has happened, but I need to ask a favour."

"You've got some cheek after what you said to me this morning."

"I know, and I'm sorry. I shouldn't have said what I did but ... long story, short, I've been trying to find Bruce Franklin for the last week or so, and I've taken a few wrong turns along the way. One of those wrong turns led me to your place this morning."

"And?"

"And I really, really need you to do something for me. I'll beg if I have to."

"What is it?"

"Mum is at home on her own and I'd rather she wasn't. Will you go over there and stay with her until you hear from me?"

"Is she in any danger?"

"I don't think so, no, but ... please, Lynn. Do this for me."

I wait for another lecture, or for Lynn to push back so I have to plead my case for a second time.

"I'll leave now," she then says.

"Thank you," I pant. "I am grateful."

"There's one condition, though."

"Name it."

"I want to know what you've been up to."

"You will. I'll explain everything, I promise."

"Very well. I'd better get off the phone."

"Yes, and thanks again, Lynn."

One problem solved, I tuck the phone back in my pocket, not quite ready to face the next but at least I've got my own accomplice for this one.

"Let's go then."

After checking that Paula's neighbour isn't watching, we slip through a sparse hedge next to the lane. The route takes us into a light thicket of trees and out to a meadow.

"Fucking countryside," Clement mumbles as we cut a path through knee-high grass.

"Not a fan?"

"No, I ain't."

All that stands between us and the rear gardens of the cottages is a wild hedgerow that we have to force our way through. Fortunately, Clement's massive frame acts like a bulldozer, clearing the path until we come out the other side, right next to a panelled fence with a gate at the rear of number one.

Clement steps up to the fence and peers over the top. He looks left and right, then reaches for the gate handle.

"Let's hope your friend ain't big on security," he says quietly whilst turning the handle.

The gate requires a shove, but it opens. I then scurry behind as Clement moves quickly towards the back door of Paula's former home. What he's yet to explain is how we proceed once we reach the door.

My answer comes almost immediately as Clement jabs his elbow against one of the small square panes of glass that occupy the top half of the door. It's just enough to crack the pane in two but not so hard the glass shatters to the ground, alerting the neighbours. He then carefully manoeuvres the two pieces of glass out of the frame and lays them next to the doormat.

"You sure you wanna do this?" he asks in barely a whisper. "It ain't exactly lawful."

"Just open the door," I hiss back.

He reaches a hand through the gap and, after a bit of twisting, turns the handle from inside and eases the door open.

A week ago, if anyone had told me I'd soon be breaking and entering Paula's home, I'd have questioned their sanity. Then again, some might question my sanity for the deed itself.

We enter the kitchen, and Clement quietly closes the back door.

"Don't look like we'll be stopping for a cuppa," he remarks, nodding towards the empty worktops. "No bleedin' kettle."

To satisfy my own curiosity, I open a couple of cupboard doors. All are completely bare.

"If you were hoping to scour the bin for evidence that might implicate Paula, you're out of luck. She's obviously taken the bin with her."

Clement grunts a reply and then opens the door leading to the narrow hallway. From memory, there's a door to the lounge and a staircase leading to the first floor. We try the lounge first but all we find are scuff marks on the floorboards where furniture once rested. What was once a cosy, welcoming room now feels anything but with its four bare walls and stone-cold fireplace.

"This doesn't bode well," I remark as we exit the lounge and turn right towards the staircase.

"As I said, Doll, if you don't look, you'll never know."

There are three doors leading off the first-floor landing: one for the bathroom and one for each of the two bedrooms. We turn right and head to the bigger bedroom at the front of the cottage. Clement opens the door but only takes a couple of steps into the room. When I reach the threshold, I can see why. Like the lounge below, all that remains is dust and a few marks on the walls.

The penultimate stop is the bathroom. There's no bin, and Clement even checks the airing cupboard but to no avail. It seems Paula was meticulous in ensuring she didn't leave even the tiniest of breadcrumbs for anyone to follow.

"Shall we go?" I suggest. "Before someone realises we're here."

"One more room to check, ain't there?"

"It's just the spare bedroom."

"No harm in looking."

Clement, ignoring my protest, pushes open the door. From my vantage point, I catch sight of the only stick of furniture we've seen since entering the cottage — a single bed with the covers pulled back.

"Now, we're getting somewhere," the big man remarks as he enters the bedroom.

I follow him in, although there's not a lot of floor space in the room. Besides the unmade bed, there's a single wardrobe and a small chest of drawers. Unlike the other rooms, this one still has a set of curtains.

Clement steps towards the bed, leans over the pillow, and sniffs at it.

"What are you doing?" I ask.

"I can smell perfume. Have a sniff."

I don't have to get too close before a familiar scent reaches my nostrils. It's the exact same scent that lingered in my bedroom back at Mum's.

"That's Paula's perfume."

"It's still strong, so she must have slept here last night."

"Why would she have all her worldly goods shipped off and then stay in her spare room? It doesn't make sense."

Clement rounds the bed and looks out of the window. After a brief pause, he turns to face me.

"You wanna hear my theory?"

"I don't *want* to hear it, no, but I suppose I should."

"My best guess is that after he emptied your mum's bank account, David Smith decided to hide out in New York until the dust settled whilst Paula kept tabs on you and your mum — just so she could report back if the Old Bill got anywhere. I reckon that's when the greedy fuckers came up with the idea of helping themselves to an extra half a million quid, and your mate Paula decided to play her part ... or your mum's part, to be precise.

"A lot of supposition but go on."

"Then, we manage to find that Goodwin bloke, and he spills the beans, but he must have called Paula — if that's even her real name — the minute we left. She was probably hanging out here for a few days until the loan money came through, and then she'd be on her toes, just like Smith."

Clement's theory isn't outlandish, but it does sound like the plot summary of a crime novel rather than a possible reality. Things like this just don't happen to people like us, but I can't think of an explanation that makes any better sense. It's reason enough to do what I should have done an hour ago and mitigate the risk to Mum.

"I need to call Mike Goodwin. Now."

Standing in Paula's spare bedroom, I look up the number for Geras Financial Planning and call it. After a heated exchange with a receptionist, I'm put through to Mike Goodwin.

"Mr Goodwin. We met this morning in the car park outside your office."

"I'm glad you called because I want to know the name of that tosser who assaulted me. I've got CCTV evidence, and I intend to press charges."

"Well, while you're on the phone to the police, you can explain your involvement in a case of attempted fraud."

"What?" he spits back.

333

"The woman you arranged an equity release loan for is not my mother, Helen Jackson. Now, I don't know if you were party to the fraud or just a gullible idiot, but, either way, I need to know if that loan has been issued yet."

There's a moment of silence, punctuated by Goodwin's heavy breathing.

"You have proof?" he then says in a more subdued tone.

"I have one hundred per cent, copper-bottomed proof that the woman you arranged a loan for is not Helen Jackson."

"Shit," he says under his breath.

"That's exactly what you'll be in if that loan has already been issued, Mr Goodwin."

"Hold on."

I'm left to listen to the frantic tapping of keys and clicking of a mouse.

"The lender sent out a final form requiring a signature," he says in a monotone voice as if reading notes on a screen. "That form should have arrived this morning — it was sent first class on Friday."

"Sent where?"

"To your mother's address."

My mind races back to the moment I opened the front door to Paula this morning. She handed over the post, but did she really just bump into the postman on the driveway and offer to take those letters to their intended recipients, or was she waiting for that form to arrive?

"Thank God," Mike Goodwin suddenly pants. "The lender hasn't received that signed form yet, so they haven't issued the loan."

"How long does it usually take once they receive all the paperwork?"

"Three working days."

"So, you can update the lender and make sure the loan isn't issued?"

"Yes, yes, I can."

"Good," I snap. "Now, if you want to prove that you were innocent in all this, I'd suggest you end this call and do whatever you need to do to permanently cancel that application."

"I will, and I am innocent. I didn't know, I swear."

"You can prove that by answering one question. Did you call the woman you thought was Helen Jackson this morning?"

"Yes, shortly after you left, intent on venting my disgust at what happened. As soon as I confirmed that you, her daughter, wanted to know why I was arranging an equity release loan, she hung up. I tried calling her back, but it went straight to voicemail."

"Can you confirm the last four digits of the number you called?"

"I can. One sec."

It's not one sec, but two clicks of a mouse.

"3481."

"My mum's phone number ends with 1909. Whoever you called, it wasn't my mother."

"I hear you, okay, and the second you get off the phone, I'll deal with it."

"Make sure you do."

With part of Clement's theory no longer just a theory, I end the call.

"You were right about that call," I say, putting my phone away. "Goodwin did call the woman he thought was Mum, shortly after we left."

"You still think it's a coincidence that Paula received a call at the same time and promptly pissed off? Now, she's nowhere to be found?"

The evidence is mounting, and as much as it turns my stomach to even consider it, I fear Clement is right.

335

"Whether it was Paula, or not, that bitch was only three days away from getting her hands on the last of Mum's money. If there's any silver lining to this, at least we stopped that."

"Explains why she was still hanging around here. She sure as fuck won't be coming back now she knows we're on to her."

"I think it's time to get the police involved."

"You do what you want, Doll," Clement replies while moving towards the chest of drawers. "But I ain't done yet."

"She's gone, Clement, just like David bloody Smith."

"We'll see about that."

He then pulls the top drawer out and tips the content on the bed: enough socks, knickers, and bras for a long weekend, but nothing more. Clement tosses the drawer aside and pulls out the next. Its contents join Paula's underwear on the bed.

"What are you looking for?" I ask.

"Dunno."

I step towards the bed and examine the scattering of makeup products and toiletries deposited from the second drawer. It's evidence, but only that Paula likes designer brands.

Clement pulls out the third drawer but doesn't add to the pile on the bed.

"Fuck," he mumbles, tossing the empty drawer aside and then standing with his hands on his hips.

"I'll check the wardrobe," I remark, for no other reason than I feel like a spare part.

Clement nods but remains silent.

I open the wardrobe door expecting it to be empty. There are, however, four garments hanging from the rail: two blouses, a pair of jeans, and a lime-green coat. I quickly scan the floor of the wardrobe, but there's nothing besides a thin layer of dust.

I turn around. "Nothing," I say in a conciliatory tone. "Let's call it a day, eh?"

"Yeah, alright."

Clement trudges back past the bed, and as I turn to step through the doorway, he pauses by the still-open wardrobe.

"One sec," he says.

"I've checked. There's nothing in there."

Ignoring my protest, he grabs the pair of jeans from the hanger and checks the front and back.

"There ain't no bleedin' pockets."

He drops the jeans on the floor and then inspects the two blouses. After a cursory check, they join the jeans on the floor. Finally, he pulls out Paula's coat. From the left-hand pocket, he withdraws half a packet of gum. From the right, nothing at all. With a heavy sigh, he then inspects the lining for an inside pocket. There's one, and it's a tight fit for his huge hand.

"What we got here then?" he says to himself, slowly withdrawing his hand.

At first glance, it looks like a credit card — it's the right size, and it seems to be made of plastic. However, the logo printed prominently on one side isn't for any financial institution I've ever heard of.

Clement flips it over and inspects it in more detail.

"Grampton Riverside," he mumbles. "What do you reckon that is?"

"I'll check. One second."

I quickly google the name. "It's a luxury hotel in Canary Wharf. Docklands."

The moment the words pass my lips, I instinctively know what Clement's response will be.

"She's obviously been kipping here, so why would she have a room card for some swanky hotel in Docklands?"

"Because ... um ..."

"She's not staying there, but I'd bet my left bollock that her partner in crime is."

"Do you really think David Smith is in London?"

"We obviously spooked your so-called friend, and she didn't have time to come back here; otherwise, we'd never have found this. Maybe she's got this room card 'cos she intended to meet up with someone as soon as she got her hands on that loan money. That ain't happening, so where do you think she's heading?"

"To the Grampton Riverside Hotel?"

"That'd be my best guess, yeah."

"And ... that means?"

"It means, Doll, we've got one final journey to make."

Chapter 39

As we approach the car, Clement holds out his hand. I stare at it blankly.

"Gimme the keys," he demands. "We ain't got time to pootle across Essex."

"But—"

"Doll. Keys. Now."

It's not his tone that convinces me to hand over the keys but the steely coldness in his eyes. Why he's so invested in finding David Smith remains a mystery, but now he's caught the scent of his quarry, it's almost as if he's been possessed by a higher force.

We get in the car, but not before Clement has rammed the driver's seat as far back as it goes.

"Just remember this is my mum's car, and I'm sure she'd like it back in one piece."

"If we manage to find this fucker, I'm pretty sure your mum wouldn't care if we brought her car back in a dozen bin bags."

"True, but let's not die trying, please."

"Have faith, Doll."

"Right, well ... do you know how to get to Canary Wharf from here?"

"Ain't got the foggiest, which is why you're navigating."

"It's pretty straightforward. M25 clockwise and then the A13 westbound."

"And how do we get to the M25?"

"I'll direct you as we go."

Clement turns the ignition key, rams the gearstick into first, and revs the engine as if he's about to drive the final leg at Le Mans. We haven't moved yet and I'm already regretting the decision to let him get behind the wheel.

"Hold tight," he says with a near maniacal grin.

I'm thrust back in my seat as Clement suddenly lifts the clutch and spins the steering wheel. Somehow, he manages to turn the car around in the lane whilst also pressing the accelerator to the floor. Mum's poor little car screams an objection on both our parts.

It's only a couple of miles to the nearest M25 junction, but those miles are all country lanes. The narrow, winding roads are no deterrent to Clement's driving style, nor is the forty miles-per-hour speed limit.

It's a relief when we finally reach the straight lanes of the M25 motorway. Clement settles the car at a steady eighty and rests his left arm in his lap. He then yawns and turns to me.

"Stick some tunes on. None of that modern bollocks, though."

I press the power button on the stereo. If this were my car, the pre-set stations would be Radio 1, Heart, and Capital, but this is Mum's car, and I'm certain her pre-set stations are an eclectic mix covering music across the last five decades. The first station confirms as much.

"Gotta love a bit of Dr Hook," Clement remarks.

As the big man taps a beat on the top of the steering wheel, I slowly unclench my buttocks and relax a fraction. I don't think I've heard it before but the song playing relates to a phone call to Sylvia's mother and the desperate pleas of a man negotiating with the telephone operator. It's not a bad tune, but lyrically, it's definitely of its time.

The song ends, and the DJ introduces the next: *Let's Dance* by Chris Montez.

"Can't stand that song," Clement complains. "Switch the station, Doll."

I lean forward, jab the next button, and sit back. Within a few seconds, I smack my hand against the power button, silencing the stereo altogether.

"What did you do that for?" Clement asks.

"I ... I didn't like the song they were playing."

"What was it?"

"*Somewhere Only We Know* by Keane."

"Never heard of it, but it can't be any worse than Let's bleedin' Dance. I'd rather stick knitting needles in my ears."

"There's nothing wrong with the song. It's just ... it's a song that meant something to me once, and I'd rather not go where it'll take me if I hear it again."

"The woman you split up with?"

"Yep," I sigh.

"Go on then. Tell me."

"Tell you what?"

"What happened? How'd it end?"

"I haven't changed my stance, Clement. I don't want to talk about it."

"Maybe that's your problem. If you can't even listen to a bleedin' song, you need to exorcise a few demons."

"Maybe, but I'm sure you don't want to hear my sob story."

"I wouldn't have asked if I didn't wanna know, but why don't you tell me how it started and then see if you feel like telling me how it ended? Deal?"

I consider the ramifications of spilling my guts to the man next to me, and maybe he has a point. I've never discussed what happened with anyone, even Mum. Admittedly, it's also an excuse to think of something other than Paula's treachery for five minutes.

341

"Her name was … her name *is* Priya, and we joined an art class at the college within a week of one another. We hit it off the moment we first met and became firm friends. Then, we had an opportunity to visit an exhibition in Bath, so we booked a hotel and planned to make a weekend of it. On the second evening, we went to a bar and enjoyed a few too many glasses of wine. Then, when we got back to the hotel, and pardon the cliché, but one thing led to another. In hindsight, that was a mistake."

"Nothin' wrong with a dirty weekend and a bit of hanky-panky, Doll."

"It wasn't a mistake per se, but if that night hadn't happened, we'd likely never have got to the point we reached."

"Which was?"

"Falling in love. Proper, head over heels, soul mate kind of love."

"Why was that a problem?"

"Priya was married. Still is."

"Ahh," Clement winces. "To a bird or a bloke?"

"A guy."

"And let me guess. When it came down to leaving him, she bottled it."

"If only it were that simple. It wasn't her husband as such, but her family. Priya's parents are first-generation immigrants, and … let's just say that their only daughter setting up home with another woman would have clashed with their religious beliefs."

"So, she ended it?"

"I'm not sure either of us ended it as such. I tried to be patient and understanding, but the longer it went on, the more it hurt. You can't imagine what it's like, knowing the person you love is living a completely separate life where you don't even feature. Priya is an accountant, her husband a doctor, and they have all the trappings of a successful, middle-class life. She had exactly what her parents dreamed of when they moved to the UK."

"Is she happy?"

"Not really, no, which is why I held out so long. I thought, given time, she'd work on her parents and slowly shift their mindset, but every time I pressed the issue, she'd tell me that the time wasn't right."

"Sounds like an excuse to me."

"That's what I thought so back in March I gave her an ultimatum — leave her husband within four weeks, or we're finished. Those four weeks came and went, and I've not spoken to her since."

Clement puffs out a long breath and shakes his head.

"That's rough," he eventually says. "But that's the risk you take when you let someone in. It's a roll of a dice, a turn of a card."

"I get that. Doesn't make it any easier, though."

"You'll be okay, Doll. Time is a healer, they say."

"Is it?"

"Nah," he snorts after a moment's thought. "It ain't."

"Are you speaking from experience?"

"Yeah."

"You lost someone?"

"Literally. She was the one, then she carked it."

"Oh ... I'm so sorry."

"It was a long time ago."

"And it still hurts?"

"It did, but not so much these days. I reckon I'll get to see her again one day."

His answer takes me by surprise. Never in a million years would I have marked Clement as the religious type.

"Do you genuinely believe that?"

"I didn't, but now I do."

"Is that why you're so ... reckless?"

"Who says I'm reckless?"

343

"You told me you mug drug dealers. I'd call that reckless, and some would call it a death wish."

"Wishing for death ain't gonna change my situation. It seems I ain't going anywhere until I've done what I need to do."

"And what exactly is it you need to do?"

"Rebalance the books."

Before I get the chance to question his vague reply, he reaches out a hand and turns the stereo back on. Keane have left the stage, mercifully.

"Now, this is a decent tune," Clement says, deftly changing the subject. "I met Suzi Quatro once — good looking bird back in the day."

"I'd be impressed if I knew who she was."

"American singer and a proper rock chick."

"Where did you meet her?"

"After her gig at The Talk of the Town. A mate of a mate invited me along to a party, and she was there."

"Never heard of the place. Where is it?"

"It's called The Hippodrome these days."

"Oh, right. How was the party?"

"Crazy. If I weren't such a gent, some of the tales I could tell would blow your mind."

Clement then reaches out his hand again and cranks up the volume. As my eardrums are blasted by Ms Quatro's guitar and her enthusiasm for *Devil Gate Drive*, my companion seems to drift off into a world of his own.

The volume remains high for the next half dozen songs, and that seems to suit both of us. Wherever Clement's mind has taken him, he seems content, whereas my mind isn't so considerate. It wants to dwell on Priya and where she is right now. I'm only able to bring my thoughts back to the here and now and more immediate concerns when we reach our junction to exit the M25.

"This is us," I shout, reaching for the volume knob. "Take the A13 exit."

"Gotcha."

Once we're on the dual carriageway heading into London, it seems an appropriate time to discuss what the hell we're going to do once we reach our destination.

"You do realise this hotel has several hundred rooms, right?"

"And?"

"All we know is that Paula had a card for one of those rooms. We don't know which one, nor do we know for sure if that's where she decided to go after the call from Mike Goodwin. Come to think of it, we don't know anything for sure — this could be just another wild goose chase."

"Educated guess, gut instinct ... call it what you like, but something tells me your mate is up to her neck in this. If I'm right, it makes sense she'd head to that hotel."

"Not if she thinks we're on to her."

"Yeah, but she don't know that we broke into her house and found the room card. As far as she's concerned, the trail is cold."

"Okay, but that doesn't address my first point. There are hundreds of rooms in that hotel, and if Paula is there, how do we know which room she's in?"

"Let's get there first, and we'll work it out once we know what's what."

"That doesn't sound like much of a plan."

"It's a better plan than you had when you hopped on a plane to New York."

"I ... okay. Fair point."

As the buildings become taller and I direct Clement to take the final exit, apprehension froths in my stomach. I've already experienced more than enough highs and lows in this quest, but this has all the potential to be the ultimate high or a terminal low. When I checked the location of the Grampton Riverside Hotel on the map, I happened to notice that it's fairly close to London City Airport, and that's unlikely to be a coincidence. If Paula and David Smith are staying at the Grampton Riverside, chances are they won't hang around now we've scuppered the second part of their plot. They're only a ten-minute taxi ride from the airport, and from there they could jet off to any number of cities in Europe.

If we miss them, it really will be the end of the line. Smith might have slipped up on occasions, but I can't see him dropping the ball again; not when there's the potential to lose everything he conned from my mother.

One way or another, today will be the last day of my search for David Smith. What it means for the man sitting next to me, however, is still anyone's guess.

Chapter 40

I use the sat nav app on my phone to guide us the last mile. I don't know if it's a good omen or not, but the traffic around the area is unusually light by London standards.

"There's an underground car park straight ahead," I comment as we pass the Grampton Riverside Hotel on our right.

Being early afternoon, we've arrived at the ideal time of day to find a parking space. Most of last night's guests have long-since left and today's won't be checking in for another hour or two. Clement comes to a stop in front of a barrier as the machine next to the driver's door churns out a ticket.

"You need to take the ticket," I say as Clement sits and stares at the barrier.

"Eh?"

"Open your window and take the ticket. The barrier won't go up otherwise."

He mumbles something under his breath but follows my instructions. We then enter the car park and pass a row of cars that probably belong to the hotel staff or residents staying for more than just one night. Clement spots an empty bay on the left and throws the car into it with limited concern for the expensive motors on either side, missing a Range Rover by a fraction of an inch.

He kills the engine and turns to me.

"You ready?"

"I don't know. I feel a bit sick."

"My driving that bad?" Clement says with a wry smile.

"Yes, but that's not the primary reason I feel like throwing up."

"What's the matter, then?"

Before answering, I take a moment to dissect the cause of my symptoms.

"Ever since I booked that flight to New York, I've been running on adrenalin and hate ... you know, barrelling forward, tunnel vision, eyes on the prize. Sitting here now, this is it — I win or lose, but either way, this is the end."

"Nerves, then?"

"I guess so. Maybe, if I'm being completely honest with myself, I never really thought I had a cat in hell's chance of finding David Smith and yet, here we are. It's like ... what's the saying? It's the hope that kills?"

"You're nervous about falling at the last hurdle?"

"In a nutshell, yes, but not for myself — for Mum."

"She'll be alright, whatever happens."

"You think?"

"Trust me. You ain't the only one looking out for her."

I respond with a quizzical stare.

"Doll, I could sit here all afternoon and list a thousand reasons why you need to have a bit of faith, but it don't work like that. You've just gotta trust me."

"I do trust you."

Clement's eyebrows arch. "Really?"

"Yes. Really."

"Then we're all set. Nothing to be nervous about."

I find a smile and undo my seatbelt.

"Perhaps I wouldn't be quite so nervous if we had a plan. Any thoughts on that?"

"Yeah, I have as it goes."

"Care to share?"

"Let's head to the hotel. I'll tell you on the way."

We get out of the car and take a slow walk back through the car park.

"So, plan-A was to try every room with the key card," Clement says.

"There are hundreds of rooms, though."

"I know, which is why I ditched that idea. If they're in there, we need to flush 'em out somehow."

"We could set off the fire alarm."

"Nice idea but that won't work. The hotel staff will probably check if there's a fire before getting the guests to leave. They ain't gonna evacuate the place on the back of one alarm."

"No, I suppose not."

We walk on in silence for a dozen yards until Clement suddenly clicks his fingers.

"You got that Paula's phone number, right?"

"Of course."

"I want you to give her a bell and tell her that we know where she is. Mention the hotel name and that you're about to call the Old Bill. Then hang up."

"Okay, I can do that, but why? If your theory about Paula being involved with David Smith is right, why alert them?"

"What would you do in their shoes, knowing the Old Bill could be minutes away? You'd get your shit together sharpish and bolt."

"And, when they come through reception, we're there waiting?"

"More or less, yeah."

"That's genius," I say, reaching a hand into my pocket. "I'll call her now."

We come to a stop just outside the car park. Having called Paula several times of late, I don't have to scroll far to locate her number. I tap the dial icon and wait to be connected.

"Shit!"

"What?"

"It's gone straight to voicemail ... do I leave a message?"

"Don't waste your breath. Hang up."

I do as Clement asks, and look up at him.

"You know what a burner phone is?" he asks.

"It's a cheap phone that criminals use to send messages and make calls. They can't be traced."

"Yeah, you got it. That Goodwin fella said he tried calling her back but couldn't get through, so I reckon she's ditched her phone."

"Great," I groan. "That's the end of ... wait. I could send her a message via Facebook. She must have another phone, and I bet it's connected to her Facebook account."

"If you say so, Doll. Means nothing to me."

"We might as well try. Give me a second."

I open up the Facebook Messenger app and tap through to my recent chats with Paula.

"Here goes."

The message is short and concise: *I know you're at the Grampton Riverside Hotel. I'm calling the police.*

I send the message and the app confirms delivery.

"Now we just have to wait for her to read it," I say, keeping my eyes locked on the screen.

"If she don't, we're back to plan-A."

Long seconds pass as I continue to stare at the screen.

"Doll?"

"She still hasn't read it."

Clement takes the opportunity to remove the cigarette packet from his pocket and light up. He takes a deep drag and whilst I don't witness it, I certainly hear and smell the long puff of smoke exiting his lungs. I close

350

my eyes and count to three for no other reason than to prolong the inevitable. When I open my eyes, the message is still unread.

"Let's go," Clement says. "It was a good idea but—"

"Yes!" I squeal as the tiny icon next to my message lights up. "She's read it!"

I keep the phone in my hand just in case Paula dares to reply but now she knows we're on to her, surely she'll run.

"We need to find somewhere in the reception to hide out," I say as we hurry along the path towards the hotel's main entrance.

"We're better off waiting outside. Whether she's alone or with Smith, only an idiot would wander through the reception without checking the coast is clear. There's bound to be more than one way out of the hotel, and we can't cover every exit."

"Good point. So, where do we wait?"

As we close in on the hotel entrance, Clement points to the huge palm trees in stone planters on either side of the doors. "We'll wait behind one of those. They won't see us till they're outside, and then it'll be too late."

"Which one?"

"The furthest one."

"Why?"

"Why not?"

Assuming it'll take more than sixty seconds to get from their room down to the reception, I glance through the glass doors more in hope than expectation. Besides two members of staff behind the reception desk and a cleaner mopping up a spill on the marble floor, there's not a soul around.

We reach the second planter and take up position behind it, leaning against the front wall of the building. With the adrenalin pumping, it's hard to think straight, but within a few seconds, a worrying thought breaks through.

"This could be a waste of time," I say in a hushed voice. "We don't know they're in the hotel, do we?"

"If they ain't, they ain't. Fretting ain't gonna change it either way."

"You missed the point of my question. I was hoping for some reassurance."

"Alright, fine," Clement sighs. "They're in there."

I roll my eyes and turn my focus back to the view beyond the palm tree. Considering we're close to Central London, it's surprisingly quiet with just the sound of the wind and the occasional blare of a car horn in the distance. There is another question I could have asked Clement — what he intends to do if David Smith does stroll out of the hotel. I might have imagined him beating Smith to a pulp and the obvious way to find out would be to ask him, but I don't want to tempt fate.

I glance at my watch but as I didn't check the time when we secured our position, I can't calculate how long we've been standing here. A minute? Two? How long do we wait before we concede defeat? If the roles were reversed, I wouldn't want to hang around more than five minutes, ten at the absolute maximum.

"I could do with a piss," Clement remarks.

"You really pick your moments, don't you?"

"I'm not desperate. Just saying I could do with one."

"And what did you expect me to say in response?"

"Nothin'. I'm just making small talk, that's all."

"Can't you talk about the weather or the price of a pint, or—"

One of the hotel doors suddenly swishes open and a female figure emerges. I can only see her from behind as she darts along the same path we just walked, but the short blonde hair is an obvious giveaway.

"That's Paula!" I hiss, jabbing my elbow in Clement's midriff with a touch too much enthusiasm. "Yes! Yes!"

My elation is short-lived. The mounting weight of evidence against Mum's best friend might only be circumstantial, but it supports Clement's theory. That, in turn, is no cause for celebration.

"She don't look like she's on the run. No luggage, not even a coat."

"She's heading towards the car park, so I presume she's collecting her car."

"Do you know what motor she drives?"

"A Mercedes A-Class. Metallic red."

"Don't suppose you noticed it when we parked up?"

"Um, no, but I wasn't really looking. Maybe I should have."

"Don't matter now. Listen, here's the plan."

I look up at Clement, incredulous. "Now you're telling me about the plan?"

"Only just thought of it. You follow her but keep your distance, and then when she gets to her motor, you need to confront her. Don't get too close, though ... keep at least ten feet away."

"But what if—"

"Just do it. Go."

I glance past the palm tree to the path. Paula is halfway along and moving at a pace. There's no time to debate Clement's plan.

As soon as I pass the hotel doors, I break into a slight jog. The entrance to the car park is some seventy yards away, but more importantly, Paula is fifty yards ahead. There's no cover between us so if she were to turn around I've nowhere to hide. It's of little consequence because I'm in no mood to hide from anyone, least of all the duplicitous bitch I'm currently pursuing.

Paula reaches the car park entrance and slips past the barrier, disappearing from sight. I happen to glance over

353

my shoulder as I get close to the end of the path and I'm relieved to see Clement is only a dozen paces behind me. How long he stays there, or what he has planned, is unknown, but I need to concentrate on following my foe.

I reach the car park barrier and duck behind the ticket machine so I can check on Paula's progress. She's walking close to the row of cars on the opposite side to Mum's, her pace noticeably slower. Then, she raises her right hand, and although I can't see what she's holding, the blipping sound of a car unlocking is distinctive enough to suggest it's a key fob. It's my cue.

Moving briskly, I close the distance between us. That, in part, is helped because Paula has slowed to an almost standstill at the rear of a black saloon car. She then stops altogether and pulls out her phone. Whilst she's staring at the screen, the yards between us become feet.

No more than ten feet, Clement said.

I stop and clear my throat.

Paula's head snaps up.

Chapter 41

I come to a stop at the rear of a white Tesla, exactly ten feet away from a stunned woman with a mobile phone in her hand.

"Gina," she gasps. "What ... what are you doing here?"

"I could ask you the same question," I reply, fighting hard to at least appear calm. "Going somewhere, are we?"

"I'm meeting with a client, and then I intended to call you and ask what the hell that message meant."

"The one about the police?"

"Yes. Obviously."

"Do I really need to explain?"

Paula's body language suddenly shifts as she stands upright, her chin jutting out.

"Yes, you do. I don't know what's going on in that head of yours, but following me here and sending threatening messages is a bit weird, don't you think?"

It seems she intends to continue the charade.

"No weirder than you moving house and not telling a soul."

"What?" she snorts. "You're threatening me with the police because I didn't inform you I was moving house? Are you serious?"

"You know that's not why I called the police, Paula. I called them because you intended to defraud an equity release company with Mum's home as collateral. Ring any bells?"

"Good grief," she groans. "I don't know where you got that crazy idea from, Gina, but as I said, I'm here with a client, so we'll have to continue this conversation later."

She slips her phone into her back pocket and shoots me a disapproving look. Either I've made a huge mistake in assuming Paula's guilt, or she's been attending acting classes. Torn between both possibilities, I don't know what to say, or what to do. Clement never got as far as telling me his plan from this point onwards.

I've nothing to lose by lobbing a final grenade and seeing what Paula's reaction is.

"Is David Smith your client by any chance?" I ask. "Presuming he's now dropped the Bruce Franklin moniker."

Paula's eyes narrow for just a second before she adopts what I presume is a puzzled expression.

"What are you on about?" she scoffs.

Just as I'm about to reply, there's a flash of movement to the side of the car Paula is standing next to. That flash then looms large behind her.

"Make a sound, and you're dead," Clement growls, so close he could bite a chunk out of Paula's right ear if he so chose.

Rather than spin around or run, Paula remains frozen to the spot, completely motionless, bar the slight trembling of her bottom jaw. Clement's sudden appearance was surprise enough to me so I can only imagine Paula's shock.

"Don't hurt me," she gulps while raising her arms in the air.

"Put your arms by your side," Clement responds. "Or I *will* shoot you."

Shoot?

If Clement has a gun, Christ knows where he got it from. I've been with him most of the day and seen no evidence of one.

Paula swallows hard and fixes me with a look I can't decipher. I guess this must be the second phase of Clement's plan, so there's no need to maintain the distance.

"I'm sorry it's come to this," I say, stepping forward. "But we need answers."

"I don't know what you're talking about," Paula pleads. "I'm just here for a meeting."

"Why didn't you tell me or Mum you were selling your house?"

"Because ... because I've had a few money worries, and I need to downsize. I never said anything because you've got enough on your plate. I didn't want to burden either of you with my problems."

"That seems a fair enough reason," I reply with a distinct lack of emotion. "Now, what about last Thursday?"

"What about it?"

"Where were you?"

"I ... err ... I can't remember."

"You said you went to the garden centre, but that's not true, is it?"

"I honestly can't remember, Gina. Maybe it was Wednesday or Friday ... what does it matter?"

"It matters because someone met with Mike Goodwin at the bungalow on Thursday afternoon, and that someone signed the final documents to instigate a five hundred-thousand-pound loan against Mum's home."

"It wasn't me."

"I don't believe you."

"It wasn't. I genuinely don't know what you're talking about."

We could stand here all afternoon, batting accusations and denials back and forth. I need hard evidence, and, more importantly, I need to know if David Smith is waiting for Paula back in the hotel.

"Shall we open the boot of whoever's car this is?" I say to Clement.

"Sounds like a good idea."

"You do the honours, Doll."

I step towards the boot of the car but keep my eyes fixed on Paula. Whatever's running through her mind right now, she's doing a reasonable job of maintaining her poker face.

The car happens to be an Audi, and it looks almost new. I run my hand under the boot sill until my fingers touch the catch. The boot lid eases open.

"If you're here for a meeting, Paula," I say. "Whose car is this, and why is there a suitcase in the boot?"

"It's ... it's, um ... my client's car. He asked me to pop down and pick something up for him."

"What did he ask you to pick up?"

"Pardon?"

"What did he ask you to pick up for him?"

"His, err ... his laptop."

I lean into the boot space and check for a laptop. It's a large space, but besides the suitcase, it's empty.

"There's no laptop," I remark, turning to face Paula. "But you know that, don't you?"

My eyes drift towards the front pocket of her jeans and a bulge.

"Those your car keys?" I ask. "Give them to me."

"Slowly," Clement adds. "Wouldn't want an accident, would we?"

Following her instructions to the tee, Paula gingerly removes the car keys from her pocket and holds them up. I snatch them from her hand and then press the remote central locking button on the fob. Twenty yards from the Audi, a set of indicator lights flash on a metallic-red Mercedes.

"Back in one sec," I say to Clement.

"We ain't going nowhere," he replies.

I hurry along the row of vehicles and stop at the back of Paula's Mercedes. It takes one quick press of a button for the hatchback to reveal the contents of its boot. I shake my head, slam the boot shut, and trot back to my previous spot on the tarmac.

"Bit of a coincidence that you've also got a suitcase in your boot," I say to Paula.

"It's been in there since I left your mum's place," she retorts.

The circumstantial evidence against Paula is mounting, but none of it directly connects her to David Smith or the attempt to set up a loan against Mum's home. I need more, and if there really is a smoking gun, it's likely to be in Paula's back pocket.

"Give me your phone," I demand. "Now."

"Why?"

"Don't ask, just give."

"Gina, I don't have time—"

"If you've nothing to hide, give me your phone."

Paula's eyes flick left and right, but she makes no attempt to reach into her pocket. Clement, on the other hand, is proactive. He reaches down and pulls the phone out.

"This what you're after?" he asks, holding Paula's phone aloft.

"That's exactly what I'm after, thank you."

Clement holds the phone out, and for a second, Paula's muscles tense as if she's planning on grabbing it herself. If that was her intention, she doesn't follow through in time.

"What's the pin?" I ask once the phone is safely in my hand.

No response.

"Give me the pin, Paula."

Silent seconds pass. Apart from making a third and likely pointless demand, I don't know what else to do.

"Time for plan-B," Clement sighs.

He follows his statement with a wink that literally goes over Paula's head. As I can't mind read, all I can do is play along.

"I think you're right," I reply.

"Anything you wanna say to her before I do the deed?"

"No," I spit. "Just do it."

"Last chance," Clement growls. "If you ain't gonna talk to us, you're no use to us."

"What ... what do you mean?" Paula asks, her voice laced with panic.

"I mean, we want David Smith, but if you can't help us find him, you'll have to take what's coming."

"Please don't hurt me."

"I ain't gonna hurt you. It'll be painless ... painless, but terminal."

Clement leans in so his mouth is within a few inches of Paula's right ear. So close, she must be able to feel the heat of his breath on her neck.

"Gina is a good soul," he then says in a low voice. "But unfortunately for you, I ain't."

Paula's chest moves up and down at a noticeable rate as she looks straight at me, her eyes pleading.

"I'm sorry it's come to this," I say, dropping my gaze to the floor. "It's not in my hands anymore."

"Say goodbye," Clement growls.

"It's ... it's, 1972," Paula suddenly splutters. "The pin is 1972."

I immediately turn my attention to her phone and enter the code. The screen lights up, and my eyes are immediately drawn to the bottom-right corner, and a red bubble hovering over the WhatsApp messaging app. I tap the icon, and the app opens.

"You've got a message from 'D'," I say as I cast my eye over the last communication. "Who's that?"

Paula closes her eyes for a long moment, choosing not to reply. I open the message.

"He, or she, wants you to hurry up. That was sent two minutes ago — any comment?"

Still no response. I scroll up to the next message.

"Received at 11.09 am today: *Fuck. Get out of there and get back here ASAP.*"

In itself, the message is benign, but the same cannot be said of the one Paula originally sent.

I read it once, and my stomach muscles tighten. To be sure I haven't misunderstood the context, I read it again. The urge to throw up is almost overwhelming. I take a few deep breaths and stare back at Paula. She can't look at me.

"Your message to 'D' at 11.08 am: *Gina found Goodwin. She knows! What do I do?*"

Her shoulders slumped, Paula continues to stare at the tarmac. I take three steps forward so my feet are occupying the patch of tarmac she's clearly fascinated by.

"It's you, isn't it?" I hiss. "You're the one who helped Smith destroy my mum's life."

Her head bows forward. No answer to my question, but, tellingly, no denial either.

"Where is Smith?" Clement then asks.

Still, Paula remains silent.

"I'll count to three, and if you don't tell me, I'm gonna pull this fucking trigger. One—"

"Room 802," Paula replies in barely a whisper.

No confession, no obvious remorse — just one solemn link between the woman we've treated like one of the family and a man who almost destroyed our family. I should be elated because the hunt for David Smith is now over, but an entirely different emotion is now close to overwhelming.

"You absolute bitch," I snarl, my muscles tensing, hands balling into tight fists.

"I'm sorry," Paula sniffles, still avoiding eye contact.

"Sorry? You're fucking sorry?"

My mum is the loveliest woman you could meet. She's kind, warm-hearted, and compassionate — not the sort of woman who easily loses her temper. Unfortunately for Paula, I haven't inherited all of my mother's best traits.

The months of pain and hopelessness suddenly coalesce into a white-hot rage in my chest. Even if I wanted to, I couldn't stop what is now inevitable. I've waited too long to release it.

My right arm cuts through the air with such venom that the speed surprises even me. What will also be a surprise is where the punch lands because I've never thrown one before. The trajectory of my fist should land it somewhere on Paula's face, but exactly where is anyone's guess. I don't care, as long as it transfers some of Mum's pain to her so-called best friend.

Flesh strikes flesh.

"Fuck!" I gasp as a sharp pain explodes across the top of my hand.

Paula doesn't so much as yelp, but that might be because her head is slumped forward, and the only thing keeping her upright is the giant of a man behind her.

I clutch my right hand and hiss breaths through my clenched teeth.

"Can't say I saw that coming," Clement remarks with a slight grin.

"Is she ... Christ, I haven't killed her, have I?"

"Nah, she's just spark out."

Without a moment's hesitation, Clement scoops up Paula's unconscious carcass and unceremoniously deposits it in the still-open boot of the Audi. Without a second glance, he then slams the lid shut and turns to face me.

"That's her dealt with," he says, casually. "She'll be out like a light for a while."

"I didn't hit her that hard."

Clement's eyebrows arch. "Yeah, you did."

"I never meant to ... you're the one with the bloody gun."

"This, you mean?"

He holds up a cylindrical cigarette lighter.

"Stick it in someone's back, and they can't tell if it's a lighter or the barrel of a shooter. Works every time."

I am relieved that he's not armed. Clement is dangerous and unpredictable enough without throwing a loaded gun into the mix.

"Okay, now Paula's out for the count, what do we do?"

"I think we've got some business to attend to. Room 802, weren't it?"

"You don't think I should call the police?"

"Only if we you wanna give Smith time to bolt."

"Err ..."

I'm struggling to think straight. With the adrenaline fading from my system, the stark reality of Paula's deceit is beginning to hit home. How could she?

"Doll?" Clement prompts. "Wakey, wakey."

"Sorry ... what do we do?"

"You should send a message on that Paula's phone, saying you're on your way back. We don't want that fucker Smith getting suspicious and bolting before we get there."

"We're going to his room?"

"Too bleedin' right we are. This is it, Doll — time to go get what you've been searching for."

Chapter 42

Clement strides at such a pace that I have to jog to keep up with him.

"What's the plan?" I pant as we approach the hotel doors.

"We go to the room, and then ... leave the rest to me."

"He's hardly going to open the door for you, is he? And he certainly won't open it for me."

"You got a key card, ain't you?"

In all the drama, I'd totally forgotten about the key card. I slap both my back pockets.

"Got it," I say with some relief.

"He's expecting his sidekick, so it'll be a nice surprise for the bloke when we pitch up."

"Surprise, yes. Nice, I don't think so."

"If you kick as hard as you punch, Doll, he'll be able to wash his balls the same time he brushes his teeth."

I smile up at Clement as we step through the doors to the hotel reception.

There was a time, not that long ago, when I fantasised about confronting the man who took everything from my mother. Looking back, it was nothing more than a fantasy because as much as I wanted to attack him, it's unlikely I'd have stood a chance if he'd retaliated.

Now, though, I no longer need to fantasise. I have a Clement at my disposal.

"This way," I say, changing course across the marble floor towards the lifts.

The position of the reception desk makes it impossible not to catch the eye of the two members of staff on duty. The woman is preoccupied, but the thirty-something male with slicked-back hair throws a smile our way. Knowing full well that Clement won't reciprocate, I do the honours. If the receptionist is curious why such an unlikely couple are about to enter the lift in one of London's most expensive hotels, he doesn't see fit to enquire.

I press the lift call button, and the doors open almost immediately. We step inside and, as I inspect the bank of buttons on the right-hand wall, I can see why the receptionist had no cause to question our right to be here — a sign confirms guests must tap their key card on a panel before they select their destination floor. I guess if you're paying the hotel's eye-watering room rates, you expect the security to be robust.

Maybe that's one of the reasons David Smith chose it.

I duly tap the key card against the panel.

"If it's room 802, I presume we want the eighth floor, right?" I ask.

"Makes sense."

I press the button, noting that the eighth floor is the highest available and likely where the most expensive rooms and suites are located. The thought of Paula and David Smith living it up in a penthouse suite on Mum's money removes any lingering regret I might have had for punching the former in the head. She deserves worse, and I'll make sure she gets it once we're done with her partner in crime.

A soft chiming sound signifies that we've reached the eighth floor, and the doors glide open. Clement's body language appears less relaxed as he steps out of the lift first. I decide against mentioning his lack of manners.

The last time we were standing on a landing together was in a dump of a building in Brooklyn, just before we paid a visit to a rude pothead. This landing couldn't be more of a contrast. Clearly the work of an experienced interior designer, the landing alone is plusher than most of the hotel rooms I've frequented over the years.

Directly ahead, a gold-coloured sign fixed to the wall confirms that suites 801-809 are to the left.

"I knew that wanker would be in a suite," I snarl. "Funded by Mum's money, no doubt."

"Keep your voice down," Clement hisses.

"Sorry."

"Give me the key card."

I hand it over without question. Perhaps in my fantasy I'd be the one to enter the room first, just to see the look of shock on David Smith's face. In reality, I'm happy to settle on seeing the terror in his eyes when Clement confronts him.

Slowly, silently, we pass the door to suite 801. Perhaps because suites are much bigger than standard rooms, there are no doors on the opposite wall. That means the next door is the one we'll be entering.

Clement reaches the door to suite 802 and comes to a stop. He then turns to face me and holds a finger to his lips. I nod once, acknowledging the request for silence, although there's nothing I can do about the frantic thumping in my chest.

This is it.

Clement cautiously slides the key card into the slot on the door handle, and in the silence, it's impossible not to hear the click as the mechanism releases the lock. He then grips the handle, and I prepare myself for what is likely to be a shock and awe entrance.

Duly, Clement drops the handle and pushes the door open, but he doesn't immediately enter the room. From my position, I can't see what he's looking at, but I'd guess he's just ensuring there are no nasty surprises waiting for us. With his attention fixed directly ahead, he then takes one stride forward, disappearing into the room.

I count to three and I'm concerned that there isn't any verbal reaction to Clement's presence. Surely, if some random stranger wandered into your hotel room, you'd react by asking what the hell they're doing there, likely in a raised voice.

This is a concern.

Clement told me to be silent, but he never told me to stand still. I shuffle a few steps and peek around the corner. At first glance, the entrance to the suite is no different to that of a typical hotel room. I can't see into the suite itself as Clement's frame is blocking the view directly ahead, but he's beyond a closed door on the left, likely the bathroom.

If David Smith is in this room, I don't understand how he can fail to notice the oversized unit standing just inside the entrance area.

Did Clement check the bathroom?

No longer willing to wait outside, I step into the room and close the door, gingerly manoeuvring the handle so the lock doesn't clunk loudly into place. Unless Smith wants to exit via the balcony, and a hundred-foot drop, his only way out is through the closed door behind me. That assumes he's in here, of course, and I'm beginning to fear he might not be.

A troublesome thought arrives. I have Paula's phone securely stowed in my pocket, but Clement speculated that she might have used a burner. We never frisked her for a second phone, and what if she regained consciousness within a few minutes? She might have called David Smith and warned him.

It's speculation, and unhelpful speculation at that — if he's not here, he's not here. I shake the thought from my mind and refocus.

Clement takes a cautious step forward, glancing around the left-hand corner where the entrance area opens out to the main suite. Going on his reaction, or lack of one, Smith wasn't lurking behind the corner, ready to scarper.

"Psst," I hiss, so quietly I can't be certain it was even audible.

Clement slowly turns his head until he's staring back at me over his left shoulder. I jab my finger towards the bathroom door and mouth five words: *Did you check in there?*

The already prominent scowl lines across the big man's forehead deepen, making it clear I'm not helping the situation. I'm about to mouth an apology when the shadow behind Clement suddenly shifts.

Too late, I realise it's not a shadow. Something or someone has emerged from a recessed section of the wall just beyond Clement's position.

The information moves across my neural network at lightning speed, processing every frame captured by my eyes: a hand holding a glass bottle, and that bottle moving along a near-horizontal plane towards Clement's head. Quick as it is, there just isn't time for my brain to send a signal to my vocal cords. I get as far as opening my mouth but by then, the information is out of date.

The bulbous end of the bottle strikes the side of Clement's head with such force, the exploding fragments pepper the left-hand wall like buckshot. A millisecond later, fat globules of water — previously contained within the bottle — spray across my face, my chest, and the door behind me.

When I move my hand to wipe one of those globules from my brow, I have to close my eyes for no more than an extended blink. That's all the time it takes for everything to change.

Clement is no longer standing in front of me. His lower legs, however, are still in view, although they're now flat against the plush carpet, motionless. The rest of him is hidden by the room's architecture.

As my eyes flick upwards, there is new and urgent information to send across the neural network. Standing over my felled friend and guardian's legs, the shadow now has form. The shadow is also holding the jagged end of a broken bottle neck in an outstretched hand, aimed in my direction.

"Open your mouth and you lose an eye," David Smith warns in his faux American accent.

The voice I've heard many times but hoped never to hear again unless deployed in a desperate plea, rings in my ears. It sets off a tsunami of adrenalin, and more hate than any human could hope to contain.

"Fuck you ... David," I snarl. "And drop the phoney accent. I know exactly who you are, and so do the police. They're on their way."

"Then step aside," he replies, letting me hear his true accent for the first time. "This doesn't have to end badly for either of us."

The police are not on their way, and I now face the true and damning reality of meeting my nemesis alone. I'm a shade over five foot while the man waving a broken bottle is six foot tall, broad-shouldered, and has the physique of a man who gets full value from his gym membership.

Most bookmakers wouldn't even bother calculating the odds of a Gina Jackson victory in this contest, they're that long.

And yet, I cannot let him get away.

"You destroyed my mother," I say, swallowing hard.

"It was just business. Helen had something I needed, and I took it. Nothing personal."

"Nothing personal? Leaving Mum at the altar whilst emptying her bank account is beyond personal. What you did was wicked."

"What's done is done," he shrugs. "All that matters is the next sixty seconds."

He's right on one count — I have no more than sixty seconds to hope that he drops his guard long enough for a literal punt. It's the longest of long shots, but I've seen bigger men collapse in a heap when their delicate testicles meet the unforgiving force of female knee or boot.

"There's no point you running," I say, trying my utmost not to let the fear show. "I know everything, and on the journey here I emailed the detective handling Mum's case. You're finished whether you leave this building or not."

"You know nothing," he spits. "Now, be a good girl and step into the bathroom."

To emphasise his point, he nods towards the door on my left.

"How about Evelyn Conroy, for starters? I met her."

"Who?"

"The widower from Bridgeport, Connecticut. You drugged her, and then stole her late husband's graduation ring."

I make a point of looking at his hand, hoping he'll do the same. All I need is one second.

"My, my," he sneers, keeping his eyes locked directly ahead. "You have been a busy beaver, Gina. I'd be impressed if I actually gave a shit. Now, I won't tell you again — get in the fucking bathroom."

He takes a step forward, keeping the broken bottle at the same height as my face. It's now worryingly close.

"No," I gulp. "Not a chance."

370

I edge backwards until my shoulder blades touch the door, countering Smith's advance. The advantage is short-lived, though, as he takes another step forward.

"You think your Mum was upset when I emptied her bank account? Imagine how upset she'll be at her only daughter's funeral."

Slowly, he moves forward until the bottle is so close, I can clearly see every shard of splintered glass. There's no time left, no opportunity to strike unless I create one.

I make a show of widening my eyes and staring beyond Smith's right hip, as if something has caught my attention. It's my hope that he turns and checks that Clement is still lying motionless on the carpet, which he unfortunately is.

He falls for my ruse and snatches a quick glance over his shoulder. I doubt I have a full second to react, but it's immaterial now because whatever time I have, it's running out. On top of the time constraint, I'm too close to the door to swing my leg back before aiming it towards Smith's groin. There's only one other option, and I need to enact it now.

In one swift movement, I fall into a squat and propel myself forward whilst simultaneously thrusting out my right arm, fist balled tightly. My knuckles are still tender from the impact with Paula's face, but Smith's genitals will prove a more malleable target.

Frame by glorious frame, I follow the trajectory of my fist as it homes in on the few square inches of fabric protecting Smith's modesty. Whether I make contact or not, my momentum will bring some part of my body, probably my shoulder, into contact with his legs. There's no going back, no way I can abort — this is a one-shot deal with no go-around, no second chance.

Two events occur in almost the same exact moment, separated by fractions of a second. My fist strikes Smith's groin exactly where I hoped, and with more potency

371

than I expected. I know it landed hard because of the pain in my hand. However much my hand hurts, it's nothing compared to the searing, white-hot pain now emanating from somewhere left of my neck.

As my shoulder crashes into Smith's shins, the pain becomes overwhelming. The man who inflicted that pain tumbles forward, and although I don't witness it, I hear him land heavily on the floor whilst the pained groaning confirms the potency of my punch.

I twist my head to try and see what's happening with Smith, but suddenly his suffering is no longer a priority. The shoulder of my jacket, previously a sandy brown colour, is now a deep shade of red.

Blood, and so much of it.

Despite the chaos of the scene and my heightened state of confusion, I know what's happened, and I know what it means. That broken bottle pierced my flesh and, if the blood is any barometer, it pierced deep.

My eyes begin to flicker like an old TV set, and the searing pain is offset by a sudden and profound coldness. Somewhere out of sight, I hear a shuffling sound which I can only attribute to Smith getting to his feet. My attack achieved what I intended, but the results were only ever going to be temporary. There was no time to plan what came next, but I hoped that once he was incapacitated, however briefly, I could deliver a kick to the head, rendering him unconscious.

That plan failed, and now David Smith is about to walk away.

I hear the sound of the door handle levering downwards, and then a blunt force thumps against my left foot. With my knee already pressed up against the wall, I'm in no position to adjust my leg.

"Fucking move!" Smith spits, banging the door against my foot twice more.

I glance towards my shoulder again. The blood is now seeping down the arm of my jacket, which would explain why I feel so groggy, so light-headed. I don't know if I *can* move. I can't even find sufficient breath to tell him to go to hell.

"Move!"

He can say it till he's blue in the face. Even if I could move, I wouldn't. It's a futile gesture, but I'm not willing to make his inevitable escape any easier. Instead, I loll my head to the right and let out a low groan.

"I'll fucking move you myself, then."

There's a sudden movement in the corner of my eye, and then Smith's lower torso comes into view. If I had the energy, it would be the simplest of tasks to roll over and throw another punch towards his groin. Before that thought has had a chance to take root, Smith grabs my left wrist and tugs my arm with almost enough force to pull it clean from its socket.

I try to scream, but the shot of pain across my shoulder is so acute it steals my breath. Ignorant or indifferent to my suffering, Smith continues tugging my wrist, dragging my sorry carcass across the carpet away from the door.

I'm not letting him go without a fight. I try to twist my body so I can kick out a leg, but then another tug drags me onto my back, and the accompanying agony drains the last molecule of resistance from my body.

He tugs again, and my head falls to the right. Because I'm now half out of the entrance area, I can finally see beyond the wall, into the main suite where Clement fell.

Where Clement fell ...

Fell.

Why is he no longer where he fell?

Maybe it's a sign of losing consciousness, or the shadow of the Grim Reaper stepping forward to gather my soul, but suddenly there's a lot less light reflecting off the gloss-white skirting board.

A swish of air, followed by a sound I can't decipher, like someone hurling a raw joint of beef against a hard surface. It takes a second or two to realise there's no longer a force gripping my wrist.

Then, a figure fills my narrowing vision.

"Doll! You still with me?"

It wasn't the Grim Reaper after all, more a guardian angel.

"S ... s ... Smith?"

"He's spark out, and I'll deal with him shortly. For now, you need an ambulance."

Clement pulls out his phone and jabs the screen repeatedly. Then, he places the handset to his ear while cupping my cheek with his free hand.

"You stay awake, Doll. You hear me?"

"Ugh ..."

"I mean it. I don't wanna give you a slap, but I will."

Those eyes that I thought so cold, so empty, are now blazing with warmth. Maybe there is a real human lurking behind them.

"Ambulance, now!" he bellows. "There's been a stabbing. Room 802, Grampton Riverside Hotel, Docklands, and be bleedin' quick about it."

He terminates the call and returns the phone to his pocket.

"Right, you," he then says. "I'm gonna sit you up and then find something to stop the bleeding. Alright?"

I can barely keep Clement's face in focus. Conversing is beyond me.

He disappears momentarily and then returns with a pristine white towel.

"This is gonna hurt a bit, but it's for the best."

I must be beyond pain because I barely feel a thing as the big man carefully sits me upright against the nearest wall. He then balls up the towel and carefully pushes it

374

under the collar of my jacket, towards the bloodiest part of my shoulder.

"That should stem the bleeding till the ambulance arrives," he says.

"Uhh ..."

"You're gonna have to do better than that, Doll. Talk to me."

"I ... I ... feel ..."

"You feel what?"

"I ... feel ..."

"For fuck's sake. Please don't say horny."

Involuntary and unexpected, the snort of laughter feels good, considering the circumstances. I'd rather die with a smile on my face than a pained grimace.

"Seeing as you're not feeling too chatty, how about you just watch?"

"Huh?"

Clement gets to his feet and then strides across the room to a set of patio doors. Blinking hard, I watch on as he slides the left-hand door open and then steps onto the balcony. After glancing down at the street, probably to check if the ambulance has arrived, he steps back into the room.

For a fleeting moment, Clement disappears from my field of vision, but when he returns he's holding David Smith's ankles. It's a shame the arsehole is unconscious and can't experience what it's like to be dragged across the floor like a rag doll.

My eyelids suddenly feel like lead. I don't think I've ever experienced such tiredness, and I want to give in. I really want to give in.

Clement comes to a stop by the patio doors. He bends over, grabs Smith under the armpits, and with almost unbelievable ease, hoists the still unconscious conman over his shoulder.

What's going on?

Reality bleeds away as I drift towards that space between consciousness and sleep. It's a surreal but painless place where I no longer feel scared, no longer feel angry. I don't much feel anything.

Nothing is real. Nothing is ...

Clement is not stepping onto the balcony. He's not ... is he? Details fade away until all I can see is the silhouette of a giant man, leaning over the balcony. I can just about make out a second, almost shapeless silhouette draped over his shoulder. Clement stoops forward, the second silhouette disappears in maybe the final blink of my eyes.

Did he ...?

My God.

Have I just witnessed ...?

The still-standing silhouette turns around, steps back through the door, and closes it. I can't fight the tiredness a second longer.

My eyelids close.

Peace.

Then, a presence.

"Job's a good'un, Doll. Time for us both to move on."

And with that, reality bleeds away.

Chapter 43

The British media frequently claim our National Health Service is inefficient. Maybe there are too many counters counting beans or too many humans in human resources, but in my recent experience, the frontline staff are the model of efficiency.

Eight days ago, two paramedics transferred me from a hotel room to an ambulance and then sped across town to the Royal London Hospital. There, the accident and emergency team took over and, at some point, I landed on a table in an operating theatre.

Of course, I was completely unaware of these events on account of being unconscious the whole time. In fact, two entire days passed before I fully regained consciousness. To me, those days never happened — one moment, I'm sprawled on the floor of a hotel room, and the next, I'm lying in a hospital bed. Fortunately, Mum was at my bedside when I returned from the two days of nothingness.

In those first tearful minutes, I realised that my ordeal had profoundly affected both of us, but in different ways. After we'd attempted a hug — not easy with several dozen fresh stitches holding together a deep wound in my upper back — I realised that the woman perched on the edge of my bed was not the same woman I left watching TV a few days prior. The dynamic of protector and protected had shifted.

I wanted to talk, ask questions, but a tall, middle-aged man with thinning hair arrived on the scene. He introduced himself as Dr Patterson, and after Mum excused herself, the doctor provided an update on my condition. It was a sobering experience.

I've no idea whose blood ended up pumping through my veins, but I lost so much of my own that I should have died, according to Dr Patterson. Swallowing hard, I tried to convey my gratitude for the NHS staff who'd collectively saved my life, but the doctor said with an injury like mine, ninety-nine times out of a hundred, their efforts would have been in vain.

Just before he left the room, Dr Patterson said, too cheerfully considering the situation, that I was a lucky girl, and someone must have been watching over me. If he meant literally, that would have been Mum, who remained at my bedside the entire two days I lost. If he meant metaphorically, a few contenders spring to mind.

After the doctor left, Mum returned with a cup of tea and a small packet of Bourbon biscuits. The tea was weak and the biscuits dry, but both were welcome.

The caffeine and sugar helped pave the way for Mum to ask a simple but pertinent question: what happened?

Groggy and heavily medicated, I struggled to unpick what I could remember and what I didn't want Mum to know.

It didn't matter.

Mum already knew more than I would ever have wanted her to know, including David Smith's fate. With a surprising amount of stoicism, she passed on what she'd gleaned from the police while I was still unconscious. To say I was stunned by how calmly she relayed the facts didn't come close. I was apoplectic when I learned about Paula's deceit, and I presumed Mum would be inconsolable. As it was, she veered between bitter and livid. On one occasion, I did pluck up the courage to ask how she was coping. Mum gripped my hand firmly before telling me in no uncertain terms that she was coping just fine, and then she made me promise not to worry.

That was easier said than done — worried has been my default state for months now. However, a visit from a member of the local constabulary helped put both our minds at rest.

Detective Constable Vicky Grant stood impassively next to my bed and confirmed that David Smith, AKA Bruce Franklin, had died on impact after falling from the balcony of suite 802 at the Grampton Canary Hotel. Of course, DC Grant asked if I could shed any light on Smith's demise, but I pleaded ignorance. I told her that all I could remember was a brief skirmish with Smith, in which I punched him in the balls, and he stabbed me with a broken bottle. That was it.

Being that London is one of the most surveilled cities on the planet, several cameras in the hotel captured two people entering the lift early in the afternoon. They then entered Smith's room using a key card. Patently, one of those people was me, and DC Grant was keen to know the name of the man who had entered the suite with me.

Who knows what strategies the police deploy when trying to eke information out of a witness or suspect, but DC Grant could have resorted to thumbscrews, and I'd still have stuck to my answer: I couldn't remember his name.

It was obvious she didn't believe me, but Mum stepped in to remind the detective, in no uncertain terms, that her daughter was the victim and David Smith was a career conman who very nearly killed her only child. The detective's face was a picture when Mum said that if she even dared to paint Smith out as a victim, she'd go to the press and tell them the whole story. That would not have painted the police in a particularly good light, seeing as a thirty-three-year-old artist managed to track down a man they'd not even bothered to look for.

I think DC Grant warmed to Mum after that and, in fairness to her, the detective listened intently as I filled in the blanks regarding David Smith's crimes both here and in America. She, in turn, revealed a few interesting details about what happened in the hours and days after the incident at the hotel.

Shortly after the ambulance arrived at the Grafton Canary Hotel to collect me, an emergency service call handler received a phone call from an anonymous male. That individual stated that a woman was lying unconscious in the boot of a black Audi saloon in the hotel car park. He then confirmed that the woman in the boot was involved with a man named David Smith, and together, they had conned Helen Jackson out of £1.9 million and then attempted to organise a fraudulent loan against her property.

After rescuing Paula Webster from the boot of the Audi, one of DC Grant's colleagues subsequently found two mobile phones and a laptop computer in the hotel room. Those devices offered enough evidence for the police to take the anonymous allegations seriously. They interviewed Paula and initially she denied any involvement. When the detective presented her with a swathe of damning WhatsApp messages to and from David Smith, Paula returned a 'no comment' reply to every subsequent question.

I don't know the detective's name, but he single-handedly redeemed my faith in the police with his reaction to Paula's strategy. He informed Paula that David Smith had booked just one airline ticket to Bern in Switzerland for the day they were due to depart together. They also tested Paula's phone and discovered the same Trojan software Smith installed on Mum's phone. It seems that the money from the sale of Paula's cottage would never have settled her mounting debts because the moment it landed in her account, David Smith intended to transfer it out.

If I hadn't arrived at the hotel with Clement and upset their plans, Paula Webster would have ended up as much a victim as a perpetrator. For that reason, and with the prospect of a much-reduced sentence, she decided to cooperate with the police and tell them everything.

And what a sad tale of betrayal it turned out to be.

Six months prior to the New York trip Paula planned with Mum, she received a message via an online dating app. That first flattering message stoked Paula's interest, and after a week of intense messaging, she went on a date with a man calling himself David Lynton-Smith — yet another moniker for the conman, David Smith.

Paula fell hard for Smith, and within six weeks, he had her under his spell. At that point, he told Paula he had just received a once-in-a-lifetime opportunity to invest in an equestrian centre in New England. Anyone scrolling long enough on Paula's Facebook profile would learn that she once owned a horse and, for much of her youth, she was obsessed with all things equine. They discussed the opportunity at length, and that's when Smith admitted he still needed to raise another hundred grand to secure his dream.

With the bait in place, Smith assumed that Paula would quickly suggest selling her cottage and investing in his supposed opportunity. He dropped enough hints about the two of them getting married, running the centre together, and living happily ever after. What Smith didn't know is how much debt Paula had accrued over the years through failed business ventures and her weakness for retail therapy. That debt equated to almost all the equity in the cottage she inherited. In short, Paula

Webster had less than fifty grand to her name, and even that modest sum was tied up in her home.

Unable to get his hands on a worthwhile sum of money, Smith backed away from the relationship, saying that it wouldn't be fair on either of them to continue with it, knowing he had to move across The Pond as soon as he'd secured the hundred grand he needed.

Thinking she was about to lose the love of her life, Paula pleaded with Smith to give her time to find the money. The obvious option would have been to ask a friend, specifically one with almost two million quid in the bank. Smith suggested as much, but Mum and Paula had only known each other for eighteen months at that point, and there was no way Mum would have agreed to it.

That's when Smith first mooted the idea of helping themselves to Mum's money. I can only guess, but I suspect he had nothing to lose at that point.

Throughout history, people have made incredible sacrifices in the name of love, but they've also committed the most atrocious acts. For that reason, it's not entirely impossible to imagine what went through Paula's mind once she got over the shock of hearing Smith's suggestion. We'll never know how he sold the idea, but Paula did admit in her police interview that initially, the plan was to liberate £350,000 from Mum's account: one hundred grand for the investment and the rest to settle all Paula's debts. From there, the couple would be free to start their new life.

Their plot, once settled, would begin with Smith bumping into Mum while she was in New York. By following our posts on social media, Paula was able to confirm we were in a gallery and all Smith had to do was follow us once we left. As soon as we stepped foot in that coffee shop, he had his opportunity to pounce.

382

Fate played no part in Mum meeting the man she thought was her soul mate.

Paula claimed that she had no idea that Smith would empty both Mum's bank accounts, but by that point, she was all in on the con. He justified the theft by showing Paula photos of another potential investment opportunity — a dilapidated beachside mansion he wanted to buy and convert into luxury vacation condos. The bigger the dream, the more Paula fell for Smith's lies.

It's easy to look at what Paula did and condemn her, not just for the cruelty but also for her rank naivety. Did she really think that once Smith had secured the money from the fraudulent loan, they'd ride off into the sunset together? People in love often make illogical decisions, and although it was nowhere near the scale of Paula's naivety, I once let love override my gut instincts.

Like Mum, I bet Paula Webster is now ruing the day she met David Smith.

As for Smith himself, the police have only gleaned minimal information about the man so far. Born in London in 1975 to an American father and English mother, David Ambrose Smith led an unassuming life up until he attended university. He was expelled in his second year after it came to light that he'd set up an investment club for his fellow students, promising returns of up to twenty per cent within six months. He claimed that his father worked on Wall Street, and he had access to insider knowledge, but it turned out Smith was running a crude Ponzi scheme and spending the investments on drink, drugs, and partying. That was the last known record of David Smith, although his name will enter the public records any day now when it appears on a death certificate.

It's hard to imagine anyone mourning Smith's death, particularly the so-far unspecified number of other victims the police believe he's conned in recent years. The thinnest of silver linings is that amongst Smith's possessions, the police found a gold graduation ring inscribed with the letters B.C.N.Y. I told DC Grant the sad tale of Evelyn Conroy, and she promised to call Evelyn and let her know they'd secured her late husband's ring. I suggested that DC Grant should also let Evelyn know that David Smith is now dead. That fact should deliver the closure she deserves.

"Do you mind if I sit here?" a grey-haired chap asks.

Of the eight chairs in the hospital reception area, the only one free is next to me.

"Not at all," I smile up at the man.

He slowly lowers himself onto the chair using a walking stick for support.

"Bleedin' hip," he says by way of explanation once he's settled. "I've been waiting nine months for a new one."

I don't know what to say, so I just offer a sympathetic smile. The old guy's use of the word 'bleedin' then reignites thoughts of a man who's occupied my mind an awful lot in recent days.

Not many people can say they've faced their own death whilst witnessing another. I'm not even sure what label I'd attach to the scene that played out on the balcony of suite 802. Revenge? Justice? Cold-blooded murder? I was in no fit state to prevent Clement from dropping David Smith from that balcony, but I've wrestled with what I might have done in different circumstances. Would I have pleaded with him to stop?

My answer came in the middle of the night while lying in a hospital bed as the potency of the painkillers ebbed away. The pain of the injury inflicted by David Smith served as a reminder that he didn't care if I lived or died when he thrust that broken bottle towards my neck. I could, and maybe should have died that afternoon, and

Smith would have fled the scene, escaping justice once more.

I remember Clement speculating that Smith was rotten to the core, and I could argue that there's undoubtedly something rotten about conning vulnerable women, but would that justify killing him? Probably not, but then Smith crossed the line. He could have killed Clement when he cracked that bottle across his head, and he didn't think twice about plunging the jagged neck of that same bottle into my flesh.

David Smith *was* rotten to the core, and if I'm completely honest with myself, I'm glad he's dead. In an unjust world where people like Smith constantly get away with inflicting pain and misery on the innocent, I can live with the justice Clement meted out.

As for the big man's whereabouts since the events in suite 802, I hoped he might pop in to say hello, but then I remembered the final words he said to me before I lost consciousness: *Time for us both to move on*.

Chapter 44

"Sorry, I'm late, darlin'," Mum pants as she crosses the floor from the hospital entrance. "It took me half an hour to find a parking space."

"It's okay. It's not as though I'm in a hurry to get anywhere."

I flash a smile at the old guy next to me and then get to my feet. For Mum's sake, I try not to wince. Whilst my injury is healing nicely, according to the nurse who replaced the dressing an hour ago, any kind of movement serves as a reminder that a now-dead man plunged a broken bottle into my flesh only eight days ago.

"Will you be okay walking?" Mum asks. "It's a good half a mile away."

"It's fine, Mum. I could do with some fresh air and stretching my legs."

"You do remember this is London?" she chuckles. "You've got sod all hope of fresh air."

"True."

We lock arms and head towards the exit. As I pass through the doors, I offer a silent prayer that I won't have cause to return for a very long time, if ever.

The streets of London are as noisy and chaotic as ever, but they're a welcome relief from the bedlam and clinical stench of a hospital ward.

"Everything okay with you?" I ask Mum as we amble back to the car.

"You mean, apart from my former fiancé and best friend conspiring to steal my life savings and my only daughter nearly dying?"

There's enough intonation in Mum's voice to suggest she's making light of the situation.

"Yeah, apart from that."

"I'm good ... all things considered."

I'm relieved but also perplexed.

"You're wondering why I'm not on the verge of a nervous breakdown, aren't you?" Mum then adds.

"Well, I wasn't going to say anything, but since you brought the subject up, I presumed you'd taken to smoking pot, you're that chilled."

Mum's snort of laughter is so loud it startles a passing cyclist.

"As if," she then replies. "But never say never."

"Okay, if it's not narcotics, what's behind your positivity?"

"Two things, I suppose. Firstly, I had a call from DC Grant just before I left home, and the financial fraud team found two of Smith's bank accounts. She said that although it might take a while, there's a good chance I'll get at least some of my money back."

"That is fantastic news," I gush.

"It is, so fingers crossed I won't have to sell the bungalow."

We come to a stop at a pedestrian crossing, and Mum presses the button to summon the green man. As we stand silently on the kerb, there's no mention of the second reason she seems in a better place, mentally.

"Well? What's the second reason?"

"If I tell you, no bitching, okay?"

"Why would I bitch about you being in a positive frame of mind?"

"Because ... I didn't mention it, but Lynn has been staying with me."

"Oh."

"And before you say anything, she *did* have an ulterior motive."

"Eh? She admitted it?"

"Yes, but it had nothing to do with money. She wanted to spend time with me — just the two of us."

"Am I allowed to ask why?"

The traffic on both sides of the road comes to a halt as the green man on the opposite post lights up. We cross over, and Mum clears her throat once we're back in our stride.

"After all these years," she then says, "Lynn and I have never really talked about what happened."

"She ran off with your husband — what's to talk about?"

"Up until last week, I'd have agreed with you. Thing is, darlin', it never crossed my mind what Lynn went through when she ran off with your excuse for a father."

"Whatever she went through, I'd say she deserved it."

"No, she didn't," Mum replies sternly.

"Why? What did she go through?"

"It's not my place to say, but what I will tell you is that my little sister suffered more than I did. Far more."

"Right, well, why has it taken so long for her to say anything?"

"Shame, I suppose ... and you."

"Me?" I snort.

"Lynn thought that at some point, you might want to build bridges with your dad, maybe be part of his life again. She never told a soul what he put her through because she didn't want you thinking ill of the man."

"Christ. I ... I had no idea."

"I'm ashamed to say that neither did I. All those years of harbouring resentment, thinking that I wasn't good enough, and in reality, I dodged a bloody great big bullet."

We walk on in silence for a few dozen yards while I process Mum's revelation.

"In a way," she then continues, "Lynn helped me get my head around what Paula did."

"How so?"

"Paula fell in love with a wrong'un, too, and now she'll pay a heavy price for that. Even if she escapes jail, what kind of life will she have? The house her parents gave her now belongs to someone else, and because she's saddled with so much debt, there's no way she'll get a mortgage. Would you want to be homeless, friendless, tarred with a criminal record, and burdened with all that guilt, particularly at her age?"

"No, I guess not."

"So, I can stay angry with her, but then I'd just be going through the same cycle I did with Lynn all those years ago. I might be soft in the head, but I'm not stupid."

"Don't tell me you're willing to forgive Paula."

"God, no," Mum scoffs. "The woman is an utter bitch, but that's her problem, not mine."

"Indeed, and for what it's worth, I think you're right."

"I think so too, and for now, I'm going to concentrate on the two people in this world I know I can rely on: my daughter and my sister. If I meet someone down the line, great, but if not, I won't lose any sleep over it."

Mum's dramatic mental shift is welcome, but I can't help but think that maybe this is for my benefit. Then again, if witnessing your child step dangerously close to death's door doesn't shift your thinking, nothing will. Whatever her reasons and whatever the outcome, Mum seems to be in a better place now than she's been in months, so I'm not about to pick at the scab.

"So, what's for dinner?" I ask breezily. "As grateful as I am to the NHS, their food leaves a lot to be desired."

"No idea. Lynn is cooking tonight."

"I see."

"We're going to do something we've never done before. We'll enjoy a nice meal together, open a few bottles of wine, and get royally drunk. Maybe we'll even stick on my *Mamma Mia!* CD and have a sing-along."

"Um, okay ... have you run this past Lynn?"

"It was her idea," Mum chuckles.

I might have to forgo the wine as I'm on antibiotics, and the prospect of listening to the *Mamma Mia!* soundtrack for the umpteenth time holds little appeal, but I'm all in favour of a nice meal and a spot of bridge building.

We reach the car and once Mum has helped me click my seatbelt into place, she delves her hand into the glovebox.

"You'll never guess what I found when I was rooting through the sideboard in the lounge?"

"I dread to think."

She pulls out a CD case and hands it to me.

"No way!" I gasp. "Our school-run CD."

Long before the advent of music streaming, Mum and I spent hours compiling our own playlist on a clunky old computer, ripping individual tracks from CDs and burning them onto the disc I now have in my hand.

"I'd forgotten all about it," Mum grins back. "When was the last time we listened to it together?"

"Gosh, probably my last few months of junior school."

"We're well overdue for another listen, then. Stick it on."

I click open the case and slide the disc into the CD player. Mum starts the car and flicks the indicator stalk. As she pulls away, Shania Twain joins us as we begin the hour-long journey back to Brentwood. We don't stop singing, laughing, and reminiscing until we reach Windsor Gardens.

One final flick of the indicator stalk, and Mum guides the car to a standstill outside the bungalow.

"Home, sweet, home," she says, somewhat wistfully.

She then turns to me and takes my hand.

"You'll think I'm mad," she says. "But I've felt your granddad's presence these last few days. Several times, I've turned around to talk to him. Then it hits me — he's not with us anymore."

"I don't think you're mad at all, and maybe Granddad is still with us ... in spirit. The doctor said someone must have been looking out for me, so who's to say it wasn't Granddad?"

"I'd love to think so," Mum says, squeezing my hand. "I really would."

We get out of the car and head inside. After kicking off our shoes in the hallway, Mum asks me to put the kettle on while she nips to the loo. I follow the aroma of spices through to the kitchen. Lynn is standing at the sink, her back to me.

"Hi," I say meekly. "Only me."

Lynn spins around and takes a few hesitant steps towards me.

"So it is," she says, wiping her hands on her apron. "And in one piece, I see."

"Just about."

"What were you thinking, you silly girl?" she scolds. "You had us both worried sick, getting yourself embroiled with that ... that dreadful man."

"Both?"

"Yes, both of us — your mother *and* me."

There's a moment of silence before Lynn reaches out and places her hand on my shoulder. Being she's the least tactile person I've ever met, I'm unsure how to react.

"I'm relieved you're okay," she says, almost softly.

"Thank you," I reply. "And ... um, I'm sorry. I haven't been—"

"Shush, now," Lynn interjects. "Clean slate?"

"Clean slate. I'd like that."

She nods once while biting her bottom lip.

"Has that kettle boiled yet?" comes Mum's voice from the doorway. "I'm parched."

Lynn suddenly snaps back to attention and then glances up at the clock.

"It's gone four," she says. "Too early to open the wine?"

"How long will dinner be?"

"An hour or so."

"Sod it," Mum laughs. "I'll get the glasses."

"Not for me," I announce. "I'm on antibiotics."

"One small one won't hurt. Come on — live dangerously."

"I think Gina has lived dangerously enough of late," Lynn replies with a wry smile. "Don't you?"

For the first time in an age, the sound of laughter bounces off the kitchen walls. It's accompanied by that feeling of warmth you only get when you're with family — even if that family is slightly dysfunctional and often at odds.

Ultimately, I don't have enough willpower to abstain, so I half-fill a glass of wine when we eventually sit down to dinner. The meal itself is spectacular — I had no idea Lynn was such a great cook or, to be fair, such good company. Maybe it's because we've shed some of the baggage of the past, and it's no longer weighing us down.

Once our plates are empty, I get up to load the dishwasher, but Mum has other ideas.

"Go and put your feet up on the sofa," she orders. "It won't take us long to finish in here."

"If you're sure, I'm not going to argue."

I thank Lynn for the fantastic meal again and head towards the lounge. I'm halfway along the hallway when the doorbell rings.

"I'll get it," I call out as I approach the front door.

When I open the door, the very last person I expected to see is on the other side.

"Oh ... hi," I splutter.

"Hi."

The longest seconds pass as we stand silently and stare at one another.

"Um, have you got a moment?" Priya eventually asks.

It could be the strong antibiotics, or the wine, or a combination of both, but my mind is suddenly a fog of confused thoughts. I've imagined standing in front of Priya a thousand times and going over the thousand different things I might say to her. Now, I haven't the first clue how to react beyond the obvious.

"Err, sure. Come in."

Without either of us uttering another word, I guide her through to the lounge and then close the door. When I turn around, I catch a glimpse of my reflection in the mirror above the fireplace. I look a right mess.

"Do you want to sit down?" I ask, unsure what else to say.

"I'm good, thanks. I can't stay long."

"Right."

Another awkward silence ensues while I try to avoid the mirror.

"I heard about what happened to you," Priya then says. "Are you ... will you be okay?"

"I'll live," I reply with a touch too much iciness in my voice. "I mean, I'm fine."

"You look great ... considering."

"I don't think Vogue will call me in for a photo shoot any time soon, but thanks."

Priya's smile, beautiful as it is, fades as quickly as it arrived.

"It must have been terrifying," she says in a low voice. "You know, being attacked like that."

"I'm not going to lie, it was ... wait. How do you know I was attacked?"

"The guy told me."

"What guy?"

"The guy who asked me to give you this."

She pulls a white envelope from her coat pocket and hands it to me. My first name is scrawled on the front in blue biro.

"He was sitting on a wall when I came home from work yesterday," Priya adds. "Honestly, I thought he was about to steal my handbag, but then he said my name and asked if I knew what had happened to you."

My curiosity piqued, I tear open the envelope and extract a single sheet of paper.

"He said you were friends," Priya says.

Without reading a single word, I shift my attention from the sheet of paper back to the woman who broke my heart.

"What did he look like, this guy?"

"Huge. Piercing blue eyes. Not the kind of guy you'd want to get on the wrong side of."

There's only one man I know who perfectly fits that description. I unfold the sheet of paper and read the shortest of short letters.

You want something in life, Doll, you've got to make it happen. This is me, making it happen.

Stay lucky — Clem

PS: If this don't work, go find yourself some new fanny. You deserve to be happy.

It's impossible to stop the smile from reaching my lips, but Clement's letter is as bittersweet as it is short. It's his parting words of advice, his goodbye.

"Are you okay?" Priya asks in response to my silence.

"Um, fine," I eventually reply, wiping away a tear I didn't expect to find in the corner of my eye.

"The letter. Was it bad news?"

"Just some advice from a friend. Read it if you like," I reply, handing her the letter.

I watch her chocolate-brown eyes slowly scan left to right and await a reaction.

"He's right," she says, folding the letter and passing it back to me.

"Which part is he right about?"

"You do deserve to be happy."

I nod a reply and tuck the letter into the pocket of my hoodie.

"He's also right about wanting something in life and making it happen."

"You think?"

Priya studies her feet for a moment before drawing a deep breath.

"The reason I can't stay long is because ... because I've got to drive to Chelmsford this evening. I'm staying with an old uni friend, Jenna, for a while."

I've no idea why this information is relevant or why Priya appears so nervous about sharing it.

"I ... I've left him," she then blurts.

"Sorry?"

"My marriage — it's over."

"Oh."

Priya draws another deep breath and takes a cautious step towards me.

"I'm going to say this now because if I don't, I'll regret it for the rest of my life. I've thought about calling or messaging you countless times over the last six months but ... but I'm a coward. I had the opportunity to spend the rest of my days with the most incredible woman, and I let her walk away because I wasn't brave enough to ... I should never have let my family dictate who I fall in love with."

Her point made, Priya deflates a little. She then studies my face for a reaction.

"You've caught me off guard," I say. "I don't really know what to say."

"You don't have to say anything, Gina, but there is something that I'd like to ask of you."

"What's that?"

"Will you consider having dinner with me next week?"

"Um ..."

"Just dinner," Priya pleads. "I don't expect anything from you, but I ... I didn't realise just how much I need you in my life until your friend told me what happened. The reality of never seeing you again, it just ... it terrified me."

My one-time soul mate stands silently before me: watching, waiting, anticipating.

"Just dinner?" I confirm.

"Just dinner."

"And I get to choose where?"

"Anywhere you like."

"Okay," I reply with a semi-smile. "It's a date."

Priya's face lights up, and just as it seems she's about to throw her arms around me, she pulls herself back at the last second. Too soon, I think, for both of us.

"Thank you," she says instead. "You've no idea what that means to me."

"I think I've got a vague idea."

Perhaps not wanting to push her luck or allow me time to change my mind, Priya checks her watch.

"I'd better get going. Message me when you've decided where and when, okay?"

"Will do."

I open the lounge door and lead Priya back up the hallway. As I reach for the door handle, her hesitancy implies there might be something else she wants to say. I give her a moment.

"Your friend, Clem," she says coyly. "You've never mentioned him before."

"No, I only met him recently."

"Oh, right. He's an interesting character. Intimidating, but interesting."

"I can't argue with that," I snigger.

"How did you meet?"

Priya's question is one I've thought about a lot myself these last few weeks. Was it really just chance that I crossed paths with Clement that day?

"I wouldn't swear by it," I smile. "But I think my granddad introduced us."

THE END...

For now.

BEFORE YOU GO

MAY I ASK A FAVOUR?

Thank you so much for reading *Terrier* – if you've got this far, hopefully you enjoyed the story. If you did, I'd be eternally grateful if you could post a (hopefully positive) review on Amazon, or even a nice five-star rating. Positive reviews and ratings are the only way independently published books like mine can compete with those from the big publishing houses.

FANCY SOME MORE OF THE SAME?

I've been writing novels since 2016 and much to my amazement, I seem to have built up a reasonable back catalogue. Whether you fancy reading the original Clement series (starting with *Who Sent Clement?*) or one of my quirky time travel novels, simply head to Amazon and search for 'Keith A Pearson'. If you do decide to take a punt on another of my books, I really hope you enjoy it.

ACKNOWLEDGEMENTS

First and foremost, I'd like to thank you for reading this novel. Without my small but loyal band of readers, I wouldn't be able to write full-time, so I owe you all for my career. I'd also like to thank my brilliant beta readers: Adam Eccles, Tracy Fisher, Lisa Gresty, Maf Sweet, Stuart Whyte, and Alan Wood. Their input and keen eye for typos helped to create a clean manuscript.

And finally, I'd like to thank my editor, Sian Philips. This is the only part of the book that Sian hasn't edited, so there's bound to be a typo somewhere on this page.

Printed in Great Britain
by Amazon

38110793R00229